# THE LIFE
# OF MADAM DE BEAUMOUNT

*and*

# THE LIFE OF
# CHARLOTTA DU PONT

broadview editions
series editor: Martin R. Boyne

# THE LIFE
## OF MADAM DE BEAUMONT

and

# THE LIFE OF
## CHARLOTTA DU PONT

broadview editions
series editor, Martin R. Boyne

# THE LIFE
# OF MADAM DE BEAUMOUNT

*and*

# THE LIFE OF
# CHARLOTTA DU PONT

Penelope Aubin

*edited by David A. Brewer*

broadview editions

BROADVIEW PRESS – www.broadviewpress.com
Peterborough, Ontario, Canada

Founded in 1985, Broadview Press remains a wholly independent publishing house. Broadview's focus is on academic publishing; our titles are accessible to university and college students as well as scholars and general readers. With over 800 titles in print, Broadview has become a leading international publisher in the humanities, with world-wide distribution. Broadview is committed to environmentally responsible publishing and fair business practices.

© 2023 David A. Brewer

**Library and Archives Canada Cataloguing in Publication**

Title: The life of Madam de Beaumount ; and, The life of Charlotta du Pont / Penelope Aubin ; edited by David A. Brewer.
Other titles: Novels. Selections | Life of Charlotta du Pont
Names: Aubin, Penelope, approximately 1679-approximately 1738, author. | Brewer, David A. (David Allen), 1969- editor. | Container of (work): Aubin, Penelope, approximately 1679-approximately 1738. Life of Madam de Beaumount. | Container of (work): Aubin, Penelope, approximately 1679-approximately 1738. Life of Charlotta du Pont.
Series: Broadview editions.
Description: Series statement: Broadview editions | Includes bibliographical references.
Identifiers: Canadiana (print) 20230180280 | Canadiana (ebook) 20230180302 | ISBN 9781554813537 (softcover) | ISBN 9781770488793 (PDF) | ISBN 9781460408155 (EPUB)
Subjects: LCGFT: Novels.
Classification: LCC PR3316.A68 A6 2023 | DDC 823/.5—dc23

Advisory editor for this volume: Colleen Humbert

*Broadview Press handles its own distribution in North America:*
PO Box 1243, Peterborough, Ontario K9J 7H5, Canada
555 Riverwalk Parkway, Tonawanda, NY 14150, USA
Tel: (705) 743–8990; Fax: (705) 743–8353
email: customerservice@broadviewpress.com

For all territories outside of North America, distribution is handled by Eurospan Group.

Broadview Press acknowledges the financial support of the Government of Canada for our publishing activities.

Canada

Cover design and typesetting: George Kirkpatrick

PRINTED IN CANADA

# Contents

# Acknowledgements

This edition of Penelope Aubin has been ridiculously long in the making and would never have been completed were it not for the labor, advice, and encouragement of Kate Novotny Owen and Nush Powell. I am grateful for all that they have done. I have also benefited from the interest and support of Eve Tavor Bannet, Janine Barchas, Scott Black, Lucian Brewer, Stephanie Insley Hershinow, Eric Johnson, Crystal Lake, Sandra Macpherson, Kirsten Saxton, Jennifer Schnabel, Debbie Welham, and Roxann Wheeler. Marjorie Mather's patience has been, as always, astonishing. And nothing I do would matter without the delightful companionship of Rebecca Morton.

Michele Abate, John Boneham, Robbie Ethridge, Isobel Goodman, Micah Hoggatt, Pasha Johnson, Scott Levi, John Levin, Sean Moore, Allison Muri, Yvonne Noble, Leah Orr, Nick Paige, Lewis Seifert, Allison Steadman, Karen Stokes, John Sullivan, Lisa Voigt, and Penelope Wilson have generously answered my queries about various aspects of this project. The maps were made by Rebecca Chapman. My translation of Prévost in Appendix B has been significantly improved by the sharp eyes of Lynn Festa, Garett Heysel, and Geoff Turnovsky. Generous grants from The Ohio State University and the Women's Caucus of the American Society for Eighteenth-Century Studies helped underwrite this project.

Finally, since, at its heart, Aubin's work showcases the heroism, resourcefulness, and general badassery of teenage girls, it seems only fitting to dedicate this book to our daughter, Lotte, who has taught me so much about those things, starting well before she was herself a teenager and continuing into her own adulthood.

★ ★ ★

*A Sea Fight with Barbary Corsairs* (c. 1681–86; oil on canvas, 107 x 92.7 cm, DPG428) by Lorenzo a Castro, reproduced on p. 40, appears courtesy of the Dulwich Picture Gallery, London. The frontispiece and title page of *The Life of Madam de Beaumount* appear courtesy of The Bodleian Libraries, University of Oxford (Douce A 136). The title page of *The Life of Charlotta*

*Du Pont* appears courtesy of Houghton Library, Harvard University (*EC7 Au164 723l[B]). The title page of *A Collection of Entertaining Histories and Novels* appears courtesy of the Kislak Center for Special Collections, Rare Books and Manuscripts, University of Pennsylvania (PR3316.A68 1739).

# Introduction

The first thing that strikes most modern readers when they encounter the work of Penelope Aubin (b. between 1679 and 1682; d. 1738) is all the scenes in which teenaged girls engage in spectacular violence in defense of their lives and bodily autonomy. In *The Noble Slaves* (1722), for example, Maria, an enslaved *"Spanish Girl, a Virgin of but 13 Years of Age,"* thwarts the Persian emperor's attempt to rape her by tearing out her own eyeballs and throwing them at him (26–33).[1] Similarly, in *The Life and Adventures of the Lady Lucy* (1726; henceforth *Lady Lucy*), Arminda foils a rapist's attempt to blackmail her into further submission when she grasps "the Pomel of his Sword, and with a sudden struggle drew it forth, and stabb'd him in the Thigh"; he flees, but "died ere Morning" (112–13).[2] In *The Life of Charlotta Du Pont* (1723; henceforth *Charlotta Du Pont*), the thirteen-year-old Charlotta, who is in the midst of being kidnapped across the Atlantic at the behest of her evil stepmother, defeats a pirate's attempt to rape her by "taking a sharp Bodkin out of her Hair" and stabbing "him in the Belly so dangerously, that he fell senseless on the Bed" (p. 150). And in *The Life of Madam de Beaumount* (1721; henceforth *Madam de Beaumount*), Belinda, the fourteen-year-old heroine, and two women she has rescued from bandits are lost and starving in the mountains of Wales. Providentially, a mother and baby goat wander by: "the Kid she laid hold of, calling to her Companions to assist her, and with a Knife she had in her Pocket, she stabb'd it. They lick'd up the warm Blood, and eat the raw Flesh, more joyfully than they wou'd Dainties at another time" (p. 106).[3] This is

---

1 Later on, when all of the characters' adventures are being told, "no part of their History was more wonder'd at than" Maria's "heroick Action ... in pulling out her Eyes to save her Virtue." That part of their story "charm'd all that heard it related" (181).

2 Lady Lucy's husband, once he learns the truth of what happened, thinks it "no wonder ... that a Lady of such Virtue should, in such an Exigence, stab a Man out of whose hands she could find no other way to escape" (123).

3 Other examples could be adduced, such as Lucinda's stabbing a pirate in the shoulder with the sword that she is wearing while dressed in men's clothing (*The Life and Amorous Adventures of* [*continued*])

not how we are accustomed to most novelistic heroines of the past behaving, perhaps especially in the other works of eighteenth-century prose fiction that we tend to encounter in the classroom. If figures like Pamela or Evelina win over the men and older women around them through their unrelenting, but fairly passive virtue, and even Elizabeth Bennet mostly dazzles with her wit and independence of mind, rather than with anything more dramatic—much less bloodsoaked—that she does, Aubin's heroines are active, uncowed forces in the world.[1] And yet they are able to exert this force without slipping into the kinds of criminality that characterize, say, a Moll Flanders or a Roxana.[2] This different relation to the world is made manifest not only in these acts of violent self-preservation but also in the sheer resourcefulness of their conduct more generally: these young women do what it takes to reduce their chances of being harmed as they move about the world and to escape from whatever captivity into which kidnappers, stalkers, or enslavers attempt to place them—e.g., cross-dressing, setting fires, climbing down ropes of knotted sheets and then jumping when the rope proves too short, throwing wine in the face of an assailant and then breaking out of a locked room, staging a crime scene to throw off pursuers.[3] Such heroics help us immediately see that the work

---

*Lucinda* [1721] 85) or Emilia's leaving the Governor of Algiers, who had threatened to rape her, "weltering in his Blood" after wounding him with his own dagger, which she also uses to kill a renegado (a Christian convert to Islam) who tried to stop her escape (*The Noble Slaves* 48–49). Similarly, another figure in *The Noble Slaves*, Clarinda, "caught a bayonet from [the] side" of her would-be rapist "and stabb'd him, before he suspected her Design" (93).

1  See Samuel Richardson, *Pamela; or, Virtue Rewarded* (1740; dated 1741); Frances Burney, *Evelina; or A Young Lady's Entrance into the World* (1778); and Jane Austen, *Pride and Prejudice* (1813).

2  See Daniel Defoe (?), *The Fortunes and Misfortunes of the Famous Moll Flanders* (1721) and *The Fortunate Mistress* (1724).

3  For instances of heroines cross-dressing, see *The Strange Adventures of the Count de Vinevil and His Family* (1721) 40–42; *The Life and Amorous Adventures of Lucinda* 51–52, 85, 87–113, and 139–41; *The Noble Slaves* 48–51, 72, 84, 144, 162, and 170; and *Lady Lucy* 23–24 and 43–47. For fire-setting, see *Count de Vinevil* 86–87. For ropes of sheets, see *Lucinda* 28 and *The Noble Slaves* 130 (and there is a plan to escape that way in *The Life and Adventures of the Young Count Albertus* [1728] 89, but another means presents itself). For wine-throwing and lock-breaking (which leads to a compound fracture in the heroine's

of Penelope Aubin does not involve the dutiful, patient endurance (and sometimes gaslighting and humiliation) of girls and young women familiar to us from lots of other canonical fiction, but rather something wilder, weirder, and frankly far more fun. Part of both the challenge and the delight of reading Aubin in the wake of the narrowing of what counts as good prose fiction that accompanied its incorporation into university literature curricula is figuring out how her work actually operates and how it might be different from, rather than merely an inferior version of, the novels with which we are more familiar. Aubin's early readers understood this difference: how else could one of them have proclaimed, regarding *Charlotta Du Pont* "this Story quite perfect"?[1] It is high time that we caught up, and the two texts included in full in this edition are an excellent place to start. Both *Madam de Beaumount* and *Charlotta Du Pont* prominently feature the resourceful heroines, wide-ranging and fast-paced adventure, and relatively non-judgmental presentation of sexual, political, and religious variety that sets her work apart from that of most of her contemporaries and makes it so exciting to consider at the present moment.

Once primed by the violence to notice how Aubin's heroines do not resemble those of most of the other eighteenth-century fiction we encounter in the classroom (which, we should recall, is a tiny and not wholly representative sample of what was actually published in the period), it becomes difficult not to see almost every aspect of her work as departing from—and potentially frustrating—our expectations. A partial list of such departures might include:

1. The unchanging nature of her characters. They don't "grow" psychologically over time in response to their experiences in the way that we are accustomed to saying that good novelistic characters should do.
2. The degree to which her plots rely on coincidence (and a depopulated world in which no one seems to exist who isn't

---

leg that "dash'd" her captor's "amorous Fires" and leaves her permanently disabled), see *The Noble Slaves* 197–98. For crime-scene staging, see *Lucinda* 31–32. All of these are on top of the cross-dressing, stabbing, and escaping that are integral parts of *Madam de Beaumount* and *Charlotta Du Pont*.

1 This phrase is written on the title page of a 1739 (most likely unauthorized) reprint of *Charlotta Du Pont*, now at the British Library.

part of the narrative) and so apparently violate the probability that we have been taught to regard as part of good storytelling.

3. The frequency with which the main story is paused when a new character is encountered in order to get that character's backstory, which often seems to echo elements in the main story. This means that the cast of significant characters in her work is larger than is often the case in other fiction and that the forward movement of the plot is regularly interrupted.

It would be easy to see these in terms of lack (and most previous scholars have done just that): Aubin's characters do not "develop," her plots are "improbable," all the secondary characters and their backstories dilute the focus on—and our investment in—the main characters, and so on. But a few moments of reflection should remind us that the criteria for "good" novels implicit in this list of what Aubin's work is missing are more the accumulated shibboleths of several generations of English classes than an accurate account of most of the prose fiction we admire and value. Plenty of characters do not develop over time because they are already heroines or villains or sidekicks or nemeses.[1] Plenty of plots involve improbable coincidences, though they often disguise it more than Aubin bothers to do. The inclusion of characters with no narrative function is actually quite rare. And providing backstory for secondary characters is hardly uncommon, though typically it is done more gradually and through dialogue. So the things that we tend to notice as different about Aubin's work are both not as different as we might initially think them, especially if we broaden our attention to include the fiction we encounter outside the classroom (think how much these characteristics describe a lot of the thrillers and fantasy and science fiction most popular today), and not as obviously shortcomings on her part as our internalized checklist for "good" novel-writing might be inclined to pronounce them. Indeed, a persuasive case can be made that these apparent absences and failings may actually be assets: a different way of approaching storytelling, rather than a failure to meet an arbitrary standard that almost no actual novels wholly achieve.

Let's start with the lack of character "development." Again and again, Aubin's characters are much the same at the close of their stories as they were at (or at least near) the beginning. If they were

---

1   Indeed, the degree to which even the most canonical, supposedly realistic characters "develop" has been seriously overstated. See Hershinow.

constant and faithful lovers, they remain so, despite all that has happened to them. If they were deceitful betrayers, they remain so (although occasionally they're afforded a deathbed repentance). To use the terms devised by E.M. Forster (1879–1970), they are "flat" characters, rather than "round" ones. In casual use (and these terms have become enough of a literary commonplace that multiple generations of students know them without ever having read Forster's *Aspects of the Novel*), this distinction tends to be treated as a hierarchy: "round" characters are self-evidently better than "flat" ones. But for Forster, they were just a way of describing two different approaches to characterization. "Flat" characters were "very useful" because their future conduct could be reliably predicted on the basis of their past behavior: they were "not changed by circumstances; ... which gives them in retrospect a comforting quality, and preserves them when the book that produced them may decay" (105–06). "Round" characters, on the other hand, were "capable of surprising in a convincing way" (118), typically because they had transformed over the course of a narrative. If Aubin's characters are "flat," it is because they are consistent. In the case of her heroes and heroines, they resist all the attempts of the world (kidnappers, assailants, coercive parents and stepparents, captivity, the threat of starvation, encounters with other cultures and religions) to alter them. Indeed, it is because of this unwaveringness that they prove themselves worthy of their beloveds. Had they changed, they would have shown themselves to be too much of this world and so tainted by it. A true heroine who has pledged her heart does not yield to the threats and bribes of others, nor to the misfortunes that may accost her. She remains faithful, through thick and thin, to the man whom she loves and to the person who she was when she was first beloved by him. The events that befall her are tests of her fidelity and in order to be a proper heroine she must not only pass each test but also be unscathed by it. This is an older way of thinking about the relation between characters and the world (it goes back to the Hellenistic prose fiction of late antiquity: the so-called Greek romances, especially Heliodorus's *Aethiopica* [third or fourth century CE]), but it is no less viable than the expectation of "character development" that has been dominant in more recent centuries.[1] Indeed, it is worth remembering that

---

1  M.M. Bakhtin (1895–1975) has influentially argued that the "chronotope" (a concept devised to "express ... the inseparability of time and space") of "adventure-time" that organizes Hellenistic *(continued)*

the model of development that has become the default, that of the *Bildungsroman*, is one of accommodation and compromise, a letting go of youthful idealism in the service of making one's way in the world as it supposedly is. For someone like Aubin, that is just a giving up, a tacit acceptance that nothing can be done about the world as it is. Aubin's heroes and heroines prefer to conduct themselves on the basis of principle, showing how the world could be if only others followed their lead.[1] Her approach may be "unrealistic," if we accept the often constrained and unimaginative understanding of human psychology that tends to accompany "realism," but it is in the service of something hopeful, perhaps even utopian: a vision of a world of enduring, unshakable love in which even the most vulnerable, for instance teenaged girls alone and surrounded by threats of sexual violence, can triumph. That is a world that many of us, both in Aubin's time and today, would prefer to the one in which we actually live.[2]

This different way of thinking about the relation between characters and the world can in turn help us see how Aubin's reliance on apparent coincidences is an alternative approach to storytelling, rather than an inferior one. A good example of the sort of coincidence that Aubin regularly employs can be found in *Madam de Beaumount* when the Count de Beaumount, after escaping from a Russian prison and fleeing "towards a Wood in

---

prose fiction, and so shapes what can even be narrated, "lies outside of biographical time; it changes nothing in the life of the heroes, and introduces nothing into their life. It is, precisely, an extratemporal hiatus between two moments of biographical time": the initial meeting of the lovers and their eventual marriage. Each lover and their devotion to one another "remains *absolutely unchanged* throughout," no matter how many adventures (enslavement, kidnappings, shipwrecks) occur between those two moments. But while all those adventures leave the lovers unaltered (they do not age, mature, change their minds, etc.), the lovers are nonetheless tested and "affirm[ed]" by what they've undergone and become curiously somehow even more themselves (84, 90, 89, 106).

1 For a pioneering half-recognition of what Aubin was up to with this strategy (albeit one shot through with condescension toward the "woodenness" of her "improbable stereotypes"), see Richetti 217–18.

2 Cf. Abigail Zitlin's description of the customary fate of novelistic heroines: "What does the world do to a girl? It impinges and encroaches, it buffets and tries. In what shape does it leave her? Repressible. Domitable. Scathed. Trammeled. Married" (512).

*Tartary*," encounters an old man, who turns out to be "*Anthony,*
... a *Capuchin* Fryar, who saved your Lady's Life, and came to
*Muscovy* on purpose to seek you out" (p. 92). The Count is two
thousand miles from home and has not been in France for seven
years, but somehow he still manages to encounter the very person
who can give him the information he so desperately craves about
the fate of his wife (or rather, who could have done so had "a Band
of *Tartarian* Robbers" not entered right then and shot Father
Anthony dead, thus precipitating yet another adventure). One of
the core presumptions of realism is that everyday events, by virtue
of their sheer frequency and statistical probability, are "easier to
believe" and more "realistic." Accordingly, since the odds of, say,
two people who have never met and yet have important information for one another being in exactly the right place at the right
time without prior planning are rather low, then, by our usual criteria, that encounter is implausible or far-fetched. As these adjec-
tives should suggest, realism is ultimately more concerned with the
plausible than the actual: what seventeenth-century French theo-
rists termed the *vraisemblable* (the truth-like) rather than the *vrai*
(the true).[1] But if one believes in divine Providence, as Aubin and
the vast majority of her initial readers seem to have done, or fate,
or even just luck, it is easy to recognize that much of what happens
in the world is improbable, at least according to our stock notions
of probability. Chance meetings with long-lost loves do occur,
however infrequently, as do last-minute rescues, shipwrecks from
which ample supplies wash up on shore, and all of the other seemingly unlikely events in Aubin's work—and since they do, there is
no reason why they should not be part of a plot that is devoted
to showing how a hero or heroine resists and triumphs over the
dangers and temptations of the world.[2] If anything, the putatively

---

1 This distinction ultimately goes back to the one that Aristotle (384–
  322 BCE) draws in the *Poetics* between poetry and history: the former
  tells us "the *kinds* of things that might occur and are possible in terms
  of probability or necessity" and the latter "relates actual events" in all
  their potential oddity (59). "Actual events" are always "possible—they
  could not otherwise have occurred," but their happening was not necessarily probable (61).
2 Cf. Paul Hunter's observation that readers "seem to take rational
  pleasure in having things happen against individual odds if the global
  odds are satisfactory; if something surprising can happen to someone
  in the world, it might just as well happen to someone singled out in a
  novel" (33).

improbable works all the better to demonstrate that triumph: if our heroine can overcome the extreme case, then presumably she would be able to deal handily with more routine (and less narratively compelling) situations as well.

Pausing to get the backstory of secondary characters when they are first encountered by the main characters was a hallmark of the heroic romances that dominated prose fiction for much of the seventeenth century, especially in France.[1] These additional stories often comprised a majority of the total page count of those romances, which could be very long indeed.[2] Because of their bulk, both individually and collectively, and the fact that what purported to be the main narrative was effectively paused each time a new story was introduced, these "interpolated" or "intercalated" accounts have often been held up as evidence that the heroic romances are now unreadable.[3] But such dismissals offer no insight into why they should once have been so compulsively readable, both in their original, lengthy French form and in the more abbreviated version we encounter in Aubin. At the heart of the objection to this mode of storytelling is a presumption that what most matters in narrative is plot, so anything that gets in the way of its forward movement is either a praiseworthy heightening of suspense or else an unnecessary digression. But that is hardly the only way to read, even today, and there is good reason to think that readers of the early eighteenth century were not nearly as devoted to tearing through plots to find out how they end as we might presume. For one thing, the basic contours of those plots were often made known before readers even began: the title pages of Aubin's work, like those of many of her contemporaries, give, in

---

1   For an engaging and accessible survey of the *roman héroïque*, see Moore 192–217.

2   Moore notes that "these secondary tales take up nearly 60 percent" of Marin le Roy, sieur de Gomberville's *Polexandre*, which, in its final version of 1638, was "over half a million words long" (194). Other heroic romances were even longer. Gautier de Costes, sieur de La Calprenède's *Cassandre* (1642–45) ran to approximately 5,500 pages in ten volumes, and Madeleine de Scudéry's *Artamène, ou, Le Grand Cyrus* (1649–53) amounted to more than 13,000 pages (almost two million words) in ten volumes. It contained twenty-seven inset narratives.

3   It is worth noting that they were still read so avidly in Louisiana in the mid-twentieth century that children were named after their heroines. See De Jean xi.

effect, capsule summaries of the narratives to come.[1] Those summaries were then used to market the book, either by pasting up extra copies of the title page as handbills or by transcribing them in newspaper advertisements. So, for example, we learn, from the title page of *Charlotta Du Pont*, that our heroine was tricked ("trepan'd") by her stepmother into involuntarily going to Virginia, captured by pirates, and freed by a Spanish warship, married someone in the Spanish part of the Caribbean, had "Adventures" there, and eventually returned to England, meeting a number of "Gentlemen and Ladies" along the way, some of whom had been enslaved in North Africa and others of whom were shipwrecked in South America but all ultimately escaped and returned safely to France and Spain. The kind of questions that our standard ways of thinking about plot presume are crucial—"What's going to happen? Will she survive?"—are answered before our curiosity can even be aroused. We know going in that Charlotta is going to undergo many ordeals and we have ideas as to the principal kinds of threats that she will encounter, though the specifics of the perils and the way in which she will navigate them remain to be discovered. But we can rest assured that ultimately she will triumph.[2] To a certain way of thinking, a title page like this is just a series of "spoilers" and tantamount to narrative malpractice. But if we once again open ourselves to the possibility that Aubin is doing something different, rather than doing something familiar badly, we can see that plot—at least in the arousing-concern-about-what-will-happen-to-our-heroine sense—isn't really the point

---

1  For reproductions of the title pages of *Madam de Beaumount* and *Charlotta Du Pont*, see pp. 57 and 117. For transcriptions of these and Aubin's other title pages, see the Works Cited and Select Bibliography. Perhaps the best known example from the period of this kind of title-page-as-plot-summary is that of Daniel Defoe's *Robinson Crusoe* (1719), which reads in its entirety (minus publication information): "*The Life and Strange Surprizing Adventures of Robinson Crusoe of York, Mariner: Who lived Eight and Twenty Years, all alone in an un-inhabited Island on the Coast of America, near the Mouth of the Great River of Oroonoque; Having been cast on Shore by Shipwreck, wherein all the Men perished but himself. With an Account how he was at last as strangely deliver'd by Pyrates. Written by Himself.*"

2  Bracht Branham notes a similar phenomenon in the Hellenistic romances: "What suspense there is can concern only means (How will they get out of this one?) rather than ends (Will they survive and be reunited?)" (172).

here. Instead, as the last sentence of the description on the title page of *Charlotta Du Pont* suggests, Aubin is devoted to providing "the greatest Variety of Events."[1]

Here we can begin to grasp the appeal of all the tales told by secondary characters as Charlotta and the other main characters encounter them. Put simply, they resemble, but do not wholly repeat, the stories of Charlotta, Belanger, and the others at the heart of the narrative and so contribute to the felt "Variety of Events." The secondary characters are, like Charlotta and Belanger, affected by the actions of greedy or oblivious parents and stepparents. They too have been kidnapped, captured, and bribed or threatened in an attempt to coerce them into doing what their captors want. They too have done extravagant and potentially illegal things in order to be with the ones they love. They too have suffered from the jealousy of others. They too have escaped from captivity through a combination of personal daring and divine Providence. Perhaps above all, they too live in a world in which young women are in perpetual danger of sexual violence. The result of all these stories echoing one another (though imperfectly so; as we shall see, secondary characters sometimes succumb to threats or temptations that the main characters resist) is a cohesive, "thick" vision of how virtuous people can navigate the world. Such a vision, with all of its detail and "Variety," in turn provides ample ways in for readers interested in imitating these characters, as Aubin's dedications, prefaces, and narratorial commentary routinely urge readers to do (see Appendix A), or in engaging with them in a kind of emotional training regimen in order to better equip themselves to deal with the manifold threats of the actual world. If all we got was the story of Charlotta and Belanger, then readers whose situations did not closely parallel those in the text might find it difficult to emulate our heroes (perhaps the readers had no stepparents or had left home voluntarily). But since we are presented with the broadly analogous stories of upwards of a dozen others, that multiplies the chances that some configuration of events will seem sufficiently familiar that such emulation or emotional training could seem attractive. In this way of thinking about the utility and benefits of reading fiction, the additional stories told by the secondary characters, far from being unwelcome excrescences, are key to the text's chances of being, as the ancient Roman poet Horace (much quoted and imitated

---

1  For the importance of "variety" to early eighteenth-century prose fiction more generally, see Loveman.

in the eighteenth century) said that all literature should be, *utile et dulce*: both useful and pleasurable. Moreover, to the extent that these inset stories are delaying our forward progress through the plot, they are "enacting on a formal level the delayed gratifications" (Moore 174) endured by the characters. They are features, not bugs.

None of these departures from our expectations would have struck most readers in the 1720s as particularly unusual, since they were all routine features of the kind of prose fiction often termed "romance" that was still widely read, if less widely produced in new versions. "Romance" is a baggy and not altogether satisfying category that has been used to describe the Hellenistic prose fiction of late antiquity, the stories of chivalry and magic common in the later Middle Ages, the lengthy *romans héroïques* of seventeenth-century France, and sometimes more recent narratives as well, none of which are interchangeable. It has often also been used as a foil for discussions of "the novel," generally to its own detriment: the novel is putatively modern, realistic, clear-eyed, etc., while the romance is supposedly the opposite. Nonetheless, many of the aspects of Aubin's work that may strike us as unfamiliar, perhaps even puzzling, were stock elements of the kind of texts typically described as romance in the later seventeenth and early eighteenth centuries: the prolonged testing of characters through adventure, the reliance on coincidence, the use of inset narratives, the solicitation of wonder on the part of its readers, even the astonishingly young heroes and heroines.[1] Where Aubin parts company with most of her predecessors, though, is in the sheer pace of her narratives—what she does in a few hundred pages would have taken Madeleine de Scudéry several thousand—and in the breadth and explicitness of her presentation.

Once we have begun to see how Aubin is taking a different approach to storytelling, rather than simply failing to meet some universal standard, we may be in a better position to recognize what her work provides that that of many of her contemporaries and successors does not. Again, any list will be necessarily incomplete, but some of the obvious candidates likely to stand out for modern readers include

1. The space and visibility that Aubin devotes to queer forms of desire.

---

1 For the centrality of romance and adventure to the history of fiction, see Black; Moretti; Probyn.

2. The way in which Aubin refrains from narratively punishing her female characters who have sexual experiences—both coerced and consensual—outside of marriage.
3. The way in which her work moves easily across the Protestant/ Catholic confessional divide that so polarized Europe in the sixteenth, seventeenth, and eighteenth centuries.

Most eighteenth-century fiction in English either wholly ignores any forms of desire or sexual identity that are not staunchly heterosexual and adhering to traditional gender norms or presents such departures from the supposed norm as monstrous. This is not to say that everyone behaves themselves in such fiction (far from it), but the default standard of men courting women in a way that ultimately results in marriage sets the terms on which other practices are judged as permissible sowings of wild oats, predatory libertinism, or simply beyond the representational pale. For most fiction of the period, phenomena like same-sex desire, desire that is not closely bound to the gender of the desired, and voluntary opting out of the marriage market are simply not part of the worlds being presented. On the relatively rare occasions when they do appear, the depictions are almost invariably unkind: mincing, effeminate men who cannot be trusted; voracious older men looking to ruin naïve youths for their own pleasure; women who have sought out each other's bodies because they are prostitutes or confined within the "unnatural" environment of a convent. Aubin probably wouldn't win any prizes from a modern LGBTQ+ organization for her work, but, compared to her contemporaries, she is far more willing to acknowledge that desire comes in many forms, not all of which fit neatly into a heterosexual marriage plot (or its dark counterpart, the libertine seduction plot) in which men are the active pursuers of passive women who can, at best, ineffectually resist, assent, or conveniently pass out. So, for example, in *The Strange Adventures of the Count de Vinevil and His Family* (henceforth *Count de Vinevil*), a "great Turkish general, nam'd *Osmin*" meets the heroine, Ardelisa, on the road. In order to avoid notice, Ardelisa has been traveling dressed in men's clothing. Osmin is "enchanted" by "the Charms of her Face, and the Eloquence of her Tongue," and so takes her and her companions prisoner and transports them back to Constantinople (now Istanbul). Once there, he addresses her: "Lovely Boy, or Maid, I know not which as yet to call you, fear not the Treatment I shall give you; my Heart is made a Captive to your Eyes, I will enjoy and keep you here, where nothing shall be wanting to make you happy." Of course, he then "clasp'd her in his Arms, and rudely opening her Breast, discover'd that she was of the soft Sex" (62–65). But his desire to "enjoy" her was aroused well before he knew she was female. Similarly, in *The Life and Amorous Adventures of Lucinda* (henceforth *Lucinda*), the titular heroine, dressed in men's clothes to keep herself safe from the "libidinous Desires" of her captors, reencounters her first love, Charles, when they both end up enslaved in Turkey. After fixing his eyes "unmoveably" on her for some time, he then embraced her "in his Arms, gave me a thousand surprizing Kisses," while acknowledging that "this manner of Address ... is not customary amongst Men, but ... I have a secret Inclination that makes me covet you in my Arms, so perfectly does your Figure represent the most dear and faithless Mistress of my Heart" (85–90).[1] Ultimately, perhaps, we might want to call Charles's desire heterosexual (he unconsciously recognizes Lucinda as the woman he loved, even if he thinks that this young man only somehow resembles her). But it is far less straightforward (and far more queer) than such recognition scenes tend to be in eighteenth-century fiction. Elsewhere, men do not typically give other men "a thousand surprizing Kisses," even if they somehow discern something unusual about them. Moreover, before Lucinda feels safe to reveal her gender and true identity to Charles, her master's daughter, Sabina (who is "not yet twenty Years of Age"), falls in love with her, thinking she is a young man. This worries Lucinda, because, without a male body, she can only offer "trifling Joys," with "no possibility of returning more substantial Bliss." That is, Lucinda cannot consent to marriage with Sabina, not only because she would be expected to convert to Islam, but also—and it seems more importantly—because she was "so incapable of performing the greatest Part of the Ceremony" (99–108). This apparent inability to imagine sex without a penis was quite common in the eighteenth century; Lucinda's regarding this as a logistical problem, rather than a moral one, is far more unusual. There are a number of other instances of various sorts of queerness in Aubin's work that we could investigate, but the general point should

---

1 Charles thinks Lucinda "faithless" because she wasn't at their planned meeting place when he arrived to run away with her. He only later learns that she was kidnapped shortly beforehand by another man, who was obsessed with her.

be clear.[1] There is a space here for queer desire (and ostensibly straight characters who are untroubled by the form their desires have taken) that is vanishingly rare in her contemporaries and a recognition that love, desire, and gender are more complicated, fluid, and personal than most people, past or present, tend to be willing to acknowledge. Aubin may not think the same way about these issues as most users of this edition do, but there is much more of a family resemblance between her and us when it comes to queerness than there is between us and most other writers of her era.

In most eighteenth-century prose fiction, women rarely show any desire, and those who do are immediately set apart from their respectable counterparts and branded as, in effect, prostitutes in all but name. A similar situation obtains for women who are seduced and then abandoned by their lovers (a far more common scenario). If someone could find her seducer and force him to marry the woman he had "ruined," then there might be a chance of a future, if not true happiness. If not, then the seduced and abandoned woman typically faced a nasty, brutish, and short descent into degrading sex work, venereal disease, and an early grave. Either way, the message was clear: pre- or extra-marital sex was something that "good" women didn't do, so any woman found to be in the vicinity of sexual activity under those circumstances (regardless of whether it was consensual) was putting her own virtue and life at risk, along with the happiness and reputation of her family. Aubin's principal heroines—the ones named on her title pages—tend to follow this rule: they are married, or at least engaged, before their adventures begin; they heroically resist all attempts during those adventures to force or persuade them into sex; and ultimately they are reunited with their husbands or fiancés (who promptly become their husbands) for a happily-ever-after filled with friends, children, and domestic bliss.[2] But

---

1 For further examples, see *The Noble Slaves* 42 and 139–41; *Lady Lucy* 45–47; and *The Life and Adventures of the Young Count Albertus* 153–54 and 158–59. For a discussion of most of these episodes, see Mounsey, "Conversion."

2 It is worth acknowledging, however, that Charlotta Du Pont's fidelity may strike unsympathetic readers as akin to Lois's protestation, in *Kiss Me Kate*, that "I'm always true to you, darlin', in my fashion" (Porter 278). After all, Charlotta marries and has children with a man whom she does not love (although she gradually comes to respect him). But we are explicitly told that she did so in order to avoid rape (which

her secondary characters often have pre- or extra-marital sexual experiences—both coerced and consensual—and live to tell the tale without even a stain on their reputations, especially if the experiences in question took place outside of Europe.[1] For example, Violetta, in *Count de Vinevil*, was kidnapped from a Venetian convent by Turks and presented, as a captive, to Osmin (the one "enchanted" by Ardelisa) to be part of his seraglio. She had a son with him and "loved him, saw him with a Wife's Eyes, and thought myself oblig'd to do so" (91–92). Indeed, even after she has been rescued and is being courted by a Christian, she acknowledges that while "'Tis true" Osmin "forc'd me to his Bed, ... 'twas the Custom of his Nation, and what he thought no Crime, ... he was tender of me; and whilst he lives, my Modesty cannot permit me to receive another in my Bed" (117).[2] There is a similar scenario in *The Noble Slaves*, in which the Governor of Algiers "treated" Eleanora "kindly, pretended to love me passionately, and forced me to his Bed; after which he deny'd me nothing, purchased and freed *Attabala* [an enslaved Black man] at my Request; and for eight years, tho he had many other new Mistresses, gave me the Preference, and loved me with the same Ardour as at first," though Providence "did not think fit to give" them a child (67–68). Indeed, Eleanora goes further than Violetta and makes advances on a fellow European captive, Don Lopez, offering to file off his chains and help him and his friend escape, in return for his being "grateful" and giving her "a Place" in his "Heart." Don Lopez, who "was too well skill'd in the fair Sex, not to perfectly understand" her "meaning," decided that "since no other means but this was left to free them," he would "wisely conceal ... his being pre-engaged" to another and give her what she wanted (56).

---

her husband-to-be had threatened) and so can infer that she is preserving what matters most about herself until such time as she could be reunited with her true love. That is, her fidelity is located in—and should be judged by—the constancy of her heart, not the activities of her body.

1 For the importance of "far-off, exotic settings" to this comparative lack of reputational consequences, see Gollapudi 681.

2 Turkish and North African men were widely regarded in eighteenth-century Europe (often, though not always with horror) as having a voracious sexual appetite that broke through "normal" boundaries and constraints and so licensed polygamy, rape, and same-sex desire as "the Custom" of their "Nation." See Bekkaoui 12–27; Colley, *Captives* 128–31.

The narrator comments, "doubtless he was not altogether insensible of *Eleanora*'s Charms ... he was a Man, and tho he was intirely devoted to *Teresa*, yet as Man he could oblige a hundred more: Life is Sweet, and I hope my Reader will not condemn him for what his own Sex must applaud in justification of themselves: for what brave, handsome young Gentleman would refuse a beautiful Lady, who loved him, a Favour?" (56–57). Once they've escaped and reached a safe house, they "began to taste the Pleasures of Liberty" (60).[1]

Let's be clear: neither of these cases, nor any of the others to which we could point, is a straightforward instance of anything we might regard as sexual autonomy, much less liberation. Violetta and Eleanora and all of their counterparts are in their respective predicaments because of coercion and assault, and they are hardly unscathed by their ordeals.[2] But they are also not wholly defined by them. Their worth does not depend on their virginity or any other sort of narrowly technical definition of chastity, which means that women in Aubin's world can not only survive rape but also subsequently feel desire, and even find love (Violetta with someone new; Eleanora with someone she thought lost to her) without being tainted by their experience. They can also find partners who don't regard them as ruined: in *The Noble Slaves*, Antonio describes how, when he set out, as a fourteen-year-old, to search for his beloved Anna, who had been kidnapped from a Venetian monastery in an Ottoman raid, he "resolved, tho she had been ravish'd by the *Turks*, and sold or presented to the Seraglio of some Villain, for that her Beauty would doubtless occasion her to be, yet I would take her to my Arms, with as much Joy and Affection, as if she had been ever mine: Yet this her tender Years made me hope to prevent" (122).[3] Aubin's twinned presumptions that her secondary characters could have rich, full lives in the wake of sexual violence and that their beloveds should not reject them as damaged goods may now seem unremarkable and the place where any compassionate response should begin. But it

---

1 Eleanora's captivity began when she was "almost fourteen" (62). She looks to be "about five and twenty" when she meets Don Lopez (55).

2 For the ways in which actual women in the period experienced, resisted, and recounted sexual violence, see Gowing 90–101.

3 Anna was kidnapped when she was "seven Years of Age" and credits her "tender Years" with "preserv[ing] my Vertue," though she suspects "the Governor" of Algiers "reserv'd me for his Use, when I was older" (73–74).

would be centuries before such possibilities were again available to novelistic heroines in Anglophone fiction.[1]

Although Aubin was herself a member of the Church of England, her narratives revolve around enough heroic, non-villainous Catholic characters, including priests and monks, that several generations of scholars presumed that she must have been Catholic.[2] She certainly does not display the hostility and paranoia toward Catholicism that, for many of her contemporaries, was what most defined being British.[3] Nor does she treat conversion from one branch of Christianity to another (as, say, Charlotta Du Pont, raised as a Protestant, does when she marries a Spanish Catholic) as perilous or disturbing. Even conversion from Christianity to Islam is presented as something that one can repent and reverse (as characters in *Count de Vinevil* [77–83] and *The Life and Adventures of the Young Count Albertus* [henceforth *Count Albertus*] do [73–79, 140–44]). This is not to say that confessional divides do not matter. They clearly do in the case of Madam de Beaumount, who ends up in Wales because of the hostility that her French Catholic father-in-law demonstrates to her Protestant beliefs. But Aubin presents us largely with a world in which what unites Christendom is far more important than what divides it—a view that, had it been

---

1  For another example of how Aubin treats premarital sex on the part of her secondary characters, consider Monsieur de Chateau-Roial's story in *The Noble Slaves*. He recounts how "I enjoy'd the Maid I so much languished for" (81), a young woman "about fifteen" named Clarinda (84) as soon as they had run away together, although he "promis[ed] to marry her so soon as we were arrived in a place of Safety" (81). He later reproaches himself for this (and for robbing the church where he was a priest in order to finance their escape), but the couple survive their North African adventures, escape safely to Venice, and seem positioned for a happy ending until he "fell sick of a Fever" and died (179). He presumes that his illness is divine punishment for his transgressions, and at his urging, Clarinda enters a convent. But she there "enjoy[ed] uninterrupted Peace, where no worldly Cares [could] enter to disturb her" (181), which seems a far better fate than awaits most women in eighteenth-century prose fiction who have sex before their weddings.

2  See, for example, Dooley.

3  For the centrality to first English and later British nationalism of being a Protestant nation beset by Catholic enemies (especially France), see Colley, *Britons* 11–54.

more widespread, might have saved millions of lives in the centuries after the Reformation.

I should stress that none of this makes Aubin our contemporary in any easy or straightforward way. She was a woman of her time, and her work is entangled with ways of thinking that most of us would find quite different, and probably at least somewhat alien or problematic: witness only her calm acceptance of the existence of slavery in the Americas and her apparent willingness to perpetuate misleading stereotypes regarding the Muslim world. Yet Aubin also regularly gestures toward ideas that most of her peers would find either incomprehensible or abhorrent but that we can recognize as at least cousins of some of the values we tend to hold dear, for instance that love and desire are messy and take many potentially valid forms. Aubin's fiction has often been dismissed as somehow more old-fashioned than that of other prominent writers of prose fiction in the 1720s, such as Daniel Defoe (c. 1660–1731) or Eliza Haywood (c. 1693–1756)—and perhaps at a formal level it sometimes is (all those inset narratives akin to what we encounter in the *roman héroïque*). But in terms of its ability to imagine a world that works differently than the actual world does—or at least the actual world as it is presented in most other fiction of the period, especially the titles that have become canonical—Aubin's work often feels surprisingly modern and not nearly as mired in the presumptions and prejudices of three hundred years ago as that of many of her contemporaries.

So what, given all this, is Aubin up to in her work? What sort of effects do these departures both from our expectations and from the expectations of her contemporaries collectively create? At least the beginnings of an answer can be gleaned from Aubin's dedications, prefaces, and narratorial commentary (see Appendix A), which repeatedly stress the exemplary qualities of her characters, how we would do well to imitate them, and how we should wonder at the marvelous workings of Providence that ultimately reward the virtuous and punish the vicious. Traditionally, these dedications, prefaces, and narratorial comments have been read as clumsy pieties: sincere but uninteresting expressions of Aubin's own religious devotion (as we shall see, this interpretation piggybacked on a substantive misunderstanding of Aubin's biography). More recently, some scholars have stressed the significant tensions between that view of Aubin and the often wild adventures narrated in the fiction itself and so recast these prefaces, dedications, and narratorial comments as tactical: savvy, possibly cynical attempts to tap into a market for virtuous women writers or to mislead the parents and guardians who acted as gatekeepers for the reading of the young into thinking that these tales were innocuous and orthodox.[1] Both positions seem uninterested in what imitating Aubin's characters might actually involve and why and for whom such imitation could be compelling. They also disregard the ways in which prefaces (and to a lesser extent, dedications and narratorial commentary) served as one of the principal ways in which prose fiction was theorized in this period. Let's consider what Aubin actually writes about her own work. Here is a selection of snippets drawn from the selections in Appendix A:

1. The preface to *Count de Vinevil* insists that it is "*a Story*" in which "*Women are really vertuous, and such as we ought to imitate*" and the closing paragraph professes that "Divine Providence ... rewarded" the good characters "according to their Merit, making them most happy and fortunate" (pp. 278, 279).

2. The preface to *The Noble Slaves* explains that because of the characters' faith in God's power, "*Chains could not hold them; Want, Sickness, Grief, nor the merciless Seas destroy them.*" Aubin claims that her "*only Aim is to encourage Virtue, and expose Vice, imprint noble Principles in the ductile Souls of our Youth, and setting great Examples before their Eyes, excite them to imitate them.*" Indeed, the opening paragraph of the text goes so far as to assert that "if we are not better'd by the Examples of the virtuous *Teresa* and the brave Don *Lopez*, 'tis our own Faults," and the closing paragraphs go even further: "The Gentlemen in this Story well deserve our Imitation; the Ladies, I fear, will scarce find any here who will pull out their Eyes, break their Legs, starve, and chuse to die, to preserve their Virtues." Ultimately, Aubin concludes that "since our Heroes and Heroines have done nothing here but what is possible, let us resolve to act like them, make Virtue the Rule of all our Actions, and eternal Happiness our only Aim" (pp. 281, 282, 283).

3. The preface to *Lady Lucy* maintains that "*the virtuous shall look Dangers in the face unmov'd, and putting their whole trust in the Divine Providence, shall be deliver'd, even by miraculous Means*" and entreats "*all marry'd Men to consider, from* Albertus's *Story, the dangerous Effects of Jealousy, and not to give credit to Appearances, but to examine well into the Truth of Things, before they treat a Wife unkindly, or abandon her; for we are very often deceiv'd, and condemn the innocent, whilst we love and caress the*

---

1  See Mounsey, "'... bring her'"; Prescott 47–51, 69–70, and 83–86.

*guilty.*" Aubin repeats this plea at the close of the narrative: "I hope it will be of use to all who read it, and prevent Men from entertaining that dangerous Enemy to Man's repose, Jealousy, and teach them to be very cautious in suspecting their Wives' Virtue, or giving credit to Appearances, which very often deceive the Wisest: and may the unhappy *Henrietta*'s Crimes and Death, make my own Sex take care to avoid the like Fate, and strive to imitate the virtuous Lady *Lucy*, that like her they may die in peace, and their Memorys be ever dear to all that know them, and reverenc'd by all Posterity" (pp. 284, 285).

In all of these (and other, similar passages), there is an underlying insistence that the best way in which readers can engage with Aubin's work is to imitate the conduct of her heroes and heroines—and shun that of her villains.

At first glance, this seems a rather odd presumption: surely those heroes and heroines are routinely thrust into situations that are far from those likely to befall Aubin's readers. For example, characters in *Lucinda, The Noble Slaves, Charlotta Du Pont,* and *Count Albertus* are all captured by North African corsairs (state-sanctioned pirates) and subsequently enslaved. Now "between 1660 and the 1730s, at least ... 6,000 Britons fell afoul of Barbary corsairs," but the vast majority were "poor, labouring men": "petty traders, fishermen, soldiers in transit to overseas postings, ... seamen" (Colley, *Captives* 44, 54), not the relatively wealthy, leisured people who could afford to purchase multi-shilling works of prose fiction. So opportunities to imitate the conduct of these characters while in North African captivity (or lost in the mountains of Wales or shipwrecked in South America) seem fairly unlikely to arise for most readers. But what if we thought more about the general form of the perils that Aubin's characters undergo than about their specific location and personnel? If we do, then it quickly becomes apparent that over and over we encounter teenaged girls who are being threatened with some sort of sexual violence—remember that the word "rape" comes from the Latin word *rapere* (to seize; cf. "raptor": a creature that seizes its prey), and so all of the kidnapping, even when it is not explicitly undertaken in the service of forced sex, is nonetheless shadowed by that possibility.[1] Aubin's readers, especially her young female readers (and there is reason to think that a substantial portion of

---

1 April London notes that "to be a woman in the Aubin world involves constant sexual intimidation" (112).

her readership was part of that demographic), may not have been at active risk of being forced into the seraglio of the Governor of Algiers or drugged and shipped across the Atlantic by an evil stepmother, but they were certainly in analogous sorts of peril on a regular basis.[1] Unwanted advances from neighbors and relatives; stepparents who wished their stepchildren out of the way in order for their own offspring to inherit more fully; parents who expected their children to renounce their first loves and marry others who could advance the family fortunes; a sense of constant vulnerability; sudden catastrophe when traveling: all these were routine experiences for teenagers and young adults in the early eighteenth century (and many of them continue to this day). Take away the exotic settings and romance names, and the predicaments in which Aubin's characters find themselves seem recognizable and familiar, and so if they could triumph over those threats through a combination of ingenuity, bravery, faith, and (where necessary) spectacular violence in their own defense, then they might well be useful models to imitate. Indeed, we could go a step further and suggest that it is precisely because Aubin's characters are

---

1   We have almost no direct evidence as to who read Aubin's work, but the general presumption in the period was certainly that prose fiction was primarily for that segment of the reading public that Samuel Johnson (1709–84) disparagingly termed "the young, the ignorant, and the idle, to whom [it] serve[s] as lectures of conduct, and introductions into life" (21). Hunter concurs, less judgmentally, arguing that "the evidence from novels themselves, from what novelists and social observers say about readers and from what readers report about their own reading experiences, all suggests that the young (males and females under the age of 25) were highly motivated toward novel reading and that they constituted the single largest age group of novel readers" (79). In the preface to *Count de Vinevil*, Aubin seems to presume that her readership will include "*our giddy Youth*" (p. 278). However, we should be cautious about presuming that this means that Aubin was writing what we would term YA fiction centuries before that category was invented (as, in effect, Mounsey contends in "'… bring her'"). Teresa Michals has argued that prior to 1900, almost all prose fiction was "written for a mixed-age audience, one that was primarily imagined not in terms of age but of social status and gender" (2). The only reader of Aubin for whom documentation survives, so far as we know, is Gertrude Savile, who read *Count de Vinevil* twice in the later 1720s when she was about thirty (49, 140). She also read *The Noble Slaves* (139–40).

defending and preserving themselves in milieux so different from the day-to-day lives of her readers that they can serve as compelling objects of imitation. Were they thrust into dilemmas that too closely resembled those of her readers, then it would be dangerously easy to get caught up in the minutiae and distracted by the particulars (e.g., "Belinda is being preyed upon by her husband's cousin, but I am not yet married and am being harassed by the miller down the road ..."). But the sheer extremity and exoticism of the situations faced by Aubin's principal characters allows their conduct to stand out. So too does their youth. Having twelve- to fifteen-year-olds as heroes and heroines was a convention of romance because it helped highlight just how exceptional and worthy of imitation they were (though the protagonists of traditional romance tended to be princes and princesses, not the children of gentry and merchants). Few young women were subject to quite as awful misunderstanding and mistreatment as, say, the Lady Lucy faced at the hands of her husband, but knowing that men could be murderously jealous and that seeming friends could betray you in ways that heightened that jealousy could be not only helpful but life-saving.[1] This goes beyond the "emotional practice" that Catherine Gallagher has seen as key to the process of sympathizing with a fictional character (getting low-risk opportunities to consider questions like "could I love Mr. so-and-so, were he to propose?")[2] into something more akin to Kenneth Burke's

---

1 Count Albertus is so enraged by what he thinks is evidence of the Lady Lucy's infidelity (some forged letters and a friend who has sex wearing Lucy's clothing) that he murders her supposed lover—his own cousin—and has Lucy kidnapped and taken out into the midst of the German woods, where he stabs her three times, attempts to shoot her in the face (scorching her eyelids), and leaves her for dead, stripping her of anything that might identify her, in a forest full of "wild Beasts" (72).

2 Gallagher contends that such "practice" hinges upon the felt fictionality of novelistic characters: the emotions aroused by sympathizing with a character took on "the same suppositional, conjectural status" as the character "in whom they supposedly originate." This "would have been especially important for women in an age when the new, affective demands of family life came into conflict with the still prevalent belief that women were not to love before they were beloved" (192). Cf. Johnson's account of "the purpose" of fiction as "not only to show mankind, but to provide that they may be seen hereafter with less hazard; to teach the means of avoiding the same snares which are laid

"literature as an equipment for living." For Burke, literature ultimately works in the way that proverbs work: to provide "*strategies for dealing with situations,*" so that when one encounters such a situation one knows what to do (11).[1] A reader's happiness, reputation, bodily integrity, and very life could depend on it.

Aubin's dedications, prefaces, and narratorial comments also stress the wonder that these stories should provoke in her readers (and she models such a response in the repeated accounts of how her characters were "surprized" by what they encountered).[2] Wonder, admiration, surprise, astonishment, and awe at marvels, miracles, rarities, and the mysterious workings of Providence: these were all important ways of engaging with both literature and the world in Aubin's time—albeit ones that have been eclipsed by

---

by Treachery for Innocence, without infusing any wish for that superiority with which the betrayer flatters his vanity; to give the power of counteracting fraud, without the temptation to practice it; to initiate youth by mock encounters in the art of necessary defence, and to increase prudence without impairing virtue" (22–23).

1  Cf. Hunter's observation that "readers, especially young readers, have always found novels a ready source of information about worlds they have not yet quite entered or circumstances still unmet.... Readers ... turned to novels to discover how the world 'really' works in matters of love, marriage, money, career, conversation, negotiation—virtually everything that we wish to feel more comfortable and sophisticated about than we ordinarily do" (91–92).

2  See the preface to *Madam de Beaumount* (the story about to begin is "*very extraordinary*" and the Count de Beaumount's actions are "*surprising*" [p. 59]); the preface to *Charlotta Du Pont* ("*the Adventures of a young Lady, whose Life contains the most extraordinary Events that I ever heard or read of*" [p. 121]); the preface to *Lady Lucy* ("*The Story I here present to the World is very extraordinary*") and its final paragraph: "And thus ends a History full of very extraordinary Events" (pp. 284, 285); and the narrator's comments at an important moment of transition in *Count Albertus*: "And now we are going to be entertained with very extraordinary Adventures, and the most strange Occurrences imaginable" (69). Cf. the title page of *Madam de Beaumount* reproduced on p. 57 ("many strange Accidents") and the ones transcribed later, (pp. 303–04) ("the surprizing Discoveries they made, and strange Deliverance thence" "with many extraordinary Accidents" [*The Noble Slaves*] and "the strange Adventures" and "wonderful Manner in which they met again, after living eighteen Years asunder" [*Lady Lucy*]).

modernity's supposed disenchantment of the world and the shift to a putatively more rational, secular, scientific way of thinking. Wonder was also "widely theorized in the period as the response that romance solicits" (Kareem 2), what with its wild adventures, statistically unlikely coincidences, and seemingly superhuman devotion and endurance. Such things rarely violate the ordinary laws of the universe (e.g., no one is brought back from the dead), but they stretch our sense of the possible and so help both the world and the heroines navigating it seem that much more exciting and special.[1] Wonder makes daily life less predictable, familiar, and boringly explicable. It gives an outlet for curiosity and a glimpse of how one's life could be other than it is. And it helps remind us that reality does not always fit within the bounds of "realism."[2]

Aubin's work poses an intriguing challenge to many of our standard ideas about "the novel," especially "the eighteenth-century novel." If we judge by most of our usual criteria, her fiction should be an abject failure. And yet it works, effectively and delightfully, which suggests that the problem lies with those criteria rather than in Aubin. In a similar vein, she usefully complicates many of our stock approaches to early women writers. One of the ironies of literary history is that despite our many (and justified) critiques of the misogyny of various aspects of the eighteenth century and our efforts to recover writers who have traditionally been marginalized or denigrated because of their gender or along gendered lines, we still often follow the lead of the eighteenth-century moralists who helped bring about that marginalization. This takes a number of forms, but chief among them is our persistent (and pernicious) tendency to divide female authors into stark dichotomies: sinners vs. saints, amatory vs. pious, public vs. private, professional vs. amateur, metropolitan vs. provincial. The usual examples of the first term in each of these dichotomies would include Aphra Behn (c. 1640–89), Delarivier Manley (c. 1670–1724), Haywood, and sometimes a few other figures who shared the Fair Triumvirate's

---

1  Lorraine Daston and Katherine Park describe wonders as marking "the outermost limits of the natural" and challenging "the assumptions that ruled ordinary life" (13, 20). They also usefully point out that wonders "demanded emotional and intellectual consent rather than a dogmatic commitment to belief" (60).

2  Cf. Scott Black's description of "the chronotope of adventure" as "a form of fiction about extraordinary experiences ... that offers readers, in turn, versions of such experiences" (3).

supposed focus on scandal and illicit desire and who wrote plays, prose fiction, and other commercially oriented forms for the unknown members of the reading public.[1] The second term in each dichotomy is reserved for the likes of Katherine Philips (1632–64), Anne Finch (1661–1720), and Elizabeth Singer Rowe (1674–1737), who were putatively more chaste, decorous, and financially independent, which meant that they could devote themselves to writing verse, conduct books, and other more respectable literary forms, often for a coterie of close friends. When it comes to scholarship on individual figures, we generally admit that the situation is more complex and nuanced than these "moralized taxonomies" (King 175) allow.[2] But this schema is still sufficiently entrenched as to be the default that gets trotted out when we need to quickly position a particular text or author.

Aubin, obviously, does not fit easily into any of these dichotomies. On one hand, the preface to *Charlotta Du Pont* presents her as the polar opposite of someone like Haywood: "*I had design'd to employ my Pen on something more serious and learned; but* [my booksellers] *tell me, I shall meet with no Incouragement, and advise me to write rather more modishly, that is, less like a Christian, and in a Style careless and loose, as the Custom of the present Age is to live. But I leave that to the other female Authors my Contemporaries, whose Lives and Writings have, I fear, too great a resemblance*" (p. 122). And yet Aubin not only was writing in a supposedly "low" commercial form (prose fiction) but was also explicitly concerned with how her work was selling.[3] Moreover, her work is, as we have seen, chock-full of adventure, violence, and other things that might

---

1 James Sterling referred to Behn, Manley, and Haywood as "*the fair Triumvirate of Wit*," playing off of John Denham's description of John Fletcher (1579–1625), Ben Jonson (1572–1637), and William Shakespeare (1564–1616) as "*the Triumvirate of wit*" (Sterling, sig. a2r; Denham, sig. b1v).

2 For examples of the uses to which these taxonomies have been put, see Prescott, especially 4–7.

3 For Aubin's attention to the market, despite her insistence in the preface to *Charlotta Du Pont* that "*I do not write for Bread, nor am I vain or fond of Applause; but I am very ambitious to gain the Esteem of those who honour Virtue, and shall ever be*" (p. 122), see the preface to *Count de Vinevil* ("*If this Trifle sells, I conclude it takes, and you may be sure to hear from me again; so you may be innocently diverted, and I employ'd to my Satisfaction*" [p. 279]); the preface to *Charlotta Du Pont* ("*The kind reception you have already given the Trifles I have* [continued]

seem at odds with any straightforward moralizing along the lines of what someone like Rowe supposedly provided.[1] But it is also concerned with the workings of Providence and how God will protect the innocent and punish the wicked. The result is that anyone coming to Aubin's fiction with a preconceived idea as to how she fits into the traditional dichotomies is likely to find themself immediately disoriented. Pious writers focused on moral improvement generally do not offer scenes as explicit and visceral (some might even say lurid) as we encounter in Aubin's work. And yet the moral intentions announced in her prefaces seem more than simply a fig leaf or marketing device (although they may well also be the latter).[2]

Given the ways in which almost any first-time encounter with Aubin today is likely to notice the inadequacy of these dichotomies as a means of describing her work, it is a bit surprising that for upward of 250 years, Aubin was generally regarded as uncomplicatedly and "strenuously pious" and working in the same vein as Rowe to provide "emotional confirmation" of "the victory of faith and virtue against an unbelieving world" (Richetti 262, 220).[3] The responsibility for this (at best) highly distorted view of Aubin and her work lies primarily with two texts from the 1730s, both of which have been taken at face value far more than they deserve.

---

published, lay me under an Obligation to do something more to merit your Favour. Besides, as I am neither a Statesman, Courtier, or modern great Man or Lady, I cannot break my Word without blushing, having ever kept it as a thing that is sacred: and I remember I promis'd in my Preface to the Count de Vineville, to continue writing if you dealt favourably with me. My Booksellers say, my Novels sell tolerably well" [pp. 121–22]); and the preface to Lady Lucy ("This is the fifth Attempt that I have made of this nature, to entertain the Publick, and not with ill Success; which has encouraged me to proceed" [p. 284]).

1  It's worth noting, however, that almost all of the alleged moral alternatives to the Fair Triumvirate are more interesting and complex than that categorization would suggest.

2  Prescott has argued that "by presenting herself ... as a virtuous opposite to her female contemporaries," Aubin "can carve a market niche for herself and suggest that her novels offer something different from the rest of the female-authored fiction being sold": her "commercial appeal lay in her virtuous difference from her 'scandalous' sisters" (50, 69).

3  I single out Richetti because his book has been particularly influential, but his understanding of Aubin is representative of most critics between approximately 1740 and 2000.

In 1739, Aubin's prose fiction was posthumously collected into a three-volume set with a preface (possibly by Samuel Richardson [1689–1761]; Appendix B2) that presented her as unabashedly seeking to "*mend … the Hearts of her Readers; … Encourage … Religion and Virtue; and … discountenanc*[e] *… Impiety and Vice.*" According to the author of the 1739 preface, Aubin is, in this aim, unlike most of her female contemporaries, who "*have been far from preserving that Purity of Style and Manners, which is the greatest Glory of a fine Writer on any Subject; but, like the* fallen Angels, *having lost their own Innocence, seem, as one would think by their Writings, to make it their Study to corrupt the Minds of others, and render them as depraved, as miserable, and as lost as themselves.*" On the contrary, she is following in the admirable tradition of "*the celebrated Mrs.* Rowe, *with whom she had an Intimacy, as we see* [in the dedication to *Charlotta Du Pont*], *and may farther reasonably infer from the Tenor of both their Writings, for the Promotion of the Cause of Religion and Virtue.*"[1] As evidence, the author of the preface quotes selectively from Aubin's prefaces and concludes that—unlike, say, Haywood—her work may be "*safely … recommended to the Perusal of Youth, without the least Apprehension of inculcating upon their Minds, those impure and polluted Images which too generally abound in Pieces of this Nature.*" As an account of Aubin, this seems startlingly incomplete and like it's ignoring a lot of potential counter-evidence. For instance, her work not infrequently includes images that the author of the preface would presumably describe (at least if they appeared in Behn, Manley, or Haywood) as "*impure and polluted.*"[2] But some combination of the greater availability of this collection than the earlier editions of Aubin's work (multi-volume sets tend to survive better) and the ways in which it assimilated her to the kind of Richardsonian moral project that would become dominant—or at least normative—among women writers in the second half of the eighteenth century made the 1739 preface's

---

1  See p. 119, n. 1 in this edition for how the "Mrs. *Rowe*" to whom *Charlotta Du Pont* is dedicated is almost certainly not "*the celebrated Mrs.* Rowe" (i.e., Elizabeth Singer Rowe) to whom the 1739 preface refers.

2  Consider only the moment in *Lucinda* when, after our heroine's master dies, she watches his body be prepared for Islamic burial, which includes "stripp[ing] off his Linen" and "wash[ing] … his Privities"— i.e., his genitals (106). While the episode is not eroticized in any way, it nonetheless depicts a scene that the author of the 1739 preface would regard as deeply unsuitable, both for heroines to witness and for "*the Perusal of Youth.*"

version of Aubin stick and so become the "common knowledge" on which most subsequent scholarship would build.

An accurate understanding of Aubin was also made considerably more difficult by the fact that the most readily available biographical information about her was Antoine François Prévost d'Exiles's description of her in several issues of his periodical, *Le Pour et contre* (for a translation of the most relevant section, see Appendix B1). Prévost (1697–1763) lived in London in the late 1720s and early 1730s—to avoid arrest in France for having left his abbey without permission—and so could plausibly have met Aubin. But the account he gives is both incorrect and seemingly malicious. According to Prévost, Aubin was the daughter of a French officer and both ugly and poor (the latter because, after her first work of prose fiction—which only succeeded because of the novelty of its having been written by a woman, her work was received coldly by the public). Out of a combination of piety and disgust with the world, Aubin turned to lay preaching and had some short-lived success as an oddity. Shortly thereafter she died. Prévost pretends to defend Aubin against an attack by *The Grub-Street Journal*, a prominent satirical weekly loosely affiliated with Alexander Pope (1688–1744)—the substance of which is that ugly women should not have the audacity to appear, much less perform, in public, but no such attack has ever been located in the pages of that journal and the effect of his putatively chivalric action is to underscore his earlier characterization of Aubin as not only ugly but also somehow defined by her ugliness. This is clearly a far from impartial account, yet because it was one of the very few from the eighteenth century readily available in print (the others being the remarks about Aubin's moral character and "*Intimacy*" with "*the celebrated Mrs. Rowe*" in the 1739 preface and Elizabeth Griffith's report, in 1777, that Aubin was "so personally unknown to fame" that "no particulars of her private life have come to my knowledge, farther than that she was the wife of a Mr. Aubin, who held a genteel employment under government, during the reigns of queen Anne and of George the first" [47]), Prévost's biographical tidbits came to be relied on by scholars who really should have known better. William McBurney, for example, whose 1957 article remains the standard starting point for most scholarship on Aubin, describes Prévost as "curiously malicious" and "sneer[ing]" yet seems to accept his description of her ugliness and presumes, on the basis of Prévost's claim that Aubin's father was a French officer (and perhaps the fact that Aubin is itself a French surname), that Aubin was "Catholic, by birth or conversion" (McBurney 246, 262, 247). On its own, this erroneous version of Aubin's biography (Aubin was English by birth, Anglican, reasonably well off, and—at the time that Prévost was writing—still alive) might simply be annoying and a sign that some scholars hadn't done their due diligence. However, coupled with our longstanding tendency to read women's writing with the default presumption that it must be autobiographical, Prévost's distortions and falsehoods (it seems improbable that they are all merely mistakes) and later generations' overcredulous reliance on them have meant that the "Aubin" discussed for most of the time since her death in 1738 bears relatively little resemblance to the historical Aubin and her work.

Aubin's actual biography has only recently been reconstructed through the meticulous archival research of Joel Baer and Debbie Welham.[1] Aubin was born sometime between 1679 and 1682 as Penelope Charleton, the illegitimate daughter of Sir Richard Temple (1634–97) and Anne Charleton. She was herself Anglican, but spent time around Catholics in Hammersmith (then a quiet town west of London, where King Charles II's Portuguese Catholic widow Catherine of Braganza [1638–1705] lived), and some of her husband's family were Huguenots— French Protestants, who had been stripped of their rights and expelled from their country in the 1680s. Penelope Charleton married Abraham Aubin in 1696 while she was still in her midteens, without parental consent, which deprived them of an expected dowry and inheritance. They had three children, all of whom seem to have predeceased their parents. Her husband was an army officer and merchant and his brothers were merchants who traded all over the Atlantic. One lived in the Caribbean and was captured and beaten by French pirates, who then stole his ship; another (who was involved in the slave trade) survived a hurricane and a shipwreck. Aubin was herself involved in the planning, and probably the financial support, of a project in 1702 to salvage a sunken treasure ship in the Caribbean. And there is reason to think that she probably carried on the family business while her husband was away fighting in the War of the Spanish Succession (at least between 1706 and 1712 and possibly earlier as well). Presumably because of these connections, Aubin was asked in 1708 to help organize a petition to Queen Anne (r. 1702–14) on behalf of a proposed scheme to

---

1 For more details, see Baer; Baer and Welham; Welham, "Delight"; "Lady"; "Particular Case."

pardon and repatriate the English pirates who were hiding out on Madagascar, in return for a share of their supposedly astonishing plunder; Aubin declined and the next year gave a deposition to the Board of Trade—the governmental body that oversaw the colonies—against the plan, at least in part because the chief organizer of the scheme was a conman and sometime pirate. She published three poems in the first decade of the eighteenth century and then apparently nothing else until 1721, when she began to both write and translate prose fiction at a rapid pace for several years (see the Brief Chronology, pp. 48–49). Somewhat unusually for prose fiction in the period, most of her work was signed. Also unusually, her work was published by a fairly stable group of booksellers (what we would call publishers) who had joined together in a "conger" to decrease the financial risks of speculative publication (see A Note on the Texts, p. 51). In 1729, Aubin established the "Lady's Oratory," a running series of public performances in which she offered satirical commentary on current events—and sometimes music or tea—to paying customers (this included mocking her principal competition, another orator named John Henley [1692–1756]). In 1730 a play of hers, *The Merry Masqueraders,* was performed briefly at the Little Theatre in the Haymarket, one of several small theaters that had sprung up in the late 1720s to compete with the established theaters of Drury Lane and Lincoln's Inn Fields that operated under royal patents. Aubin died in 1738, a year before the publication of the collection that would so shape her posthumous reputation.

As her biography should suggest, Aubin was worldly. She understood how global commerce worked and the threats posed to it by natural disasters and piracy. She also understood the realities of dynastic and religious politics, as is evidenced by her early poems in praise of Queen Anne and the Duke of Marlborough (1650–1722; Anne's principal and most successful general in the War of the Spanish Succession, which is, of course, the war in which Aubin's husband fought). So whatever departures from those actualities that we get in her work are most likely deliberate choices on her part, rather than the result of ignorance or misunderstanding. With that in mind, let's conclude by briefly exploring two important and highly charged issues of the 1720s that figure prominently in Aubin's work (North African captivity and lingering Jacobite support for the deposed Stuart family) so that users of this edition can better assess the ways in which she is engaging with and transforming them and how her approach compares to that of other writers of the period.

As the summaries of various scenes given earlier should indicate, much of Aubin's work features characters who were captured and sold into slavery—or threatened with such a fate—in the Ottoman Empire (which was centered in present-day Turkey but controlled almost the entire eastern Mediterranean, including much of the Balkans and most of the Black Sea, and which extended as far east as present-day Iraq), its North African client states (Algiers, Tunis, and Tripolitania),[1] or Morocco. Slavery was an integral part of most Mediterranean states and their economies. Navies (especially those of France, Genoa, the Papal States, and Venice) relied on enslaved people—both prisoners and Muslim captives—to row their galleys. Farmers and artisans regularly turned to enslaved labor to keep their operations going. The governments of the North African or "Barbary" states (especially Algiers) depended heavily on their corsairs capturing European ships and raiding coastal European villages and then selling or ransoming the resulting captives (the rulers took a cut of such sales and ransoms and taxed whatever valuables were seized at the time of capture). Some European nations, especially Malta and Spain, engaged in similar practices. And elite men in the Islamic part of the Mediterranean kept enslaved captives, both male and female, for sexual exploitation, sometimes individually and sometimes in established seraglios.

Unlike the slavery that was key to the settler societies of the Caribbean and much of North and South America (and so to the European powers that had colonies in the New World), Mediterranean slavery was not overwhelmingly racialized. Nor was it typically hereditary, and it was possible for a captive to be ransomed by their family, church, or state in a way that was not available to the vast majority of enslaved people in the Americas. This is not to say that skin color did not matter (especially fair or dark complexions were sometimes prized or denigrated, and captives from certain regions tended to be put to particular kinds of work). But specific sorts of people were not presumptively slaves or enslavable simply because of their ancestry or skin color in the way that persons of African descent were for European settlers in most of the Americas. Instead, slavery throughout the Mediterranean was wholly tied up with religion and politics. The North African corsairs focused their attacks on ships from and villages in Christian nations, especially those with whom they had

---

1 Algiers, Tunis, and Tripolitania correspond roughly with the coastal portions of present-day Algeria, Tunisia, and Libya.

Lorenzo a Castro, *A Sea Fight with Barbary Corsairs* (c. 1681–86), oil on canvas

not signed treaties, and the Maltese and Spanish did the same with Muslim ships (as did other European nations on a more occasional basis). At the same time, though, the Mediterranean was one of the most important and profitable areas of the world for trade, so European nations that sought that trade regularly and knowingly put their sailors (and the passengers on their ships) at risk.[1] The result was that, as mentioned earlier, at least six thousand

---

1  In 1700, British trade in the Mediterranean was worth as much as all the trade with India and North America "put together" (Colley, *Captives* 34).

Britons were captured between 1660 and the 1730s by corsairs operating out of North Africa, and they were a small fraction of the total number of Europeans who were taken.[1] Some were ransomed and got to return home; some escaped; a few converted to Islam and gained some measure of freedom and occasionally even wealth; a majority probably died in captivity after treatment ranging from the comparatively humane (if still profoundly unjust) to the almost unimaginably cruel.[2] One of the principal consequences of all this for our understanding of Aubin is that British readers of the 1720s were significantly more likely to know about Mediterranean slavery (and perhaps even know someone—most likely a man—who was once captive in the Mediterranean) than they were to know about the Caribbean and North and South American plantation slavery that is far more familiar to us. Most ransoms for British captives were raised through churches (both the established Churches of England, Ireland, and Scotland, and those of the various Protestant Dissenting sects), which, because of more or less compulsory church attendance, meant that "virtually every man, woman, and child in Britain and Ireland ... was exposed to arguments, assertions and rudimentary information about Muslim North Africa, the Ottoman Empire more generally, and commercial and naval activity in the Mediterranean. Not since the Crusades, had the power and content of Islam been ventilated in these islands at such a broad and popular level" (Colley, *Captives* 76).[3] And when ransomed captives returned, there were often public ceremonies, such as a procession of 280 men wearing the remaining rags of their "Moorish" clothing through the streets of London in December 1721, to which the closing paragraphs of

1  Robert Davis has estimated that "between 1530 and 1780 there were almost certainly a million and quite possibly as many as a million and a quarter ... European Christians enslaved" in North Africa (23). Davis's figure derives from the fact that the enslaved population was fairly stable (about 35,000 at a time) but required an influx of approximately 8,500 new captives every year to offset deaths, ransoms, and conversions.
2  Under the dominant interpretation of Islamic law, "only unbelievers could be enslaved in the first place," which may partially explain the attraction of converting (Colley, *Captives* 115).
3  It is worth remembering that that power was not just a threat to Europeans at the level of individual ships and their passengers. An Ottoman army pushed far enough north to besiege Vienna, the capital of the Habsburg Holy Roman Empire, in 1683.

*The Noble Slaves* may refer (see p. 282). For most of Aubin's original readers, "slavery" probably conjured up something done to Europeans by Muslims in the Mediterranean, rather than something done by Europeans to persons of African descent on both sides of the Atlantic. This is not to say there was no awareness of the latter; there certainly was. But for most Britons of the 1720s, what we tend to think of first when we think of slavery was decidedly secondary to what happened every day in the Mediterranean.

The sense that many of Aubin's initial readers had of the Islamic Mediterranean as a potent threat was complicated by a growing fascination in the period with "oriental" fashion and customs, including the drinking of coffee (which was almost unknown in Europe prior to 1650 and ubiquitous by Aubin's time). Largely spurred on by the translation of what we often call *The Arabian Nights* first into French in 1704–06 and then almost immediately into English, there was a vogue in the early eighteenth century for stories of Turkish and Persian opulence, sensuality, and magic, which, while often wildly fanciful, could make the Islamic world come off as not only alluring but also offering kinds of freedom not available to most people in Europe. Aubin does not go as far down that road as some of her contemporaries, but the unsettling attractiveness of many of the Muslim men in her work may owe a debt to this fascination. So too may some of the glowing descriptions of beautiful objects to be found (and sometimes weaponized) in the seraglios into which her heroines are thrust.

But the attention of Aubin and her readers was not just devoted to threats abroad. Domestic dangers were also a perennial source of concern (and fodder for stories, albeit often in coded ways to avoid prosecution for seditious libel). The greatest of these was the ongoing threat of Jacobitism (the desire to reinstate the Stuart rulers who had been deposed in the Revolution of 1688–89). Because Elizabeth Tudor (Queen Elizabeth I, r. 1558–1603) died without any children, the throne of England passed to her first cousin twice removed, James Stuart (already King James VI of Scotland, r. 1567–1625), who became King James I of England (r. 1603–25). After his death both nations continued to be ruled by a single monarch, James's eldest surviving son, Charles, who became King Charles I (r. 1625–49). For a variety of reasons, including Charles I's high-handed attempt to govern without Parliament and to impose English religious ritual on the Scots, a series of civil wars broke out in the late 1630s and engulfed England, Scotland, and Ireland (then effectively an English colony) until the early

1650s. Toward the end of that period, Charles I sought refuge with the Scots who, after lengthy negotiations, turned him over to the English, whose Parliament (purged of Royalists) tried him for treason and executed him in 1649. England then briefly experimented with being a republic and then lapsed into a military dictatorship under Oliver Cromwell (1599–1658). After Cromwell's death the nation was thrown into chaos, and by 1660, powerful factions in England were soliciting Charles I's son, who had been in exile on the Continent, to return and be crowned King Charles II (he, of course, thought he had been king since his father's execution). The monarchy was restored in 1660 with widespread support, though some of that early enthusiasm soon waned. Charles II (r. 1660–85) had thirteen or fourteen children, but none of them with his wife, Catherine of Braganza, and so the throne was set to pass to his younger brother, James. However, James had converted to Catholicism, so there was a strong push in the years surrounding 1680 to exclude him from the throne (a crisis that saw the invention of something like modern political parties). Ultimately, that campaign failed and James succeeded his brother and put down a rebellion from one of his nephews (Charles's eldest illegitimate child, also named James [1649–85]) to become King James II of England and James VII of Scotland in 1685 (r. 1685–88). However, because he was not only personally Catholic (and poised to establish a Catholic dynasty) but also seemed devoted to undoing the exclusion of Catholics from public life that had been a central feature of Protestant rule for more than a century, James quickly alienated many of his most powerful subjects, especially as his admiration for the absolutist approach to monarchy being pursued by King Louis XIV of France (r. 1643–1715) became clear. In 1688, they invited James's staunchly Protestant nephew and son-in-law, William, Prince of Orange and Statholder (steward) of the Dutch Republic, to assist them in preserving liberty and "true religion." William landed on the southern coast of England with a Dutch army and marched toward London. James panicked and fled, the members of Parliament who had invited William to England declared the throne abandoned, and then, in early 1689, asked William and Mary (James II's eldest daughter, who was married to William), to assume the role of joint sovereigns. However, James II did not relinquish the throne quite that easily, and the fighting that had been largely avoided in England (which is part of why the Revolution of 1688–89 has often been described by the English as the "Glorious" or "Bloodless" Revolution) devastated Ireland and Scotland over the next few years and created resentments, especially in Northern Ireland, that last to this day. A significant minority of the English and even more of the Scots and Irish thought that the accession of King William III (William II in Scotland) and Queen Mary II was an illegitimate jumping of the line of succession, which it was, if the son that had been born to James II shortly before the Revolution was in fact his child—there were rumors that an unrelated baby had been smuggled in as part of a Catholic plot. Those who still supported James II and thought him their rightful monarch were called Jacobites (from the Latin version of James, *Jacobus*). They plotted, schemed, and forged alliances with the Catholic powers of Europe, especially France—though perhaps not quite as much as the Williamites feared they were doing (there was a lot of paranoia in the decades following the Revolution). Mary II died in 1694, after which William III ruled alone until 1702. All of Mary's pregnancies ended in miscarriage, so the throne passed to her younger sister, Anne (another devout Protestant). All of Queen Anne's children (five live births out of seventeen pregnancies) died while she was still a princess, which meant that, legally, the line of succession reverted to the deposed James II/VII or, after he died in 1701, to the son just mentioned (yet another James), which in turn meant that the prospect of a Catholic dynasty was again on the horizon. This was unacceptable to the English Parliament, which passed the Act of Settlement in 1701 barring Catholics or anyone married to a Catholic from holding the throne, thus, in one fell swoop, disqualifying the first fifty-seven heirs in the line of succession. The next Protestant in line was Sophia, the Electress of Hanover (in northern Germany), who was the second youngest child—of thirteen—born to James I's eldest daughter. However, Sophia died a scant two months before Anne and so her position as heir apparent passed to her son, Georg Ludwig, who became King George I of Great Britain and Ireland in 1714 (England and Scotland had joined to form a United Kingdom in 1706–07). By bringing in a German, who spoke relatively little English and often seemed to care more about Hanover than Britain, simply because he was the closest Protestant heir, Parliament effectively ended the Stuart dynasty (George I [r. 1714–27] was technically the great-grandchild of James I, just as Mary II and Anne had been, but he was so culturally different from his predecessors that it seemed as if an era had ended).

The reason that all of this political history matters for our thinking about Aubin is that with the Act of Settlement and the accession of George I, the chances of the monarchy passing peacefully back into Stuart hands became vanishingly small: George had two legitimate children who each had children of their own, so the prospect of a Hanoverian dynasty stretched out into the indefinite future. The Jacobites decided to take more drastic measures. In 1715, there was a Jacobite uprising in which an army of Scots (and a few English) loyal to James II/VII's son (the would-be James III/VIII) captured almost all of Scotland and began to advance into northern England before being defeated. The Jacobites who survived had their property confiscated and were tried for treason and sentenced to death, though most were pardoned in 1717 by an Act of Parliament. Not content with this result, in 1719, another group of Jacobites launched an uprising, this time with Spanish help (though not nearly as much as they had anticipated). A small force of Spanish marines and Jacobite exiles landed in Scotland and fought a few battles before again being defeated by the British army, though the Scottish Highlands remained largely outside of governmental control for close to a decade. And then again, in 1721–22, a group of English Jacobites planned a *coup d'état* in which they would seize important buildings in London, capture the royal family, and murder other prominent state officials. The plot collapsed when the Duke of Orleans (1674–1723), then serving as the regent of France for the underage King Louis XV (r. 1715–74), informed the British government that the Jacobites had asked him for military aid. The leading conspirators were arrested and tried (possibly with manufactured evidence) and either executed or forced into exile. In the course of just seven years there were three Jacobite campaigns to overthrow the Hanoverians and forcibly restore the Stuarts to power (and rumors of still more). None of them ultimately succeeded, but their failure was hardly guaranteed at the time; had they succeeded they would have, depending on one's point of view, either dragged Britain back to the horrors of Protestants being burned at the stake for heresy or undone the appalling injustice of the Revolution of 1688–89 and the subsequent exclusion of the Stuarts from their divinely ordained role as monarchs. Either way, the stakes were huge. When Aubin presents us with characters who are Jacobites (in both of the texts in this edition, plus *Lady Lucy*), it is a move that is highly charged. We can't be certain where Aubin's political sympathies lay (there were plenty of people who regarded the Stuarts as having a better claim to the throne and more charisma than the Hanoverians, who nonetheless were not willing to fight a civil war on their behalf). But the inclusion of these explicitly Jacobite figures—typically gentleman bandits and pirates—is something that both sets Aubin apart from most of her contemporaries (who, if they were presenting Jacobites as anything other than dastardly traitors tended to do so in coded, allegorical ways) and usefully reminds us that for all of the delicious over-the-topness of her work, it is nonetheless deeply engaged with the world in which she and her initial readers were living. Aubin's work may not be "realistic" in our customary (often narrow and bland) sense. But in its engagement with the perils posed, especially to young women, by a world of sexual violence, grasping families, slavery, piracy, and political upheaval, it is movingly, profoundly real. And in the sympathy, even admiration, that Aubin shows for various types of people (Catholics, Jacobites, "fallen" women, the queer, even some Muslims) who were being actively vilified by her government, her Church, and most of her fellow British subjects, she is demonstrating a courage and compassion that are rare in any age—and certainly not part of how we have tended to regard the "moral" women writers of the eighteenth century. Aubin both deserves and amply rewards far more attention than scholars have traditionally been willing to accord her. At least judging by her sales, her earliest readers not only understood what she was doing but also savored it. We would do well to follow their lead.

# Penelope Aubin: A Brief Chronology

c. 1679–82 Penelope born to Ann Charleton, mistress of Sir
Richard Temple
1696 Penelope Charleton marries Abraham Aubin and
becomes Penelope Aubin; they marry without the
consent of their parents, which deprives her of a
£1,000 dowry and gets him disowned
1697 First child born (Marie)
1699 Second child born (Abraham)
1701 Third child born (Penelope)
1702 Aubin advises Thomas Fairfax, Baron of Cameron,
and Richard Savage, Earl of Rivers, regarding a
proposed expedition to the Caribbean to salvage a
sunken treasure ship; she may also have invested in
this venture; as part of this, she meets with a pirate,
Peter Dearlove
1703 The Aubins sue Penelope's mother in the Court of
Chancery for her withheld dowry and a secret inheritance from her father that they never received
1706 Abraham commissioned as a second lieutenant in
the army
1707 Publishes *The Stuarts: A Pindarique Ode. Humbly
Dedicated to Her Majesty of Great Britain* (November)
1708 Publishes *The Extasy: A Pindarick Ode to Her Majesty
the Queen*
Meets with the backers of a plan for the British
government to pardon and repatriate English pirates
hiding out in Madagascar in return for a share of
their supposedly fabulous wealth, but declines their
request to help with a lobbying campaign on behalf
of this plan
1709 Publishes *The Wellcome: A Poem, to His Grace the
Duke of Marlborough* (March)
Gives a deposition that helps the Board of Trade
decide to reject the plan to pardon and repatriate
the Madagascar pirates
1712 Abraham retires from the army
1720 Abraham's brother is attacked by French privateers
in the Caribbean; the local officials in Martinique
(where he and his crew are taken) are not helpful

| 1721 | Publishes *The Strange Adventures of the Count de Vinevil and His Family* (July) |
| --- | --- |
| | Edits and publishes Thomas Gibbs's translation of Marin le Roy, sieur de Gomberville's *La Doctrine des moeurs* (Paris, 1646) as *The Doctrine of Morality; or, A View of Human Life, According to the Stoick Philosophy* (August) |
| | Publishes *The Life of Madam de Beaumount, a French Lady* (mid-October) |
| | Publishes *The Life and Amorous Adventures of Lucinda, an English Lady* (late October; dated 1722 on the title page). Unlike the rest of her prose fiction, this text appeared without Aubin's name on the title page, though it was advertised with *The Strange Adventures of the Count de Vinevil and His Family* and *The Life of Madam de Beaumount*, so potential readers might have been able to guess at its authorship |
| 1722 | Publishes *The Noble Slaves* (March) |
| | Publishes a translation, with new names for the characters, of Louise-Geneviève Gomès de Vasconcellos, Gillot de Beaucour's *Les Mémoires de la vie de Madame de Ravezan* (Paris, 1678) as *The Adventures of the Prince of Clermont, and Madam de Ravezan* (March), though the title page claims the translation was "by the Author of Ildegerte"; *Ildegerte Reyne de Norwege, ou L'Amour magnanime* (Paris, 1694) was written by Eustache Le Noble, and we do not know who was responsible for its 1721 translation into English, nor whether they had any connection to Aubin |
| | Publishes a translation of François Pétis de la Croix's *Histoire du Grand Genghizcan* (Paris, 1710) as *The History of Genghizcan the Great* (July) |
| | *The Strange Adventures of the Count de Vinevil* reprinted in Dublin |
| 1723 | Publishes *The Life of Charlotta Du Pont, an English Lady* (July) |
| 1726 | Publishes *The Life and Adventures of the Lady Lucy* (March) |
| | Publishes a translation of Robert Challes's *Les Illustres Françoises* (The Hague, 1713) as *The Illustrious French Lovers* (September; dated 1727 on the title page) |

The unsold sheets of *The Doctrine of Morality* are reissued under a new title: *Moral Virtue Delineated*
*The Life and Adventures of the Lady Lucy* reprinted in parts

1728    Publishes *The Life and Adventures of the Young Count Albertus, the Son of Count Lewis Augustus by the Lady Lucy* (January)
Abraham draws up a will but does not mention their children, which suggests that they may all have been dead by this point
*The Strange Adventures of the Count de Vinevil* reprinted
*The Life of Madam de Beaumount* reprinted

1729    Publishes a translation of Marguerite de Lussan's *Histoire de la comtesse de Gondez* (Paris, 1725) as *The Life of the Countess de Gondez* (January)
Establishes the Lady's Oratory in April; it runs regularly through November, with a final performance in February 1730

1730    *The Merry Masqueraders*, Aubin's only play, performed for two or three nights in December at the Little Theatre in the Haymarket; on the final night, Aubin spoke "a new Epilogue"
*The Noble Slaves* reprinted in Dublin

1732    Publishes *The Merry Masqueraders*; it is advertised as being a reprint of a Dublin edition, but the latter, if it existed, is not extant

1733    The unsold sheets of *The Merry Masqueraders* are reissued by a different bookseller under a new title: *The Humours of the Masqueraders*

1734    *The Merry Masqueraders* reprinted as *The Masquerade; or The Humourous Cuckold*
Antoine François Prévost d'Exiles offers an incorrect and seemingly malicious account of Aubin in his periodical, *Le Pour et contre*

1736    *The Life of Charlotta Du Pont* reprinted
*The Noble Slaves* reprinted twice in Dublin
Prévost returns to the topic of Aubin in *Le Pour et contre*, telling the tale of a supposed squabble between two booksellers over the rights to publish a manuscript of hers

1738    Aubin dies (April)

# A Note on the Texts

*The Life of Madam de Beaumount* was first published in mid-October 1721 by the "Castle Conger" of booksellers: Elizabeth Bell, John Darby, Arthur Bettesworth, Francis Fayram, John Pemberton, John Hooke, Charles Rivington, Francis Clay, Jeremiah Batley, and Edward Symon.[1] Somewhat unusually for prose fiction, it bore Aubin's name on the title page.[2] It was also—and this, too, was unusual—"adorned" with what an early advertisement described as "a curious frontispiece" (see p. 56).[3] A second edition of *The Life of Madam de Beaumount*, financed by a slightly different configuration of the conger, came out in 1728, and the text was included in

---

1   A "conger" was a group of booksellers (what we would call publishers) who jointly financed publications and then shared in their profits or losses. Congers were a means of managing the financial risk of publishing (then, as now, most of the cost of publishing a book was incurred speculatively up front and may or may not have been made back, much less made back promptly). The term "conger" comes from a kind of large eel that devours all of its smaller competition. The names of the booksellers are listed (with one exception) in descending order of their seniority in the Stationer's Company, the guild for the book trades.

2   Leah Orr has calculated that "in the period 1690–1730, approximately 70 percent of the fiction published did not name the real author on the title page" (75). This figure is a combination of outright anonymity, the use of a pseudonym, the pretense that the narrative was written by one of its characters, and the provision of an authorial name inside the book itself—perhaps at the close of the dedication. Since extra copies of title pages were pasted up as advertising and their text was often used for newspaper advertising (which is how provincial readers typically found out about new books), only providing a name inside the book could make it effectively anonymous for most potential readers until it had been purchased. And a substantial majority of prose fiction in the 1720s was purchased (or borrowed from friends and relations); the commercial circulating libraries that were such a big part of later eighteenth-century novel reading were only just getting going and were not yet established in London.

3   The frontispiece was designed and engraved by John Pine (1690–1756), who produced the frontispieces for four other works of Aubin's as well: *The Strange Adventures of the Count de Vinevil* (*continued*)

*A Collection of Entertaining Histories and Novels* (1739), a three-volume set of Aubin's work put out by yet another configuration of the conger. Appearing in multiple editions was, of course, a sign of commercial success, since a new edition would not be printed until the previous edition was either close to sold out or completely so.[1] The text was then serialized by George Buckeridge in fifteen (probably weekly) parts in 1741.[2] Later in the century, it was reprinted twice under the title *Belinda; or, Happiness the Reward of Constancy*. Nowhere do the latter indicate that this was a decades-old text. Indeed, one of the editions of *Belinda*, probably published in the early to mid-1760s, claims that it provides "a SERIES of the most INTERESTING and SURPRIZING EVENTS ever yet made publick." The 1721 first edition was printed in a duodecimo format, as were the subsequent editions, including the 1739 collection, except for one of the editions of *Belinda*, which was in octodecimo (also known as eighteenmo). "Duodecimo" means that the book in question is comprised of sheets of paper folded and cut to each form twelve leaves and so twenty-four pages (an octodecimo would be folded and cut to yield eighteen leaves, and so thirty-six pages, per sheet). In the case of the first edition of *The Life of Madam de Beaumount*, six sheets of paper were required for each copy, with a typical page measuring 13 x 6.9 cm (approximately 5⅛ x 2¾ inches). The book sold for 1 shilling and ninepence, a fairly typical price for a volume of that length, especially one that contained an illustration (paper was the single largest expense in eighteenth-century book production, so price closely correlated to the number of sheets required).[3]

The first edition of *The Life of Charlotta Du Pont* came out in early July 1723. Unlike Aubin's other prose fiction, *Charlotta Du*

---

and *His Family, The Life and Amorous Adventures of Lucinda, The Noble Slaves*, and her translation of Louise-Geneviève Gomès de Vasconcellos, Gillot de Beaucour's *Les Mémoires de la vie de Madame de Ravezan*.

1 Orr notes that "at least a quarter of the works of fiction" published between 1690 and 1730 "did not sell well enough to be reprinted at all" (56).

2 Publication in parts allowed readers who couldn't afford the price of an entire book at once to acquire it piecemeal over time (although sometimes at a greater total cost).

3 For typical prices and how they correlate to length, see Orr, *Novel Ventures* 36. See "A Note on Money" (p. 55) for how to convert this price to an approximate modern equivalent.

*Pont* was published by a single individual, Arthur Bettesworth, rather than a conger—although Bettesworth was a member of the Castle Conger. A second edition, put out by Bettesworth and his son-in-law, Charles Hitch (another member of the later configurations of the Castle Conger), appeared in 1736, and the text was included in the 1739 *Collection of Entertaining Histories and Novels*. Another edition was published in twenty-five (probably weekly) parts in 1739 without any publication information, which suggests that it was probably not authorized by the copyright holders (i.e., it was "pirated").[1] This edition also omitted Aubin's name. Similarly to what happened with *The Life of Madam de Beaumount*, *The Life of Charlotta Du Pont* appeared, with minor changes, under a new title (again with no attribution to Aubin) in 1770: *The Inhuman Stepmother; or, The History of Miss Harriot Montague*. *The Life of Charlotta Du Pont* then reappeared in 1800, as part of a series, *English Nights Entertainments*, under the title *The Life, Adventures and Distresses of Charlotte Dupont, and Her Lover Belanger; Who, it is supposed, underwent a greater Variety of real Misfortunes, and miraculous Adventures, than any Couple that ever existed*. The 1723 first edition was printed as a duodecimo, using twelve sheets of paper per copy, with a typical page measuring 13.2 x 7.2 cm (roughly 5¼ x 2⅞ inches). It sold for 2 shillings in a sheepskin binding and 2 shillings and sixpence for a calfskin binding (both prices are slightly on the low end for a book of that size). Subsequent editions were also in duodecimo, except for the unauthorized 1739 edition, which was in octavo (a format comprised of sheets folded to each yield eight leaves and so sixteen pages).

The texts of *The Life of Madam de Beaumount* and *The Life of Charlotta Du Pont* in this edition follow the 1721 and 1723 first editions, although in each case a few obvious errors have been corrected, following the 1739 collection if it made the same correction. I have otherwise left the text unaltered, even when it is inconsistent (as it is with several characters' names). There are a

---

1 The following year, this edition was advertised as "printed for, and sold by" Elizabeth Applebee in the back of another book she published, but it is unclear why she should have brought out *The Life of Charlotta Du Pont* in the first place. If she had permission either from Bettesworth and Hitch or from the Castle Conger, she would most likely have indicated that on the title page. Instead, the publication information at the bottom simply reads "*LONDON*: Printed in the YEAR 1739."

number of other changes made in the 1739 collection but they are all attempts to regularize Aubin's style and so reveal more about what her posthumous editor (possibly Samuel Richardson) thought was good English than they do about what Aubin actually wrote.

The texts in the appendices are taken from their respective first editions, with the exception of the selection from the Abbé Prévost's *Le Pour et contre*, which I present in translation (Appendix B1).

With all of these texts, I have added apostrophes and quotation marks, in keeping with modern North American usage, where it seemed likely that they could help prevent confusion (eighteenth-century printing uses apostrophes somewhat differently than we do, and quotation marks, when employed at all, tend to run down the left side of a page, rather than enclose specific lines). I have glossed, on their first appearance in a text, all the words and references that I thought could benefit from a note, but if you are puzzled by a word that goes unglossed, try reading it aloud. Chances are it is just an unfamiliar spelling (e.g., "waste" for "waist").

# A Note on Money

In the early eighteenth century, British money comprised pennies (or pence), shillings, and pounds. There were 12 pence to a shilling and 20 shillings to a pound. Often these would be referred to by their Latin abbreviations: d. [*denarii*] for pence, s. [*solidi*] for shillings, and l. or £ [*librae*] for pounds. Most transactions were done with silver coins, although for large sums gold coins, banknotes, or bills of exchange would be used.[1] Some specific coins had other names, such as a crown (5 shillings) or a guinea (21 shillings). Converting prices from the eighteenth century to the present is quite difficult because the relative costs of things have changed so much: food and clothing used to cost much more, and labor, housing, and real estate much less than they do now. But multiplying early eighteenth-century prices by 200 to 300 should yield an approximate equivalent in current British money, which can then be easily converted into the currency with which you're most familiar.[2] It is important to remember, however, that a far smaller percentage of the population had the kind of disposable income necessary to regularly buy books than is now the case (although then, as now, determined readers could often find ways to gain access to considerably more than they could actually afford to purchase).

---

1  A bill of exchange is a written order to someone, typically a merchant or banker, to pay a named person a particular sum on a particular date. It effectively works like a postdated check.

2  See Hume. For the value of other nations' currencies in the period, see McCusker.

# THE
# LIFE
## OF
## Madam *de Beaumount*, *Douce* *A. 136.*
### a *French* LADY;

Who lived in a Cave in *Wales* above
fourteen Years undifcovered, being forced to fly *France* for her Religion; and
of the cruel Ufage fhe had there.

## ALSO
Her LORD's Adventures in *Mufcovy*,
where he was a Prifoner fome Years.

## WITH
An Account of his returning to *France*, and
her being difcover'd by a *Welfh* Gentleman,
who fetch'd her Lord to *Wales*: And of many ftrange Accidents which befel them, and
their Daughter *Belinda*, who was ftolen away
from them; and of their Return to *France*
in the Year 1718.

## By Mrs. *AUBIN*.

*Superanda omnis Fortuna ferendo eft.* Vir. Æneid.
*Fortem pofce animum, & mortis terrore carentem.*
Juvenal. Sat. 10.

## LONDON:
Printed for E. BELL, J. DARBY, A. BETTESWORTH,
F. FAYRAM, J. PEMBERTON, J. HOOKE, C. RI-
VINGTON, F. CLAY, J. BATLEY, E. SYMON. 1721.

Notes to the facsimile title page on the preceding page:

"*Superanda omnis Fortuna ferendo est*" comes from the ancient Roman poet Virgil's *Aeneid* 5:710 and translates as "whatever Fortune sends, we master it all" (176). It is part of a speech in which Nautes, a seer, tries to console Aeneas after the Trojan women, stirred up by the goddess Iris, have set fire to their ships in order to end their time as refugees, even though they have not yet reached Italy, where it has been prophesied that Aeneas will found a great nation.

"*Fortem posce animum, & mortis terrore carentem*" comes from the ancient Roman poet Juvenal's *Satire* 10:357 and translates as "ask for a heart that is courageous, with no fear of death" (397). The "&" is not usually part of the text. The quotation appears toward the end of a lengthy demonstration that prayer is useless (because the gods are going to do what they think best). However, if you still want to ask for something, it is better to "pray for a sound mind in a sound body" and "ask for a heart that is courageous, with no fear of death, ... that can put up with any anguish, ... that longs for nothing" than to make any of the usual requests, such as for money, power, glory, longevity, or beauty. Such a mind, body, and heart are at least things "you can give yourself."

# PREFACE TO THE READER.

*The Air has infected some of the neighbouring Nations with the Plague,*[1] *and swept away the astonish'd Inhabitants by thousands; but in our Nation it has had a different Effect, it has certainly infected our Understandings: A Madness has for some time possest the* English, *and we are turn'd Projectors,*[2] *exceeded the* French *in extravagant Whimseys, and parted with our Money as easily, as if we had forgot that we were to live a day longer; we are grown false as* Jews *in Trading,* Turks *and* Italians *in Lust,* Libertines *in Principle, and have more Religions amongst us, and less Sincerity, than the* Dutch.[3] *The Knavish Part of us are employ'd at present in getting Money; and the Thoughtless, which are the major part, in searching for something new to divert their Spleen: the Tales of Fairies, and Elves, take with them, and the most improbable things please best.*

*The Story I here present the Publick withal, is very extraordinary, but not quite so incredible as these. This is an Age of Wonders, and certainly we can doubt of nothing after what we have seen in our Days: yet there is one thing in the Story of* Madam de Beaumount *very strange; which is, that she, and her Daughter, are very religious, and very virtuous, and that there were two honest Clergymen living at one time. In the* Lord de Beaumount's *Story, there is yet something more surprising; which is, that he loved an absent Wife so well, that he obstinately refused a pretty Lady a Favour.*

*These Circumstances will, I suppose, make the Truth of this Story doubted; but since Men are grown very doubtful, even in those Things that concern them most, I'll not give myself much trouble to clear their Doubts about this.*[4] Wales *being a Place not extremely populous in many Parts, is certainly more rich in Virtue than* England, *which is now improved in Vice only, and rich in Foreigners, who often bring more Vices than Ready Money along with them.*[5] *He that would keep his*

---

1 There was an outbreak of bubonic plague in southern France in 1720–22. It killed about 100,000 people (between one-quarter and one-half of the population of the affected areas).

2 Devisers of dubious business ventures.

3 These were all common national stereotypes in the early eighteenth century.

4 Moralists regularly complained of a growing skepticism regarding the literal truth of scripture.

5 When Georg Ludwig, Elector of Hanover, became King George I of Great Britain in 1714, a number of Germans accompanied him and took senior positions in the court.

*Integrity, must dwell in a Cell;*[1] *and* Belinda *had never been so virtuous, had she not been bred in a Cave, and never seen a Court.*

Wales *has produced many brave Men, and been famed for the unshaken Loyalty of its People to their Princes, and Bravery in Fight, scorning to bow their Necks to Slavery,*[2] *or be conquer'd; why may it not produce a Woman virtuous and wise, as the Men are courageous?*

*In this Story I have aim'd at pleasing, and at the same time encouraging Virtue in my Readers. I wish Men would, like* Belinda, *confide in Providence, and look on Death with the same Indifference that she did. But I forget that this Book is to be publish'd in* London, *where abundance of People live, whose Actions must persuade us, that they are so far from fearing to die, that they certainly fear nothing that is to come after dying: some of these not speaking good* English, *will not, perhaps, read this; I shall therefore refer them to their own Countries for virtuous Examples, and present this Story to the true-born* English, *and* Antient Britons,[3] *to whom I wish Increase of Sense and Virtue, Plenty of Money, good Governours, and endless Prosperity.*

Penelope Aubin.

---

1 The home of a hermit.
2 Tyranny.
3 The Welsh, who had been pushed to the margins of Britain by the Anglo-Saxon invasions.

# THE LIFE OF MADAM *DE* BEAUMOUNT, &C.

## CHAP. I.

Not far from *Swansey*, a Sea-Port in *Wales*,[1] in *Glamorganshire*, there dwelt a Gentleman whose Name was Mr. *Lluelling*; he was descended of a good Family, and had a handsome Estate of about 500 *l. per Annum*, all lying together in that Place, on which he liv'd comfortably and nobly, doing much good; a Man whose generous Temper, and good Sense, made him beloved by all that knew him: He had been once a Member of Parliament, travell'd in his Youth, bred at the University,[2] and in fine,[3] was a most accomplish'd Gentleman. It is not therefore to be doubted, but that he had many Opportunities of marrying, but he always declin'd it, and seem'd, tho ever gallant and complaisant,[4] yet indifferent to the Fair Sex; he was thirty-six Years of Age, and wisely prefer'd a Country Retirement before noisy Courts, and Business; his Person was very handsome, and his Conversation and Mein[5] perfectly genteel and agreeable. This Gentleman, in the Year 1717, one Evening, in the Month of *May*, was walking alone by the Sea-side to take the Air, and passing over some little Hills, came at last to the Top of one much higher than the rest, where standing still to view the lovely Prospect of the neighbouring Fields and Valleys, which were now all in their greatest Pride, adorn'd with lovely Flowers, and various Greens; he saw just opposite another Hill, and in the side of it a Door open, before which there stood a Maid of such exquisite Beauty, and Shape, and in a Habit[6] so odd and uncommon, that he was both extremely surprized and charmed: he stood still, not daring to approach her, lest he shou'd surprize, and make her fly from him. She seem'd very thoughtful, but at length, looking up, she saw him, and immediately retired, shutting the Door after her. He continued musing for some time, and having well observ'd the Place, return'd home, resolving to go back thither early the next Morning; he pass'd that Night without once closing his Eyes, such strong

---

1  See map, p. 115.
2  Oxford or Cambridge.
3  To sum up.
4  Obliging and ready to please.
5  Look and bearing, especially as it reveals something about one's character.
6  Clothing.

Impressions had her Beauty made in his Soul, that he thought of nothing but the bright Vision. At break of day he rose, forbidding his Servants to attend him, and hasten'd to the Hill, from whence he descended into the Valley, where he sought for a convenient Place to conceal himself, at some little distance from the Cave, resolving to watch the opening of the Door, and observe what past there. Having found a low Tree, he climbed up into it, and did not wait long before he saw a proper Lad[1] come forth with a Basket on his Arm; he went towards the Town, as if he were going to fetch Provisions: soon after a Maid Servant came out with a Broom, and swept before the Door of the Cave, drest in a Red-Petticoat, a *French* Jacket and Coif;[2] and in some time after she went in, he saw a Lady in a rich Night-Gown, and Nightcloths, something in years, but very beautiful, attended by the young Virgin he had seen the day before, who was drest in a cherry-colour Silk Petticoat, flower'd[3] with Silver, a white Sattin Waistcoat, ty'd down the Breast with red and Silver Ribbons, her Neck was bare,[4] and her Hair was carelesly braided, and tied up in green Sattin Ribbon: upon her Head she wore a fine Straw-Hat, lined with Green and Gold, and a Hatband suiting:[5] she appear'd to be about fourteen, was fair as *Diana*;[6] her Eyes were black, her Face oval, her Shape incomparable; she wore a Sweetness and Modesty in her Look, that would have charm'd the coldest Breast, and check'd the boldest Lover from proceeding farther then he ought. Their Habits, Speech, and Mein, spoke them Persons of Quality, and Foreigners.

"Come my dear Child," *said the Lady*, "let us take a Walk over the Hills this sweet Morning, 'tis all the Diversion our sad Circumstance permits us to take." "Why, Madam," *answer'd the fair* Belinda, *for so was the young Lady call'd*, "can there be any Pleasures in the World exceeding those this sweet Retirement gives us? How often have you recounted to me the Miseries and Dangers that attend a Life led in crowded Cities, and noisy Courts: had you never left the quiet Convent for the World, or

---

1  Handsome young male servant.
2  A close-fitting cap that covers the hair.
3  Embroidered with flowers.
4  In the eighteenth century, a woman's "neck" extended down to the (often low) neckline of her dress. If she wished, she could cover up her exposed décolletage with a kerchief tucked into her bodice.
5  Appropriate for those materials and colors.
6  The Roman goddess of the hunt and the moon, famous for both her beauty and her virginity.

changed your Virgin State, how happy had you been. Our homely Cell, indeed, is nothing like the splendid Places I have heard you talk of; but then we are not half so much exposed to those Temptations you have warn'd me of: nothing I dread but only this; should Providence take you from me, I should be so sad and lonely, that I fear my Heart would break." "My Child," *the Lady answer'd*, "our Lives are in the Almighty's Hands, and we must still submit; you can't be wretched whilst you are innocent, and I still hope your Father lives, that we shall meet again, that we shall leave this dismal Place, return to *France*, and live to see you happily disposed of in the World. 'Tis now fourteen Years and six Months since we have lived securely in this lonely Mansion, a tedious Task to me; you know I dare not return to *France* a second time, having been once betray'd, and with much Difficulty escaped from my Enemies' hands: I want[1] only some faithful Friend that could go thither for me." By this time they were past on so far, that Mr. *Lluelling* could hear no more; he came down from the Tree, and follow'd gently after, soon overtook, and thus address'd himself to them: "Ladies," *said he*, "be not surprized, I am a Gentleman of this Place, one who am able to serve you, my Estate and Heart are at your Command; sure I have been very unfortunate in being so long ignorant of my being near you. I have overheard your Discourse, and am come to offer myself and Fortune to you." Here he threw himself at *Belinda*'s Feet: "To this fair Creature," *said he*, "I dedicate the remainder of my Life; I and all that's mine shall be devoted to her Service. Speak, lovely Maid," *said he*, "whose Eyes have robb'd me of a Heart, may I presume to hope?" *Belinda*, much confused, look'd first on him, then on her Mother, remaining silent, seized with a Passion she had been a Stranger to till that moment: the Lady well perceiving it, answer'd thus; "Rise, Sir, since Heaven, who has till now preserved us from all Discovery, has permitted you to see us, and, as I conjecture, more than this time, so that it would be in vain to forbid your coming where we are; I consent to accept the Friendship which you offer, not doubting but you are what you appear, a Person of Birth and Fortune." He bow'd, and taking *Belinda* by the hand, said, "Madam, you shall find me all you can wish; let me now have the Honour to wait of you[2] home to your Cell, and there we may be more at liberty to talk." The Ladies consenting, they went back together to the Cave, the inside of which was most surprizing

---

1 Lack.
2 Accompany you.

to Mr. *Lluelling*; there he found five Rooms so contrived, and so richly furnish'd, that he stood amazed. "In the Name of Wonder," *said he*, "Ladies, by what Inchantment or Art was this Place contrived, from whence is this Light convey'd that illuminates it, which seems without all cover'd o'er with Earth, and is within so light and agreeable?" The Lady answer'd, "When you have heard our Story you will be satisfied in all. At our landing on this Place, we found a Cave, or little Cell, but not like what it now is; the Seamen belonging to the Ship that brought us here, contrived and made it what you see; the Damask[1] Beds, Scrutores,[2] and all the Furniture you find here, I brought with me from *France*: the Light is from a Sky-light on the top of the Hill, covered with a Shutter and Grate, when we think fit to shut day out; a Pair of Stairs leads to it in the midst of the Rooms which you see lie in a kind of round: the Building is contriv'd an Oval, part lined with some Boards, to defend the Damps from us; but yet in Winter 'tis no pleasant Dwelling." "Madam," *said he*, "I have a Seat,[3] and more convenient House that shall be proud to receive you, and I shall not cease to importune you, till you grace it with your Presence; I shall therefore deny myself the Pleasure of staying with you longer, and fetch my Coach to bear you thither." At these Words he took leave.

When he was gone, the old Lady, looking on her Daughter, spake thus to her; "Now, my dear Child, what do you think, Providence provides us here at last a Friend; and, if I am not deceiv'd, a Husband for you: What think you of this Gentleman?" "Alas! Madam," *she reply'd*, "I know not what to think, I wish I had not seen him; for if he proves deceitful, as Men, you say, often do, sure I should be unhappy." They continued this Discourse, breakfasted, and before Noon saw Mr. *Lluelling* return with a Coach, and Servants, to fetch them to his House to dinner; he wisely left his Coach on the farther Hill, and came alone to them: his Importunities were so great, they could not refuse him; so staying only to dress, they went with him. The Ladies' Habits, tho not made after the *English* Mode, were rich, and such as were hardly ever seen in that part of *Wales*, being what the Lady brought from *France* with her. When arrived at his House, they were entertain'd in a manner suiting the noble Nature and Hospitality of the Antient *Britons*; nothing was wanting to show

---

1 Fabric with a design woven into it.
2 Writing desks.
3 Large country estate.

the Master's Respect. How much the young Lady was surpriz'd, it is almost impossible to imagine, since she had never been abroad before, or convers'd with any Stranger. After dinner, Mr. *Lluelling* carried the Ladies into a Drawing-Room, where the Pictures hung of his Ancestors: Stately, and so furnish'd was the Place, it might have taken up some Hours to have view'd it with Delight. Here Wines, Sweetmeats,[1] and Tea, were placed, and the Servants withdrawing, he seated the Ladies, and himself, and then said, "Now, Madam," *addressing himself to the Mother*, "may I, without offending, beg to know your Quality, the Adventures of your Life, and the true Cause of your dwelling in the obscure Place I found you." "Yes," *answer'd she*, "your Curiosity is just, and I readily agree to all you ask." Then she began the Narrative of her Life in this manner.

## CHAP. II.

"I was born in *Normandy*;[2] my Father being a *French* Nobleman, his Name was the Count *de Rochefoucault*: my Mother was an *English* Lady, who came over with the unfortunate Queen of *England*, Wife to King *James* II[3] to whom my Mother's Father was a loyal, and faithful Servant, tho a Protestant: He was a Lord, but could give no Fortune with my Mother, but her Beauty and Virtue. My Father being at Court at *Paris*, and visiting at *St. Germains*,[4] there saw, and fell in love with her, in the end marry'd, and brought her to his Seat in *Normandy*. I was born the first Year of their Marriage, and by my Mother secretly bred up a Protestant; we talking together in *English*, which she taught me; for which reason I was not much esteem'd by my Father's Family, when it came to be known.[5]

When I was ten Years of Age, it pleased God to take away my dear Mother, whose Virtues had made her dear to all that knew

---

1   Desserts.
2   Province in northern France, along the English Channel.
3   Mary of Modena (1658–1718), whose husband, James II, was deposed in 1688–89. See Introduction, pp. 43–44.
4   King Louis XIV of France (r. 1643–1715) allowed James II to estab-lish a court-in-exile in Saint-German-en-Laye, a town west of Paris and close to Louis's new palace at Versailles.
5   French Protestants were stripped of all their rights in 1685 (and had been persecuted for several years before that).

her; but my Father's Grief was such, that it overcame his Reason, and in a short time threw him into a deep Consumption,[1] of which, to my unutterable Grief, he died, leaving me, his only Child, an Orphan of but twelve years of Age. He left me a great Fortune in Lands and Money, in the Care of three Catholick Noblemen, his own Relations, whom he strictly enjoin'd to take care of me, and never force my Inclinations in any thing, or force me into a Convent; but no sooner was he laid in the Ground, but they shut me up in a Monastery of Poor *Clares*,[2] as they pretended to have me convinced of my Errors in Religion, but, in truth, with design to wrong me of my Fortune. Here I continued a Year, being very kindly treated by the Abbess and Society, who were most of them Ladies born of good Families, and perfectly well bred; amongst these was one, whose Name was *Katherine*, Daughter to Monsieur *de Maintenon*, the Governour of *Normandy*. With this young Lady I contracted a strict Friendship; to her I open'd all the Secrets of my Heart, and we loved so tenderly, that we were inseparable: we lay together,[3] and she had told me all her Griefs, confessing she had, and did still love, a young Gentleman who was a Colonel and Relation of her Mother's; which coming to her Father's Knowledge, who was related to the King,[4] and a Man very ambitious, had so offended him, that he had sent him away to the Army, and forced her into this Convent. This Lady had an only Brother, who was call'd the Count *de Beaumount*, who was young, gay,[5] handsome, witty; and in fine, every thing that's charming; his Soul was noble, and full of Truth and Honour. This young Lord came frequently to the Grates[6] to visit his Sister, whom he tenderly loved: by this means he saw, and loved me; his Conversation charm'd me, and I quickly found I more than lik'd him: in fine, he declared his Passion, and I at last yielded to fly with, and marry him, on condition that his Sister should go with me. Nothing now was wanting but an Opportunity to effect our Design, which we did in a few days, in the manner following: The Count went to the Gardener who used to look after the Monastery Garden, and with Gold bribed him, to

---

1  Wasting disease, such as tuberculosis.
2  Franciscan order of nuns.
3  It was not uncommon for unmarried women to share a bed (for warmth, for companionship, to save money).
4  Louis XIV.
5  Light-hearted.
6  Men were not permitted to enter convents, so they conversed through grates with the relatives whom they were visiting.

get another Key made to the Garden Gate, with which my Lover enter'd when he pleased, concealing himself in one of the Arbours till my Companion and I came to walk. We soon agreed on the Day, and Hour, when we should escape; the Evening of the appointed Day, he brought a Chaise[1] with six Horses, to a Village near the Convent, and in the dusk came in it to the Garden Gate, which was the hour we used to be at Vespers:[2] I and Sister *Katherine* feigning ourselves not well all that day, got leave to be absent from Prayers; this gave us an Opportunity of getting to the Count, who received us with Transport:[3] he carry'd us in two hours time to the Chevalier *de Alancon*'s House, which was twenty Miles off; there we alit, and were received gladly: this Gentleman was Father to the Colonel whom Lady *Katherine* loved, and therefore was glad of this Opportunity to oblige the Count *de Beaumount*, hoping it might be a means to procure his Son's Happiness, who was his only Child, and whom he loved excessively: the Count having also promised me to consent to his Sister's Marriage, had made choice of this Gentleman, as most proper to assist us in this Affair. Here having changed our Habits, and put on others which the Count had provided for us, we were entertain'd with a splendid Supper; after which, the Count prest me in so passionate a manner, to make him happy, by marrying him that Night, that I condescended[4] to his Request, and the Chevalier's Chaplain made us one. The next Morning the Chevalier *de Alancon* sent away a Servant Express to the Army, to give his Son notice of Lady *Katherine*'s Escape, and that he should come immediately Home *incognito* to marry her. The Count *de Beaumount* that Evening returned home to see how our Flight was taken, and how his Father resented it, promising a speedy return to us; which he soon did, for the next morning he came back, and acquainted me with all that had past. 'My Father,' *said he*, 'no sooner saw me enter the Room, where he was sitting with some Noblemen at Ombre,[5] but he rose, looking fiercely upon me, and addressing himself to them, said, "Messieurs, I beg leave to withdraw with my Son for a few Minutes." I follow'd him into his Closet,[6] where we no sooner enter'd, but he shut the Door, and said; "Son, I am highly troubled to think that you have done

---

1  A light, fast carriage.
2  Evening prayers.
3  With overwhelming excitement.
4  Agreed.
5  A card game.
6  Private room, used as a study or a place to be alone.

a Deed so unadvised, so rash, and I fear ruinous to yourself, and disgustful to me: are you marry'd without my Consent, and to a Heretick? what will the King say? Cou'd you not find a Wife of our own Faith and Family? but you must rob a Convent for one? Where is your deluded Sister? have you match'd her too? Alas! alas! my Son, what Grief and Confusion[1] will you bring upon us?" My Surprize was so great to see my Father so calm, that I could scarce answer; but throwing myself at his feet, embracing his Knees, I implored his Pardon, and his Blessing, saying, "My honour'd Lord, and Father, the Lady I have marry'd, is our Equal both in Birth and Fortune; vertuous, young, and will, I doubt not, be every thing you can desire: let not her Religion, which is not a fault in her, but the Misfortune of her Education, make you prejudiced against her, I shall soon prevail with her to be what I am; if not, our Children shall be bred as you desire: she was no Nun, but wrongfully detain'd there by her Guardians, who will no sooner hear who she belongs to, but they will resign her Fortune; and now, my Lord, compleat my Happiness, permit me to bring my Bride to pay her Duty, and receive my Sister, who, both by Promise and Affection, is engaged to the brave *Alancon*, a young Gentleman whose Worth excells all Titles, who will be to you another Son, and make her happy." "Rise Son," *said my Father*, "I will endeavour to be easy." At these Words he took me up, and opening the door, return'd to the Company, I following; he said nothing of my Marriage to them: in the morning I pay'd my Duty to him in his Chamber, and told him I was going to fetch you to him; he bid me go.' This News overjoy'd us all, and the Chevalier, my Sister *Katherine*, the Count *de Beaumount*, and I, taking Coach, went to the Castle, where my Father-in-law received us with such Goodness, and with an Air so obliging, that I was amazed: an Apartment was immediately assign'd me, the same my Mother-in-law had in her Life-time. Our Wedding was kept as became our Quality,[2] and in few days I had the Satisfaction to see my dear Sister, whom I tenderly loved, made happy as myself, being marry'd to the Colonel, who being come Post[3] to his Father's, was by him brought to us, and marry'd in my Father's Presence with full Consent.[4] And now we appear'd to be the happiest Family

---

1 Ruin.

2 In accordance with our social rank.

3 As fast as possible (like the horses who carried the mail).

4 The terms "brother" and "sister" were used to refer both to siblings by birth and siblings by marriage. Similarly, "father" and "mother" could refer both to one's birth parents and the parents of one's spouse.

in the World: my Guardians no sooner heard of my Marriage, but they waited on my Father and Husband, and in few days deliver'd my Fortune into their hands.

For some Months my Father treated me with all the Kindness imaginable; when it began to be whisper'd that I was with Child: then my Sister began to importune me, when we were alone, to change my Religion, which I evaded to answer to, as much as possible, beginning to suspect that she was put upon so doing, and this made me very thoughtful, and apprehensive of some Misfortune.

One Morning my Father-in-law enter'd my Chamber, and with a very serious Air began to talk to me in this manner: 'Daughter, I have been very indulgent to you, and do now assure you that I love you extremely, of which I can give you no better Proof than what I am going to propose to you: You have been bred in an Error, and your Religion is false; I have provided those that shall instruct you in the Truth, and I expect that you hearken to them, and embrace it; and if you mean to live happy, and be dear to me, you must be a *Roman* Catholick, otherwise the King has commanded me to part my Son and you. I have said enough, I hope, to convince you that it is absolutely necessary that you comply with my Desires.' At these Words he went out of my Chamber, leaving me in great Confusion and Disorder. At this Instant my dear Lord came in from walking in the Park, and was much surprized to find me in Tears; he clasp'd me in his Arms, and pressed me earnestly to tell him what was the cause of my Grief. 'Forbear, my Dearest,' said I, 'do not ask many Questions, we must be parted, and be wretched, the King will not permit you to caress a poor Orphan, and sleep in the Arms of a Heretick; I must change my Faith, or lose all that is dear to me upon the Earth: Hard choice!' He wiped away my Tears, kiss'd and comforted me all he was able, using all his Eloquence to persuade me to comply; and I must confess it was more difficult to me to refuse him, than all the World; not Racks, nor Flames[1] could move my Soul, so much as one of those tender things he said to me: and now I was daily visited by learned Priests, and such who, as Relations or Friends, thought themselves obliged to assist in my Conversion; but having been educated in an intire Abhorrence of the Church of *Rome*, I gave little heed to their Arguments, and resolved to continue

---

1  Both racks (torture devices that painfully stretched the body) and flames (burning at the stake) were used by the Inquisition to convince Protestants to renounce their supposed heresy.

firm to the Opinion[1] I had been bred in, which they soon discovered, and took my Silence for Obstinacy: with which, acquainting my Father, they so wrought with him, that he grew to hate me, and believed nothing could be done with me whilst my Lord was present: he therefore resolved to part us, hoping by this means to shock my Resolution, and make me yield to his Desires. In order to this, he procures a Commission for a Regiment of Horse[2] for the Count his Son, with a Letter from the King, commanding him to repair to his Command immediately: this his Father deliver'd to him, telling him withall, that he had provided him an Equipage,[3] and all things suiting his Quality, and that he must not fail to be ready by the next morning to be gone.

This News was, as you may imagine, like a Sentence of Death to us both: as for my part, fearing to declare my Grief, lest it should encrease the Count's, I remained silent, and restrain'd all but my Tears, which flow'd incessantly. This sight so moved my Lord, that at last he resolv'd to expose himself both to the King's and his Father's Displeasure, rather than leave me; but upon Reflection, I dreaded the Consequence so much, of so rash an Action, that I proposed an Expedient: 'My dear Lord,' said I, 'my Mother's Brother in *England*, the Lord —[4] will no doubt gladly receive and take care of me; send me thither, with part of our Fortune, there I shall enjoy my Religion without Molestation, and be safe from all my Enemies, till you return; which Heaven grant may be soon, and to both our Comforts.' This Proposal he with much Reluctance agreed to, and the next morning told his Father that he could not consent to part thence under seven days, in which time he wou'd take care to remove me out of *France*, being fully determin'd not to leave me in my Enemies' power; which the old Lord was forced to yield to, finding it was in vain to oppose him, and being glad that we should be separated so far asunder. The Count *de Beaumount* was resolved to see *France* no more till his Father died, designing that I should go to meet him in *Flanders*,[5] by the way of *Holland*, so soon as I should have lain-in;[6] he therefore call'd in all the Ready Money

---

1  Religious conviction.
2  A position as an officer in a regiment of cavalry (here as its commander).
3  Uniforms and equipment.
4  Dashed-out names were often used to suggest that reference was being made to a real person (who, if named outright, might sue for libel or otherwise retaliate).
5  Region in what is now northern Belgium.
6  Given birth and recovered.

he could raise, which he turn'd all into Gold, and borrow'd some of his Friends, giving me Jewels and Money, to the value of fifty thousand Crowns:[1] he hired a Vessel at *St. Malo*'s,[2] putting aboard of it all the rich Furniture of my Apartment, and all my Clothes and Linnen; and at last my Sister and he brought me aboard, my Father-in-law having first took leave of me, and again made me large Offers, if I would turn Catholick, and stay in *France*, which I modestly rejected; and the Wind being fair, in this fatal[3] Vessel my dear Lord and I took leave of each other. And first I embraced my dear Sister, who took our Separation so heavily, that I believe it hasten'd her Death, which happen'd not long after; and then my Lord, with Eyes full of Tears, took me in his Arms, where he held me some time before he was able to speak, then said, 'Farewel, my dear *Belinda*, may Guardian Angels guard you, and the dear Pledge[4] you carry with you; may God defend you from the Danger of the Sea, and bring you safe to Land, and to my Arms again; judge by yourself what Pangs I feel, and spare to torture me by saying more.' I could not answer him one word, but fainted in his Arms: my Sister urged him to be gone, saying, it would be wiser to depart, than continue the tragick Scene; which he would not do till I reviv'd, and then I faintly said, 'My Lord, farewel, remember we are Christians, born to part, let us as such support our Afflictions, and live in hope to meet again, if not here, yet in Heaven; Farewel.' He repeated his Embraces, and at length yielded to go. The Ship set sail for *England*, designing to reach the Port of *London*; but as we were at Sea, the Wind veer'd about, a dreadful Storm arose, and with much Difficulty the ninth day of our being at Sea, we made this Point of Land, and in the Evening got ashore near the Cave where you found us: there we look'd for some Place to secure our- selves and Goods in, and found this Cave, which doubtless had been contrived by some Hermit in antient Times, and was the Work of past Ages; it was all ruinous, and cover'd over with Weeds, but the Seamen soon clean'd and fitted it up as you see; I liked the Place for its Privacy, and resolved to tarry here till I could write to *London*, to my Uncle, whom I very well knew and loved, he having been several times in *France* to visit my Mother. The Captain of the Ship went to *Swansey*, bought Provisions, sent away my Letters,

---

1  A crown is an *écu*, a large silver French coin worth about 2 shillings at the time.
2  Port on the northern coast of France (see map, p. 115).
3  Fateful.
4  Their unborn child, who is a sign of their devotion to one another.

and in some days we receiv'd an Answer, little to our Satisfaction; I trembled when I open'd the Seal, seeing the Direction in a strange Hand, and found it was writ by a Gentleman who was something related, as it appear'd, to my Uncle; who receiving my Letter, answer'd it, informing me my Uncle was long since dead in *Scotland*, being forced to fly *England*, all his Estate being seized by the Government on account of his Loyalty to King *James*, and carrying on Designs for his Service;[1] therefore he advised me to return to *France*, and not venture to come to *London*. Upon this News, I resolved to continue in the Cave, with my two Servants, my Maid, and a Boy, whom I had brought from *France*, *Maria* having been a Servant to my Mother, and a Native of *England*; the Boy *Philip* was preferr'd[2] by my Uncle to my Mother's Service, when he last visited her in *France*; for which reason I always took care of these Servants, and thought they wou'd be most proper for my Service here, speaking the Language.

And now, in few days, the Captain having bought what he wanted, and repair'd his Vessel, set sail for *France* again, to give the Count *de Beaumount* an account of all that had happen'd to us; but, to my great Misfortune, the Ship (as I have been since inform'd) founder'd[3] at Sea, so that my Lord could never be inform'd what was become of me. Here I was brought to bed of[4] this Daughter by a Country Midwife *Philip* fetch'd from a Village hard by;[5] and having in two Years no News from *France*, I resolved to venture back thither myself: so I took the Boy with me, leaving *Maria* with the Child, and in a small Vessel, which I found at *Swansey*, and hired to carry me over to *St. Malo*'s, I got Passage, leaving *Philip* at *Swansey*, to return back to the Cave, he being only fit to fetch Provisions, and what the Maid and Child wanted.

At my landing at *St. Malo*'s, I went to a Friend of my Husband's, whose House we were at, at my leaving *France*; there I got a Man's Habit, and so disguised, took a Post Chaise[6] for the Chevalier *de Alancon*'s, where being safe arriv'd, I discover'd[7] myself, and was

---

1 Acting as an agent for the son of James II, who hoped to reclaim his father's throne. In the eyes of the government, this made him a Jacobite spy. See Introduction (pp. 44–46).
2 Promoted.
3 Filled with water and sank.
4 Gave birth to.
5 Nearby.
6 Fast coach used to carry passengers and the mail.
7 Revealed.

receiv'd with all Demonstrations of Friendship; and here I learn'd that my dear Sister was dead of a Fever the Year I left *France*; that the Count *de Beaumount*, having the News of the Ship's being lost, and hearing nothing from me, came back from the Army to his Father's, and concluding me dead, fell into a deep Melancholy; at last quarrell'd with his Father, resign'd his Commission, quitted the *French* Service,[1] and was gone for *Sweden*, where he had obtain'd the Command of a Regiment under the King of *Sweden*, who was engag'd in a War with the Czar of *Muscovy*,[2] and that no News had been heard of him since: 'This,' *says the Chevalier*, 'has so incensed your Father-in-law against you, Madam, whom he looks upon as the principal Cause of this his great Misfortune, in losing the Comfort of his Son's Presence, that I would not for the World he shou'd find you here, for I know not what his Passion would transport him to do; I therefore advise you to get back to *St. Malo*'s as soon as possible, and return to *England*; I will do all that's possible to send word to the Count of your Safety, and the Place of your Residence.' After Supper I went to Bed, much distracted in my Thoughts: the next morning early, I set out again for *St. Malo*'s; but at Noon, entering into an Inn to refresh myself, I was seized for a Spy, carry'd before a Magistrate, who soon perceiv'd I was a Woman, and, in fine, knew me, and immediately confin'd me in his House, till he sent to Monsieur *de Maintenon*, who by the next morning arriv'd at *St. Malo*'s, and coming into the Room where I was, accosted me in this manner: 'So, Madam, I think myself very happy in seeing you once again in *France*, you have made me one of the most unfortunate Fathers in the World; I have by your means lost an only Son: you fled hence for Conscience, and I, to satisfy Justice, shall confine you here the rest of your days.' He gave me no time to answer; for I was pinion'd,[3] and put into his Coach, with four of his Servants to guard me: nor did they suffer[4] me to rest, or eat, for twenty four Hours, in which time we stop't but twice to change Horses. At length they brought me to a ruinous old Castle, near the Sea-side, where they left me in the hands of a Man, whose grim Aspect spoke him a Goaler;[5] this Man, his Daughter, and Wife, were all that dwelt in

---

1  The French army.

2  Russia. The Great Northern War between Sweden, Russia, and its allies was fought between 1700 and 1721.

3  Bound.

4  Allow.

5  More commonly spelled "gaoler": a jailer.

this dismal Place; they drove me up into a Room that was in the Top of an old Tower, and there lock'd me in, like a wild Beast in a Den: and here I sat down and reflected on my Condition."

Here Mr. *Lluelling* interrupted the Lady, saying, "Madam, thank Providence you are now here, and at Liberty; come, we will defer to some other time, to finish this dismal Story: Supper is upon the Table, let us eat and forget all past Sorrows, to-morrow I will beg to hear the rest." So presenting her his Hand, he led her to the Table. After Supper the Ladies would have taken leave, and return'd to the Cave; but he so importunately desired their stay there, that they at length consented, and were lodged in an Apartment altogether suitable to their Quality.

## CHAP. III.

In the Morning the Ladies were waked by a Concert of Musick, playing under their Window; with which the young Lady was much delighted, having never heard any thing so charming, or of that nature before. "Madam," *said she,* "what an agreeable Part of the World are we come into? why did you not sooner bring me into Company? what a ravishing thing is Society? for Heaven's sake do not return to our unwholesome lonely Cave. We want not a Fortune to pay for all the Conveniences of Life, why shou'd we fly Company? we are in a Nation where you have no Enemies to fear." The old Lady smiled, saying, "Alas! my Child, you little know what you have to fear, and what mighty Cares attend a marry'd Life; tho I hope God will, in pity to my Sufferings, make you happy, and grant you a long Series of Years free from Misfortunes." At these Words a Maid Servant enter'd the Chamber with *Maria,* who was come to attend her Ladies, and to inform them that Mr. *Lluelling* begg'd the Honour of their Company to Breakfast: they dress'd, and went down into a Parlour they had not seen the day before; and here the Lady *Beaumount* was surprized with the sight of her Mother's Picture, amongst many others, which were all drawn by the hands of celebrated Masters; "My God," *said she,* "how came this lovely Picture here? Alas! my dear Mother, little did I think ever to see that Face again!" Mr. *Lluelling, interrupting her, said,* "Madam, that Lady was by my Father courted, and beloved so dearly, that when she left *England,* he seem'd to have lost all he valued, fell sick, and soon after died; my Mother having left him a Widower, dying in Child-birth of me, whom he left an Orphan about three Years old. This melancholy Account I have had of his

Death, but little thought I shou'd have seen a Daughter of that Lady's, or shared my Father's Inclinations, in loving one descended from her." "Fair *Belinda*," said he, turning to the young Lady, "do not by a cruel Absence from me, kill me too." *Belinda* blush'd: "Believe me," said her Mother, "she is much inclined to stay with you; and if all your Actions correspond with what we have already seen, I shall never desire to take her from you." At these words he bow'd, saying; "May I be hated by Heaven and you, and may she scorn me, when I cease to love, to honour, and take care of you and her. Madam, till now, I never loved, my Heart has been indifferent to all the Sex; but from the moment I first look'd on that Angel's Face, where so much Innocence and Beauty shines, I have not asked a Blessing in which she was not comprehended; make her mine, and I have all I wish on Earth." Here Tea, Chocolate, and Coffee, was brought in, so they turn'd the Discourse.[1]

After Breakfast they walked into the Gardens, and being come to a lovely Banquetting-House,[2] they went into it, and sat down. Here Mr. *Lluelling* importun'd the Lady to finish the Story of her Misfortunes: "Madam," said he, "I left you in a dismal Place last night, pray glad me with an Account of your Deliverance thence." "I will," said she; so continued her Relation in this manner.

### CHAP. IV.

"Being left, as I before told you, imprison'd, and all alone, faint, hungry, and bereft of all Comfort, I did, as most People do, when their own Prudence can help them no farther; look'd up to God, whose Power can never be limited, and from whom only I could expect my Deliverance: lifting up my Hands, I cry'd, 'Now, my God, help me; I am perfectly resign'd to thy Will, accept my Submission, encrease my Faith and Patience, in proportion to the Evils thou hast decreed me to suffer; be to me Food, Liberty, and a Husband; and to my Child a Father and Mother.' Here a Flood of Tears interrupted, I could speak no more; after which I grew calm, found my Faith encrease, my Fears abate, and my Soul seem'd arm'd for all Events. Thus, Sir, I experienced that great Truth, That we have nothing more to do, to be happy and secure from all the Miseries of Life, but to resign our Wills to the Divine Being; nor

---

1 Changed the subject.
2 Separate building on an estate used just for eating (and perhaps enjoying the view).

does Providence ever appear more conspicuously than on such Occasions. I fell soon into a sweet Slumber, which in few Hours so refresh'd me, that I awoke a new Creature. About ten in the Evening, the Wife and Daughter of my Goaler came into the Room, bringing me some sour Sider to drink, and a piece of Bread: a poor Repast, alas! after such a Fatigue as I had undergone! but I took it chearfully, and thankfully. The Women seem'd to compassionate[1] me, and after an Hour's Discourse they both wept with me; they were Persons of mean Capacities and Education, but were not altogether void of Good-Nature and Humanity. Here I remain'd for two long Years, and was delivered by a strange Accident: My Food being very mean, and my Grief great, I soon fell into a languishing Sickness; at length the good Woman inform'd her Husband, that she believed me near Death, and therefore thought it concern'd their Consciences to fetch a Priest to me; which he consenting to, the Daughter was sent for a Fryar, who was Curate of the Parish. The good Man, whose Outside was mean, as his Inside was rich, soon came; but believe me, Sir, his Understanding and Goodness was such, that it might justly have preferr'd him to a Mitre:[2] his Name was Father *Benedict*; he was the Son of a Lord, and had refused all Dignities, purely out of his great Humility, for which reason he chose to live in this obscure Place. He approach'd me with such Compassion in his Looks, as encouraged me to hear him without Prejudice: I was then so weak I could not rise; he ask'd me many Questions, how I came there, why I was thus confined; and being truly inform'd of all, spoke of my Father-in-law with much Dislike: 'God forbid,' *said he*, 'our Faith should be propagated by such detestable Means as these; Madam, I am sensible of your Wrongs, and will deliver you, or die in the Attempt.' He never urged me farther as to my Religion, but advising me to Secrecy, not thinking the Women proper to repose[3] Confidence in; he came every day to visit me, bringing in his Bosom Wine and Meat to comfort and strengthen me, which, with the reviving Hopes of Liberty, soon restored me to Health: and now he study'd how to compleat his good Work, by getting me thence, which he thus effected: He came to me one afternoon, bringing another Brother of his Order with him, who had a double Habit on; in this religious Disguise I dress'd myself, and Father *Benedict* going into the Room where the Goaler's Wife and Daughter were sitting, who, at his coming, as

---

1  Pity.
2  Ceremonial headdress of a bishop.
3  Place.

usual, left my Chamber; he held them in discourse whilst Father *Anthony* and I went down, and past the Gate by my Goaler, who civilly bid us Good night. I was conducted by this good Father to a little Hermitage[1] on the top of a Hill near the Convent[2] he belong'd to: Father *Benedict* came soon after to us, and here we consulted what to do; they agreed that I should stay there for some days concealed, that then Father *Anthony* should go with me to *Grandvil*,[3] from whence he should send me to *England*, that being a Sea-Port less frequented, and consequently less dangerous for me, than *St. Malo*'s. I stay'd in this Hermitage five days, they bringing me Food: no Search was made after me, because the Goaler fearing to be ruined, when they mist me, went away to Monsieur *de Maintenon*, and told him I was dead of a Spotted Fever,[4] and they were forced to dig a Grave, and throw me into it the same Night, for fear of Infection; of which News he was very glad, and Christian Burial being not allow'd to Hereticks,[5] he did not regret the manner of my Burial, but rewarded the Goaler, who return'd joyful to his miserable Home. The good Father *Anthony* and I, set out for *Grandvill*; my Cowle and Frock, with a long pair of Beads ty'd to my Hempen Girdle,[6] made me appear a perfect *Capuchin*:[7] We arrived safe at a Convent, where, being refresh'd, we went to the Port; there we found a *Guernsey*[8] Ship just ready to depart for *Southampton*;[9] and here the good Priest, to compleat his Generosity, gave me a Purse of Gold to pay for my Passage, and assist me to get to my home: he gave me many Blessings at parting, and I return'd him innumerable Thanks, promising ever to pray for him and Father *Benedict*, which I am bound to do. I arrived in *England* on the 17th of *March*, 1707–8,[10] and from *Southampton* hired Horses and a Guide to this

---

1 House of a hermit (or, more broadly, any secluded dwelling).
2 Monastery. The term was not gendered in the period and so could refer equally well to an association of monks as to one of nuns.
3 Port on the northern coast of France (see map, p. 115).
4 Infectious disease, such as typhus, that produces purplish spots on the skin.
5 Generally Protestants could not be buried in Catholic graveyards.
6 Belt made of rope.
7 Member of an order of Franciscan friars devoted to living simply and serving the poor.
8 Island in the English Channel that belongs to Great Britain.
9 Port on the southern coast of England (see map, p. 115).
10 The calendar officially began on 25 March, so dates falling in the first quarter of the year sometimes gave both the legal (*continued*)

Place: at the Post-House,[1] I parted with and discharged the Man and Horses, and walked to my dear Cave, where my Child and Servants received me with such Transport, as if I had been risen from the Dead: and here I resolved to stay the remainder of my days, unless Providence, by some Miracle, restores my dear Lord to me, of whom I have never been able to get any Tidings, not daring to return to *France* again." "Madam," *answer'd* Mr. Lluelling, "I will be the Person who shall do you that Service, be pleased only to consent to remain in my House, where you are from this day Mistress; send for your Furniture from the Cave, and make this, which is far more commodious, your Abode, and I will forthwith to *France*, to learn all that is possible of your Lord." The Ladies accepted with Joy his Offer, and now he pass'd some Days agreeably with them, whilst all things were getting ready for his departure to *France*. In this time he study'd both how to divert them, and secure the young Lady's Heart, with whom he long'd to talk in private, hoping to be satisfy'd what Sentiments she had of him; to do which, he sought a fit Opportunity.

## CHAP. V.

The young Lady was now, by the little God *Cupid*, render'd more thoughtful than usual, and loved to retire from Company, often frequented the Grove, and shady Walks. One Evening, while some Ladies whom Mr. *Lluelling* had brought acquainted with his Guests, were playing at Cards with the Lady *Beaumount*, *Belinda* stole into the Garden to walk alone; her Lover, whose Eyes watch'd all her Steps, soon follow'd. "Now, fair *Belinda*," *said he*, "Fate has given me the happy Moment I have so long wish'd for; here we are alone, no Spys to overhear: Ah! tell me, charming Maid, what may I hope? Am I beloved again?[2] or must I die unbless'd? Tho I must be all my days the most unhappy of Mankind, if you refuse me that fair Hand; yet believe me, lovely Virgin, I would not force your Inclination for an Empire, nor occasion you one moment's Uneasiness, tho to enjoy you, which would be to me the greatest Bliss my Soul could know: speak, and

---

year (here, still 1707) and the generally accepted, beginning-the-calendar-in-January year (in this case, 1708).
1   Inn that keeps horses for rent (and to which one could return horses that one had rented elsewhere).
2   Is my love returned?

78   PENELOPE AUBIN

let that charming Mouth pronounce my Doom." *Belinda* quite unpractised in the cunning Arts of her ingenious[1] Sex, her Face o'er-spread with Blushes, answer'd, "Sir, the Passion of Love, I think, I am a Stranger to; but this I own, I have a grateful Sense of all the generous Treatment we have received from you: I don't dislike your Person, nor disapprove your Passion, if sincere, but do not think myself of years to chuse a Husband; my Mother must dispose of me, for she has both Wisdom and Experience, 'tis her Commands must guide my Choice." "Ah! must I then," *said he,* "owe that to her Commands, that I would only owe to you? Say, should she command you to receive another in your Arms, wou'd you consent to see me wretched, cursing my Fate, and dying at your Feet, and make another happy with my Ruin?" "Press me no more," *she cry'd,* "you have urg'd me to a Point I cannot answer to."[2] At these words she fainted in his Arms; Joy and Fear, at that Instant, did so divide his Soul, he knew not what he did: he took her in his Arms, and bore her to his own Chamber, laid her on his Bed, and there, in Transports, view'd her reviving Beauties, saw the Roses return to her pale Cheeks, and her Eyes open to behold the Man she lov'd; and here he gain'd a Promise from her to be his. Here they join'd Lips and Hands, for Fate had join'd their Hearts before, and bound themselves in sacred Vows, to be for ever true to one another; then he, reflecting on his Indiscretion, led her to her Chamber, where, repeating his Protestations and Embraces, he left her. Full of Joy he rejoin'd the Company, where he appear'd so gay and chearful, that it was easy to imagine something more than usual had happen'd to him. In some time, the Company taking leave, the Lady *Beaumount* ask'd for her Daughter, and was told she was not well in her Chamber; thither the Lady went, and found *Belinda* so disorder'd, that she was much surpriz'd, but could not guess the Reason, till *Maria,* who had seen from the Window Mr. *Lluelling* carry her in his Arms into the House from the Garden, whisper'd[3] her Lady, which fill'd her with such Suspicions, that she was almost distracted; she desired *Belinda* to go down to Supper, and take the Air, thinking it wiser to conceal her Thoughts, than ask Questions, hoping to discover by their Behaviour what had pass'd. No sooner did *Belinda* enter the Parlour, where her Lover waited their coming to Supper, which was then upon the Table, but his Eyes sparkled,

---

1 Clever and inventive.
2 A decision I cannot make.
3 Whispered to.

and her Colour chang'd, and both trembled; at Supper his Eyes were continually turn'd upon her, and hers cast down: he seem'd more tender and officious than ever, she more shy. After Supper they walked into the Garden, and there Mr. *Lluelling* thus put an end to the old Lady's pain: "Madam," *said he,* "you are, I am certain, too clear-sighted, not to have observed something in my Looks and Behaviour this Evening, that must inform you, that the charming *Belinda* and I have had an Interview alone, much to my Satisfaction, nor do I doubt but somebody has whisper'd it to you already; I saw at Table how you watch'd our Eyes and Looks, and to prevent all Suspicions that may ruin our Peace, I tell you, she has this happy Day made herself mine, and to morrow-morning, if you bless me with your Consent, we will be marry'd; for I cannot leave *Wales* before I have secured my Charmer from the Temptations she might be expos'd to in my Absence, which, when a Wife, she will be freed from." The old Lady gladly consented, and the next Morning they went privately in the Coach to a Village, where the Ceremony was perform'd to the Satisfaction of all Parties. The next day it was publick Talk, and Mr. *Lluelling* show'd his Joy, by treating all his Country Relations and Tenants for ten days together; all which time he kept open House.[1] In this Juncture there came down from *London,* to pay him a Visit, a young Gentleman who was his Cousin-German,[2] and had long wish'd his Death, no doubt, because he was his Heir, if he died without Issue. This young Man, Mr. *Lluelling* had always lov'd and bred up as his Son, having bought him Chambers in the *Temple,*[3] where he, like most Gentlemen of this Age, had forgot the noble Principles, and virtuous Precepts, he brought to Town with him, and acquir'd all the fashionable Vices that give a Man the Title of a fine Gentleman: he was a Contemner[4] of Marriage, cou'd drink, dissemble, and deceive to Perfection; had a very handsome Person, an excellent Wit, and was most happy in expressing his Thoughts elegantly: these Talents he always employ'd in seducing the Fair, or engaging the Affection of his Companions, who doated upon him, because he was cunning and

---

1 Supplied food, drink, and other hospitality to all visitors, regardless of whether he knew them.
2 First cousin.
3 Enrolled him as a student in either the Inner Temple or the Middle Temple (two of the four Inns of Court, the traditional law schools in London).
4 One who is contemptuous or scornful.

daring, could always lead them on to Pleasures, or bring them nicely off, if frustrated in any vicious Designs.[1] His Name was Mr. *Charles Owen Glandore*: this Gentleman was received by his Kinsman with much Joy and Affection; he assured him he shou'd not be slighted or forgotten, tho he was marry'd; he brought him to his Lady, recommending him to her Favour. And now the time approach'd when Mr. *Lluelling* was to go for *France*, all things being ready; he thought none more proper than his Kinsman (who had by this time gain'd the Lady's Esteem) to take care of his Affairs in his Absence; he therefore desired him to stay, till his Return, with his Wife, and Mother-in-law, who would by that means be eased of some Care and Trouble; and so taking leave, in the most tender manner, of his charming Bride, he set sail for *France*, in a small Vessel which he hir'd on purpose to go for *St. Malo*'s, and wait his Return, proposing to be back in *Wales* in a Month or Six Weeks' time.

## CHAP. VI.

Mr. *Lluelling* being now gone, Mr. *Glandore*, his young Kinsman, had the Pleasure of entertaining the Ladies, and frequent Opportunities of being alone with *Belinda*: his Kinsman's Fortune was all at his Command, and having unfortunately cast his Eyes on her, whom he no sooner saw, but he loved; he strove to gain her Affection, and charm her Vertue asleep, by all the Arts imaginable: he dress'd magnificently, gave them new Diversions every day, was gay and entertaining, study'd how to gratify all her Wishes; and in fine, was so assiduous and tender of both the Ladies, that had *Belinda*'s Heart not been pre-ingaged, he would certainly have gained both that and her Mother's Consent. Being now grown intimate and familiar with both, *Belinda* did not scruple sometimes to walk with him in the Gardens, Grove, and Fields; and when her Mother was engaged with grave Company,[2] courted these Opportunities of slipping out with him, whom she believed honourable and virtuous as herself, and loved as a Brother. He being perfectly skill'd in the Arts of his subtle Sex, resolved never to discover his base Design to her, till he was well assured she

---

1 Law students were notorious for their pursuit of extracurricular pleasures (studying law was an easy way for a young gentleman to get to live in London at parental expense).

2 Reserved and serious visitors.

liked him, and a fit Opportunity offer'd in a Place where he might ruin her, without being prevented; for he was resolved to enjoy her, tho by Force, and determined to run all Dangers rather than miss of what his headstrong Passion persuaded him he could not live without. He knew the time was but short before Mr. *Lluelling* would return, and therefore he must be quick in executing what he design'd; he had a Servant whom he had left in Town, who was a Pimp to all his Pleasures, a Fellow who was wicked, bold, and in fine, such a one as was fit to carry on any vitious[1] or base Design, secret and proper for his vile Purpose: him he sent for; he came down, and they contrived the poor *Belinda*'s Undoing. At the bottom of the Grove, which was a quarter of a Mile distant from the House, was a fine Summer-House;[2] hither one Evening he led her, whilst her Mother was engaged at Cards with some Ladies who were come to visit her.

When *Belinda* and he came to the Grove, he persuaded her to go up into the Summer-House, into which they were no sooner enter'd, but he shut to the Door, saying, "Madam, be not surprized, but hearken to what I am going to say, and answer me." Here he threw himself upon his Knees; "Charming *Belinda*," *said he*, "I love you, I even die to possess you; oblige me not to use Force, where I would use only Prayers, make me this moment the most transported, the most happy Man alive, or else I must convey you to a Place where I shall make you comply, and perhaps make us both wretched: here we can have Opportunities without being discover'd, and may enjoy one another without publick Scandal and Noise; but if I take you hence, I must live with you in Obscurity, and if we are discover'd, kill your Husband in my own Defence and yours; or dying, leave you to his Reproaches, and publick Disgrace. You are, I know, with Child,[3] and therefore need fear no Discovery." Here he drew forth a Pistol; "Look not round about," *said he,* "for Help, Death stands between this Door and him that dares to enter; I have those at hand that make all safe for me to act." *Belinda,* who had now no other Arms but Prayers and Tears, to defend her Virtue withal, threw herself at his Feet, saying, "Oh! cruel, faithless Man, what Joy can you receive in the Ruin of a Person who can ne'er be lawfully yours? Consider the sad Consequence of such a Deed, which you will doubtless repent of: By Heaven, I'll never give Consent, and if you force me like a

---

1 Vicious.
2 Building used for recreation in warm weather.
3 Pregnant.

Brute, what Satisfaction will you reap? I shall then hate and scorn you, loath your Embraces, and if I ever escape your hands again, sure Vengeance will o'ertake you; nay, you shall drag me sooner to my Grave, than to your Bed; I will resist to Death, and curse you with my last Breath: but if you spare me, my Prayers and Blessings shall attend you, nay, I will pity and forgive you." "I'm deaf to all that you can plead against my Love," he cry'd, "yield, or I'll force you hence." "No," says she, "I'll rather die; now, Villain, I will hate you: help and defend me Heaven."

Here he seized her Hands, his Man at the same instant entering, gagg'd and bound her; then they blindfolded her, and Mr. *Glandore* carry'd her down, putting her into a Coach, where, drawing up the Canvasses,[1] he held her in his Lap, whilst his Man drove them over the Hills across the Country, with design to reach a Village fifty Miles distant, where Mr. *Glandore* had procured a Place to receive them; being an old ruinous Castle, where none but an old Man and his Family resided, who spoke nothing but *Welsh*, lived on what was produced about the Place, and never saw a Market-Town, so that he could keep her there without fear of Discovery. To be enabled for this, he had taken a considerable Sum of Money of his Kinsman's in the Coach, and had besides some Fortune of his own: they chang'd Horses on the Road twice, all things being before provided, and travell'd all night, he taking the impudent Liberty of kissing her as he pleased. About five in the Morning they were in sight of this dismal Place; here he stopt the Coach: she being swooned away in his Arms, he unbound and gave her some Wine; but before he could bring her to herself, he saw four Men in Vizards,[2] well mounted, coming up to the Coach, which made him leap out, to be upon his Guard: his guilty Conscience made him tremble, for tho he was brave on other Occasions, yet now he was not so; Heaven that had permitted him to act this Villany, still protects Innocence, and had prepared its Judgments to o'ertake him. These Men were Robbers, who lived concealed in these desolate Mountains; they went to seize him, he resisted, his Man coming down to help his Master, was shot dead, and in the Dispute the unfortunate *Glandore* was kill'd.

During this Scuffle, the unhappy *Belinda* reviv'd; they dragg'd her out of the Coach, which whilst they were rifling, a Company of Clowns,[3] who were going to a Fair, about twenty Miles thence,

---

1  Canvas blinds.
2  Masks.
3  Rural laborers.

with Horses to sell, came up, at whose Approach the Thieves fled. By these honest Countrymen the Lady was relieved, but they could speak nothing but *Welsh*, so that she could not make them understand one word: one of them got up into the Coach-box, and drove the Lady to his Landlord's House, where he gave an Account of what had past: the Son of the Gentleman was at home, but his Father was elsewhere; he was a very accomplish'd young Gentleman, well bred, handsome, about 20 Years of Age: he and his Father, who had in this Place purchased a small Estate, lived very private, for Reasons that shall be hereafter declared: he was known by the Name of Mr. *Hide*. He received the young Lady in a manner so courtly, that it was easy to guess he had been educated in Palaces, and convers'd with Princes; having treated her in the highest manner with Wine and Food, he begg'd to know who she was: she prudently conceal'd her Name, Family, and all the Transactions of her Life, telling him only that she was coming this way with her Brother, who was the unfortunate Gentleman, whom the Thieves had kill'd, and came from *Swansey*, to which Place she begg'd he would send some of his Servants back with her, and it would be the greatest Favour he could do her. This he promised to do, but, alas! the blind God[1] had already wounded his Breast; he gazed upon her with Transport, and resolved not to part with her on any Terms. The Coach being clean'd and put up[2] by the Servants, they found the Sum of Gold *Glandore* had put up[3] in the Seat, and honestly brought it to the Lady, who genteelly gave them five Guineas[4] to drink: this Largess, the Greatness of the Sum, which was fifteen hundred Pieces,[5] and her Habit, made Mr. *Hide* conclude she was some Person of Distinction; which the more inflamed his Desires to know who she was. He entertain'd her magnificently, but put off from day to day her Departure, saying she must stay till his Father came, and then he would wait on her home himself. She too well guess'd the reason of his prolonging her stay, and having so lately escaped from the hands of a desperate Lover, was dreadfully alarm'd at this new Misfortune: he

---

1 Cupid.
2 Put in the stable.
3 Hidden.
4 Gold coins worth 21 shillings each (one pound, plus an additional shilling).
5 Generic term for coins, but that here seems to mean pounds, because we later learn that the amount being carried in the coach, prior to Belinda's gifts, was £1,500.

behav'd himself with such Modesty and Respect, that she cou'd not complain, but still she fear'd it was like *Glandore*'s Cunning, only to procure an Opportunity to undo her: she was wholly in his power, having none but Servants in the House, who spoke nothing but *Welsh*; this made her very reserved. At last he declared himself to her, as they were sitting together after Dinner, the Servants being all withdrawn: "Madam," *said he*, "Providence that brought you hither, did it, I hope, for both our Happiness; I no sooner saw you, but my Soul adored you; I am by Birth much nobler than I appear to be, our Years are agreeable, I will omit nothing that can gain your Affection, nor think any Pains too much, or Time too long to obtain you. Charming Fair, why do you fear and avoid me? why treat me with such Coldness and Reserve? Am I disliked, and must I languish, sigh, and beg in vain? Never can I cease to love you, till I cease to live; permit me then to hope, if not, I am resolved to die a Victim to your Disdain; forbid me not to follow you, for I must disobey, I cannot bear your Absence, nor consent to live, and see a happy Rival possess you." Here he seiz'd her Hand, and in a great Disorder kiss'd it. "Forbear Sir," *said* Belinda, "I never can be yours, I am already marry'd, and with Child." Here she related to him, how *Glandore* had stolen her away.

At these Words a death-like Paleness overspread his Face, a cold Sweat trickled down his Cheeks. "My God," *said he*, "it is enough; Madam, I will no more importune you, fear nothing from me, Virtue and Honour are as dear to me as you; since you cannot be mine, I ask no more, but that you'll stay and see me die, and not detest my Memory, since Vice has no share in my Soul." Here he fainted, and was by the Servants carry'd to his Chamber: *Belinda* wept, her Heart was young and tender, and the Honour he had shown, touch'd her Soul so nearly, that she much lamented his Misfortune, and cou'd not consent with ease to let him die; therefore she strove with Reason to assuage his Grief, and cure his Passion: but in vain, he fell into an intermitting[1] Fever, and grew so weak, that he cou'd not rise without Help, yet would every day be taken up, and brought into the Parlour where she sat. And here we must leave them, and return to enquire after the Lord *Beaumount* and Mr. *Lluelling*.

---

1  Intermittent.

## CHAP. VII.

Mr. *Lluelling* arrived safe at *St Malo*'s, *July* the 30th, 1717, and went, as the Lady *Beaumount* had directed, with a Letter to the Gentleman's House, where she had been received at her being in *France*, but he was dead; so that he was obliged to go thence without much Information of what he wanted. But it being now a time when *France* and *England* were at Peace, he had nothing to fear; he went therefore directly to *Coutance*,[1] and there lodg'd at the best Inn, where he enquired for the Governour Monsieur *de Maintenon*: they told him he was long since dead, but the young Marquiss, his Son, was still alive, but had quitted all his Employments, being retired into the Country. "Is he a single Man?" *said Mr. Lluelling*. "Yes, Sir," *said the Inn-Keeper*, "he is a Widower for the second time, having bury'd his second Lady about two years ago; he has a Daughter of his Wife's by a first Husband, who is one of the beautifullest Children, and will be the greatest Fortune[2] in this Province."

Mr. *Lluelling* was impatient to see him, so stay'd no longer there than that Night: the next morning he set out with his two Servants which he took along with him from *Wales*, and arrived that night at a Village which was about three Miles short of the Marquiss's Seat: it being late, he stay'd at the Village that night, and the next morning went to the Marquiss's, whom it was no easy matter to speak with, for he was deny'd to all Company,[3] but some particular Friends. Mr. *Lluelling* sent him word, by his Gentleman who was call'd to him,[4] that he came from *Wales* express, to bring him News of some Persons whom he would be much overjoy'd to hear of.

The Marquiss no sooner received this Message, but he came down and receiv'd him in much Disorder; he was dress'd in Mourning, and look'd like a Man half dead: "My Lord," *said he*, "I doubt not but I shall be welcome, since I come from your virtuous Lady *Belinda*;[5] she lives, has a Daughter, who is my

---

1 Now Coutances; town on the northern coast of France (see map, p. 115).

2 Heiress.

3 He had his servants say he was not at home. This was thought a more polite way of avoiding visitors than refusing to let them in.

4 Through a servant who came to see what was wanted.

5 It was not uncommon for a mother and her first-born daughter to have the same name (at least prior to the daughter's marriage, if she married).

Wife, to present to you; such a one, that you may glory to be the Father of." Here he presented him a Letter from his Wife, at the sight of which, the Tears ran down his Face, and he fainted away, Joy having so overpower'd his Faculties, that they lost their Power to perform their Functions. Mr. *Lluelling* supported him till he recover'd, and then he broke out into these passionate Expressions: "My God, am I alive! do I wake! can this be true! Is my *Belinda*, my Joy, my All, still living? Is the precious Pledge of our mutual Affection born, and preserved to this Day: Oh! mitigate my Transport, or strengthen my Faculties! Do I here find a Son?" *Here he embraced Mr.* Lluelling. "Oh! welcome, welcome, ten thousand times; I want Expressions[1] to speak my Gratitude to my God and you."

Here they sat down, the Marquiss call'd for Wine, and now Mr. *Lluelling* related to him all the Adventures that had befallen his Lady since their parting: but when he related Monsieur *de Maintenon*'s cruel Usage of her, the Marquiss wept. "And now, my Lord," *said Mr.* Lluelling, "I should be glad to know your Story, but we will defer that to some other time; 'tis Joy enough to me that I find you here alive." *The Marquiss answer'd,* "That Story will serve to entertain us in our Journey to *St. Malo*'s, and Voyage to *Wales*: I must now order my Affairs to go thither, for my Impatience to see my dear *Belinda*, and my Child, is such, that I can think of nothing else." Mr. *Lluelling* was entertain'd here so magnificently, that he was even surprized. The young Lady, Daughter-in-law to the Marquiss, whose Name was *Isabella*, was so beautiful and witty, that Mr. *Lluelling* thought her equal to his Wife: she was then thirteen, and the Marquiss was very fond of her, she begg'd to accompany her Father, to see her new Mother and Sister, and at last prevail'd to go with them. In few days all things were ready for their departure, the Servants were order'd to repair to the Marquiss's Seat at *Coutance*, to be ready to receive their Lady; the whole Country[2] rang of this strange Adventure: the Marquiss set out, attended by only two of his own Servants, and Mr. *Lluelling*'s two, with the Lady *Isabella*, and her Woman: they arrived at *St. Malo*'s, and the next morning set sail with a fair Wind for Wales, in the Vessel that attended Mr. *Lluelling*.

And now being aboard, he importuned the Marquiss to relate his Adventures in *Sweden*, which he willingly condescended to, and began the Narrative of his Misfortunes in this manner:

---

1  Lack adequate language.
2  Province.

## CHAP. VIII.

"You have heard how, my Father and I quarrelling, I left *France*, supposing my dear Wife dead; and considering him as the principal cause of her Death. I had continued with him about six Months before I resolved to be gone; I was fallen into so deep a Melancholy, that I was regardless of every thing,[1] but fearing my Death, he so importuned me to reassume my usual Chearfulness and Gayety, that at length he obliged me to discover my Resentments, declare the Reasons of my being uneasy in his Presence, and Resolution to continue no longer in *France*. I had writ several Letters to my Wife's Uncle, but receiving no Answer, I concluded him also dead, and therefore order'd all my Affairs to depart for *Sweden*, determining to seek a noble Death in the Field, under that glorious Monarch, the last King of *Sweden*.[2] I took no more but three Servants to attend me, having remitted Money sufficient to purchase an Employment, and answer my Expences. I no sooner arriv'd at *Stockholm*, but I obtain'd the Command of a Regiment, and after having courted Death in many Skirmishes and bloody Battles, I was unfortunately in the last that brave King fought with the Czar,[3] taken Prisoner; my whole Regiment, and the greatest part of the Army, being destroy'd, I fell full of Wounds amongst the Slain: but upon the *Muscovites* stripping the Dead,[4] they found some Signs of Life in me, and judging by my Habit that I was some Person of Distinction, they carried me to a Tent near the General's, where they dress'd my Wounds, and with Cordials[5] brought me to the use of my Reason again, to my great grief. I continued so ill and weak, for three Months, that they had small hopes of recovering me: in this time I was removed to a Town call'd *Toropierz*,[6] where the General had a Country-Seat. In this Place I was very civilly entertain'd, the General having taken a great liking to me, and here he much persuaded me to enter into the Czar's Service, saying, that being a Native of *France*, and no Subject of *Sweden*,

---

1   Paid attention to nothing.
2   Charles XII (r. 1697–1718), widely admired for his military brilliance.
3   The Battle of Poltava (1709), won by the Russians (see map, p. 116).
4   Stealing valuables from corpses.
5   Alcohol-based medicines supposed to stimulate the heart, which were used to revive those who had fainted.
6   Toropets; town about 250 miles (410 km) west of Moscow (see map, p. 116).

having paid for my Employment there,[1] he thought I was under no Obligation to the King of *Sweden*, and that his Master should engage me to his Service, by giving me a Command under him. I answer'd, That having voluntarily drawn my Sword in the King of *Sweden*'s Defence, Honour obliged me never to quit it; that I was highly obliged to him for his generous Offers, and should upon all Occasions return the Obligation. He smiled, seeming to applaud my Resolution, but told me he should, he believed, find an Advocate that should prevail with me, otherwise he should set a Ransom so great upon me, knowing my Worth, that he believed he should have the pleasure of my Company long; and since he could not engage me to serve his Prince, he would, if possible, prevent my fighting against him.

At these Words he took me by the Hand, and led me to his Wife's Apartment,[2] where were his two Sons, and Wife, with his only Daughter, a Maid of fourteen Years of Age, beautiful as Nature ever form'd; she was tall, slender, fair as *Venus*, her Eyes blue, bright, and languishing; her Hair was light brown, and every Feature of her Face had a Charm; but, Son, her Conversation was enchanting, as I afterwards experienced. The General presented me to his Sons, two lovely young Men, whose Looks and Habit spoke their Worth and Quality. 'Here Children,' *said he*, 'is the bravest Enemy our Emperor has; a Man who is so dear to me, that if you can make him our Monarch's Friend, you will oblige me in the most sensible manner;[3] use all your utmost Skill to gain him.' Then he took *Zara*, his fair Daughter, by the Hand, presenting her to me, 'Here is the dearest thing I have in the World,' *said he*, 'I give you leave to love her; nay, will bestow her upon you, to secure your Friendship: if her Eyes cannot prevail, our Eloquence cannot succeed.' Here he left us, and from this Day I was caress'd[4] by all the Family; and *Zara*, the charmingest Advocate that ever sued to gain a Heart,[5] try'd all her Arts, she danced, sung, dress'd, and trying to ensnare me, unfortunately lost herself, for, alas! she loved me, and had not my whole Soul been fill'd with the bright Idea of my *Belinda*, it would have been impossible for me to have

---

1  In many European armies, one could—or was required to—purchase a commission in order to serve as an officer and in some one did not need to be a citizen of that country.

2  Set of rooms used by a particular individual within a larger house.

3  Strongest way possible.

4  Treated with affection.

5  Attempted to win a heart.

resisted her Charms. At length I generously told her, as we were sitting alone in a Drawing-Room, it being the cold Season of the Year, when we were obliged to sit in warm Rooms; 'Charming *Zara*,' *said I*, 'it would be cruel and ungrateful in me, not to deal ingenuously with you; I own you are the most lovely, the most accomplish'd Maid my Eyes ever saw, there is nothing wanting in you to make a Man compleatly happy; you have Wisdom, Beauty, and Virtue, and God never made any Work more perfect: but, alas! Fairest of your Sex, I am a Man unworthy of that Affection, which given to another, would set him above Monarchs; my Choice was long since made, my Heart is a Captive to one like yourself, who was my Wife; one in whose Arms I slept more glorious and content, than Eastern Kings; a Lady who is no more, yet one whose Memory is so dear to me, that I am grown insensible to all your Sex: her bright Idea fills my Mind, in Dreams I'm nightly happy, pursue her Shadow, and embrace her heavenly Form; and when awake, still long for Death, in hopes to meet her in the glorious Regions where the happy Souls shall meet again: look then no more upon a Wretch, who can make no Returns to your invaluable Bounties.' *Zara* beheld me all this while as one amazed, the Roses forsook her Cheeks, and finding I had done, she thus began: 'Unfortunate *Beaumount*, are you enamour'd of a Ghost? Must the Dead rise to rob the wretched *Zara* of your Heart? Why did you not forewarn me e'er I was undone? Ye Powers, why does my Vengeance stay to stab[1] the Wretch that is a Witness to my Folly; I never loved before, she whom you loved is buried in the Grave: Can you consent to sacrifice me to her Ghost? Can you enjoy a Shadow? consider e'er you bid me die; I will not live and be despised.' 'Forgive me Heaven,' *said I*, 'may a Thought like that ne'er enter your Soul; may *Zara* live, and be most happy, gladly I'd die to save your Life, but cannot make a second Choice.'

Here we were interrupted, and after this she shunn'd me, and for some Months kept much within her Chamber, grew sick, and alter'd, which much alarm'd the Family; and I confess, my Thoughts were much confused; sometimes I thought to marry her, and run all hazards to make her happy: but then *Belinda* might be still alive, and then I were undone, and my Peace lost for ever.

One Morning *Barintha*, *Zara*'s *Governess*, came hastily into my Chamber: 'Sir,' *said she*, 'if you will ever see my Lady more, come now, for she's expiring.' I follow'd her, and found *Zara* in the

---

1  Refrain from stabbing.

Agonies of Death; she fix'd her dying Eyes upon me, grasp'd my Hand, and faintly cry'd, 'Farewel, cruel, but faithful *Beaumount*, adieu; I go to seek the Ghost of her that murders me; I loved you, could not live without you, and therefore drank a poisonous Draught last night to free me; forgive me, Heaven, since Life was insupportable: ah! pray for me, dear Cause of my sad Fate, I'm going I know not where.' Here her Tongue falter'd, her Agonies encreased, and in few Moments she expired. At this Instant my Grief was such, that had I not been a Christian, I had surely ended my Life and Misfortunes together; I kiss'd her pale Face and Lips a hundred times, wept over her, and then retreated to my Chamber, threw myself upon my Bed, refused to eat, and by next morning was seized with a violent Fever, which robb'd me of my Reason for some days, at the end of which, my Disease being something abated, I saw *Zara*'s two Brothers enter my Chamber, with four Soldiers; the eldest loaded me with Reproaches for his Sister's Death, to which I was unable to reply through Weakness. At last they took me out of my Bed, pinion'd me, and set me upon a Horse, the four Soldiers riding by me as a Guard: they went with me over dreadful Mountains and Hills, whose Tops were covered with Snow, and after three Days, and two Nights travelling, in which time they never enter'd any House or Inn, but laid me bound upon the Ground, whilst the Horses fed and rested, giving me Brandy, Bread, and Meat, out of their Snapsacks;[1] we at last arrived at an old Tower on the Borders of *Muscovy*, where they deliver'd me into the hands of a Goaler, who lodg'd me in a close[2] damp Room, loading me with Irons.[3] Here I remain'd ten Months sick, and had not God's Providence preserved me miraculously, I had doubtless died.

Three Months after my Arrival, a young Gentleman was brought Prisoner to this dismal Place, by order of the Czar, who having much Gold to fee[4] the Goaler, had the Liberty of walking up and down the Prison; we convers'd together, he much pitied my Misfortune and ill Treatment, and promised to procure my Enlargement,[5] either by his Interest with the General, or Force.

1  Knapsacks.
2  Closed up.
3  Shackles.
4  Pay. In the eighteenth century, prisons generally allowed jailers to charge inmates for their upkeep. Often if a prisoner was able to pay more, he received better treatment or more privileges.
5  Release.

His Friends who sollicited for him at Court, being unsuccessful, gave him notice that his Case was desperate: upon which we took a Resolution to kill our Goaler, and fight our way out. Accordingly the next Morning we seiz'd him as he enter'd my Chamber, and having knock'd him down with the Bar of a Door that we found in my Room, we dispatch'd him, took the Keys, and rush'd by the Centries who kept the Out-Gate; and not knowing where to go, we fled o'er the Mountains towards a Wood in *Tartary*,[1] to which he guided me, where none but Robbers and Out-Laws lived. My Fetters[2] much hinder'd my Speed, being extremely weak, but Fear gave me Strength, so that we reached the Wood before night, believing it more safe for us to put our Lives into the hands of Theives, than our merciless Enemies. Here we laid down under a Tree to rest, not being able to go farther, and slept some Hours, tho in danger of Death every minute, from the wild Beasts who went howling about the Woods for Prey, or more barbarous Men; but God kept us, and awaking, we thought we perceived, at some distance, a Light. Necessity, being in great want of Food, made us venture to the Place. We saw a little Cave, in which a venerable old Man sat reading by a Lamp; we enter'd, saluting him in the *Muscovite* Language, with 'God save you, Sir, take pity of us who are fled from our Enemies, out of a Prison, destitute of Food or Comfort, grant us a Retreat for a few Days, or at least a few Hours; we are Christians, Catholicks, and one of us a Native of *France*.' At these words the old Man rose from his Seat, embraced us, and stirring up the Embers, made a Fire, and gave us Wine and Bread, telling us we were welcome: we inform'd him whence we came, the Causes of our Confinement. At last he turned towards me; 'Countryman,' *said he*, 'tell me what Family you are descended from, what Province you were born in.' I inform'd him, then he caught me in his Arms as a Man lost in Wonder. 'My Lord,' *said he*, 'I have sought you long, and can disclose Wonders to you; my Name is *Anthony*, I am a *Capuchin* Fryar, who saved your Lady's Life, and came to *Muscovy* on purpose to seek you out.' Here he recounted to us how *Belinda* came to *France* in search of me; how my Father imprison'd her! but e'er he could finish his Story, a Band of *Tartarian* Robbers enter'd

---

1  A very loose term for Central Asia that was applied to regions extending from the Crimea to Mongolia (see map, p. 116). Given the subsequent encounter with Persian merchants, Beaumount and his companion probably fled toward the Caucasus.

2  Ankle shackles.

the Cell, seized us, and he importuning them for us, was unfortunately shot by one of the barbarous Villains. They ty'd us back to back, and carry'd us some Miles farther into the Wood, where there were about a hundred of them encamped; and now we were again Prisoners: here they lived with their Women all in common,[1] lodging only in Tents, and chiefly supporting their Lives with robbing all Passengers that came near the Wood; yet tho Barbarians, we found some Humanity amongst them; they gave us Plenty of Food, took off my Fetters, and offer'd us our Freedom, if we would consent to live with them; which we accepted, and for some days were obliged to ride out with them, at the head of twenty or thirty *Tartars*, where we robb'd, getting considerable Booty from some *Persian* Merchants, who were going to *Muscovy* with rich Merchandize. The *Tartars* were so well pleased with our Behaviour and Conduct, that they gave us what we pleased of the Plunder: by this means we were trusted with good Horses, which, tho small, yet were fleet as the Wind.

We did not design to stay here, but sought an Opportunity to escape, which Providence favour'd us withal in this manner: One morning, at break of day, we went out with a Party in search of a Caravan that we had Information was to pass by that Road; it consisted of about fifty Merchants, Passengers, and Soldiers of several Nations, who were coming from *Persia* to *Muscovy* with Merchandize. We no sooner saw this Company coming up, but the *Tartars* began to shrink; they saw their Enemies well arm'd and numerous, and did not think themselves strong enough to attack them: we set Spurs to our Horses, leaving them in this Consternation, and calling to the foremost of the Caravan, in a suppliant manner throwing down our Arms, desired to be heard. Seeing us but two, they stopp'd, and upon our declaring ourselves Friends, receiv'd us. We then gave an Account of our Adventures with the *Tartars*, and enquired if any of them were going to *Sweden* or *Germany*: there were two Gentlemen and their Servants going to *Hungary*; these we went along with, leaving the rest: and the young *Muscovite* Lord, not knowing how to provide for himself, I offer'd to carry him with me to *France*, and there take care of him, which he gladly consented to.

Being arrived in *Hungary*, having now but little Money left of what we brought with us of the Plunder we got amongst the Robbers, we were obliged to sell some rich Diamonds we had

---

1 That is, the men shared all of the women, rather than paired off with them in monogamous marriages.

saved, and hid in our Clothes; and with this Money we procured ourselves Horses, with a couple of Servants to attend us, and so set out for *France*, whither I was now determined to return, being weary'd with the many Misfortunes I had met with abroad: and at the end of six Weeks we arrived safely at *Coutance*, where I found my Father dead, and all my Relations and Friends overjoy'd to see me. I was sorry my Father died e'er I had seen him, to have ask'd his Pardon for my Rashness in leaving him, tho he was to blame; yet I believe God punished me for my Disobedience, and 'tis to that Cause that I attribute all my Misfortunes in *Muscovy*.

Being now settled in my Father's Estate, and Posts of Honour,[1] by the King, to whom I paid my Duty at my first Arrival in *France*; he received me with his accustom'd Goodness, reproving me gently for leaving his Service, saying, 'My Lord, Love is an Excuse, I own, for doing many rash inconsiderate things: I don't approve your Father's Proceedings with your Wife; but I and your Country had done you no wrong. 'Tis true, your Father used my Name, which was not well done, but I protest I was ignorant of all, till since your departure from *France*; and had you address'd yourself to me, be assur'd I would have made you easy and happy. I here give you all your Father's Posts of Honour, and doubt not but you'll as bravely and faithfully discharge the Trust I repose in you, as he did.' Here the King embrac'd me, and during his Life, I was so happy to have his Favour. I now thought only of my *Belinda*, and examining all my Father's old Servants, discover'd the Castle where she had been imprison'd; I went thither, found the Goaler dead, but his Wife and Daughter told me she died there of a Spotted Fever, fearing to confess the Truth, that she had escaped from them. I writ to *St. Malo*'s to my Friend, at whose House she had been; he was dead, and I could learn no News of her there.

Thus I remained two whole Years in Suspense; at last tired with the Importunities of my Friends, I resolved to marry again. It was now nine Years since I parted from *Belinda*, and I concluded it was impossible that she should be still alive, and I hear nothing from her; nor had I any Hopes till last week, when a Fryar came to me, who is just arrived from *Muscovy*, where he had seen Father *Anthony*, before I met with him in *Tartary*, and he told me he related to him the cause of his coming thither thus; That Father *Benedict*, soon after he return'd from *Granville*, where he had sent my Wife away, falling sick, enjoin'd him to go to *Sweden* in search of me, in case he died, which he did soon

---

1 Positions in the royal court that were prestigious but unpaid.

after: and this was the occasion of my meeting that good Father in the Wood, who learning in *Sweden* that I was in *Muscovy* a Prisoner, came thither, but could not discover where I was, so retired to this dismal Place, where we found him; where he begged in the neighbouring Villages, his holy Habit securing him from Injuries. But I concluded, not being able then to get any Information of her, she was dead; and in compliance with my Friends' Importunities, marry'd a Lady who was a young Widow, of a great Family and Fortune, having only this lovely Daughter: but, alas! I found myself so miserable now, that I cannot describe the Tortures of my Mind. I never enter'd my Bed with this Lady, but I shiver'd; she loved me tenderly, but I fancy'd *Belinda*'s Ghost pursued me; every Place where she had trod, each Room, brought some new thing to my Remembrance: I talk'd and started in my Sleep. In fine, tho I did all that I was able to conceal my Distraction, all the World perceived it; and my Wife, who was a Lady of great Wisdom and Goodness, and most unfortunate in being mine, was so sensibly touch'd, that she fell into a Consumption, and after having languished for two Years, all Means proving unsuccessful to preserve her, she died. In her last Agonies, as I was weeping by her, for indeed I highly respected, tho I cou'd not love her with Passion, and omitted nothing that could oblige or help her; she pull'd me to her, fix'd her Lips on mine, then sigh'd deeply, 'My dear Lord,' *said she*, 'I thank you, you have done more for me, than for your loved *Belinda*; the Constraint you have suffer'd upon my account, is the greatest Obligation; I am now going, I doubt not, to Rest, and hope to meet you again in Glory; let my Child be your chief Care; and if the tender Affection I have borne you, merits any thing, show your esteem of me, by your Love to her. I die, 'tis true, by having had too deep a Sense of your Misfortune, in not loving me; but, my Lord, believe me, 'tis with Pleasure that I leave the World, since it will set you free: could you have loved me, as you did *Belinda*, I should have been desirous to live long; but since you cannot, I wish to die.' Here she again embraced and kiss'd me, then turn'd to her Confessor, who stood on the other side the Bed; 'Father,' *said she*, 'I have now done with the World, and all its Weaknesses; I'll grieve no more for mortal things, but fix my Thoughts on Heaven.' We all withdrew but the good Father, and in about an hour she departed, leaving me most disconsolate. For some Months I kept my Chamber, and then resolved to retire, and quit all publick Business; I went to the King, took my leave of him, recommending the *Muscovite*

Lord to him, to whom he gave a Company of Dragoons:[1] then I retired to my Country-Seat, where you found me."

Thus the Marquiss finish'd his Relation; they past the remainder of this Day, and the next, very agreeably. In the Evening of the fifth Day, the Sky began to darken, the Wind blew, and about midnight a dreadful Storm arose; at length the Pilot was obliged to quit the Government[2] of the Ship, and let her drive before the Wind.[3] At break of day they found themselves in the *Irish* Seas,[4] and not far from Land; their Rigging was all torn, their Mast shatter'd, and it was in vain for them to attempt going for *Wales*, before they had repair'd their Vessel, and refreshed themselves; therefore they made in for Land, and cast Anchor at *Wexford*,[5] in the County of *Rosse*, in *Ireland*. They went ashore with the Captain, and lodged at an Inn whilst the Sailors refitted the Ship.

## CHAP. IX.

In the time of their stay at *Wexford*, they were curious to see the Country, and the Marquiss and Mr. *Lluelling* frequently rid out to view the adjacent Towns and Villages, leaving the young Lady *Isabella* with her Servants. One Evening they lost their way returning home, and wandering about, found themselves near a Wood: it was almost dark, and they knew not whither to go; they therefore made a stand,[6] consulting what to do. At last they espy'd an old Man with a Candle and Lanthorn[7] coming towards them, in very poor Habit, and a Beard down to his Breast.[8] "Honest Man," *said Mr.* Lluelling, "can you direct us to some safe Place to lodge in to-night? or put us in the way to *Wexford*?" "To *Wexford*, Sir!" *said he*, "you cannot reach that to-night: in the morning I'll put you in the way; but for to-night, if you'll accept a Lodging in my

---

1 Mounted infantry that primarily used firearms rather than lances or sabers.
2 Stop trying to steer (usually in order to avoid further damaging or sinking a ship by working against the force of a storm).
3 Sail in whatever direction the wind blew.
4 The water that separates Ireland and Great Britain.
5 Port on the southeastern coast of Ireland (see maps, pp. 115 and 116).
6 Came to a stop.
7 Lantern.
8 Eighteenth-century men tended to be clean-shaven, except in special circumstances like shipwrecks or being a hermit.

poor Cottage hard by, you are welcome." They gladly accepted his Offer, and follow'd him into the Wood, tho something afraid, lest he should betray them into the hands of Robbers, of which there are many times Gangs that retreat to such Places. At length they came to a poor Clay Cottage,[1] where a Boy stood at the Door; the good Man bid them alite, which they did, taking their Pistols in their hands, the Boy taking their Horses: they found the Place neat, and not destitute of Necessaries; the Man entertain'd them handsomely, bringing out Venison-Pasty,[2] Wine, and dry'd Tongues.[3] "Gentlemen," *said he,* "eat heartily, and spare not; we'll drink the King's Health[4] before we part." The Marquiss and Mr. *Lluelling* began to imagine there was some Mystery in this Man's living here, and were upon their guard; they appeared very merry, and guest by their Host's Behaviour, that he was a Man of Quality. When they were well warm'd with Wine, they all began to be free, the old Man toasted the King's Health, they pledged him.[5] "My Lord," *said Mr.* Lluelling, "methinks 'tis almost as good living here as in *France,* or *Wales*; Faith, I can't treat you better when you come to *Swansey.*" At these words, the Stranger look'd upon them, saying, "Gentlemen, are you Natives of these two Places? they are both well known to me." Here they were interrupted by the Boy, who inform'd his Master some Friends were come; he presently stept to the Door, where they heard the sound of Horses' Feet: after some time he return'd to them, saying, "Gentlemen, I beg pardon for leaving you, but it was to take leave of some Friends who are going for *France.*" It was now midnight, and he genteelly said, "Gentlemen you are weary, will you be pleased to go to bed?" They finish'd their Bottle, and were conducted up stairs, to a Room where they could but just stand upright for the Ceiling; but the Softness of the Bed, and Fineness of the Sheets, made amends: however they could not sleep, their Minds were so fill'd with Curiosity to know who this Man was. They talk'd all night; the Marquiss mention'd *Belinda* several times, and *Isabella,* saying, "My dear Child will repent her

---

1  Cottage with walls built of clay.
2  Pie filled with venison.
3  Ox or cow tongues dried with salt and smoke in order to preserve them.
4  Drink a toast to the King. It was a common way of expressing one's political allegiances (did one drink to the Hanoverian on the throne or the Stuart in exile?), but could also be used to disguise those allegiances, if necessary—drinking to "the King" didn't require specifying which king.
5  Drank the toast that he proposed.

leaving *France*, and be much concerned for us this night." This their Discourse was overheard by the old Man, who lay in the next Room; they heard him up early, and rose: coming down stairs, they found Breakfast ready for them. "Now Gentlemen," *said their Host*, "I must be impertinent, and ask some Questions before we part: I last night heard one of you name *Belinda*, and find you are lately come from *France*; I had a Sister of that Name, who dying, left a Daughter, of whom I would be glad to hear some Tidings: Come you from *Normandy*?" "By Heaven," *said the Marquiss, embracing the old Man*, "you are the L—[1] the Uncle of my dear *Belinda*, that charming Virgin, Fate made me the happy Husband of." Here they sat down, recounting, in a pathetick[2] manner, all their Adventures: the Marquiss concluding, said, "And now, Sir, tell us what Providence brought you here." "Sir," *said he*, "I will: My Loyalty to my Prince brought me under some Misfortunes, at last I was forced, with my only Son, to fly to *Scotland*; there we lay concealed a while, till I had received a great Sum of Money, that I had taken Methods to have remitted to me. From thence we hired a small Vessel, and sailed for *Wales*, where I thought I shou'd be secure from all Discovery; there I changed my Name, purchased a small Estate, and have lived happily, tho obscurely, ever since, making several Voyages to *France*, hither, and elsewhere, upon Business to serve my Friends. I came to *Ireland* some Months ago, and chose this Place to reside in, my Habit, and my Servants, making us pass undiscovered; the Gentlemen you heard me speak to, are gone to take Shipping, and I design to go for *Wales* with the first Opportunity." "We will go together," *said Mr.* Lluelling, "where we shall fill our expecting Wives' Hearts with Joy." They parted, the L— not thinking it proper to go along with them by day-light, sending his Boy to guide them to *Wexford*, where they arrived to the great Joy of the Lady *Isabella*, who had been almost distracted for fear her Father and Brother-in-law had been killed. In few days after, the Ship being ready, the Marquiss and all the rest went aboard, with the L— who came to them disguised; they set sail for *Swansey*, where they soon arrived in good Health.

---

1   It is unclear whether the dash in "L—" is supposed to be standing in for the remaining letters in "Lord" or if it is just an accidental compression of "Lord —," as the man in question is called elsewhere. If the former, perhaps the suggestion is that there is something dangerous about referring directly to an aristocrat who had served as a Jacobite spy and been reported as dead.

2   Emotionally moving.

# CHAP. X.

Mr. *Lluelling* conducted the Marquiss and the L— with the young Lady and Servants, to his House; where being arrived, he saw the Servants look upon one another, and a general Sadness and Silence seemed to reign in every Face and Room. "Where is your Lady, and her Mother?" he demanded. None answer'd. At length, "Sir," *said a Boy trembling, that had been bred in his House*, "my Lady is stolen away, as we suppose, by your Kinsman Mr. *Glandore*; we have heard nothing of her this Month and more: the old Lady has taken it so to heart, that she has kept her bed ever since, and is more likely to die than to live." "Show me to her," *said Mr.* Lluelling, "and let us join with her in Sorrow." "My God," *continued he*, "where shall we find Faith in Man? Can neither the Tyes of Blood, Friendship, Interest, nor Religion, bind Men to be just: but alas! he lived too long in that curs'd Town, where Vice takes place of Virtue, where Men rise by Villany and Fraud, where the lustful Appetite has all Opportunities of being gratify'd; where Oaths and Promises are only Jests, and all Religion but Pretence, and made a Skreen and Cloak for Knavery; a place where Truth and Virtue cannot live. Oh! curse on my Credulity, to trust so rich a Treasure to a Wolf, a lustful *Londoner*." He wou'd have gone on, if the Marquiss had not interrupted him, begging him to be patient, and at least procure his Happiness, by bringing him to *Belinda*. To her Chamber they went, where she was lying in her Bed so weak, that it was even dangerous to let her know her Happiness. The Marquiss threw himself upon the Bed by her, weeping, and embracing her in his Arms, cry'd, "My God, I thank thee, that my longing Arms again do hold my dear *Belinda*; spare her, I beg thee, some few Years longer to enjoy the mighty Blessings thou hast granted us: look up, my Dear, and bless thy ravish'd[1] Husband with a tender Look, let my Soul leap to hear thy well-known Voice, and thy Tongue tell me I am welcome." "Am I alive! and do I wake!" *she cry'd*, "do I behold my dear Lord again! it is impossible! let me behold him till my Eye-strings[2] crack, and my Life ends in Rapture; what Thanks, what Returns, can I make to Heaven? let all my Faculties exert themselves, and all united praise my God." Here she fainted, Joy having overcome her wasted Spirits; Cordials were brought, and she was recover'd from her Fit, and then she began to weep. "Alas! my Lord," *said she*, "were I able, I

---

1 Overcome with strong emotion.
2 Nerves in the eyes that supposedly cracked at the moment of death.

would ask you a thousand Questions, but I hope now to live and enjoy your dear Company again; but we have lost our Child, dishonourably stolen." "Ah! Son," *said she, turning to Mr.* Lluelling, "you were deceived, and left a Villain to supply your Place." At these Words she saw *Isabella*: "What fair Virgin," *said she,* "is that, my Lord? Have you more Daughters? and has some other Woman slept in your dear Arms?" "My Dear," *said he,* "I have been marry'd since we parted, believing you were dead; but the Lady was so happy as to die before I was bless'd with the knowledge of your Safety: this is a Daughter of hers, by a former Husband; she is as dear to me as *Belinda,* and I brought her, to present her to you, as the greatest Blessing Heaven can send you, next my Life, and *Belinda*'s Safety." Then he turn'd to Mr. *Lluelling;* "Fear not, my Son," *said he,* "I will find and fetch *Belinda* back, if yet alive, and use[1] the Ravisher as he deserves." Then the Servants were all called up, and examined; they inform'd them of *Glandore*'s being seen with her in the Summer-House, and of some Places where they were seen together on the Road; so they concluded she was carried Northward, and the L— said, "My Estate lies that way, Nephew, if you please to stay with my Neice, my Kinsman and I will go together; we know the Roads and Country, and shall soon trace the Robber to his Den, I doubt not." The Servants said they had rid all about the Country, but could get no Intelligence where they were.

The next morning, the Lord — whom we must henceforward know to have gone by the Name of Mr. *Hide,* for he was Father to the young Gentleman who had *Belinda* in keeping, set out with Mr. *Lluelling* and three Servants, well arm'd, and went the Road to his House, which was in *Merionethshire,*[2] near the River *Wie*; they got Information on the Road of the Coach, and so continued to go towards Mr. *Hide*'s, where they found young Mr. *Hide* dangerously ill: he receiv'd his Father with all Joy and Affection, and after some Discourse, related to them the Adventure of the young Lady's being brought thither, with the manner of her being rescued from *Glandore,* and his, and his Servants being kill'd by the Highwaymen. Then Mr. *Lluelling,* impatient to know where she was, interrupted him, asking to see her. "Are you then," *said* Mr. Hide, "the happy Man to whom *Belinda* is Wife? Why do you ask me for her? I sent her home to you three days since, in your own Coach, guarded by three of my Servants, not being

---

1 Treat.

2 County in northwestern Wales (see map, p. 115).

able to persuade her to stay here, till I was either dead, or able to see her home myself." At these Words Mr. *Lluelling* was even Thunderstruck; he look'd on the Lord — "Am I then," *said he*, "born to lose her? What can become of her now?" "Doubt not," *said the young Gentleman*, "Heaven will preserve her; such Perfection, such Vertue and Beauty, Angels attend upon; I am undone for ever by the sight of her, before I knew she was another's I adored her, and now die a Victim to her Charms: her Virtue I ne'er attempted, but honour'd and protected her, hoping to die respected of her; and tho 'twas worse than Death to lose the sight of her, yet I consented to our Separation, and sent her away; since which I find my Illness encreased, and hope my End is at hand." Mr. *Lluelling* look'd upon him with Jealousy and Rage: "Is *Belinda*," *said he*, "so unfortunate, to raise me a Rival in every Man of Worth that sees her: Why did she not rather die in the Retreat I found her; let me but find her once again, and she shall never quit my Sight; I'll guard and keep her with such care, that all my lustful Sex shall ne'er be able to seduce, or steal her from me." Here the old Lord interpos'd: "My Friend and Kinsman," *said he*, "you wrong your Lady and my Son; Why do you rave? Has he not done nobly by you? If he loved her before he knew that she was pre-ingag'd, it was no Crime, but his Misfortune; and his honourable Treatment of her since, renders him highly deserving your Compassion and Esteem. Come, let us wisely search for her, and return to your Home, where she, by this time, may be arrived. Come, my Son, vanquish the Frailty of your Mind, and then your Body will recover; *Belinda* has a Sister, fair as herself, a Horse-litter[1] shall be provided to carry you with us to *Swansey*, there Company, and the lovely *Isabella*, will, I hope, compleat your Cure, and make you happy." All Things were strait got ready for their return thither, where being arrived, there was no News of *Belinda*. And now we shall leave them to go in search of her, and give an Account of what had happen'd to her.


## CHAP. XI.

*Belinda* being on the Road with her Attendants, about ten Miles from Mr. *Hide*'s, the Coach going gently over a dangerous Mountain, was met, and set upon, by a Band of ten Robbers, who stopp'd the Coach, and kill'd one of the Servants, and two of the

---

1  Bed slung between two horses, used to transport invalids.

Horses; took the other two Servants, whom they bound hand and foot; then they pulled *Belinda* out of the Coach, and searching that, found the Sum of 1490 *l.* in Gold, *Belinda* having used only ten Pounds of the Money *Glandore* had brought in the Coach, which ten Pounds she had given Mr. *Hide*'s Servants, and the Clowns that rescued her. There was one amongst the Thieves that seem'd to be much respected by, and commanded the rest. He put *Belinda* into the Coach again, and going into it himself, bid her be silent, and no harm should come to her. One of the Thieves got up into the Coach-box,[1] and with the four remaining Horses drove the Coach down the Mountain into a deep Valley; then he drove to a Wood about two Miles from that Place, and being enter'd into the thickest part of it, they stopp'd, took the Horses out,[2] and left the Coach: the Captain leading Mrs. *Lluelling*, they came to an old ruined Stone Building, where an old Church was remaining, and part of the House.

Here these Robbers lived, it being a place desolate of all Inhabitants, and long since abandon'd: here they locked the two Servants they had taken Prisoners into a Room, and then pulling off their Vizards, they saluted[3] Mrs. *Lluelling*, and told her she was welcome: But, good Heavens! what a Surprize was she under! when she saw the Captain of the Robbers' Face, and knew him to be a young Gentleman whom she had once seen at Mr. *Hide*'s with Letters, and had been by him caress'd in an extraordinary manner; he soon perceiv'd she knew him. "Madam," *said he*, "you will not be half so much surprized as you now seem to be, when I tell you, that I no sooner saw you at Mr. *Hide*'s, but I loved you; I am a Man nobly born, but unfortunate; we are all Gentlemen, most of us outlaw'd, except three really Thieves, whom we are join'd with. We have for our Royal Master's, and Religion's sake, been ruined; our Estates, or our Fathers', which was our Birth-right, confiscated; we have try'd to get our Bread abroad, but like the poor Cavaliers, were look'd on as burdensome wherever we came.[4] Thus made

---

1 Driver's seat at the front of or on top of a coach.
2 Unhitched the horses.
3 Kissed.
4 The "robbers" are Jacobites and probably Catholics (and so doubly unwelcome in Hanoverian Britain). The Cavaliers were supporters of Charles I in the Civil Wars of the 1640s. They frequently complained that their loyalty was insufficiently rewarded, both during the Interregnum and after the restoration of the monarchy in 1660. For other Jacobite

desperate, since *Lewis* the Fourteenth dy'd,[1] we return'd to *England*; we had most of us a Being[2] when first we came, but our Friends are since impoverish'd: our Spirits are great, therefore we have chosen this desperate way to maintain ourselves. At the harmless Country Peoples, where we lodge in couples, we pass for Jacobites, and honest Tories, great Men disguised, &c. and when we have got a good Booty, and are flush of Money, they imagine we have receiv'd Supplies from abroad. News we often do indeed receive from foreign Parts, but Money never: we would, if a Change came, venture into the World again, and live honestly. We never murder any Man, or rob a poor Traveller; we hold Correspondence with some Servant or other, in every Gentleman's Family in the Country, and seldom miss of Intelligence where great Sums of Money are stirring. This Place is our Rendevouz, here we divide our Plunder, and then we separate. You see, Madam, the Confidence I repose in you; I believe you are a Lady of Quality; I admire your Person, I am not your Inferior in Birth, and therefore since I have purchas'd you with the hazard of my Life, hope you will not grant me the Possession of your Person with Reluctance; I will maintain you nobly, and run all Dangers to preserve, provide for, and please you."

Here one of his Companions enter'd, saying, "Sir, Dinner is ready." He took her by the hand, she not daring to resist, and led her to a large Room, where was a Table spread, and great Store of cold Meats, with Plenty of Wine: she was plac'd by the Captain at the upper end, and now he and his Companions gave a loose to Joy; Mirth and Good-humour reigned. *Belinda* could not eat, her Soul was fill'd with all the dreadful Imaginations of Ruin and Misery; but after they had eaten plentifully, they all withdrew to sleep, and she and the Captain were left alone: he press'd her earnestly to yeild to him, but she refused him with such soft Words and Resolution, that he forbore to treat her rudely, trying to win her to his Embraces gently; for tho Necessity had made him a Robber, yet it could not make him a Brute; he had been well born and educated, and retain'd some Remnants of Honour. At night he left her there, and went out with his Band, leaving with her two Women, who were in appearance Servants to them: to these

---

highwaymen see Aubin, *The Life and Adventures of the Lady Lucy* 50–51; Monod 111–19.

1  Louis XIV died in 1715. His successor, Louis XV (r. 1715–74), was initially less inclined to aid the Stuart cause.

2  Enough money to get by.

she address'd herself, saying, "You are Women, your Hearts must be tender and pitiful! I am a Wife, brought hither by Misfortune, torn from a fond Husband, and a doating Mother. Oh! help me in this great Distress, assist me to escape, and bring me to them, and you shall be rewarded to your Satisfaction." The eldest of the two reply'd, "Madam, we gladly would, but cannot serve you; we are Strangers in this Place like you; we were brought here by Force, blindfold and taken far from hence: 'tis now eight Months since we were brought to this sad Place. Here we have been ruined, and are made subservient to the Lust and Humour of these desperate Men; we both were Gentlewomen born in *France*, tho we speak *English*: this is my Neice, I was a single Woman, had no Relation whom I thought so well deserved my Love as she. I had a handsome Fortune, and we lived together; and having some Business to go for *England*, I took her with me: we took along with us our Necklaces, Rings, Clothes, and what we had most valuable to appear in, with Money to defray our Charges. The Vessel we came over in, was bound to *Southampton*, but a Storm drove us upon this Coast; we got into *Swansey*, and from thence hired Horses to carry us cross the Countries thither, with a Guide. In the way we were set upon by this Band of Robbers; they stopp'd us, took us off our Horses, carry'd us, our Boxes, and all off along with them, and brought us to this Place. Our Guide they bound, and left behind, and now threaten us with Death, if we attempt to leave them. Alas! we know not where to fly to, this Place is destitute of all Inhabitants; besides, some of our Band is always watching near this Wood: we are Strangers to this Country, have no Friends here to make inquiry after us; we came only to trade, which I often did, and so learned *English*, and now despair of ever seeing our native Land and Friends again."

This Story nearly touched Mrs. *Lluelling*'s Heart. "Find a way for our Escape," *said she*, "and I will procure your safe return to *France*." Here she related to them all her own Adventures, at which they seem'd astonish'd; but when she named her Father and Mother, they fell a weeping, and embracing her Knees, declared that they had been Servants to her Grandfather, the Governour of *Normandy*, the eldest having been many years Housekeeper to her Grandmother, the Marchioness of *Maintenon*. "My dear Lady," said she, "what would I refuse to do to serve you? I will set you at Liberty, or die in the Attempt." Here they consulted what to do, Mrs. *Lluelling* resolving not to stay there all that night, fearing the Men's return. There was in the Chapel many Disguises, with which the Robbers used to conceal themselves; of these they chose three, which were old ragged Coats, Shoes, Hats, &c. being Beggars' Habits; they took Soot and Grease, and made an odd kind of Pomatum[1] to rub their Faces and Hands; and thus accouter'd,[2] with long oaken Sticks in their Hands, they ventur'd into the Wood, leaving the dismal Dwelling, empty of Human Creatures. They went on, trembling at every Noise or Rustling of the Trees, seeking a Path, but could discover none: they still went forward, till they had pass'd through the Wood, and then they discover'd the open Country, where they could discern nothing but dreadful high barren Mountains, and lonely Valleys, dangerous to pass: they had no Food with them, nor any Money, for the Robbers never left that behind them in that Place.

Thus they wander'd over the Mountains till Night approach'd, weary and faint for want of Food; and when it grew dark, they could go no farther; back they neither dar'd, nor would return. *Belinda* had a Soul too noble to submit to gratify a Villain's Lust. "Come my Companions," *said she*, "let us lie down on the cold Earth, and trust that Providence that still preserves those that put their Confidence in it; 'tis better far to perish here, than live in Infamy and Misery: 'tis true, our Bodies are enfeebled by the want of Sustenance, but Sleep will refresh our tired Spirits, and enable us to prosecute our Journey; recommend yourselves to God, his Power is all-sufficient, and when Human Means are wanting, can supply our Wants by Miracle." Here she fell upon her Knees, and cry'd, "My God, encrease my Faith, pity our Distress, and send us Help: but if thou hast decreed us to die in this Place, support us under the mighty Tryal, and give us Grace to be entirely resigned to thy Will, and send thy Angels to receive our Souls." Her Companions remain'd silent, admiring the Constancy of *Belinda*, who seemed then scarce fifteen; they laid down and slept profoundly, Weariness making them rest, tho under the most racking Apprehensions of the greatest Dangers. At break of day they arose, but knew not which way to go.

Thus they wander'd three Days and Nights: the Evening of the third day, they discovered, at a considerable distance, a small Town; but now, alas! they were no longer able to stand. "My merciful God," *cry'd the almost dying* Belinda, "must I perish now, when Help is so near? Why do my fainting Limbs refuse to bear me to that Place, where Food is to be had, and Drink to quench my raging Thirst, which Water will no longer do? My

---

1 Pomade: a paste for the skin or hair.
2 Dressed and equipped.

craving Stomach sickens with the cold Draught, and casts it back again." Here she fainted, *Lisbia* and *Magdalena*, for those were the Women's Names that accompany'd her, look'd ghastly[1] upon her, and fell down by her.

Thus the Almighty try'd her Faith and Patience, but design'd not she, who fled from Sin, should perish: a She-Goat, with a little Kid, at her recovering from her Trance, stood by her; she catch'd at it with her eager hands, the Goat fled, but the Kid she laid hold of, calling to her Companions to assist her, and with a Knife she had in her Pocket, she stabb'd it. They lick'd up the warm Blood, and eat the raw Flesh, more joyfully than they wou'd Dainties at another time, so sharp is Hunger! Refresh'd with this, they slept that night much better, tho it was now pinching cold, it being the latter end of *October*. It snow'd hard towards morning, which so benumb'd their Limbs, that they were not able to walk; and here they sat eating their strange Breakfast of raw Flesh, till it was almost Noon, making many vain Attempts to rise and walk: but then the Sun breaking out, they made a shift to creep along towards the Town. But, alas! when they thought they were almost there, they met with the River *Wie*; they saw no Bridge or Boat, and it was impossible for them to get over it on foot: they went as far as they were able by the River-side, ready to sink down at every step; at length they sat down, and wept sadly. *Belinda* believing herself near Death, her Constitution being more tender and delicate than the *French* Women's, with a weak Voice thus exhorted them: "My Friends," *says she*, "I need not tell you that we are all born to part, and die; I believe our time is short, and that in few hours we shall be released from the Miseries of this Life: how necessary is it for us then, to improve those few Hours Providence gives us, to prepare for Eternity? My Life has, I thank God, been pass'd in Retirement; I have not been exposed to the Temptations of the World, yet have I not been free from Errors: you have lived long, I beg therefore that you would apply yourselves earnestly to him that must condemn, or save us, out of whose mighty Hand none can deliver us; and remember that now is the Moment when eternal Happiness is to be obtain'd or lost."

Here she cou'd proceed no farther, but fell back in a Swoon. At this Instant a poor Fisherman brought his Nets down to dry them on the Shore; and seeing three poor Men together, two of them weeping over him that was lying down, he drew near, and overheard their Complaints. The Man spoke but bad *English*, but

---

1  Full of fear.

he understood it much better; he found the Person dying was a Woman disguised, because they wrung their Hands, and lamented her, crying, "Our dear Lady is dead, what shall we do?" The good Man look'd about to see if his Boat was coming in, which he had left his Boy to bring thither, who at that Instant brought it to the Shore; the good Man leaped into it, and took out a Bottle of Brandy, which he quickly brought, and pour'd some of it down *Belinda*'s Throat, at which she recovered; the two Women drank likewise. He told them his House, tho a poor one, was but a Mile farther, and invited them to it; but, alas! they were not able to walk thither: he and his Boy were obliged to help them into his Boat, in which he carry'd them to his Cottage, where they were kindly received by his Wife, to whom the Fisherman told how he found them; the good Woman warm'd a Bed,[1] and got them into it, giving them good hot Broth. And now being much refreshed, *Belinda* told her who she was, and that she lived at *Swansey*. "Alas! Madam," *said the good Woman*, "you are a great way from home, but I will send my Husband thither, to give your Friends notice." "He shall be well rewarded," *said* Belinda. The next morning the Fisherman set out for *Swansey*, and *Belinda* fell very sick; *Lisbia* and *Magdelaine* recover'd soon, but she remain'd so weak, that she could not walk. In five Days the Fisherman reach'd Mr. *Lluelling*'s, whom we must now return to speak of.

### CHAP. XII.

Mr. *Lluelling*, the Lord —, and his Son, being arrived at *Swansey*, and finding no News of *Belinda*, they took all the Methods possible to find her out, but in vain. Mr. *Hide* was so weak that he could not accompany his Father, and Kinsman, who rid out every day in search of *Belinda*; the Marquiss, who could not part one hour from his dear Lady, and the lovely *Isabella*, kept him company: her Charms soon touch'd his Soul, and he at last began to imagine, that if *Belinda* was found again, and happy, he could be so with her Sister. *Isabella* grew insensibly[2] to be fond of him, her Virgin Heart that never felt Love's Flame before, was warmed, and every thing he did, was charming in her Eyes: he now was able to walk into the Garden, and tho very weak, was well-bred, obliging, gay, and entertaining. The Marquiss was extreme fond of him, and was

---

1 Put a container of hot coals between the sheets.
2 Without noticing.

pleased to see the growing Affection betwixt Mr. *Hide* and *Isabella*; nothing was wanting but *Belinda*'s Presence, to make this Family compleatly happy: and now the fortunate Moment came, they so much wish'd for; the Fisherman arrived, and gave an account of her being at his House with two Friends, with the manner of their coming thither: but, good Heavens! what Transports fill'd Mr. *Lluelling*'s and her Mother's Soul? It was late at night when this News was brought, and impossible to travel by reason of the Snow and Darkness, yet it was with difficulty that the Marquiss restrained his Son from venturing.

In the morning they set out at the break of day, the Marquiss, Lord —, and Mr. *Lluelling*, in the Coach and Six, with five Servants, and the Fisherman well horsed: the old Lady would fain have gone, but her Weakness was such, that she, Mr. *Hide*, and *Isabella*, were constrained to stay at home. In three days Mr. *Lluelling*, and the rest, arrived at the Cottage, where he was bless'd with the sight of his dear *Belinda*; she was in bed, very weak, but when she heard his Voice, she started up, and when he came to the bed-side, threw her Arms about his Neck, and both remain'd silent for some Moments, whilst Tears of Joy shew'd their Affection: then he recovering, said a thousand tender Things, such as fully express'd his Fondness. Her Father next embrac'd her, saying, "See here, *Belinda*, your transported Father, who never saw a day like this! now my God has crowned my Age with Blessings, exceeding Expectation, and almost Belief. What Thanks are we obliged to render our Creator, for the mighty Blessings he has this day bestow'd upon us?" She bow'd, but being faint, could scarce reply, when Mr. *Lluelling*, looking tenderly upon her, said, "Alas! my *Belinda*, may I hope that I shall sleep again within those Arms? Has no vile Ravisher usurped my Right, and forced you to his hated Bed? Has not that lovely Body been polluted with his curs'd Embraces? tho I believe your Mind still pure, and that your Soul loath'd, and abhor'd the damning Thought; yet forgive me, if I tremble at the dreadful Idea of so curs'd an Act, and long to know the Truth." *Belinda*, lifting up her Eyes, look'd on him with Disdain; "Are you my Husband?" *she cry'd.* "Do you know me? and can you believe me capable of so vile, so base a Crime, as yielding up my Honour to a Ravisher? No; I would have pre-fer'd the cruellest Death to Infamy; or if by Force compell'd, wou'd ne'er have let the impious Villain live for to repeat his Crime; or I would have urged him to destroy me, pursued him with Reproaches, till with my Blood he should have bought his Peace, and wash'd away my Stain: believe me, I am innocent as when you took me first a Virgin to your Bed, and your Suspicions are unkind." Here she fainted, he held her in his Arms, ask'd pardon for his Rashness, and with fervent Kisses seal'd his Peace[1] upon her Lips and Hands. And now they thought of removing her to *Swansey*: this was a Place not fit for her to stay in, Physicians, and all Things wanting, could not here be had. He had forgot to bring Clothes and Linnen thither, and till she was to rise, took no notice of hers, and her Companions' Habits; but when he saw *Lisbia* bring her Beggar's Coat, and other Accoutrements, he, and the Marquiss, and Lord —, were much surprized, and diverted; and indeed it was a pleasant Sight to see her, and her Female Attendants, so dress'd, enter the Coach.

And now nothing remained but to reward the honest Fisherman and his Wife; Mr. *Lluelling* gave them ten Pieces of Gold, a Sum they had never been Masters of before in their whole Lives; he told them if they would come to *Swansey*, he would give them a House to live in. They return'd him Thanks, but said they had lived in that Cottage thirty odd Years, and had rather continue there; but if he wou'd give their Boy *Jack* a new Fisher-boat against he was marry'd,[2] which was to be shortly, they should be bound to pray for him to their Lives' end. He agreed to their Request, bidding the Fisherman come to *Swansey*, and chuse such a one as he best liked, and he would pay for it: so they parted thence, and in three days came in Safety to *Swansey*, where *Belinda* was received with excessive Joy by her Mother, and the rest. *Isabella* admired her Sister's Beauty, tho somewhat changed by Sickness, when she saw her dress'd in her own Clothes. Habits were given to the Women her Attendants, and none but Mr. *Hide* feared to look upon her; she turn'd towards him smiling, "My generous Lover and Friend," *said she*, "look not upon me with such Disorder; believe me, your Treatment of me was so generous and noble, that had I not been disposed of, nor known Mr. *Lluelling* before, I declare, Mr. *Hide* should have had the first Place in my Esteem: but here is another to be disposed of, my charming Sister, who has, in my Eyes, superior Charms; give her that Heart which I must now refuse, and make her happy." "Speak, my dear Sister," *said she*, "shall he be heard? and do you not think him worthy your Love?" *Isabella* blush'd, and the Marchioness answer'd, "Her Father and I approving it, I dare answer for my dear *Isabella*, she will be guided by us." Mr. *Hide* made a low Bow. "My Lord,"

---

1 Ended their argument.
2 In anticipation of his marriage.

*said he,* "may I presume to hope so great an Honour as seems here design'd me?" "You may," *answer'd the Marquiss,* "I shall be proud to call you Son." From this Hour Mr. *Hide* paid his Addresses to *Isabella,* and Content reigned in every Face, and now *Belinda* gave an Account of all that had happened to her, from her being taken by the Robbers, to her Arrival at the Fisherman's.

Two days after her return home, the two poor Servants that were taken by the Thieves with her, and left lock'd up in a Room, when she fled from the ruinous House in the Wood, came to *Swansey,* and told, How having found themselves there alone, and hearing nobody stir, or come to relieve them for two days and a night, they resolved to force their way out, at all Adventures; and searching about to find the best Place to make their Escape at, one of them pull'd a great Stone out of the Wall, at which they both crept out: they saw nobody, and rambled all about the House, and ruin'd Church; there they found several Boxes and Trunks, but most of them empty: examining more curiously, they found a Trap-door in the Chancel,[1] which, lifting up, they ventur'd to go into a Vault,[2] where was much Treasure, as Plate,[3] Jewels, Money, and Clothes; they took as much as they could well carry in their Pockets, and departed, going over the Mountains till they thought they were safe, and there they lay that night. The next day, knowing the Country, they went home to their Master, Mr. *Hide*'s House, and from thence came to *Swansey,* to give him an Account of all.

Upon this Information, and Mrs. *Lluelling*'s, Mr. Lluelling resolved to send to the High-Sheriff, and raise the County, to apprehend this Gang of Thieves;[4] but *Belinda* entreated him to spare the Captain of the Robbers.

According to his Desire, the Sheriff gave Orders, and Mr. *Lluelling* heading the Hue-and-Cry, Mr. *Hide*'s Servants guiding them, they went directly to the Wood, where they apprehended two of the meanest of the Crew, that is, two real Thieves; who inform'd them, that the whole Band returning thither two days

---

1 The part of a church where services are performed.

2 Space beneath the floor of a church.

3 Serving pieces or utensils made of gold or silver.

4 There was no official police force in the eighteenth century, so when a suspect was on the loose, the high sheriff (the local representative of the crown for everything pertaining to criminal law) would issue a "hue and cry" calling for all residents of the county to aid in the search and apprehension.

after *Belinda*'s Escape thence, and finding the two Women, and Mr. *Hide*'s two Servants gone, they feared being discovered, and had therefore changed their Lodgings, and retired to a Place more secret, and almost impossible to be discovered, taking part of their Treasure with them, and were resolved to go off to Sea, if they were too closely pursued to live longer there; and had left them behind to give Intelligence. They said moreover, That they had look'd narrowly upon most of the Mountains for *Belinda* and the Women, and missing them, hoped they had perished in some of the dismal Valleys, or tumbled down from some Precipice, and kill'd themselves. "Our Captain, indeed," *said one of them,* "is a brave Gentleman, and storm'd dreadfully at us, saying, he would give his Life willingly to save the Lady, and that if we did not find, and bring her safe back, he would kill us: which we little regarded; for tho we let him at present head us, and command, 'tis only because he is boldest, and will venture where we don't care to go: but should we be taken and imprison'd, we should not scruple to hang him, or any of his Friends, to save ourselves." "Villains that you are," *cry'd Mr.* Lluelling, "if possible, I will save him, and hang you." They were pinion'd, and the House and Church searched narrowly, where some Plate and Clothes were found, and afterwards put into the Sheriff's Hands, to be restored to the Owners, upon publick Notice given, and their appearing; and after much search, being able to discover no more of the Thieves, Mr. *Lluelling* dismiss'd the Assistants, and return'd home, the two Thieves being first lodged in the County Goal. Some days after, a Man brought a Letter, directed to the *French* Marquiss, Monsieur *de Maintenon*; he gave it to one of the Servants, and departed: the Marquiss open'd it before the Family, and read the Contents, which were as follows

My LORD,

*It is with the utmost Confusion I inform your Lordship, that I am the unfortunate Sir C.O. known here only as Captain of a Band of Robbers, amongst whom are Mr. T. B., Sir A. D., the two A—rs, and two Gentlemen more, unknown to you. I am perfectly sensible of the Danger and Sinfulness of this wretched Course of Life I at present follow, and would gladly leave it for any honest way of getting Bread. I throw myself at your Feet, to implore your Pity and Pardon for the Rudeness I offer'd Belinda, which I heartily repent of. I know your Generosity and Goodness, and resolve to put my Life into your Hands, by coming to you; and if you think me worthy to live, dispose of me as you please, I will follow you into France, and draw my Sword no more,*

*but for yours, and my Master's*[1] *Service: if you condemn me to Death,
send me to a Prison, and you will take away a Life, that, whilst I continue in Sin, must be burdensome to*

Your Devoted Friend,
and Old Acquaintance
*C. O.*

## CHAP. XIII.

The Marquiss was much surprized at reading this Letter, knowing the Gentleman very well: he ask'd Mr. *Lluelling*, his Lady,
and Lord — Advice; they all agreed that they would, if possible,
save him and the rest. The next day the Captain of the Robbers
came, and Mr. *Hide* embraced him, and so did the Marquis, Mr.
*Lluelling*, and L—; they had the Diversion of his relating to them
all his dangerous and bold Adventures: he lay there that night,
next morning Mr. *Lluelling* went to the Port, and hired a Vessel to
carry him and his Companions to *Spain*, the Marquiss giving him
Letters of Recommendation to some Great Men there, who were
his Friends. He made him deliver up all the Things of value he
had left in his Hands, of his Robberies, and part of Mr. *Lluelling*'s
Money, and gave him Bills[2] for a handsome Sum of Money to
support him and his Friends, till they could be provided for in the
Army, which they desired to be received into:[3] this the Marquiss
generously gave out of his own Pocket, with some Gold for their
present Occasion, till they came to *Barcelona*, the Bill being drawn
on a Merchant there, with whom he held a Correspondence.

The rest of the unfortunate Gentlemen, who, by their Captain's
Advice, were all near at hand, went aboard the Vessel, to which
the Marquiss, Mr. *Lluelling*, L—, and Mr. *Hide*, went with the
Captain, and there they supp'd merrily, and parted; the Marquiss,
and his Son, L—, and Mr. *Hide*, returning home. Next morning
the ship sailed with a fair Wind, and *Wales* was delivered from a

---

1  The would-be James III, the Stuart claimant to the throne.

2  Bills of exchange, written orders to someone, typically a merchant or
   banker, to pay a named person a particular sum on a particular date.
   They effectively work like postdated checks. Such bills were used to
   facilitate financial transactions when sending coins was either impractical or dangerous.

3  Like France, Spain backed the Jacobites and would sometimes accept
   them into its army.

Band of Gentlemen Thieves, and the unfortunate Gentlemen from hanging.

And now nothing remain'd to compleat this Family's Felicity, but *Isabella*'s Marriage with Mr. *Hide*, which in some days after was consummated; this Wedding was very splendid, all sorts of innocent Diversion, as Dancing, Feasting, and musical Entertainments, compleated the Festival. The Country-People had their share in it, and much pleased the Ladies with their odd Dancing and Songs: the *Welsh* Harpers came from all parts of the Country, blind and lame, and the Halls echo'd with the trembling Harps.[1] The Marquiss, who had heard the most harmonious Concerts of Musick in *Rome* and *France*, confess'd he had heard nothing more diverting, or seen an Entertainment where there was less Expence, or more true Mirth; saying, "Were the *Welsh* Language as agreeable and musical as their Harps, I should love to hear them talk, and prefer it to *French.*" The Marquiss and his Lady resolved to continue here till Mrs. *Lluelling* was brought to bed, which she was in the *March* following, on the 17th of which, she was happily delivered of a Son. After she was up again,[2] the Marquiss thought of returning to *France* with his Lady, but desired he might have his little Grandson and his Nurse with him; the L— and Mr. *Hide* likewise resolving to go with him, and settle there, sold their Estates. Mr. *Lluelling* and *Belinda* offer'd to accompany their Father and Mother, and spend the Summer in *Normandy*. And now it being the Year 1718, on the 2d of *May* they went aboard a Ship they had hired to carry them, and arrived safe on the 9th, in the Evening, at *St. Malo*'s, from whence they set out for *Coutance*, and in few Days arrived at the Marquiss's Seat, where they were entertain'd nobly. The two *French* Women, *Lisbia* and *Magdelaine*, went joyfully to their Home, returning many Thanks to the Marquiss and Ladies. Mr. *Lluelling* and his Lady, found *France* so charming, that they continue there.

Thus Providence does, with unexpected Accidents, try Men's Faith, frustrate their Designs, and lead them thro a Series of Misfortunes, to manifest its Power in their Deliverance; confounding the Atheist, and convincing the Libertine, that there is a just God, who rewards Virtue, and does punish Vice: so wonderful are the Ways of God, so boundless is his Power, that none ought to despair that believe in him. You see he can give Food upon the

---

1 Wandering blind harpers often performed for the Welsh elite. The harp is one of the traditional symbols of Wales.
2 Recovered.

barren Mountain, and prevent the bold Ravisher from accomplishing his wicked Design: the virtuous *Belinda* was safe in the hands of a Man who was desperately in love with her, and whose desperate Circumstance made him dare to do almost any thing; but Virtue was her Armour, and Providence her Defender: these Tryals did but improve her Vertues, and encrease her Faith.

Such Histories as these ought to be publish'd in this Age above all others, and if we would be like the worthy Persons whose Story we have here read, happy and bless'd with all Human Felicity; let us imitate their Virtues, since that is the only way to make us dear to God and Man, and the most certain and noble Method to perpetuate our Names, and render our Memories immortal, and our Souls eternally happy.

*FINIS.*[1]

---

1 Latin: the end.

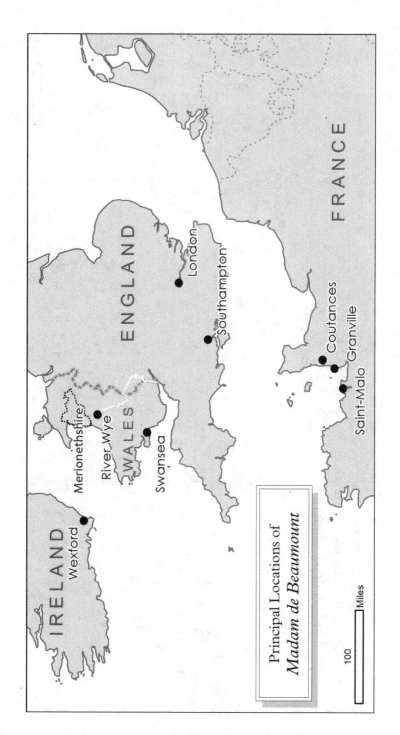

Principal Locations of
*Madam de Beaumount*

IRELAND

Wexford

WALES

Merionethshire

River Wye

Swansea

ENGLAND

London

Southampton

FRANCE

Coutances

Granville

Saint-Malo

100 ⃞ Miles

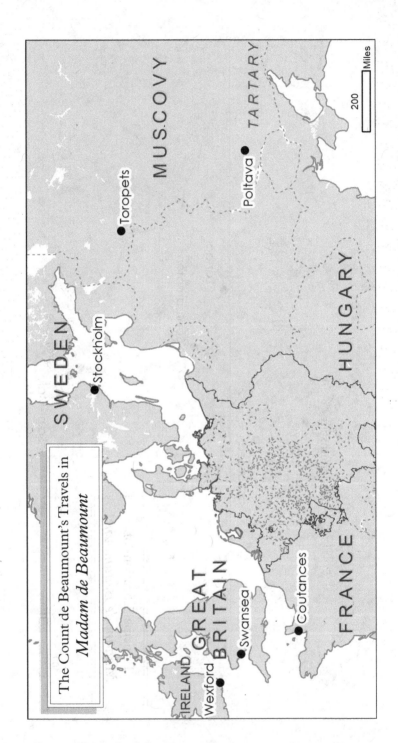

The Count de Beaumount's Travels in
*Madam de Beaumount*

SWEDEN

Stockholm

MUSCOVY

Toropets

Poltava

TARTARY

HUNGARY

IRELAND

GREAT BRITAIN

Wexford

Swansea

Coutances

FRANCE

200 Miles

# THE
# LIFE
## OF
## Charlotta Du Pont,
## An *English* LADY;

Taken from her own MEMOIRS.

Giving an Account how she was trepan'd
by her Stepmother to *Virginia*, how the Ship
was taken by some *Madagascar* Pirates, and
retaken by a *Spanish* Man of War. Of her
Marriage in the *Spanish West-Indies*, and
Adventures whilst she resided there, with her
return to *England*. And the History of several Gentlemen and Ladys whom she met
withal in her Travels; some of whom had
been Slaves in *Barbary*, and others cast on
Shore by Shipwreck on the barbarous Coasts
up the great River *Oroonoko*: with their E-
scape thence, and safe Return to *France* and
*Spain*.

A History that contains the greatest Variety
of Events that ever was publish'd.

---

## By Mrs. AUBIN.

---

LONDON:
Printed for *A. Bettesworth* at the *Red Lion* in *Pater-
Noster-Row.* M.DCC.XXIII.

To my much honoured Friend Mrs. *ROWE*.[1]

MADAM,

I have long waited an Opportunity to give some publick Testimony of the Esteem and Respect I have for you. The Friendship you and Mr. *Rowe* have shewn to me and my dead Friend, have laid me under the greatest Obligations to love and value you; but your particular Merit has doubly ingaged me to honour you.[2] In you I have found all that is valuable in our Sex; and without Flattery, you are the best Wife, the best Friend, the most prudent, most humble, and most accomplish'd Woman I ever met withal. I am charm'd with your Conversation, and extremely proud of your Friendship. The World has often condemn'd me for being too curious,[3] and, as they term it, partial in my Friendships; but I am of *Horace*'s Mind, and take no Pleasure in Variety of Acquaintance and Conversation: Two or three Persons of Worth and Integrity are enough to make Life pleasant.[4] I confess I have little to recommend me to such, except the grateful Sense I have of the Honour they do me, and the Love I bear their Virtues; and I account it my good Fortune to have found such Friends, amongst

---

1  Since at least 1739, this has been presumed to be Elizabeth Singer Rowe (1674–1737), the famously pious poet and novelist (Appendix B2, p. 302). But the biographical details mentioned do not correspond with that "Mrs. Rowe," whose husband had been dead for eight years by the time *Charlotta Du Pont* came out and whose father was not "Dr. *Barker*, Dean of *Exeter*," but rather Walter Singer, a Dissenting minister turned clothier. Either this is all opportunistic positioning on Aubin's part (aligning herself with a fellow writer of impeccable morality and making it sound like they were friends) or else she was simply referring to a different "Mrs. Rowe." Aubin's biographer, Debbie Welham, has been unable to find anyone named Barker associated with Exeter who had a daughter who married a Mr. Rowe ("Delight"141).

2  We do not know who this "dead Friend" was, though William McBurney (252n18) suggests it may have been Thomas Gibbs, whose translation of Marin le Roy, sieur de Gomberville's *La Doctrine des moeurs* as *The Doctrine of Morality* was seen through the press after his death by Aubin.

3  Fastidious.

4  The ancient Roman poet Horace (65–8 BCE) often wrote about friendship. The specific reference here is probably to *Satires* 1.9, in which Horace's patron, Maecenas, is described by an envious social climber as "a man of few friends and right good sense" (109).

whom I esteem you in the first Rank. I need say nothing of Mr. *Rowe*, but that he has such Excellencys as prevail'd with you, who are an admirable Judge, and endow'd with as much Sense and Virtue as any Woman living, to prefer him before all the rest of Mankind: and your Choice is sufficient to speak his Merit. May Heaven prolong your Lives, and continue your Felicity, that your Friends may long enjoy you, and the World be better'd by your Examples. You act as your learned[1] Father taught, and are in all kinds an Honour to the antient noble Familys from whence you are descended. Forgive this Rapture, my Zeal transports[2] me when you are the Subject of my Thoughts; and I had almost forgot to entreat the Favour of you to accept the little Present I here make of the Adventures of a Lady, whose Life was full of the most extraordinary Incidents. I hope it will agreeably entertain you at a leisure Hour, and I assure you I dedicate it to you with the utmost Respect and Affection, and am, Madam,

Your most sincere Friend,<br>and devoted humble Servant,<br>*Penelope Aubin.*

---

1 [Aubin's note:] Dr. *Barker*, Dean of *Exeter*. [Dean: clergyman in charge of an Anglican cathedral, in this case Exeter Cathedral in the town of that name in southwestern England.]
2 Overwhelms.

# THE PREFACE.

Gentlemen and Ladys,

   *The Court being removed to the other Side of the Water, and beyond Sea, to take the Pleasures this Town and our dull Island cannot afford; the greater part of our Nobility and Members of Parliament retired to* Hannover[1] *or their Country-Seats, where they may supinely sit, and with Pleasure reflect on the great Things they have done for the publick Good, and the mighty Toils they have sustained from sultry Days and sleepless Nights, unravelling the horrid Plot:[2] whilst these our great Patriots enjoy the repose of their own Consciences, and reap the fruits of their Labours, and enlarged[3] Prisoners freed from Stone Walls, and Jailors taste the Sweets of Liberty; I believed something new and diverting would be welcome to the Town, and that the Adventures of a young Lady, whose Life contains the most extraordinary Events that I ever heard or read of, might agreeably entertain you at a time when our News-Papers furnish nothing of moment. The Story of Madam* Charlotta du Pont, *I had from the Mouth of a Gentleman of Integrity, who related it as from his own Knowledge. I have join'd some other Historys to hers, to imbellish, and render it more entertaining and useful, to incourage Virtue, and excite us to heroick Actions, which is my principal Aim in all I write; and this I hope you will rather applaud than condemn me for. The kind reception you have already given the Trifles I have published, lay me under an Obligation to do something more to merit your Favour. Besides, as I am neither a Statesman, Courtier, or modern great Man or Lady, I cannot break my Word without blushing, having ever kept it as a thing that is sacred: and I remember I*

---

1  George I was Elector of Hanover, in northern Germany, before he became King of Great Britain and Ireland. He made extended (and widely criticized) trips back to Hanover, including one in the summer of 1723, and when he did so, a number of courtiers went with him.

2  Jacobite coup attempt. It was squelched in the exceptionally hot and stormy summer of 1722 before it got very far. One of the principal conspirators was executed in May 1723 (after having been promised immunity in exchange for his testimony), and another was sent into exile in June. See Introduction, p. 45.

3  Set free. Parliament had recently abolished "the Mint," a sanctuary in London in which, because of a legal loophole, debters could take refuge and avoid arrest. As part of that legislation, Parliament offered amnesty to debtors who owed less than £50. Close to six thousand availed themselves of the offer and so were able to exit the Mint and move about freely.

*promis'd in my Preface to the Count* de Vineville, *to continue writing if you dealt favourably with me.*[1] *My Booksellers say, my Novels sell tolerably well. I had design'd to employ my Pen on something more serious and learned; but they tell me, I shall meet with no Incouragement, and advise me to write rather more modishly, that is, less like a Christian, and in a Style careless and loose, as the Custom of the present Age is to live. But I leave that to the other female Authors my Contemporaries, whose Lives and Writings have, I fear, too great a resemblance.*[2] *My Design in writing, is to employ my leisure Hours to some Advantage to my self and others; and I shall forbear publishing any work of greater Price and Value than these, till times mend, and Money again is plenty in* England.[3] *Necessity may make Wits, but Authors will be at a loss for Patrons and Subscribers whilst the Nation is poor. I do not write for Bread, nor am I vain or fond of Applause; but I am very ambitious to gain the Esteem of those who honour Virtue, and shall ever be*

Their devoted humble Servant,<br>
Penelope Aubin.

---

1   See Appendix A1, p. 279.

2   This putative "resemblance" had been a stock charge against women writers since the late seventeenth century. Supposedly women could not write convincingly about love and desire unless they were themselves promiscuous.

3   The bursting of the South Sea Bubble (the meteoric rise and then crash of the stock of the private company used to manage the national debt) in 1720 sent the country into recession for much of the next decade.

# THE LIFE OF *CHARLOTTA DU PONT*.

## CHAP. I.

Towards the end of King *Charles* the Second's Reign, when a long continuance of Peace, and his merciful Government, had made our Nation the most rich and happy Country in the World; a *French* Gentleman, whose Name was Monsieur *du Pont*, being a Protestant, left *France*, and came and settled near *Bristol*[1] with his Wife.[2] He had been Master of a Vessel; with which making many prosperous Voyages to the *West-Indies*, and other places, he had gain'd a competent Estate; and was now resolv'd to sit down in quiet, and pass the remainder of his Life at ease, in a Country where he might enjoy his Religion without molestation. Having dispos'd of all he had in *France*, and remitted the Money by Bills[3] into *England*, to some Merchants his Correspondents[4] here, he chose to settle near this Sea-Port, where he had some acquaintance with the most considerable Merchants, with whom he had traded; having been several times in *England* before, and perfectly skill'd in our Language. He put part of his Money into the publick Funds,[5] and with the rest purchas'd a House and some Land, on which he liv'd with his Wife, and some Servants, as happily as any Man on Earth could do; and nothing was wanting[6] but Children to make him completely blest. He had been marry'd eight Years, and had no Child; but he had not liv'd in this healthful Country above two Years, when his Lady with

---

1  Port in western England (see map, p. 275).

2  Charles II's reign ended with his death in February 1685. Later that year, Protestants were officially forbidden to practice their religion in France (although Louis XIV had been making them feel extremely unwelcome since at least 1681). This prompted hundreds of thousands of French Protestants (or Huguenots) to emigrate to other Protestant counties, including England.

3  Bills of exchange, written orders to someone, typically a merchant or banker, to pay a named person a particular sum on a particular date. Such bills were used to facilitate financial transactions when sending coins was either impractical or dangerous. They effectively work like postdated checks.

4  Business partners in other places.

5  Government bonds (one of the few kinds of relatively safe investments then available).

6  Lacking.

much Joy told him, she was with Child; at which News he return'd thanks to Heaven with transport,[1] and she was at the expiration of her time[2] happily deliver'd of a Daughter, whose Life is the subject of this History, being full of such strange Misfortunes, and wonderful Adventures, that it well deserves to be publish'd. They gave her the Name of her fond Mother, *Charlotta*;[3] and the Child was so beautiful, that every body that saw her, admir'd her.

'Tis needless to tell you, that Monsieur *du Pont* and his Lady bred her up with all the Care and Tenderness imaginable: But it pleas'd God to deprive this little Creature of her dear Mother, before she was five Years old; for Madam *du Pont* fell sick of a Fever, and dy'd. And now *Charlotta* was left to her Father's Care, who, deeply concern'd for his Lady's Death, look'd on her as the dear Pledge[4] which was left him, of their mutual Affection; and was so doatingly fond of her, that he resolv'd never to marry again, but to make it the business of his Life to educate and provide for her, in the most advantageous manner he was able.

The Child was beautiful and ingenious, and shew'd so great a Capacity, and so quick an Apprehension in all she went about, that he had reason to hope great things from her. Nor were his Expectations frustrated; for before she was ten Years old, she cou'd play upon the Lute and Harpsicord, danc'd finely, spoke *French* and *Latin* perfectly, sung ravishingly, writ delicately, and us'd her Needle with as much Art and Skill, as if *Pallas*[5] had been her Mistress.[6] Mons. *du Pont* blest Heaven hourly for her, and delighted in her more than he indeed ought to have done, fancying he could not out-live the loss of her. She was so obedient to his Will, that his Commands were always obey'd, and she never once offended him. But Man is a frail Creature, and there are unlucky Hours in Life, which, if not carefully arm'd against, give us opportunitys of being undone. A Merchant of *London*, in whose Hands

---

1  Rapture.

2  End of her pregnancy.

3  There was a character named Charlotte de Pontais added to the 1722 version of Robert Challes's *Les Illustres Françoises*. Aubin would translate this text in 1727. It is unknown whether she encountered it prior to writing *Charlotta Du Pont*. There is no similarity between the stories of the two heroines.

4  Token.

5  Epithet often used to refer to Athena, the ancient Greek goddess whose portfolio included weaving.

6  Teacher.

Monsieur *du Pont* had a great Sum of Money, dy'd, and he was oblig'd to make a Journey to Town, to look after it, and get it out of the Executrix's Hands, who was look'd upon to be no very honest Woman. He would not venture to take *Charlotta* with him, for fear she should be disorder'd with the Journey, or get the Small-pox,[1] which she had not as yet had; so he left her with a discreet Gentlewoman, whom he had taken into his House after his Wife's death, to manage his Servants, and breed her up. And being come to *London*, to a Friend's House, where he lay, in the City,[2] and was joyfully receiv'd by him, he did not only take care of his Money-Affair; but was also resolv'd to take a little diversion during his stay in *London*, where he had not been for many Years; and accordingly he went to Court, and to the Play-houses.[3] His Friend and he being together one Evening at a Play, two very handsom well-drest Gentlewomen came into the Pit,[4] and sat down before them: one of these Ladys was very beautiful and genteel, the other seem'd to be her Companion. Monsieur *du Pont* felt a strange Alteration in himself at the sight of this Woman: he soon got into discourse with her, presented some Oranges and Sweet-meats[5] to them, and found her Conversation as bewitching as her Face and Mien.[6] His Friend kindly caution'd him, but in vain. In fine,[7] the Play being done, he prevail'd with these Ladys to see 'em home, and ask'd his Friend to go along with him, which he unwillingly consented to: so they usher'd the Ladys to a Coach, into which being enter'd, the Ladys bid the Coachman drive to a Street in *Westminster*; where, being come, they alighted; and the Gentlemen being invited in, came into a very handsom House, genteely furnish'd. Here they

1  In an age before widespread inoculation, smallpox could be deadly (and even when it wasn't, it could leave facial scars that could imperil a young woman's marriage prospects).
2  The area of central London that used to be surrounded by the medieval walls. Traditionally its inhabitants were thought to be devoted above all to trade.
3  In Westminster, an area in western London that was both the seat of government and a destination for various sorts of pleasure-seekers.
4  The seating area of the theater immediately in front of the stage. It was where wits, would-be wits, and sex workers looking for clients were thought to gather.
5  Desserts.
6  Look and bearing, especially as it revealed something about her character.
7  To sum up.

staid Supper, which was serv'd up by two Maid-Servants, being cold Meat, Tarts, and Wine. And now entering into a more free Conversation, the Lady who appear'd to be the Mistress of the House, being her who was the youngest and most beautiful, told them she was a Widow, having bury'd her Husband about two Years before, who was a Country Gentleman, and had left her a moderate Fortune, and no Child: That finding the Country too melancholly for her, she had come to *London* with this Lady, her Aunt, who was a Widow also; but having had an ill Husband, was not so well provided for, as her Birth and Fortune deserv'd: That they had taken a House in this part of the Town, as most airy and retired, and had but few Visiters: and then excus'd her self with a charming air of Modesty, for having admitted these Strangers to this freedom, to which indeed Monsieur *du Pont* had introduc'd himself with much importunity. In fine, they past Supper in a very agreeable Conversation, and then respectfully took leave, after having obtain'd the two Ladys' permission to repeat their Visits, and continue the acquaintance Chance had so happily begun. One of the Maids having call'd a Coach, Monsieur *du Pont* gave her half a Crown,¹ and enter'd into it with his Friend, who pleasantly ridicul'd him all the way home, telling him, these Ladys were, doubtless, kept Women and Jilts:² but Monsieur *du Pont* was so inflam'd with Love for the young Widow, that he was deaf to all he said, yet seem'd to hearken to him, and turn the Adventure into a Jest, saying, he did not design to visit them any more.

Being come home, and gone to bed, the tormenting Passion depriv'd him of Rest, and he lay awake all night, thinking on nothing but this charming Woman. In short, he visited her the next Evening, was entertain'd with so much Modesty and Wit, that he lost all Consideration, and resolv'd, if possible, to gain her for his Wife. And now 'tis fit that we should know who she was; and that we relate this fair one's Life and Adventures, whom we shall call *Dorinda*, in respect to her Family.

## CHAP. II.

She was the younger Daughter of a Country Gentleman, of a good Family and Estate, and tho well educated, and very witty and accomplish'd, yet being wantonly inclin'd, she at the Age of

---

1  2½ shillings.
2  Prostitutes.

thirteen, fell in love with a young Officer of the Guards,[1] who came to the Town her Father liv'd in, to visit some Relations. This gay[2] young Rake, who had a Wife and two Children in *London*, made Love[3] secretly to this lovely unexperienc'd Girl; and having prevail'd with her Maid to let him meet her in a Grove behind her Father's House, there he pretended honourable Love to her, and promis'd to marry her. In fine, having gain'd her Affections and ruin'd her, and fearing her Father wou'd revenge the Injury he had done him, if he came to the knowledge of it; he one Evening took leave of her to go for *London*, pretending that so soon as he was arriv'd there, he would employ some of his Friends to get him a better Post, for he was at that time but an Ensign;[4] and then he would write down to his Relations to move his Suit to her Father, and get his consent to marry her. But alas! the deluded *Dorinda*, young as she was, too well discern'd her Lover's base design, and was distracted with Shame, Love, and Revenge. She reproach'd him, letting fall a shower of Tears, in Words so tender and so moving, that had he not been a harden'd Wretch, and one of those heroick Rakes that have been vers'd in every Vice this famous City can instruct our Youth in, he would have relented; but he was a complete Gentleman, had the eloquent Tongue of a Lawyer, was deceitful as a Courtier, had no more Religion than Honesty, was handsom, leud, and inconstant; yet he pretended to be much concern'd at leaving her, and made a thousand Protestations of his Fidelity to her. In short, he set out for *London* the next Morning before Day, and left the poor undone *Dorinda* in the utmost despair; yet she did not dare to disclose her Grief to any but her treacherous Maid, who had been the Confident of their Amour.

Some Months past without one Line from him, by which time she had convincing Proofs of her being more unfortunate than she at first imagin'd, for she found she was with Child: this put a thousand dreadful designs into her Head, sometimes she resolv'd to put an end to her wretched Life, and prevent her Shame; but then reflecting on the miserable state her Soul must be in for ever, she desisted from her dismal purpose; and at length, finding it impossible to conceal her Misfortune much longer, she resolv'd to go for *London*, in search of the base Author of her Miserys. In order to this, she got what Money she could together, and one Evening,

---

1  The most elite regiments of the English Army.
2  Light-hearted.
3  Courted, either for seduction or marriage.
4  The lowest rank of officer in the infantry.

having before acquainted her Maid with her design, she pack'd up their Clothes, and what Rings and other things she had of value; and when all the Family were in bed, the Maid got two of the Men-servants' Habits,[1] which they put on, and so disguis'd, each carrying a Bundle, they went away from her Father's House by break of day; the Maid having order'd her Brother, to whom she had told their Design, to meet them a little way from the House with Horses, on which they mounted, and he being their Guide, went with them five and twenty Miles, which was near half of the way to *London*. There they parted from him, paying him well for his trouble, and he took the Horses back. Nor did they fear that he would make any discovery, because of being so much concern'd in assisting them in their flight.

They lay at the Inn that Night which he had carry'd them to, from whence a Stage-Coach[2] went every other day to *London*, and was to set out thence the next Morning. In this Coach they went, and having chang'd their Clothes at a By-Alehouse[3] before they came to this Inn, and given the Men's Habits to the Fellow with their Horses, they appear'd to be what they really were; and *Dorinda*'s Beauty made a Conquest of an old Colonel, who, with his Son, a Youth, was in the Coach, and soon enter'd into discourse with her. She wanted not Wit; and her Youth, and the fine Habit she had on, inform'd him she was a Person of Birth.[4] He ask'd her many Questions, and made her large Offers of his Service. At last, having been nobly treated by him at Dinner, and being now within five Miles of *London*, the unfortunate *Dorinda*, who knew not where to look for a Lodging, nor how to find out the cruel *Leander*, for so we will call the Officer that had undone her, ventur'd to tell the Colonel, that she was a Stranger to the Town, and should be oblig'd to him very highly, if he could help her to two things, a Lodging in some private House of good Reputation, and a sight of *Leander*, whom she suppos'd he might have some

---

1  Outfits.

2  Coach that offers paying customers transportation at set times along a set route. In order to travel quickly, its driver changed horses at regular intervals and predetermined locations. The latter were called "stages." Often they were inns.

3  Out of the way alehouse. Alehouses were traditionally the least elegant sort of drinking establishment, offering only ale (rather than the wine and food of a tavern or the lodging of an inn).

4  Of noble or gentle birth (that is, someone from a respectable family of landed wealth).

knowledge of, being an Officer. The old Gentleman was indeed no stranger to him, nor his Vices, and immediately guess'd the blushing *Dorinda*'s unhappy Condition; he joyfully told her, he was his intimate Friend and in his own Regiment; that he would carry her to a Lady's House who was his Relation, and should serve her in all things she could desire. *Dorinda* look'd on this as a Providence: But, alas, it was a Prelude to greater Misfortunes and her entire Ruin. For this Colonel, now believing her already ruin'd, had his own Satisfaction in view, and pitying her Condition, knowing his Friend was already marry'd, thought it would be a Deed of Charity in him to take care of and keep her himself. In order to which, so soon as the Coach came to the Inn in *Holborn*,[1] he had a Hackney[2] call'd, into which he sent his Son and a Servant that he had with him, who rid up one of his Horses, home to his own House, and went with the Lady and her Maid to a House at *Westminster*, where a useful Lady liv'd, that is in plain *English* a private Quality-Bawd,[3] who used to lodge a Mistress for him at any time; a Woman who was well bred, and a very Saint in appearance, and liv'd so privately that her Neighbours knew nothing of her Profession; she pass'd for a Widow-Gentlewoman who let Lodgings to People of Fashion; she kept a Maid-servant, and had always one handsome young Woman or other a Boarder with her, who she pretended were her Kinswomen out of the Country, being call'd Aunt by one, and Cousin by another, as she directed the poor Creatures to stile her. The House was neatly furnish'd, and had no Person in it at that time but the ruin'd *Miranda*, who afterwards went with *Dorinda*, and was with her at the Play, when Monsieur *du Pont* met with them. The Colonel presented *Dorinda* to this good Lady, giving her a great Charge to be careful of and kind to her: And indeed the Procuress, Mrs. ——[4] seeing her so young and handsome, and so well rigg'd,[5] was mighty glad of her Company, and resolv'd to use all her devilish Arts to gain her Esteem and Friendship, in hopes to make a good Penny of her. Some Wine and a Supper

---

1 Area in northern London where stagecoaches from the north would often end their journeys.
2 Horse-drawn cab.
3 Woman who arranges extramarital sex, typically with prostitutes, for money.
4 Dashed-out names, such as "Mrs. —," were often used to suggest that reference was being made to a real person (who, if named outright, might sue for libel or otherwise retaliate).
5 Well dressed.

were soon got, and the Colonel pressing *Dorinda* to know who she was and her Circumstances, got her to own to him that his Friend had promis'd her Marriage, and ruin'd her; but she would not tell him her true Name, nor from whence she came, but with Tears besought him to bring *Leander* to her, which he promis'd to do the next Morning; so took leave, much charm'd with *Dorinda*, and in his own thoughts condemning his Friend's baseness.

He went to his own home to his Wife and Family, and the poor distracted *Dorinda* was conducted with her Maid to a handsome Chamber; where, the Door being lock'd, and she and her Servant being laid in bed,[1] she began to reflect on her own Condition and Actions. It is impossible to describe in words what she felt when she consider'd, that she had left her tender Parents, blasted the reputable Family she belong'd to, since none but must guess the Cause of her sudden Flight; that she was now in a strange place, and in the Hands of those she knew nothing of; that in case *Leander*, from whom she had little Cause to expect any good, refus'd to marry and take care of her, she was ruin'd to all intents and purposes; could no more return to her home and family, nor had with her half enough to provide long for her and the helpless Infant she was likely to bring into the World. She shed a flood of Tears, and wish'd for Death a thousand times, and pass'd the Night without closing her Eyes. Thus by one imprudent Action we often ruin the Peace and Quiet of our lives for ever, and by one false step undo our selves. I wish Mankind would but reflect how barbarous a deed it is, how much below a Man, nay how like the Devil 'tis, to debauch a young unexperienc'd Virgin, and expose to Ruin and an endless train of Miseries, the Person whom his Persuasions hath drawn to gratify his Desire, and to oblige him at the expence of her own Peace and Honour. And surely if our Laws be just, that punish that Man with death who kills another, he certainly merits that or something worse, that is, eternal Infamy, who betrays the foolish Maid that credits his Oaths and Vows, and abandons her to Shame and Misery. And if Women were not infatuated, doubtless every Maid would look on the Man that proposes such a Question to her, as her mortal Enemy, and from that Moment banish him from her Heart and Company. Forgive this Digression. *Dorinda*'s Condition and Wrongs must inspire every generous Mind with some concern and resentment against Mankind.

---

1 It was not uncommon for unmarried women to share a bed (for warmth, for companionship, to save money).

The Colonel, who dream'd of her all Night, and was on fire to possess her, sent for his Friend *Leander* in the Morning to a Tavern, told him of his Adventure, and ask'd him what he meant to do with her, and who she was: But to this last Question he was dumb, well knowing that the wretched *Dorinda* was the Colonel's own Niece, being his Sister's Daughter. He said she was a Country 'Squire's Daughter in another Town, and that he could do nothing for her, but give her a piece of Money, and remove her to a cheap Lodging, and send her back to her Father's when she was up again.[1] But the Colonel reprov'd him, and said he would himself pay her Lodging, and contribute something towards providing for her: nay, in short, that if he would quit her Company, he would keep her. But *Leander* was startled at this proposal, fearing he would discover who she was, and that it would be a Quarrel betwixt them, and his Ruin. He desir'd some time to consider of that; and concluded to go immediately with him to see her. They found her up, her Eyes swoln with weeping: At the moment *Leander* enter'd the Chamber, she swooned; his Love reviv'd, he catch'd her in his Arms; and the Colonel, disorder'd with this sight, went down Stairs, and left them alone with none but the Maid, who shutting the Door, left them together. 'Tis needless to relate what passionate Expressions pass'd on her side, and Excuses on his. In fine, he told her she was in an ill House, that the Colonel had bad designs upon her, and that he would that Evening fetch her away and take care of her; that she should not discover who she was, as she valu'd her own Peace and his Life. In fine, poor *Dorinda*, born to be deceiv'd, gave credit to all he said, and follow'd his Directions. The Colonel and he went away together; and in the Evening *Leander*, having gone to an obscure Midwife's at St. *Giles*'s,[2] and took a Lodging for her, fetch'd her away and carried her thither, pretending great Fondness. Here she continu'd some time, never stirring out of doors. He continually visited her, and told the Colonel he had sent her into the Country. At last she was deliver'd of a dead Child, and lay long ill of a Fever. And now *Leander* being quite tir'd with the Expence, propos'd to her to return home. She urg'd his Promises and Vows to marry her, till he was oblig'd to disclose the fatal Secret to her, that he was marry'd already. But what Words can express her Resentments and Disorder at that instant? In short, he left her in this Distraction, and that Evening sent her a Letter to call him[3] in a Coach alone

---

1  After she had recovered from giving birth.
2  A poor, disreputable neighborhood in western London.
3  Come to him.

at a Tavern he appointed, saying he had thought of a means to make her easy. She imprudently went, and there he had hir'd two Bailiffs to arrest her with a fob Action.[1] She was by them carry'd to a Spunging-House,[2] and there kept whilst he sold his Post,[3] and with his Family went into the Country; having the Night he trepan'd[4] her, took away from the Midwife's her Clothes, Money and Jewels, and discharged[5] the Maid; who not daring to return to her Friends or Mistress's Father's, went down to an Aunt she had in another Shire:[6] And when *Leander* had dispatch'd his Business and was gone, the Officers told her he had releas'd her, and she might go where she pleas'd. She was so weak she could scarce walk, nor knew one step of the way, or the name of the place she was in. One of these Fellows was so moved with her Complaints, that he led her to the Midwife's House as she directed, having learned the name of the Street during her abode with her. The Midwife, who knew nothing of what she had suffer'd, receiv'd her with amazement, and soon gave her an Account how *Leander* had taken away all her Clothes, and sent away her Maid, which so afflicted *Dorinda* that she went half dead to bed; and in the Morning, not knowing what other Course to take, having neither Clothes nor Money, and the Midwife being poor, giving her to understand she could not long entertain her, she resolv'd to seek out the generous Colonel. In order to which she desir'd the Midwife to go with her in a Coach to the Lady's House at *Westminster*, to which he had at first carry'd her: They went, found the House, and were receiv'd by Mrs. —— with much Civility and Kindness; the Colonel was sent for, and came before Dinner: he took her in his Arms with transport, protested never to part with, but take care of her to death.[7] She related to him *Leander*'s base usage of her. He told her he had sold his Post, and left the Town: And in

---

1 Legal action pursued under false pretences (e.g., having someone arrested for a debt that they do not actually owe).

2 Sponging house: jail, often located in a private home, where debtors would be temporarily held after arrest (in the hope that their friends or family would scramble to pay the debt before a longer-term confinement became necessary).

3 Army officers routinely purchased their commissions and then sold them to an underling when they retired or were promoted.

4 Tricked.

5 Fired.

6 County.

7 Until death.

short, the Midwife being treated[1] and rewarded for bringing her thither, took leave. The best Rooms in the House were order'd for *Dorinda*, and the Colonel did that Night sleep in her Arms: Thus her first Misfortune involv'd her in a worse. Some Months she liv'd in this manner, being richly cloth'd and bravely[2] maintain'd by her old Gallant, who doted upon her. In this time she contracted a great Friendship with a young Woman in the House, *Miranda*, who was very handsome, good-natur'd, and about the Age of Twenty: They were continually together, and lay in one bed when the Colonel did not come to lie there. By this means they became so intimate, that *Miranda* gave her an Account who she was, and how she came there.

## CHAP. III.

She told her she was the Daughter of an eminent Divine,[3] who had seven Children, and very good Preferments[4] in the Country; but living very high, and breeding his Children up at a great rate, provided no Fortunes for them, so that dying before they were placed out in the World, they were left to shift, and she being one of the youngest, being then about thirteen, was taken by a Lady to wait on a little Daughter she had about seven Years old, and with the Family brought up to Town; that in a Year's time her Master, who was a young Gentleman, ruined her; and fearing her Lady should discover the Intrigue, persuaded her to quit her Service, pretending Sickness, and that *London* did not agree with her; and take leave of her Lady to return to her Mother, who kept a Boarding-School in the Country to maintain her self and the Children, two of the Boys being yet at School, and two Girls at home. But she went not to her Mother as she pretended, but into a Lodging her Master had provided for her. In this House, he for two Years maintain'd and kept her Company; but at last growing weary, gave her a small Allowance, so that by the Bawd's persuasions, she admitted others to her embraces, and was at this time maintain'd by a Merchant in the City, and concluded her Story with many Tears; saying, she did not like this Course of Life, and wish'd she could find a way to leave it; but that the Bawd always

---

1  Provided with food and drink.
2  Lavishly.
3  Clergyman.
4  Well-paid positions in the Church.

kept her bare of Money by borrowing and wheedling it out of her, and that they were always poor and wanting Money, living, as she saw, very high in Diet;[1] that she had had several Children, but had but one alive, and that was at Nurse at *Chelsey*,[2] being a little Girl, about three Years old, which she had by a young Lord, who took care of it. *Dorinda* promised to serve her in all she was able.

And now a strange Turn happen'd in her Affairs: for the Colonel's Brother-in-law, *Dorinda*'s Father, having made all the Inquiry after his Daughter that was possible in the Country, and offer'd a Reward to any that should inform him what was become of her, was at last acquainted with the manner of her going to *London* by the Maid's Brother who had procured the Horses for them; on which news he came away for *London* in search of her; he arrived at his Brother,[3] the Colonel's House, tells him his business, and begs his Assistance to find her out, knowing nothing who had debauch'd her at first, nor why she fled; tho he too rightly guess'd that must be the occasion of her withdrawing her self. The Colonel, who had never seen his Niece *Dorinda* in the Country, having not been at his Brother's House for many Years past, was a little sur-prized at the Circumstances of Time and Place where he met with this young Woman, and long'd to get to her to question her about it. It was Night when his Brother arrived, so he was obliged to delay satisfying his Curiosity till the Morning; then he went to *Dorinda*, and telling her the reason of his coming, and that her Father was come, she swooned, and by that too well convinc'd him, that he had lain with his own Niece, and not only committed a great Sin,[4] but dishonoured his Family. He at this moment felt the stings of Guilt, and bitter Repentance; he resolved never more to commit the like: And now of an amorous Lover, who used to teach her Vice, he became a wise Monitor, and preached up Virtue and Repentance; and told her, he would that Day remove her from that ill House, and place her in the Country, give her a Maintenance to live hon-estly, and, if possible, dispose of her[5] to advantage; that he would

1 Spending a great deal on expensive food.
2 Chelsea: village on the western edge of London (and so a good place to keep an illegitimate child out of sight and yet close enough to visit).
3 The terms "brother" and "sister" were used to refer both to siblings by birth and siblings by marriage.
4 The Church of England's Book of Common Prayer forbade a man from marrying (and so, implicitly, from having sex with) his "Sister's Daughter."
5 Marry her off.

endeavour to reconcile her to her Father, provided she would never disclose what had pass'd between them. She gladly agreed to all: And here Providence was so merciful as to give her an opportunity of being happy again; but, alas, Youth once vitiated is rarely reform'd, and Woman, who whilst virtuous is an Angel, ruin'd and abandon'd by the Man she loves, becomes a Devil. The Bawd had prevented all these good Designs from coming to effect, by introducing a young Nobleman into her Company, the most gay agreeable Man in the World, who was very liberal to the Procuress, and made *Dorinda* such large Presents, and used such Rhetorick, that she could not resist his Sollicitations, but yielded to his Desires. She was for this Cause deaf to Reason, and acquainted *Miranda* and Mrs. —— what had pass'd between her Uncle and her: So it was agreed that she should go where her Uncle desir'd, get what she could, and return to them. In the Evening the Colonel came and took her, and her Clothes away, and carry'd her to *Chelsey* to a Widow Gentlewoman's House that was his Friend. The next Morning he return'd with her Father, having told him, that *Leander* had ruin'd her; and that having fled to *London*, she had found a Lady of his Acquaintance out, where she had been taken care of for four Days past, having been abandon'd and ill used by *Leander*. That he had heard of it from this Lady but the Day before his arrival, and counsell'd him to forgive her, and take her home again, or continue her with this good Lady to live privately, and allow her something. This was what the Colonel had contriv'd, and taught *Dorinda* to say. The Father heard this with great Grief, and swore to take Revenge upon *Leander*; but that Heaven prevented, for they had news of his Death soon after, being thrown from off his Horse as he was hunting, and kill'd on the spot, in which Heaven's Justice was sadly manifested.

Now doting upon the unfortunate *Dorinda*, he consented to see and provide for her, but not to carry her home to his Wife and other Daughters, lest it should publish[1] his Misfortune more: but resolved to allow her a convenient Maintenance to live with this Gentlewoman, and at his return to say, that she was run away with, and married to a Person much below what he expected, belonging to the Sea;[2] and that he had done what he thought fit for her, and left her in Town. This, he thought, would silence his Neighbours and afflicted Wife, who had been long indisposed with the Grief she had fallen into on her account.

---

1 Publicize.
2 One whose livelihood comes from the sea, e.g., a fisherman or a sailor.

'Tis needless to relate what pass'd between the Father and Daughter at their first meeting; the disorder both were in was extraordinary: but having promised to allow her thirty Pounds a Year, on condition she lived soberly and retir'd in this Gentlewoman's House, and dispatch'd some other Affairs that he had to do in Town, he return'd home; and she remain'd some Days in this place, her Uncle visiting, and frequently admonishing her to live well and repent of her Follies. But she could not bear this Confinement, but long'd to see her young Lover and Friend *Miranda* again: In short, she watch'd her opportunity one Morning, when the Gentlewoman went out to a Friend that lay sick, who had sent for her; and pack'd up her Clothes, call'd a Boat,[1] and left a Letter on the Table for her Uncle, to tell him, she was gone to Town to live, to the House where he had placed her in before, where she should be glad to see him; and so went away to Mrs. —— where she was joyfully receiv'd. The Colonel soon receiv'd the news of her Flight, and the Letter, and went to her, and used all Arguments to persuade her thence, but to no purpose; so she continued there, and had variety of Lovers; learning all the base Arts of that vile Profession: till at last, having been so cunning as to have laid up a thousand Pounds, besides a great Stock of rich Clothes, a Watch, Necklace, Rings, and some Plate,[2] having liv'd in several Lodgings, and been kept by several Men of Fashion, she took *Miranda*, and furnish'd a House, kept two Maid-servants, and *Miranda*'s pretty Girl, and liv'd genteely, being visited by none but such Lovers as could pay well for their Entertainment. These were *Dorinda*'s Adventures past, and the Circumstance in which Monsieur *du Pont* found her; he visited her every Day, and could not think of leaving London without *Dorinda*. She wisely considering with her self how precarious the way of Life she followed was, resolved to marry him, but cunningly delay'd it in order to encrease his Passion; pretending that she could not marry so soon after the death of her first Husband, being but two Years a Widow. Monsieur *du Pont* confess'd his design of marrying her to his Friend; and tho he was much averse to it, yet having no particular knowledge of her, he could not alledge any thing to deter him from it but his own Conjectures. In fine, Monsieur *du Pont* in two Month's time got her consent, and taking his Friend along

---

1 Given the filth and crowding of the streets, it was often more convenient to go from one part of metropolitan London to another by water, along the Thames.

2 Tableware or serving pieces made of gold or silver.

with him, one fatal Morning went to her House, from whence she, accompanied with her Friend and Confidant *Miranda*, went with them to St. *Martin*'s Church, where the Knot was ty'd, and the unfortunate *du Pont* seal'd his ruin. They return'd to her House, where they din'd merrily, and Monsieur *du Pont* lay that Night. In a few Days after their Marriage, he importuned her to go home with him into the Country, which she was no ways averse to, because she fear'd the Visits of her Customers, some of whom could not be well deny'd admittance by reason of their Quality,[1] and Power over her; which would discover all to him. He was much pleas'd at her appearing so ready to comply with his desires; and now they prepared for going. At her request, he consented to give *Miranda* the best part of the Furniture in the House, which she design'd to continue in, and follow the unhappy Trade she had so long been versed in, tho in reality she was much averse to it, and wish'd from the bottom of her Soul, that she could meet with some honest Man that would marry her, to whom she would be true and virtuous, being no ways addicted to Vice, but reduced to it by Misfortune and Necessity.

And now *Dorinda* thought to go privately to her Uncle the Colonel, to acquaint him with her good fortune, in hopes he would now appear to credit her. She pretended to him great Repentance for her past Follies, and he gladly receiv'd her, visited her Husband, and own'd her for his Niece; sent down word to her Parents, who were over-joy'd to hear she was reclaim'd, and so well dispos'd of. Her Mother came to Town to see her long lost Child. And now, had she had the least spark of Virtue, she had been truly happy. Monsieur *du Pont* at last carry'd her home in the Stage-Coach, having sent her Clothes, Plate, and what else they thought fit by the Waggon,[2] and return'd five hundred Pounds, which she had call'd in from the Goldsmith's where she had plac'd it,[3] by Bills to *Bristol*. They arriv'd safe, and she was welcom'd by all his Friends, and treated handsomely. She pretended to be charm'd with *Charlotta* his beautiful Daughter. And for some Months they liv'd very happily.

---

1  Social rank.
2  A means of ground transportation that was slower and cheaper than the stagecoach.
3  Goldsmiths (who were used to issuing and receiving bills of exchange and whose shops had better security than the average home) sometimes allowed customers to deposit their savings in their vaults.

## CHAP. IV.

But, alas, a virtuous Life and the quiet Country were things
that did not relish well with a Woman who had liv'd a Town-life.
*Dorinda* wanted Pleasure, and soon fix'd her wanton Eyes upon
a young Sea-Captain who used to visit at Monsieur *du Pont*'s.
This young Gentleman had been exchanged with a Merchant's
Son in *France*[1] who was related to Monsieur *du Pont*, and so
became intimate with him, and many French Captains of Ships
and Merchants. He was very handsome and lov'd his Pleasures,
being a true Friend to a handsome Woman and a Bottle. *Dorinda*
soon made her self understood by him, and he as soon answer'd
her Desires, and made Monsieur *du Pont* the fashionable thing,
a Cuckold.[2] She grew big with Child, and was deliver'd of a
Daughter, which Monsieur *du Pont*, who had discover'd something of her Intrigue with the young Captain, Mr. *Furley*, did not
look on with the same tenderness as he did on *Charlotta*; for which
reason she now beheld her with much Indignation and Dislike,
tho she conceal'd her Malice and seem'd fond of her. *Charlotta*
did all she was able to please her; but now having got a Child
of her own, *Dorinda* wish'd her out of the World; and her little
Darling *Diana* growing every day more lovely in her Eyes, and her
Husband seeming more reserv'd to her, and to take little notice
of the Child, so enrag'd her, that she resolv'd to get *Charlotta* out
of her way if possible, that *Diana* might inherit all the Fortune.
Captain *Furley* went a Voyage or two to *France* and *Holland*, and
returning, when he came back to visit her, she made known her
wicked design to him, and in fine, gain'd him to assist her in it.
They contriv'd to send her beyond Sea[3] by some Captain of his
Acquaintance, and he pitch'd upon a French Master of a Ship,
who was used to trade to *Virginia* and the *Leeward-Islands*,[4] a Man
who was of a cruel avaritious Disposition, and would do any thing

---

1 The captain had been sent to France, presumably by his family, to
   live and work with Monsieur du Pont's relative, and that relative's son
   had been sent to England. This practice allowed trade networks to be
   strengthened and extended through personal ties (an important consideration in an age when one's perceived creditworthiness depended
   on how well and how widely one was known).
2 Husband whose wife has been sexually unfaithful.
3 Overseas.
4 The northern portion of the islands in the eastern Caribbean, including Saint Martin, Antigua, and Guadeloupe.

for Money; his Name was Monsieur *la Roque*. *Furley* expected him hourly in that Port. Mrs. *du Pont*, and her Husband, and *Charlotta* had often gone together on board Ships to be treated by Merchants and Masters her Husband's Acquaintance, and sometimes without her Husband with some other Friends, and particularly *Furley*. Captain *la Roque* being arriv'd at *Bristol* with his Ship, which was bound to *Virginia*, *Furley* acquainted him with their design on *Charlotta*, and offer'd him such a Bribe as easily prevail'd with the covetous Frenchman to undertake to effect it. So soon as he was ready to sail, he gave them notice; and now the fatal Day was come when the innocent lovely Virgin, who was in the thirteenth Year of her Age, was to be deprived of her dear Father and Friends, and exposed to all the Dangers of the Seas, and more cruel relentless Men. Monsieur *du Pont* going to take a Walk with a neighbouring Gentleman, Captain *Furley* came with the French Captain to invite Mrs. *du Pont* and *Charlotta* on board; she in obedience to her Mother-in-law's[1] Desires went with her in the Captain's Boat, and being come on board they were highly treated, and something being put into some Wine that was given *Charlotta*, she was so bereft of her Senses, that they put her on the Captain's Bed, and left her senseless, whilst they took leave of him and went on shore in a chance-Boat[2] which they call'd passing by the Ship, which weigh'd Anchor and set sail immediately.[3] And now Mrs. *du Pont*, as they had contriv'd, so soon as they were on shore, began to wring her Hands and cry like one distracted, pretending *Charlotta* was drown'd:[4] She alarm'd all the People as she went along, saying, that she fell over the side of the Boat into the Sea, and no help being near, was drown'd: None could contradict her, because no body could tell what Boat they came in from the Ship, the Boat being gone off before she made the out-cry. Being

---

1  In the eighteenth century, mother-in-law could also mean stepmother.
2  Boat that happened to be passing by (a busy harbor would have a number of boats ferrying people back and forth to shore).
3  There are two similar abductions in Aubin's *The Noble Slaves*: Emilia is invited by a deceitful relative to "a Treat" on board a ship and then drugged with opium-laced wine and transported involuntarily to Quebec (12–14), and Charlot is invited by her (supposedly repentent) rapist on board a ship that he claims will take them both to England. Instead, she is taken to Tripoli and sold to an "*Arabian* Captain, or Chief of a Tribe" (158–59).
4  In the eighteenth century, it was rare to know how to swim, so falling out of a boat could quickly result in drowning.

come home, she threw her self upon her bed; and her Husband being inform'd of this sad News by the Laments of the Servants at his entring into his House, and going up to her, asking a hundred Questions of the manner of it; she so rarely[1] acted her part, that he believed she was really griev'd, and *Charlotta* certainly drowned; which so struck him to the Heart, that he was seiz'd with a deep Melancholy, and spent most part of his Days in his Closet[2] shut up from Company, and the Mornings and Evenings walking alone in some retir'd place, or by the Sea-shore; so that *Dorinda* flatter'd her self that she should soon be a Widow, and return to her dear *London.*

And here 'tis necessary that we leave them, to inquire after the innocent *Charlotta*, who waking about Midnight, was quite amaz'd to find her self on a Bed no bigger than a Couch, shut up in a Closet, and hearing the Seamen's Voices, soon discover'd the fatal Secret, and knew that she was in the Ship: she knock'd loudly at the Cabin-door, upon which a young Gentleman open'd it, a Youth of excellent Shape and Features, in a fine Habit; he had a Candle in his Hand, and seem'd to view her with Admiration. "Lovely Maid," (said he) "what would you please to have?" "I beg to know, Sir," (said she) "where my Mother[3] and Captain *Furley* are, and why I am left here alone?" He remain'd silent a Moment, and then bowing, answer'd, "Madam, I am sorry that I must be so unfortunate as to acquaint you with ill News the first time that I have the Honour to speak to you: They are gone ashore, and have sold you to the Captain.[4] I am a Passenger in this Ship, and shall, I hope, be the Instrument of your Deliverance out of his cruel Hands. I was onshore when you were left here, but having seen you come on board, I made haste back, and finding the Ship just

---

1 Exceptionally.

2 Private room.

3 The term "mother" could refer to any woman who stood in a parental relation to a child.

4 The situation is a bit murky, but it seems that Dorinda and Captain Furley have paid the captain of the ship to transport Charlotta to Virginia, where he could effectively sell her as an indentured servant. Strictly speaking, indentured servitude was different from being enslaved, because it was supposed to be for a limited period of time and something one entered into voluntarily, but in practice most indentured servants were treated little better than enslaved people and their employers often found ways to extend and transfer their indentures without consent.

under sail, upon my entrance into it ask'd him where you was; on which he told me with joy, that he had you safe in his Cabin, having receiv'd a good Sum to carry you with us to *Virginia*. I love you, *Charlotta*, with the greatest Sincerity, and will lose my Life in your defence, both to secure your Virtue and your Liberty. This is not the first time I have seen you." At these words he sat down by her, press'd her Hand, and kiss'd her. But what Words can express her Confusion and Grief! She fetch'd a great Sigh and fainted, at which the young Gentleman ran and fetch'd some Cordial-Water[1] from his Chest, and gave her; at which reviving, she fell into a Transport of Sorrow, calling on Heaven to help and deliver her. He waited till her Passion was a little mitigated, and then began to reason with and comfort her, telling her, she must submit to the Almighty's Will, and that she should look upon his being in that Ship as an earnest of God's Favour to and Care of her: That he was in Circumstances that render'd him capable of serving her; that his Name was *Belanger*, and that his Father and her's had been intimate Friends, being a Merchant who lived at St. *Malos*, but was dead about seven Months before, having left him and one Daughter in Guardians' Hands, he not being yet of Age: That these Guardians us'd him and his Sister ill, having put her into a Monastery[2] against her Will, being ingaged to a young Gentleman whom they would not let her marry, pretending that he was not a suitable Match in Fortune, and that she was too young, being but fourteen, to dispose of her self; which they did with no other design, as he suppos'd, but to keep her Fortune in their Hands as long as they could, in hopes that both he and she might die single, and leave all in their Power, being his Uncles by his Father's side, and Heirs to the Fortune which was very considerable, in case they dy'd without Issue. That old Monsieur *Belanger* having Effects to a great Value in *Virginia* in the hands of a Gentleman who was Brother to Madam *Belanger* his deceas'd Mother, he was going to this Uncle to get them, and to ask his Assistance to deal with his Guardians, whom he had left, because he had some reason to fear that they design'd to poison him; having been inform'd by a trusty Servant who had liv'd with his Father long, and was now left in his House at St. *Malos*, that he had over-heard them contriving his Death; that he had taken with him a good Sum of

---

1 Alcohol-based medicine supposed to stimulate the heart, which was used to revive those who had fainted.
2 Religious community. Belanger's sister was thrust into what today would be called a convent.

Money, and some Merchandize to trade with in *Virginia*. And thus Monsieur *Belanger* having acquainted *Charlotta* with his Circumstances, concluded with many promises to take care of her in the Voyage, get her out of the Captain's hands, and marry her when he came to *Virginia*. She heard him attentively, and answer'd with great modesty, That if he did protect her from being injur'd by others, and acted in delivering her as he pretended, both she and her Father, if they liv'd to meet again, would endeavour to be grateful to him: That she had now resign'd her self to God, and was resolv'd to submit to what he pleas'd to permit her to suffer, and to prefer Death to Dishonour. He embrac'd her Knees, and vow'd to preserve her Virtue, and never suffer[1] her to be wrong'd or taken from him whilst he had a Drop of Blood left in his Veins, but to merit her Favour by all that Man could do, which he as nobly perform'd as freely promis'd. And now poor *Charlotta* had none but him to comfort her; and tho she strove all she was able, yet Grief so weaken'd her, that in few Days she was confin'd to her Bed. 'Tis needless to relate all that the tender Lover did to render himself dear to the Mistress of his Heart; he tended and watch'd[2] with her many Nights, sat on her Bed-side, and told[3] the tedious Hours, alarm'd with every change of her Distemper, which was an intermitting[4] Fever: he fee'd the Surgeon largely[5] to save her, and at last had the Satisfaction to see her recovering; Youth and Medicines both uniting, restor'd the charming Maid to Health, and *Belanger* to his repose of Mind; who now seeing the Ship not many Leagues[6] from the desired Port, flatter'd himself that she should be his. But, alas, Fate had otherwise determin'd; their Faith and Virtue was to meet with greater Trials yet and the time was far off before they should be happy.

---

1 Allow.
2 Stayed up with her when she could not sleep.
3 Counted.
4 Intermittent.
5 Paid well.
6 One league equals three miles (4.8 km).

# CHAP. V.

A Pirate-Ship came up with them in forty five Degrees of Latitude,[1] bearing English Colours,[2] which seem'd to be no Merchant-Ship, but a Frigate[3] with thirty Guns, well mann'd, and they soon discover'd who they were by their firing at them and putting up a bloody Flag,[4] bidding them surrender with their dreadful Cannon. The French Captain *la Roque* did on this occasion all that a brave Man could, nor did Monsieur *Belanger* fail to show his Courage, but fought both for his Mistress and Liberty till he was wounded in many places, and retiring into the Cabin to have his Wounds dress'd, found the affrighted *Charlotta* lying in a Swoon on the Floor: at this sight he forgot himself, and catching her up in his Arms fell back with her, and having lost much blood, fainted; mean time the Villain *la Roque* was kill'd on the Deck, and the Enemies entring the Ship, soon master'd the few that were left to oppose them, and coming into the Cabin, saw the fair *Charlotta* and her Lover holding her clasp'd in his Arms as if resolv'd in Death not to part with her. The Pirates, for such they were who had taken the Ship, being *English, French* and *Irish* Men belonging to the Crew at *Madagascar*,[5] were moved at this sight; particularly a desperate young Man that commanded the Pirate-Ship, he was charm'd with the Face of the reviving *Charlotta*, who lifting up her bright Eyes ravish'd his Soul; he rais'd her up in

---

1  See map, p. 275.

2  The English "Red Ensign" (a red flag with the traditional flag of England—a white background with a red cross—in its upper left corner).

3  Fast warship with three masts, square-rigged sails (i.e., sails perpendicular to the length of the hull), and all of its cannon on a single deck. A thirty-gun frigate (typically, fifteen cannon on each side) is on the small end but could easily sink almost any civilian vessel.

4  Red flag hoisted by pirates and corsairs as an indication that no mercy would be shown to anyone who resisted, so it would be wise to give up immediately.

5  Pirates had been using the east coast of Madagascar as a base from which to attack shipping in the Atlantic and Indian Oceans since the early 1690s. As a result, it was rumored (largely incorrectly) to be a place of fabulous wealth, and there were periodic schemes put forth for the British government to pardon and repatriate the pirates in return for a share of their plunder. Aubin testified against such a scheme in 1709 (see pp. 37–38).

his Arms, forcing *Belanger*'s Hands to let her go, he being still senseless: She look'd upon him with much amazement, but was silent with fear. The Pirate-Captain comforted her with tender Words, then she fell at his Feet, and intreated him to pity her Companion, that Gentleman. He presently order'd some Wine to be given him, had him laid on a bed, and his Wounds dress'd; then left her with him, whilst he gave orders how to dispose of the Goods and Men that were left alive in the Ship, commanding the richest Merchandize, some Provisions, and the Guns, and Pouder[1] in it, to be carry'd aboard his own Ship, and the Men and Merchant-Ship to be dismiss'd with what he thought sufficient to support them till they reached *Barbadoes* or *Virginia*, excepting no Person but the fair Virgin and her Lover. Whilst he saw these things done, and search'd the Ship, *Charlotta* had time to bewail her sad state and her Lover's, who was now so overwhelm'd with Grief and Pain that he could scarce utter his Thoughts in these moving Expressions: "My dear *Charlotta*, 'tis our hard Fate to be now left here alone in the Hands of Men whose obdurate Hearts are insensible to pity, from whom we can expect nothing but ill usage, did not your angelick Face too well convince me that they will spare your Life. Oh! could I find a way to secure your Virtue, tho with the loss of my Life, I should die with pleasure: but, alas, you must be sacrific'd, and I be left the most unhappy Wretch on Earth, if Providence does not prevent it by some Miracle or by Death. Say, my Angel, what can we do?" *Charlotta* shedding a flood of Tears, reply'd, "My dear Preserver, my only hope on Earth, all a weak Virgin can do to preserve her Honour, I will do, and only Death shall part us; but let me caution you to say you are my Brother, for the Pirate Captain seems to look on me with some concern; I fear Affection: and if so, should he discover ours to one another, it might ruin us, and cause the Villain to destroy you to possess me, who being left in his Hands when you are gone, shall be forc'd to what my Soul abhors more than Death." *Belanger* pressing her Hand, reply'd, "Alas, there needed only that dreadful Thought to end me"; and so fainted: her Shrieks brought the Pirate-Captain who was an *Irish* Gentleman (whose Story we shall relate hereafter) down to the Cabin-door, who seeing her wringing her Hands over the pale young Man who lay senseless, began to suspect he was her Lover, and was fir'd with Jealousy: however he ran to her, and lifting her up in his Arms, ask'd her, who this Person was for whom she was so greatly concern'd? She answer'd,

---

1 Gunpowder.

He was her Brother, that they were going from *France* to *Virginia* to a rich Uncle, having been cheated by their Guardians of their Fortune in *France*. And then she fell on her Knees, and besought him with Tears to land them on that Coast, or put them into the next Ship he met with bound to that place or near it. Appeas'd with hearing he was her Brother, tho doubtful of the Truth, he embrac'd her, and promis'd to do what she desir'd; commanding his Surgeon and Crew to do all that was necessary to save the young Man's Life and recover him. Cordials being given him, and his Wounds carefully dress'd, he got Strength daily. Mean time the Captain had them carefully watch'd to discover whether he was her Brother or not, resolving to get rid of him if his Rival: but *Charlotta* being on her guard, so well behav'd her self, that he could get no Satisfaction for some time. He daily importun'd her with his Passion for her in *Belanger*'s Presence, on whom she was continually attending; and told her, If she would consent to marry him when they came a-shore at the Island of *Providence*,[1] which was at that time the Pirates' Place of Rendezvous, he would make her the richest Lady in Christendom, and give her Brother a Fortune, having such immense Treasures bury'd there in the Earth of Jewels and Gold, as would purchase them a Retreat, and all things else they could desire in this World. To all these offers she gave little answer, but modestly excus'd her self from making any Promises, saying she was too young to marry yet, and would consider farther of it when they came a-shore, yet thank'd him for his generous Treatment of them. These Delays still more enflam'd him; he grew every day more earnest and importunate, and often proceeded to kiss her in *Belanger*'s Presence, whose inward Grief can hardly be describ'd, which his Face often betray'd by turning pale, whilst his enraged Soul sparkled in his fiery Eyes when he saw his Mistress rudely folded in another's Arms. One day *Charlotta*, willing to change the Discourse of Love, begg'd the Pirate-Captain to inform her who he was, and how he came to follow this unhappy Course of Life; "perhaps," said she, "being convinced you are well descended, as your Gentleman-like Treatment of us inclines me to believe, I shall esteem you more." Glad to oblige her, he began the Story of his Life in this manner.

---

1 In the 1710s, the island of New Providence in the Bahamas was used by pirates as a base from which to attack shipping in the Atlantic and the Caribbean (see map, p. 275).

## CHAP. VI.

"I was born in *Ireland*, divine *Charlotta*, of a noble and loyal Family, who fighting for King *James* II were undone: my Father fell with Honour in the Field, our Estate was afterwards confiscated, and my poor Mother, a Lord's Daughter, left with three helpless Children, of whom I was the eldest, expos'd to want.[1] I was then eighteen, and had a Soul that could not bear Misfortunes, or endure to see my Mother's condition; so I took my young Sister, who was but ten Years old, and fair as an Angel, and leaving my Mother, and my Brother, but an Infant, at a Relation's House, who charitably took them in, escaped from my ruin'd Country and Friends to *France*, hoping to get some honourable Post there, under that hospitable generous King who had receiv'd my Prince. When we arriv'd at St. *Germains*,[2] having spent what little our kind Friends had given us at our first setting out from home, we were receiv'd but coldly. My Sister, indeed, was by a *French* Lady taken to be a Companion for her eldest Daughter, something so like a Servant, that my Soul burn'd with Indignation. I waited long to get Preferment, living on Charity, that is, eating at others' Tables. At last I fell in company with some desperate young Gentlemen, who, like me, were tired with this uncertain course of life, some of whom had been bred to the Sea:[3] we agreed to go separately to *Brest*,[4] and seize in the night some small Vessel ready victual'd,[5] and equip'd for a Voyage, some of us having first gone aboard as Passengers.[6] This Design we executed with so good success, that

---

1 Many Catholic Irish fought in support of the deposed James II in the early 1690s as he attempted to use Ireland as a staging ground from which to regain his throne. After William and Mary's army put down the rebellion, they seized the estates of the Jacobite leaders and gave them to Protestant supporters of the new regime. In the wake of this defeat, tens of thousands of Irish emigrated to France. See Introduction, pp. 43–44.

2 Louis XIV allowed James II to establish a court-in-exile in Saint-Germain-en-Laye, a town west of Paris and close to Louis's new palace at Versailles.

3 Trained as sailors or fishermen.

4 Port in northwestern France.

5 Stocked with food.

6 Pirates sometimes employed Jacobite rhetoric, probably more to protest the current government's crackdown on piracy than out of any real loyalty to the Stuarts (see Bialuschewski).

finding a small Merchant-Ship bound for *Martinico*,[1] we sent five of our Companions, being in all fourteen, as Passengers, on board with our Trunks of Clothes; and pretending to take leave of them, all follow'd, staying till Night drinking Healths with the *French* Captain, who suspected nothing, and had but eight Hands aboard of twenty six that belong'd to the Ship, which was design'd to weigh Anchor, and set sail the next day: we seiz'd upon him first, and then on his Men, singing so loud that they were not heard to dispute by the Ships who were lying near us in the Harbour: we bound and put them all under Hatches, and set sail immediately, resolving to make for the Island of *Jamaica*,[2] where we hoped to sell the Merchandize we had in the Ship, which was laden with rich Goods; and having made our Fortunes there, to go for *Holland*, and settle our selves as Merchants, or look out for some other way to make our selves easy, and gain some Settlement in the World. When we were got to Sea, we fetch'd the Captain up, and told him partly our design: he beg'd to be set ashore with his Men, at some Port of *France*; pleading he had a Wife and seven Children, and was undone if we carry'd him thence in that manner. So we consented to his desire, and at break of day gave him one of the Boats, and six of the Men to carry him to Land, which I suppose he got safely to, having heard nothing more of him.

And now we put out all the Sail we could, and had a prosperous Voyage, till we came near *Jamaica*: there we met a Pirate-Sloop[3] well-mann'd and arm'd, carrying *French* Colours:[4] we were now most of us sick, and in great want of fresh Water and Provisions. They gave us a Signal to lie by,[5] and we supposing them to be Friends, obey'd, joyful to meet a Ship to assist us: but they soon made us sensible of our mistake, sending their Boat's Crew on board, who seiz'd us and our Ship, and carry'd us all fetter'd[6] to the Island of *Providence*; where, in short, we grew intimate with these and other Pirates, and consented to pursue the same course of life. They did not trust us in one Ship together, but dividing

1  Martinique, an island in the eastern Caribbean that was a French colony.
2  Then an English colony.
3  Small ship with one mast and sails rigged fore-and-aft (that is, parallel to the length of the hull).
4  Aubin's brother-in-law's ship was attacked in 1720 by pirates flying French colors.
5  Come as much to a stop as they could without anchoring.
6  Chained or shackled.

us, took us out with them. Ten of us have already lost our Lives bravely; three are marry'd, and command Ships like me; we have vast Treasures, and live like Princes on the spoils of others. 'Tis true, 'tis no safe Employment, for we are continually in danger of death: hanging or drowning are what we are to expect; but we are so daring and harden'd by custom, that we regard it as nothing. For my own part, I am often stung with remorse, and on reflection wish to quit this course of life: I am asham'd to think of the brutish Actions I have done, and the innocent Blood I have spilt, makes me uneasy, and apprehensive of Death.

And now, sweet *Charlotta*, I have told you my unhappy Story, 'tis in your power to reclaim and make me happy: promise then to be mine, and I will marry you, and take all the Treasure I am Master of, and with your Brother sail for *Virginia*; from thence we'll go for *Ireland* as Passengers. You shall acquaint your Uncle that we have been taken by Pirates, and left on that place; for my Ship shall in the night make off, and the Boat having landed us, shall return to it; so that we and our Wealth shall be left without fear of discovery." Then he address'd himself to *Belanger*, saying, "Sir, I have treated you, for your Sister's sake, kindly and generously: I expect you should lay your Commands upon her to consent to my request: I would not be obliged to use the Methods I can take to procure what I now sue for; but if I am constrain'd to use force, it will be your own Faults." At these Words he went out of the Cabin much disorder'd, and left them in great Perplexity; a death-like Paleness overspread their Faces, and they sat silent for some Moments: Then *Belanger* fetching a deep sigh, casting his Eyes up to Heaven, said, "Now, my God, manifest thy Goodness to us, and deliver us." *Charlotta* would have spoke, the Tears streaming down her pale Cheeks, but he stopp'd her from declaring her sad Thoughts, saying softly, "Hush my Angel, we are watched, betray not the fatal Secret that will bring Death to me, and ruin you." They compos'd their Looks as much as possible; and three Days pass'd, in which the Pirate-Captain grew so importunate[1] with *Charlotta*, that she was forced to declare her self in some manner, and told him she was engag'd to a Gentleman in *France*. At last he grew enrag'd, and told her, he was too well acquainted with the reason of her coldness towards him; and since fair means would not do, he would try other methods. At these words he call'd for some of the Crew, who seizing on *Belanger*, put him in Irons,[2] and carry'd him down into the

---

1 Relentlessly persistent.
2 Shackles (restraints for the wrists) and/or fetters (restraints for the ankles).

Hold. *Charlotta* transported with grief at this dismal sight, threw her self at the Pirate's feet, and told him, "'Tis in vain, cruel Man, that you endeavour to force me to consent to your desires, I have a Soul that scorns to yield to Threats; nay, Death shall not fright me into a compliance with your unjust Request: I have already given my Heart and Faith to another, and am now resolv'd never to eat or drink again, till you release my Husband, for such he is by plighted Vows and Promises,[1] which I will never break: no, I will be equally deaf to Prayers and Threats; and if you use force, Death shall free me. This is my last resolve, do as you please." At these words she rose and left him, and sat down with a look so resolute and calm, that his Soul shook: he sat down by her, and reason'd with her: "*Charlotta*," said he, "why do you force me to be cruel? I love you passionately, and cannot live without you: Heaven will absolve you from the Vows you have made, since you shall break them by necessity, not choice; that Sin I shall be answerable for: my Passion makes me as deaf to Reason, as you are to Pity: I beg you would consider e'er it is too late, and I am drove to use the last extremity to gain you. Your Lover's life is in my power: be kind, and he may live, and be happy with some other Maid; if you refuse my Offers, he shall surely die; I give you to this night to resolve."[2] At these words he left her, setting a Watch at the Cabin-door, and taking every thing from her that could harm her. Then he went to the Quarter-deck, and calling for *Belanger*, who was brought up to him loaded with Irons, he us'd Threats, Intreaties, and all he could think of, to make him consent to part with *Charlotta*, and assist him to gain her; all which he rejected with scorn and disdain. At last he was so enrag'd, that he caus'd *Belanger* to be stripp'd, and lash'd in a cruel manner, who bravely stifled his Groans, and would not once complain, lest *Charlotta* should hear him, and be driven to despair. But the Pirate's Rage did not end here; he had him carry'd down and shewn to her, the Blood running down his tender Back and Arms, and gag'd, that he might not speak to her: but she, doubtless, inspir'd with Courage from above, supported this dreadful sight with great Constancy and Calmness: "'Tis the Will of Heaven," said she, "my dear *Belanger*, that we should suffer thus: Be constant, as I will be, God will deliver us by Death or Miracle." The

---

1  It was widely held that a couple that had exchanged promises to marry one another were, in effect, married (or would be as soon as they had sex), regardless of whether the official church ritual had been performed.

2  Decide.

Pirate order'd him back to the Hold, some Brandy being given him to drink, which he refus'd. And now he resolv'd to gratify his Flame, by enjoying *Charlotta* at Midnight by force: in order to which he left her under a Guard, and return'd not to her till the dead of night, when, being laid on the Bed in her Cabin weeping and praying, almost spent with extream Grief and Abstinence, he stole gently to her, having put on *Belanger's* Coat, in hopes to deceive her the more easily; then laying his Cheek to hers, he whisper'd, "Charming *Charlotta*, see your glad Lover loosen'd from his Chains, flies to your Arms." She, as one awaken'd from a horrid Dream, trembling, and in suspence, lift up her Eyes amazed, and thought him to be *Belanger*; when he, impatient to accomplish his base design, proceeding to further Freedoms beyond Modesty, discover'd to her the deceit, which she, inspir'd by her good Angel, seem'd not to know; but taking a sharp Bodkin[1] out of her Hair, stab'd him in the Belly so dangerously, that he fell senseless on the Bed. At this instant a Sailor cry'd out, "A Sail, a Sail; where's our Captain?" This alarm'd all the Crew, and the Gunner running to the great Cabin[2]-door, which the Captain had lock'd when he went in, knock'd and call'd; but only *Charlotta* answer'd, he was coming. Mean time the Ship they had seen coming up, gave them such a Broad-side,[3] as made the whole Crew run to their Arms: a bloody fight ensu'd, and *Charlotta* consulting what to do, believing the Pirate-Captain dead, and being well assur'd the Ship that fought with that she was in, must be some Man of War[4] or Frigate come in pursuit of the Pirates, because she first attack'd them, resolv'd to disguise her self, and go out of the Cabin to see the event, hoping the danger they were in would make them free *Belanger*. She catch'd up a Cloak that lay in the Cabin, and a Hat, and so disguis'd open'd the Door; but seeing a horrid fight between the Ship's Crew and the *Spaniards*, who had now boarded her, (for it was a *Spanish* Man of War, who was sent out to scour the Pirates in those parts, and having met the *French* Ship out of which *Charlotta* had been taken, and by them got Intelligence of this Pirate-Ship, was come in pursuit of them) she did not dare to venture farther than the Door. Mean time the Pirate-Captain recovering from his

---

1 Long hairpin.
2 Located at the stern. Typically spanning the entire width of the ship and with windows overlooking its wake, the great cabin was generally reserved for the captain or his most honored guests.
3 Fired all of the cannons on one side of the ship at the same time.
4 Naval warship, especially a large one.

swoon, got up, so wounded and faint with loss of Blood, that he could scarce craul to the Door, from which he push'd *Charlotta*, whom he did not at that instant know: he call'd for help, but seeing the Enemy driving his Men back upon him, Sword in hand, he endeavour'd to take down a Cutlass that was near him, and fell down. And now the *Spaniards* having master'd the Pirates, who were almost all kill'd or grievously wounded, gave over the slaughter; and having secured those that were alive, the *Spanish* Captain, who was not only a brave, but a most accomplish'd young Gentleman, with some of his Officers, enter'd the great Cabin, in which *Charlotta* and the half-dead Pirate were: she immediately cast off her disguise, and threw her self at his Feet, begging him in the *French* Tongue, to pity and protect her, and a young Gentleman whom the Pirate had put in Irons, in the Hold, whose life she valued above her own. He gaz'd upon her with admiration; her Beauty and Youth were such Advocates, as a gallant *Spaniard* could not refuse any thing to: he took her up in his Arms, promis'd her all she desired, and commanded the young Gentleman should be immediately look'd for, and, if living, set at liberty. *Belanger* had heard the Guns and Noise, and none but a brave Man can be sensible of what he felt whilst he lay bound in Chains, whilst his Mistress's Distress and Liberty were disputed, he was even ready to tear his Limbs off to get free from his Fetters; but Heaven preserv'd his Life by keeping him thus confin'd, who else had been expos'd to all the dangers of the Fight. The *Spaniards* soon found and freed him, bringing him up to the Cabin, where *Charlotta* receiv'd him with transport; and *Gonzalo* the *Spanish* Captain, and his Friends, gave him joy of his Freedom. The Pirate-Captain, at her Intreaty, was taken care of by the Surgeon, his Wound dress'd, and he put to bed, being almost senseless, and in great danger of death. And now a sufficient number of Men, with a Lieutenant, being left on board the Pirate-Ship, *Belanger* and *Charlotta* having all that belong'd to them restor'd by the brave *Spaniard*, went on board his Ship, where they were highly treated, and might in safety bless God, and enjoy some repose.

The *Spanish* Ship was bound for the Island of St. *Domingo*,[1] from whence our Lovers hoped to get passage to *Virginia*, little

---

1 Also known as La Española; often anglicized as Hispaniola (see map, p. 275). Somewhat confusingly, Santo Domingo was also the name of the Spanish colony that occupied the eastern two-thirds of the island (roughly equivalent to the present-day Dominican Republic), the capital city of that colony, and the Real Audiencia *(continued)*

foreseeing what changes of Fortune they were to meet with in the Island they were going to. There was on board the *Spanish* Ship a young Gentleman named Don *Antonio de Medenta*, the Son of the Governor of St. *Domingo*, who went, attended by two Servants, as a Volunteer, to shew his Courage, and for Pleasure. He was very handsom, and of a daring and impatient Temper, ambitious and resolute, much respected by all that knew him, his Father's Darling, and, in short, a Man who could bear no Contradiction. He was so charm'd with *Charlotta*, that he was uneasy out of her sight; and tho he at first check'd his Passion, as knowing she was promis'd to *Belanger*, yet it daily increasing, he began to hate him as his Rival, and meditate how to take her from him. It is the nature of the *Spaniards*, we all know, to be close and very subtle in their designs, very amorous, and very revengeful: this Cavalier[1] wisely conceal'd his Passion from her, and contriv'd to get his Ends so well, that he effected it without appearing criminal. In their passage to St. *Domingo*, they met a small *French* Merchant-Ship bound to *Virginia*, whose Captain was acquainted with *Gonzalo*: They saluted,[2] and the *French* Captain came on board; where seeing Monsieur *Belanger*, he appear'd very joyful. "Sir," said he, "I have a Lady on board, who has left France to follow you, the charming Madamoiselle *Genevive Santerell*, your Guardian's Daughter, who sensible of the Injurys her Father has done you, and constant in her affection to you, is a Passenger in my Ship: I will go fetch her." *Belanger* stood like one thunder-struck at this News, and *Charlotta* look'd upon him with Disdain and Shame; whilst Joy glow'd in Don *Antonio de Medenta*'s Face. And now 'tis fit that we should know the unfortunate Maid's Story, who thus follow'd him that fled from her.

## CHAP. VII.

You have been already inform'd that this young Lady was Monsieur *Belanger*'s Guardian's Daughter, and by consequence his first Cousin; they had been bred up together and design'd for one another: she was fair, wise and virtuous, but yet could not charm *Belanger*'s Heart tho he did hers; she lov'd him before she

---

[royal audience; a judicial division of the Spanish Empire] that included the island of Cuba, present-day Puerto Rico, and Florida.

1  Stylish gentleman who knew how to fight.

2  Greeted one another, typically by firing cannon or lowering a flag.

was sensible what Love was, and her Passion encreas'd with her Years: her Father did not fail to approve her Choice, because it secur'd the Estate to the Family, and *Belanger* treated her always with much Respect and Tenderness as his Kinswoman and a Lady of great Merit, but declin'd all Promises of Marriage; she was but little younger than himself, and had refus'd many advantageous Offers, declaring she was pre-ingag'd. She was much concern'd at her Father's wicked Designs against him, and tho she too well perceiv'd he did not love her as a Lover ought, which indeed her Father hated him for, yet she so doted on him that she resolv'd to serve and follow him to death, flattering her self that since she could not discover he lov'd any other Person, Time and her Constancy would gain her his Affection. When he left *France* to go for *Virginia*, she resolv'd to follow him so soon as she could get an Opportunity, in order to which she got what Money she could together, and went disguised like a Man on board this *French* Ship, where she made her self known to the Captain, having left a Letter for her Father to acquaint him where she was gone. She soon came a-board the *Spanish* Ship, and seeing *Belanger*, who could not possibly receive her uncivilly, she ran to him with a Transport that too well manifested her Affection for him. "Are we again met," said she, "and has Heaven heard my Vows? Nothing but Death shall separate me from you any more." "Madam," said he extremely disorder'd, "I am sorry that you have risk'd your Life and Honour so greatly for a Person who is unable to make you the grateful Returns you merit; my Friendship shall ever speak my Gratitude: but here is a Lady to whom my Faith is engaged. Too constant *Genevive*, how is my Soul divided between Love and Gratitude!" At these words *Charlotta*, who was inflam'd with Jealousy and Distrust, seeing how beautiful her Rival was, and reflecting that they had been long acquainted and bred up together, that it was his Interest to marry the *French* Lady, address'd her self to her in this manner, "Madam, your Plea and Title to his Heart is of much older Date than mine; 'tis just he should be yours: and that I may convince you that my Soul is generous and noble, I will save him the confusion of making Apologies to me, and resign my Right in him." "Yes, base, ungenerous *Belanger* who have deceiv'd me, return to your Duty, I will no more listen to your Oaths and Vows, leave me to the Providence of God; I ask no other Favour of you and this Lady, but to assist me to get a Passage home to *England*." *Belanger* was so confounded, he knew not what to do; he strove all he could to convince *Charlotta* of his Sincerity, and at the same time not quite to drive a Lady to despair for whom he had a tender regard. Madam *Santerell*, too sensible that he did not love her, and distracted to see her Rival so ador'd, and her self so slighted and expos'd, did all she was able to augment her Rival's uneasiness; and now *Belanger* was so watch'd and teiz'd[1] by both, that he was at his wit's end. He desir'd to go into the *French* Ship with the two Ladies to go for *Virginia*, but Don *Medenta* secretly oppos'd it, resolving to take *Charlotta* from him; in order to which he got the *Spanish* Captain to get *Belanger* to go on board the *French* Ship to be merry, which he suspecting nothing did, leaving the two Ladies sitting together in the great Cabin. In some time after the *Spanish* Captain stepping out of the room goes into his Boat, and returning to his own Ship, whispers[2] Madam *Santerell*, whom Don *Medenta* and he had acquainted with their design, and who had willingly agreed to rid her self of her Rival, to go on board the *French* Ship immediately, which she did. In the mean time *Belanger* missing *Gonzalo*, ask'd for him, and was told he was gone to his own Ship, at which he was surpriz'd; but when he saw the Boat come back with one Woman only, his Colour chang'd, and knowing Madam *Santerell* when she came nearer, he began to suspect some Treachery; he gave her his Hand to come into the Ship, saying, "Where is *Charlotta* that you are come alone?" "I have brought your Trunks and Things," said she, "because she is coming on board when the Boat returns." Whilst they were talking the Boat made off, the Trunks being handed up. He storm'd like a Madman, calling for the *French* Captain's Boat: mean time the *Spanish* Ship made off with all her Sails, being a Ship of War and a good Sailer, which the little Merchant-Ship, which was heavy loaden, could not pretend to overtake. Having thus lost the divine *Charlotta*, whom he lov'd as much as Man could love, he lost all patience, reproaching Madam *Santerell* in the most cruel terms, nay even cursing her as the Cause of his Ruin and Death; whilst she endeavour'd to appease him with all the tender soft Expressions imaginable, pretending that she was innocent and knew nothing of the *Spaniard's* design. "Ah! cruel *Belanger*," (said she) "do not repay my Affection with such unkind treatment: have I not follow'd you, and left my native Country, and all that was dear to me, exposing my self to all the Dangers of the Seas and various Sicknesses incident to change of Climates: In fine, what have I not done to merit your Esteem? And are these the Returns you make me? Must a Stranger rob me of your Heart? Consider what this usage may reduce me to do: If Fate to punish

1 Vexed.
2 Whispers to.

you, has taken her from you, must I bear the blame? 'Tis just
Heaven, that in pity to my Sufferings decrees your Separation; and
if you cannot love me, yet 'tis the least you can do to use me civilly
and send me back to my home, that I may retire to some Convent,
and spend my unhappy Life in Prayers for you, for I will pray for
and love you to death." At these words she fainted and fell down
at his Feet. *Belanger* touch'd with this moving sight, almost forgot
his own Griefs, and laying her on his bed in his Cabin, reviv'd her
with Wine and Cordials; and seeing her open her Eyes, he took
her kindly by the Hand, saying, "Charming *Genevive*, forgive me
the rash Expressions I have us'd: urg'd by my Despair I knew not
what I did or said; I own the Obligation I have to you, and have
all the grateful Sense of it that you can wish; you are dear to me
as the Ties of Blood and Friendship can make you, and tho Fate
has permitted me to give my Heart to another, yet you shall ever
be the next to her in my Esteem." These tender Speeches, with
many others of the same kind, in some sort comforted the afflicted
Lady, who concluded in her self that she should in time, having
got rid of her Rival, get his Affection; in order to which she behav'd
her self so towards him, and treated him with such Respect and
Tenderness, that he was oblig'd to conceal his Grief for *Charlotta*'s
loss, and appear tolerably satisfy'd: yet he was almost distracted in
reality, and determin'd to go in search of her so soon as he could
get a-shore at *Virginia*, and find a Ship to carry him to the Island
of St. *Domingo*, to which he knew the *Spanish* Ship was bound,
designing to leave Madam *Santerell* with his Uncle. Thus resolv'd
he seem'd pacify'd, and in few Days they got into the desir'd Port,
and were receiv'd by his Uncle with much Joy. He promis'd upon
hearing his Nephew's Story, to assist him in all he was able, to
oblige his Guardians in *France* to do him and his Sister Justice.

And now Monsieur *Belanger*'s whole Business was, to get a
Bark[1] to carry him to the Island where he suppos'd his Mistress to
be; but the inward Grief of his Mind, and the Constraint he had
put upon himself, had so impair'd his Health, that he fell sick of a
Fever, which brought him so low that he was ten Months before
he was able to go out of his Chamber, his Illness being much
increas'd by the Vexation of his Mind: all which time Madam *de
Santerell* waited on and tended him with such extraordinary Care
and Tenderness, that she much injured her own Constitution, and
fell into a Consumption,[2] at which Monsieur *Belanger* was much

---

1 Small ship.
2 Wasting disease.

concern'd. In this time he contracted a great Friendship with a young Gentleman, his Uncle's only Son, a young Man of extraordinary Parts and Goodness, handsome and ingenious; his Name was *Lewis de Montandre*,[1] which was the Name of Monsieur *de Belanger*'s Mother's Family: He was about twenty two Years old, and had travel'd most parts of *Europe*. To him Monsieur *Belanger* made known all his secret Thoughts, and Design of going to St. *Domingo* in search of *Charlotta*, and he offer'd to accompany him thither and to assist him in all he was able. And here we must leave Monsieur *Belanger* to recover his Health, and relate what befel *Charlotta*, who was left in Seignior *de Medenta*'s Hands and Power.

## CHAP. VIII.

When she found the Ship under sail, and discover'd that she was betray'd and robb'd of *Belanger*, she retir'd to her Cabin, cast her self on her bed, and abandon'd her self to Grief. "My God," said she lifting up her delicate Hands and watry Eyes, "for what am I reserv'd? What farther Misfortunes must I suffer? No sooner did thy Providence provide me a Friend to comfort me in my Distress, and deliver'd me out of the merciless Hands of Pirates, but it has again expos'd me helpless and alone to Strangers, Men who are more violent and revengeful in their Natures than any I have yet met withal. Perhaps poor *Belanger* is already drown'd in the merciless Sea by the cruel *Medenta*, to whom, unless thy Goodness again delivers me, I must be a Sacrifice." Whilst she was thus expostulating with Heaven, the amorous *Spaniard* came to her Cabin-door, and gently opening it, sat down on the bed by her, and seeing her drown'd in Tears, was for some Moments silent: at last taking her Hand he kiss'd it passionately, and said, "Too charming lovely Maid, why do you thus abandon your self to Passion? Give me leave to convince you that you have no just cause of Grief, and that I have done nothing base or dishonourable; your Lover had ungratefully left a Lady to whom he had been engag'd from his Infancy, one who highly deserv'd his Esteem, and so lov'd him that you see she has ventur'd her Life and Fame to follow him: To you he was a Stranger, and being false to her he had known so long, you have all the reason in the World to doubt his Constancy to you. Your Rival had resolv'd to rid her self of you, and you were hourly in danger

---

1   One of Abraham Aubin's commanders in the British Army was François de Rochefoucauld, Marquis de Montandre, a Huguenot refugee.

of Death whilst she was with you. Believe me, *Charlotta*, the fear of losing you whom my Soul adores, made me take such measures to secure your Life, and restore to the Lady her faithless Lover. I am disingag'd, and have a Fortune worthy your Acceptance. This Day, this Hour, if you'll consent, I'll marry you to secure you from all fears of being ruin'd or abandon'd by me; and till you permit me to be happy, I'll guard and wait on you with such respect and assiduity, that you shall be at last constrain'd to own that I do merit to be lov'd, and with that lovely Mouth confirm me happy." She answer'd him with much reserve, wisely considering in her self, that if she treated him with too much rigor, he might be provok'd to use other means to gratify his Passion; that she was wholly in his Power, and unable to deliver her self out of his hands. In fine, some days past, in which she was so alter'd with Grief, that her Lover was under great concern, he treated her with all the Gallantry and tender Regard that a Man could use to gain a Lady's Heart; he let nothing be wanting, but presented her with Wines, Sweetmeats,[1] and every thing the Ship afforded, offering her Gold and Rings, and at length perceiv'd that she grew more chearful and obliging, at which he was even transported. The Weather had till now been very favourable; but as they were sailing near the *Summer-Islands*,[2] a dreadful Storm or Hurricane arose, and drove them with such Fury for a Day and a Night, that the Ship at last struck against one of the smallest of them, and stuck so fast on the Shore that they could not get her off, which oblig'd them to get the Boats out, and lighten the Ship of the Guns and heaviest things,[3] in doing which they discover'd that the Ship had sprung a Leak; this made them under a necessity of staying on this Island for some Days to repair the Damage. The Captain, *Charlotta*, Don *Medenta*, and all the Ship's Crew went on shore; they found it was one of those Islands that was uninhabited, so that they resolv'd to go thence as soon as they could to *Bermudas*;[4] but Providence had decreed their

---

1 Desserts.

2 The Sommer (or Summer) Islands was a common name for Bermuda (see map, p. 275). However, many of the subsequent references to these islands seem to presume that they are far closer to the Caribbean than Bermuda is, so it's possible that Aubin was using this phrase to refer to some other group of islands, such as the Lesser Antilles.

3 When a ship runs aground, it is often necessary to unload heavy cargo or cannon so that its hull does not extend as far down into the water.

4 This seems to refer to the inhabited portion of the Sommer Islands (we now refer to the entire archipelago as Bermuda).

stay there for some time. The Night they landed about Midnight, the Sky darken'd extremely, and such a Storm of Lightning and Thunder follow'd, that the Ship took fire, and was consum'd with all that was left in it; the affrighted *Charlotta*, who had no other covering to defend her but the Tents they had made of the Tarpaulins and Sails, now thought her Misfortunes and Life were at an end; her Lover and all the rest recommended themselves to God, not expecting to survive that dreadful Night. Some of the Ship's Crew venturing to look out after the Ship, were lost, being blown into the Sea, and the Morning shew'd the dismal Prospect of their flaming Ship, which lay burning on the Shore almost intirely consum'd. All the hope they now had left, was that some Boats or Barks would come to their Relief from the adjacent Islands. The Storm being over towards Evening, after having taken some Refreshment of what Provisions and Drink they had left which they had brought on Shore, they ventur'd to walk about the Island, on which was plenty of Fowl and Trees. Don *Medenta* leading *Charlotta*, they wander'd to a Place where they saw some Trees growing very close together, in the midst of which they perceiv'd a sort of Hut or Cottage made of a few Boards and Branches of Trees, and coming up to it saw a Door standing open made of a Hurdle of Canes;[1] and concluding this Place was inhabited by somebody, curiosity induced them to look into it. There, stretch'd on an old Matrass, lay a Man who appear'd to be of a middle Age, pale as Death, and so meagre and motionless, that they doubted whether he was living or dead, his Habit was all torn and ragged, yet there appear'd something so lovely and majestick in his even dying look, that it nearly touch'd their Souls. Don *Medenta* going into this poor Hut, took him by the Hand, and finding he was not dead, spoke to him, asking if he could rise and eat, who he was, and other Questions, to all which he made no answer, but look'd earnestly upon him. Mean time *Charlotta* ran and fetch'd a Bottle of Rum, returning with such incredible speed that only that ardent Charity that inflam'd her generous Soul could have inabled her to do; Don *Medenta* pour'd some of this Rum into his Mouth, but it was some time before the poor Creature could swallow it; at last he seem'd a little reviv'd, and said in *French*, "God preserve you who have reliev'd me"; he could say no more, but fainted: Don *Medenta* repeating his charitable Office, gave him more Rum, whilst *Charlotta* fetch'd some Bread and Meat; he swallow'd a Mouthful or two, but could eat no more. By this time the Captain and other Officers came up,

---

1  Portable barrier woven out of thick, flexible reeds or grasses.

and were equally surpriz'd at so sad an Object; two of the Seamen were order'd to stay with him that Night, and the next Morning *Charlotta* and the rest return'd to visit him, impatient to know who he was, and how he came in that condition. He was come a little to himself, and receiv'd them in so courtly a manner, tho he was unable to rise up upon his Feet his Weakness was so great, that they concluded he was some Man of Quality; and after some Civilities had pass'd, Don *Medenta* beg'd to know who he was. "I will," said he, "if I am able, oblige you with the recital of a Story so full of Wonders, that it will merit a place in your Memories all the Days of your Lives; you seem to be Gentlemen, and that young Lady's Curiosity shall be gratify'd." Don *Medenta* bowing, seated *Charlotta* and himself on the Ground by him, the Captain and the rest stood before the Cottage-door; and the Stranger having taken a Piece of Bisket[1] and a Glass of Wine, being very faint, began the Narrative of his Life in the following manner.

## CHAP. IX.

"I was born in *France* at St. *Malos*, my Father was a rich Merchant in that Place, his Name was *du Pont*, I was the youngest of two Sons which he had, and being grown up to Man's estate,[2] my Father was mighty sollicitous to see me dispos'd of advantageously, hoping I should marry such a Fortune as might provide for me without lessening his own, so that my elder Brother might be advanced to a Title which he design'd to purchase for him,[3] or some great Employ. This he was continually rounding[4] in my Ears. But, alas, my Soul was averse to his Commands, for I had already engaged my Affections to a young Lady whom I had unfortunately seen when I was but fifteen, at a Monastery to which I had been sent by my Father, to see a Kinswoman who was a profess'd Nun[5] there; visiting her, I saw this fair young Pensioner,[6] who was then about

---

1  Ship's biscuit, a hard, dry, unleavened bread that has been baked twice and so kept well at sea.
2  Having become an adult.
3  Some titles of nobility (those of the *noblesse de robe*) could be purchased in France.
4  Whispering or muttering.
5  One who has taken permanent vows to join a religious order.
6  A woman who pays to live in a convent (and so, as far as the Church is concerned, can leave whenever she or her family wishes).

fifteen Years old; she was beautiful as an Angel, and I found her Conversation as charming as her Face; her Name was *Angelina*: and the Monastery being at a Village not above ten Miles distant from *St. Malos*, I used secretly to visit her at least once or twice a Week, so that I got her promise to marry me so soon as I was settled in the World. She told me she was the only Daughter of an old Widow Lady who lived fifty Miles distant, was extreme rich, and had placed her there, because the Abbess was her Mother's Sister; that her Fortune was left her at her Mother's disposal. This was her Circumstance, which oblig'd me, being a younger Brother, to defer marrying her till I had got some way so provided for, that I might venture to take her without asking our Parents' consent: and this delay was our undoing, for when I was twenty, an old Widow-Lady came to my Father's on some Money-Affairs, and was lodg'd at our House, where she took such a fancy to me, that she boldly sollicited my Father to lay his Commands upon me to marry her, which offer he readily accepted; and having laid all the Advantages of this rich Match before me, concluded with injoining me with the strictest injunctions to marry her forthwith. I pleaded in vain that I was preingag'd to another. He told me in a rage, I must take my Choice, either to consent or go out of his Doors immediately, protesting he would never give me a Groat,[1] and disown me if I was disobedient to his Commands. But when I proceeded in the humblest manner to make known who the Person was to whom I was preingag'd, Good Heavens! how was I surpriz'd to find it was this Lady's Daughter? And now the fatal secret being known, *Angelina* was in few days remov'd out of my sight and knowledge, being taken away from the Monastery, and sent I knew not whether. Some Months past in which I busied my self in making inquiry after her, but all in vain; at last, quite weary'd out with my Father's Threats and the Widow's Importunities, I consented to be wretched and marry'd her, whom in my Soul I loath'd and hated; nor had I done it, but in hopes to get to the knowledge of the place where my dear *Angelina* was conceal'd from me, resolving never to consummate my Marriage with her Mother; which way of proceeding so enrag'd her, that we liv'd at continual variance: yet shame withheld her from declaring this Secret to the World; together with spight, because she would continue to plague me by living with me. At last, by the means of one of the Servants, whom I brib'd, (having now all her Fortune at command, which I took care to manage so

---

1 Originally, an English silver coin worth 4 pence. By Aubin's time, it had become a shorthand for a very small sum of money.

well, that I laid by a great Sum of Money to provide for me and *Angelina*, with whom I resolv'd to fly from *France* so soon as I could find her) I got knowledge that she was lock'd up in a Convent near *Calais*;[1] on which I converted all my Money secretly into Gold and Bills of Exchange, resolving to set out for *England* with her so soon as we could get off, having there an Uncle at *Bristol*, my Father's Brother." At these Words *Charlotta* look'd earnestly upon him, surpriz'd to find he was her Cousin-German.[2] But he continu'd his Discourse thus: "But now I was in a great Dilemma how to get to the Speech of her[3] to inform her of my Design, as likewise how to get away from my Wife, who was continually hanging upon me and following of me, fearing she should discover whither I was going, being certain she would remove *Angelina* from the Convent. I therefore pick'd a Quarrel one Evening with my Wife about a Trifle on purpose, and the next Morning took horse by break of day, attended with only one Servant in whom I could confide, and set out for *St. Malos*, where being arriv'd, I hir'd a Vessel to carry me to *Calais*, fearing to be follow'd if I had gone by land; the Wind was contrary for some days, so that my revengeful Wife had time to send for *Angelina* from the Convent. At my arrival there, I had the Mortification to find her gone, but none could, or indeed would, inform me whither she was carry'd: this so exasperated me against my Wife, that I resolv'd not to return home any more: So I went directly to my Father's, and staid there a Month, pretending Business with some Masters of Ships that were expected to come into that Port. Mean time my Wife got intelligence where I was, and came to me: I receiv'd her civilly before my Father; but at Night, when we were in bed, we fell into a warm dispute, which ended in a Resolution on my side to leave her for ever, with which I acquainted her; but then she fell to Intreatys, and in the softest Terms laid before me my Ingratitude to her, and how wicked my design was upon her Daughter; pleading, that as she was my Wife, she had all the reason in the World to keep me from the Conversation of a Person whom I lov'd better than her self; that she had made me master of a plentiful Fortune, and conceal'd from the World the high Affront I had put upon her, in refusing to perform the Duties of a Husband to her. To all which I answer'd, That as for the Ceremony of our Marriage, I look'd upon it as nothing, since I was compel'd to it; that I had deny'd my self all converse with her

---

1  Port in northern France.

2  First cousin.

3  Opportunity to speak with her.

as a Wife, because I would not commit a Sin, by breaking my sol-
emn Vows and Engagements with her Daughter, whom I had made
choice of before I saw her; and since there was no other way left to
free me, I resolv'd to declare all to the World, and annul our
Marriage, and restore what Money and Estate I had remaining in
my hands to her. At these Words she flew into a violent Passion.
'Well then' (said she) 'since you will thus expose me, I'll do my self
this Justice, to remove *Angelina* from your sight for ever; be assur'd
you shall never see her more in this World.' She that moment leap'd
out of Bed, call'd for her Servant, and put on her Clothes; and tho
I us'd many Intreaties to deter her, nay proceeded to Threats, yet
she persisted in her Resolution, and going down to my Father,
acquainted him with all that had pass'd between us, desiring him to
prevent me from following her, which he, being highly incens'd
against me, too well perform'd: for he came up to my Chamber,
where I was dressing in order to follow her, but he kept me there in
discourse whilst she took Coach and was gone I knew not whither,
nor could I for some days hear any news of her. Mean time my
Father and Brother continually persecuted me on her account,
bidding me go home and live like a Christian; nay they employ'd
several Priests and the Bishop of the place to talk to me, so that I
was now look'd on with much dislike; and being weary of this
schooling, I set out for home, where I found my Wife sick, which
indeed so touch'd me, that I repented of having us'd her so
unkindly, and resolv'd to treat her more respectfully for the time to
come. A whole Year past, all which time she languish'd of a lingring
Fever and inward Decay, Grief having doubtless seiz'd her Spirits. I
us'd her with as much Tenderness as if I had been her Son; we
never bedded together, but kept two Apartments. In fine, she dy'd,
and on her Death-bed, some Hours before she expir'd, took me by
the Hand as I sat on her bed-side, and said these Words to me,
which are still fresh in my Memory, '*Du Pont*, I am now going to
leave you, and I hope to be at rest; I have lov'd you as tenderly and
passionately as ever Wife did a Husband; and tho I committed a
great Folly in marrying a Person who was so much younger than
my self, and pre-ingag'd, yet no vitious Inclinations induc'd me to
it, as my Behaviour to you since must convince you. I flatter'd my
self, that Gratitude and my Behaviour towards you, would have
gain'd your Love, but was deceiv'd. I have never been to blame in
all my Conduct towards you, but to my Child I have been cruel
and unkind; for fearing a criminal Conversation[1] between you if

---

1 Adultery.

you came together, I us'd all my endeavours to keep you asunder, and finding that even the Convents could not secure her, provok'd by your ill usage, at last I resolv'd to send her out of *France*, which I effected by means of a Captain of a Ship which was bound to *Canada*,[1] who took her with him with a Sum of Money, promising to see her there dispos'd of in Marriage to some Merchant or Officer in those Parts, which we doubted not but she would readily consent to, finding her self among Strangers, and bereft of all hopes of seeing you any more. I have never heard of her since. This Action I heartily repent of, and to expiate my Fault, I shall leave you all my Fortune, with a strict Injunction, as you hope for everlasting Happiness hereafter, to go in search of her, and employ it in endeavouring to find her; and if she be marry'd, give her part to make her happy: and may that God, whose merciful Forgiveness and Pardon I now implore, direct and prosper you, and bring you safe together, if she be yet single. I can do no more, but ask you to accept of this my last Action as an atonement for all the Trouble I have occasion'd you, and not hate my Memory.' I was so struck with hearing *Angelina* was sent so far off, and so disarm'd of my Resentments by the sight of my Wife's Condition, who was now struggling with Death, that the Tears pour'd down my Face, and my Soul was so oppress'd, that I swooned; which so disturb'd her, that her Confessor,[2] who was present at this Discourse, order'd me to be carry'd out of the Room." Here he seem'd faint, and Don *Medenta* gave him some Wine; after which he continu'd his Relation in this manner. "Recovering from my swoon, I soon discover'd by the Out-cries and Lamentations of the Servants that my Wife was dead. I behav'd my self with all the Decency and Prudence I was able on this occasion, and bury'd her suitable to her Birth and Fortune; after which I thought of nothing but my Voyage to *Canada*, having inform'd my self of the Ship and Captain's Name, who carry'd away *Angelina*; which was not return'd, or expected back to France in three Years, being gone a trading Voyage for some Merchants at *Diep*.[3] I left my Father to take care of the Estate, who sent my Brother to reside there; made my Will, and having provided my self with Money, Bills of Exchange, and all other Necessaries, I went a board a Merchant Ship call'd the *Venturous*,

---

1 Then a French colony.
2 Catholic priest to whom a believer regularly confesses their sins and from whom they receive absolution and instructions on what penance to perform.
3 Dieppe: port in northern France.

bound for those Parts to trade, not doubting but that we should meet with the Captain there who had convey'd *Angelina* thither, and then there was no question but I should make him confess where he had left her. We had a prosperous Voyage for some Weeks, but coming near *Newfoundland,* we unfortunately met a Pirate-Ship who boarded and took us after a fierce dispute which lasted three Hours, in which our Ship was so shatter'd, that she sunk as they were rifling of her; in which Accident several of the Pirates perish'd, and all the Passengers and Sailors belonging to our Ship, except my unfortunate self and Surgeon, who were taken up by Ropes into the Pirate-Ship, where we were put in Irons into the Hold, I suppose because they were in an ill Humour at the loss of their Companions and the Ship. Some days past before we had the Favour of being brought up upon the Deck, and our Irons taken off. We were both very sick; as for my part, I was so afflicted at being prevented from going my intended Voyage, that I was care-less of what became of me. There was amongst the Pirates some that look'd like Gentlemen, but they all talk'd and behav'd them-selves like desperate Villains, Oaths and Curses were as common as in a Gaming-House, they drank like *Germans,* and discours'd like Atheists and Libertines; they ask'd us many Questions, who and what we were, to all which we answer'd cautiously. I told them, if they would set me on any Shore thereabouts, from whence I might travel by Land, or get Shipping to *Canada,* I would promise if I liv'd to return to *France,* to remit a thousand Pistoles[1] to any part of the World, or Person they should name; they took little notice of my offers, but let us have the liberty of walking in the day-time on the Decks, and at Night they put us under Hatches. At last we arriv'd at the Island of *Providence,* where they were receiv'd by their Companions with much Joy. We remain'd in this wretched Place ten whole Months, in which time they us'd us like Slaves, with many others whom they could not prevail with to take up their des-perate manner of living. At last, wearied with this way of Life, we desir'd to go out in one of their Ships, desiring them to treat us as we should deserve by our Bravery and good Behaviour: They con-sented; and now all my hopes were that I should meet a welcome Death to free me from the Miseries of Life, or find some way to escape from them. There were beside my self and Friend, six Gentlemen, three of whom were *Spaniards,* and the other three

---

1 Small Spanish gold coins (perhaps better known to us as "doblóns" or doubloons) worth roughly 16 shillings. The name was sometimes also used to refer to the gold coins of other nations.

*English*, who, like us, went with them thro necessity; the Ship was a Frigate of 30 Guns, and carry'd 140 Hands: they design'd to cruise near the *Havana*,[1] in hopes to catch some of the *Spanish* Ships coming out thence: As we lay cruising at some distance, a dreadful Storm arose, which at last tore our Ship in pieces near this Island where we now are; every Man was oblig'd to shift for himself; I catch'd hold of a Plank, floating on which, it pleased Providence to cause the Winds and Waves to cast me on this Place much bruis'd; here I have been three Weeks. I made this Hut with some old Planks and what I found on the shore, to secure me from the Cold and Storms; this old Matrass and Coat I also found; all my Food has been the Eggs of Sea-Fowls and Birds, which I have daily gather'd up on the Sands and in Holes in the Rocks and hollow Trees; but the anguish of my Mind, with the Bruises I receiv'd in my Stomach in the Shipwreck, had at last reduced me to such Weakness, that I could no longer rise on my Feet to seek for Food; and when divine Providence brought you here to my Relief, I had been three whole Days without tasting any sustenance, and had by this been freed from my Miseries." Then he fetch'd a deep sigh, concluding his Story with these Words: "Yet I am in duty bound to thank God and you, and hope, since he has prolong'd my stay on Earth a little longer, that he will make Life supportable, by furnishing me with means to find her out, without whom I must be ever wretched."

And now *Charlotta* acquainted him who she was, and in few Words of the manner of her coming to that Place; at which he was fill'd with Admiration: But he was so amaz'd when he heard that Monsieur *Belanger* and Madam *de Santerel* had left *France* in such a manner, that he could scarce credit it, they being his intimate Friends; yet she in the relation spar'd to mention Don *Medenta*'s Treachery, or *Belanger*'s Love to her, saying only he was gone to *Virginia* in a *French* Ship. And now the Conversation turning to be general, every Person spoke their Sentiments of *Du Pont*'s Adventures; some days pass'd with much anxiety, Provisions were husbanded, and their fears of wanting daily increas'd; yet *du Pont* mended, and Company render'd their solitary way of living in this desolate Place more supportable; they were hourly in expectation of seeing some Ship pass by to the adjacent Islands, having plac'd a white Cloth on the Top of a Stick on the most eminent part of the Island, to give notice of their Distress: thus they spent three whole Weeks, in which time most of the Victuals they had sav'd were

---

1 In the eighteenth century, Havana was routinely referred to as "the Havana."

spent, and the dreadful Apprehensions of Famine appear'd in every Face, and every one walk'd about looking what they could find to eat, in hopes to satisfy Nature without diminishing the small Stock of Provisions they had left. Don *Medenta*, who was one of the most vigilant in searching out something to give *Charlotta* fit for her to eat, went one Morning to the farthest part of the Island, which was about seven Miles over, and there ascending a high Rock, stood looking on the Sea, and saw a Boat fasten'd in a little Cliff of the Rock, out of which Cliff a Blackmoor[1] Man came, and launching out the Boat, put off to Sea, making towards another Island. Don *Medenta* concluded this Person liv'd somewhere in this Rock, and resolv'd to search about it in hopes to discover some Persons there, by whom he might be assisted and his Friends, to get from this dismal Island, or at least to wait the Man's return, or find out his abode, in order to return thither that Evening. He found it very dangerous to descend on that side of the Rock next the Sea, and was long e'er he could find the Place out of which he saw the Man come forth; but at last he perceiv'd a sort of a Door, which seem'd to shut in a Place that was the Entrance of a Cavern in the Rock: but it was fast lock'd, and he could not discern through the Keyhole any thing but a glimmering Light, yet he heard a human Voice like a Woman's, talking to a Child, but he understood but little of it, because it was a Language he could not speak much of, being *English*; he waited some Hours, but finding the Man did not return, he went away, and hasten'd to *Charlotta* with the glad Tidings that he had found a Boat, and Persons on the Island. Both she and the whole Company were agreeably surpriz'd with this News; and the Captain, Monsieur *du Pont*, Don *Medenta* and *Charlotta*, all resolv'd to make their Evening's Walk to this Place.

## CHAP. X.

According to the Resolution taken in the Morning, *Charlotta* and the rest walk'd to the Rock in the Evening, and getting up to the top of it, saw from thence the black Man standing at the entrance of his Cave, with a white Woman who seem'd to be very young and very handsom; she had a *Molotta*[2] Child in her Arms about a year

---

1  A term for a Black African or a person of Black African descent (more commonly, "blackamoor"). Now considered offensive.

2  Mulatto: a term for someone with one Black parent and one white parent. Now considered offensive.

old, her Gown and Petticoat was made of a fine Silk. Don *Medenta* call'd to them in *French*, at which the Man look'd up; and *Charlotta* spoke in *English* to the Woman, desiring her to come up and speak to her; on which the Blackamoor push'd the Woman in, and returning no answer, shut the door upon himself and her. Don *Medenta* and the rest concluded, that they fear'd being discover'd; so they all descended the Rock and went to the Door, resolving to force it open if they could not gain entrance otherwise, and remove their Fears by speaking gently to them, and acquainting them with their Distress. They knock'd and call'd at the Door for some time; but hearing a noise within, and no answer, they broke open the Door with much difficulty, and entring, went thro a narrow Passage in the Rock, so strait that but one Person could go a-breast; at the end of which they came into some strange Rooms fashion'd by Nature, tho cleans'd of Moss and loose Stones by labour: Into these Light enter'd by the Holes that were in some places open thro the top of the Rocks; but some part of the Caves, or Caverns (for they were scarce fit to be call'd Rooms) were very dark. In the biggest Room was a Lamp burning, and here they saw two Chests lock'd, and on a Shelf some Platters and Bowls made of Calibash-shells,[1] with two or three wooden Spits; and some Sticks were burning in a corner of the Room, in a place made with Stones pil'd round, and opening in the front like a Furnace, on which stood a Pot, wherein something was boiling. There likewise hung up some Fishing-tackle and a Gun with a Powder-horn, as also a Bow with a Quiver of Arrows. In a place which was shut with a Door, like a Cupboard, stood Bread and Flower, and on the Table (for there was a very odd one, and Stools, which seem'd to be of the Negro's own making) stood a Basket with some clean Linen[2] for a Child, and some Canvas cut out for Slaves' Jackets and Drawers. In another Room they saw a Quilt and Coverlids[3] lying on some Rushes on the Floor; but they could find no living Creature, at which they were much amaz'd. They call'd, and spoke in the softest terms, desiring them to come forth, if hid there, promising to do them no harm; but in vain. At last they heard a Child cry, and following the sound of the Voice, went thro a narrow Turning on the right Hand, which brought them to a Place where a Door was shut, before which lay a terrible Bear: Don *Medenta*, who was the foremost, carrying the Lamp in

1 Upper shells of turtles; more commonly, calipash.
2 Underclothes such as shirts, shifts, and drawers (loose-fitting underwear).
3 Coverlets; bedspreads.

one hand, and his Sword in the other, being presently more apprehensive of *Charlotta*'s danger than his own, she being next behind
him, ran at the Bear, designing to kill it, if possible, before it could
rise; but was stop'd by the sound of a human Voice which came
from that Beast, saying, "For Heaven's sake, spare my life, and I'll
do all you'll have me." At these words the Negro came out of the
Bear's Skin, and threw himself at *Medenta*'s Feet, who took him up;
and *Charlotta* bid him fear nothing, they being Persons in distress,
that wanted his assistance, and would pay him nobly for serving
them. Then he open'd the Door he had lain before in the Beast's
Skin, and brought forth the young Woman and Child, whom
*Charlotta* embrac'd, whilst the poor Creature wept for joy to see a
Christian white Woman. And now they were all chearful, and the
Negro being told, that they wanted nothing but his assistance, to
carry one of them to any of the adjacent Islands that was inhabited
to get them some Provisions, and hire a Vessel to carry them to the
Island of St. *Domingo*, he readily promis'd to do it: "My Boat, says
he, will carry no great weight, being a small Canoe which I made
my self; but it will carry me and one more, with some small quantity of Provisions." And now they were all impatient to know how
this beautiful Woman and black Man came to this place; which they
found she seem'd not willing to declare whilst the Negro was present: and therefore *Charlotta* beg'd that she might accompany her
whilst he brought the Boat round to the other side of the Island, to
take in one of the Sailors; not thinking it safe to trust Don *Medenta*,
or one of the Gentlemen with him, in so slight a Vessel. This the
Negro did not seem to be pleas'd withal, but yet dar'd not refuse it.
He us'd to drag his Boat up out of the Water into a Cleft, where it
was impossible to be seen. And now the transported Woman, with
her tauny Child, accompany'd *Charlotta* to her Tent, and in the way
recounted her sad Story in these Words.

"My Name is *Isabinda*: I am the Daughter of a Planter in
*Virginia*, who has a great Plantation there, is extremely rich; and
having no more Daughters than my self, bred me up in the best
manner, sending me to *England* for Education, from whence
I return'd at thirteen years old. I was courted by several, and
by one in particular whom I liked, and my Father did not disapprove of; but it was my unhappy Fate to be miserably disappointed of all my hopes. Amongst a great many Negro-Slaves
whom my Father had to work in our Plantation, he you saw was
one, who appearing to be bred above the rest, and more capable of being serviceable in the House, was taken into it. He was
about twenty Years old, handsom and witty, could read and

write, having (as he pretends)[1] been a Prince in his own Country, and taught several Languages and Arts by a *Romish*[2] Priest, who was cast ashore at *Angola*,[3] from whence he came. He behav'd himself so well, that he gain'd my Father's Favour, and us'd often to wait on me when I walk'd out in an Evening, or rid out, running by my Horse's side; in short, he was ever ready to do me Service. We had a Pleasure-boat, having a City-house at *James*-Town; and when I was there, I us'd often, with my Companions, to go on the Water in the Evenings for pleasure, and then he us'd to steer the Boat. He made himself the little Boat you saw here, on pretence to go out a fishing for me, which much pleas'd my Father, the fashion and usefulness of it being extraordinary; for it sails swift, and bears a rough Sea beyond any thing we had ever seen. He us'd to catch Fish very dexterously, as he did every thing he went about: He could paint, understood Navigation, the Mathematicks; and in short, was so beloved by my Father, that he would have freed him, had he not fear'd losing of him. And now *Domingo*, for that is his Name, became enamour'd with me, and lift up his aspiring Eyes to my unhappy Face: His Passion increas'd with time, and at last he resolv'd to possess me, or die in the attempt. Had he but once given me the least Intimation of his Passion, I should have acquainted my Father with his Insolence, and his Death would have prevented my Ruin: but this he knew, and therefore so well kept the Secret to himself, that no body suspected it. He had taken care to provide some Bread and Money, by selling some Tobacco, and little Mathematical Instruments and Pictures he had made, my Father having given him a little piece of Ground to plant, to buy him Linen, allowing him to go finer drest than other Slaves. He also permitted him, when we went to the Town, to sell Trifles that he made. In fine, he waited only an opportunity to get me into his little Boat, which he thus effected: One Evening, the Sea being very calm, he sat in the Boat a fishing, having hid the Bread and Money in it; I walking down with my Maid, to see what he had caught for my Supper, he persuaded me to step into the Boat, and sit down. 'Now, Madam' (said he) 'you shall see Sport.' He was pulling in a little Net; I sat down, and the Maid stood on the Shore. He, in dragging the Net, loosed the Boat from the Shore, which beginning to drive out to Sea, surpriz'd me; but he

---

1 Claims (not necessarily falsely or with an intention to deceive).
2 Catholic.
3 Region in southwestern Africa where the Portuguese had established a colony, largely for slave-trading.

bad me sit still, and fear nothing. I sat very patient for some time, till at last seeing him hoist the Sail, and go farther from Land, I began to be frighten'd; he pretended to be so too, and persuaded me he could not help it, that the Wind and Stream drove the Boat against his Will. He pull'd a little Compass out of his Pocket, by which he steer'd. We were two Nights and Days thus sailing, in which time we pass'd by some Islands, on which he pretended he could not land, because, as I since discover'd, he knew they were inhabited, and had before mark'd out this desolate Place to carry me to. At last he brought me hither half dead with the fright, and faint, having eat only a little of the Bread, and drank out of a Bottle of Wine which he had in the Boat, in which he had put his Tools for making Mathematical Instruments, and Colours for Painting. When we were landed, he seem'd mighty sollicitous where to find a Place for me to lie down, and Food for me; and brought me into the Cavern in the Rock: There being seated on his Jacket, on the Ground, we eat what Fish he had in the Boat, broil'd on a Fire he made with Sticks, having a Tinder-box in his Pocket. After we had eat he told me his Design. 'My dear Lady,' said he, 'I love you to madness, and was resolv'd to possess you or die: Tho my Out-side is black, and distasteful, I fear, to your Eyes, yet my Soul is as noble and lovely as your own. I was born a Prince, and free; and tho Chance made me a Slave, and the barbarous Christians bought and sold me, yet my Mind they never could subdue. I adore you, and have long design'd what I have now effected. No human Creature dwells here besides our selves, and from this place you never must expect to return.' Here he proceeded to kiss me, my Distraction was such, that I swooned; he took the advantage of those unhappy Minutes, when I was unable to resist, and, in fine, has kept me here two whole Years, maintaining me by carrying what he makes to the adjacent Islands; where he sells his ingenious Work to the Inhabitants, and brings back Provisions and Clothes for us: from thence he brought all you see in our miserable Habitation; and to employ me, he brings Work from these People. I make Clothes for the Slaves, and by this means, and his Fishing and Shooting, we have Food enough. I had a Pearl Necklace, and some Rings in my Ears and on my Fingers, of value, when he brought me here; which he sold, and traded with the Money. I have had but this Child by him, which he doats on. He is a Christian, and would gladly marry me. He is so jealous, that whenever he discovers any body landed on the Island, he always locks me up, if he goes out; and lives in continual fear, lest my Father should make any discovery where we are, and send some to take me from him; in case of which I believe he would certainly kill me. He told me of your being here some days since, and warn'd me not to venture forth; which indeed I long'd to do, in hopes to meet with somebody to converse withal, being weary of living such a solitary miserable Life. When he found you were resolv'd to enter our Being,[1] which he thought secure, he put me into the Room you saw me in, and placed himself before it in the Bear's Skin; a Stratagem he had invented long before, supposing no body would venture to search farther, when they saw so terrible a Creature in so dismal a Place. He had stuff'd the Legs, Feet and Head of the Beast; so that placing himself in the Belly of it, it appear'd alive, especially in so dark a Place. The two large Chests you saw, he found on the Shore some Months since, in which there are much rich Clothes, Linen and Treasure, the Spoils of some unhappy Ship that was doubtless shipwreck'd on this Coast.

And now I have acquainted you with all my unhappy Story, and must implore your Assistance to persuade *Domingo* to leave this Place, and take us with you, or else help me to escape from him; tho I would now willingly consent to be his Wife, having Treasure sufficient to purchase us a good Settlement in any Place. If he be ever found by any body from *Virginia*, my Father will surely put him to death, but *Domingo* will kill me first; and to live thus is worse than Death." Here she wept, and *Charlotta* embracing her, promis'd never to part with her. "No, my dear *Isabinda*," said she, "we will part no more; *Domingo* shall be carry'd hence to the Place we are bound to, where he may safely and lawfully possess you; since you now love, as I perceive, and have forgiven him his Crime in getting you, we will assist him to be happy. The selling human Creatures, is a Crime my Soul abhors; and Wealth so got, ne'er thrives. Tho he is black, yet the Almighty made him as well as us, and Christianity ne'er taught us Cruelty: We ought to visit those Countrys to convert, not buy our Fellow-creatures, to enslave and use them as if we were Devils, or they not Men." Don *Medenta* join'd with her in opinion; and the Captain and all agreed to have them marry'd, and take them along with 'em. And now being come to their Tent, they sat down to eat, poor *Isabinda* being so transported with such charming Conversation, that *Charlotta* could not refrain praising God in her Heart, for sending her such a sweet Companion.

---

1 Home.

## CHAP. XI.

About the close of the Day *Domingo* return'd with the Sailor, with the joyful Tidings that there was a *Spanish* Ship at the Island they had been at, and that the Captain had promis'd to come the next Morning in his Long-boat[1] to fetch them away, his Name being Don *Manuel des Escalado*, a particular Friend of *Gonzalo*'s and Don *Medenta*'s. This News reviv'd them all, and now *Charlotta* talk'd to *Domingo*, offering him to take him and *Isabinda* to St. *Domingo*, and see them marry'd in the *Spanish* Ship the next day: and Don *Medenta* promis'd that the Governor his Father should permit them to settle there; "and then," said he, "*Isabinda* may, if you think fit, write to her Father, and let him know where she is." *Domingo* gladly accepted of this Proposal, being so over-joy'd to hear that *Isabinda* consented to marry him, that he fell prostrate on the Ground, and return'd Thanks to God in so passionate a manner, that it mov'd all the Company. But *Charlotta* being still deeply concern'd for the loss of *Belanger*, seeing her self going to be carry'd to a place where she should be no longer able to resist Don *Medenta*'s desires, where his Father commanded every thing, and from whence there was no possibility to escape without his Knowledge; a Place where she must either yield to be *Medenta*'s Mistress, or Wife, and should be necessitated to break her Vows and Faith given to *Belanger*; resolv'd to try the force of her Eloquence and Power over *Medenta*, to prevail with him to land her at *Virginia*, or at least give her his faithful Promise to send her thither by the first Ship that went from *St. Domingo*. In order to this, she ask'd him to walk with her alone a little way that Evening, which he gladly did; and then she began to break her Mind to him in the most soft and moving Terms imaginable: "Tho we are not of one Religion" (said she) "yet we are both Christians; I have given my Faith to another, how can I be yours without a Crime? I have all the grateful Sense that I ought of your Civilities towards me, and wish my Heart had not been pre-ingag'd, that I might have been yours; but since I cannot break through my Engagements with him, permit me to be just, and be assur'd that I will ever love and esteem you next himself whilst I live. He will undoubtedly come to *St. Domingo* to look after me; and with what Confusion shall I see him, when marry'd to you? Besides, your Father and Family will abhor me as beneath you; it is altogether unfit for you to marry a poor *English* Maid, whose Family and Education you

---

1 Largest boat carried by a ship.

are a stranger to, and who has no Fortune to recommend her to the Honour of being your Wife; so that should I consent, we must be wretched." Don *Medenta* return'd this answer: "Lovely *Charlotta*, on whom I have plac'd all my Love, and in whom my whole Happiness in this Life consists, I can no more consent to part with you than with my Hopes of future Happiness, or my Faith. It is impossible for me to live without you; *Belanger* merits not your Love, he is false to another, and with him you must expect a Curse: besides, 'tis in vain to dispute, I am resolv'd never to part with you: I have a Father who is so tender of me, and so generous and good in his Nature, that he will be glad to see me happy, and be fond of you, because you are mine; my Family will follow his Example; I have a Sister fair and wise as your self, she loves me dearly, and shall be your Companion and Friend: Your Virtue is a Portion,[1] and I have Wealth enough to make us happy; and, to remove all obstacles, you shall not set your Foot out of the Ship we are design'd to go on board of to-morrow Morning, till I have wedded and bedded you; which if you consent not to, I must first bed, and then marry you, for you are in my Power, must and shall be mine; and by this gentle Compulsion, I'll remove your Scruples, and acquit you of your Promises to the treacherous *Belanger*, my now hated Rival." At these Words he let go her Hand in a kind of disorder, and walk'd hastily back towards the Tent. She follow'd, much distracted in her Thoughts; he stay'd till she overtook him, but went along with her home without speaking another Word. After Supper, *Charlotta* retiring to bed, could not close her Eyes all Night; and having in that time well weigh'd and consider'd all he said, resolv'd to consent to marry him, chusing rather to yield to be his with Honour, than reduce him to treat her in a manner she dreaded worse than Death. Madam *de Santerel's* following *Belanger*, and his Negligence, as she constru'd it, in going into the *French* Ship, and leaving her behind, had a little piqu'd her; and her Circumstances, being in *Medenta's* hands, oblig'd her to agree to be his; nor did she dislike him, he was beautiful, had a great Fortune, was nobly born, and finely bred. She rose, determin'd to compose her Thoughts, and, if possible, banish the Passion she had for *Belanger* out of her Soul; but that was impossible.

Don *Medenta* next Morning appear'd with an unusual Gravity in his looks; the Long-boat soon arriv'd with the *Spanish* Captain, and all the Gentlemen he had on board, and was receiv'd very joyfully; all things worth carrying away were already pack'd up by the

1  Dowry.

diligent Sailors, and soon sent a-board; and then the Boat returning in the Evening, Don *Medenta, Charlotta, Isabinda*, the Moor
*Domingo*, Monsieur *du Pont, Gonzalo*, and all the rest went into
it, bidding adieu to the desolate Island, and arrived safe to the
Ship, where they were welcom'd with the Guns[1] and good Wine:
The next Morning they weigh'd Anchor, and the Ship set sail for
the Island of *St. Domingo*; then Don *Medenta* earnestly sollicited
*Charlotta* to marry him, and was seconded by Mons. *du Pont*, and
the good Father who was Chaplain to the Ship, a Fryar whose
Name was *Ignatius*, to whom he had declared his Reasons and
Resolutions; at last she yielded, and was that day marry'd, as was
also *Isabinda* to her amorous Moor, who on this occasion behav'd
himself so handsomly, and express'd such satisfaction and transport, that every body was charm'd with him. In few Hours they
reach'd the Island, and then *Charlotta* was conducted by Don
*Medenta* to his Father's Castle, where she was surpriz'd at the great
Attendance and sumptuous Furniture; the Governor receiv'd his
Son with great Joy and Affection, and when he presented *Charlotta*
to him, begging his Blessing and Pardon for marrying without his
consent, he took her up and embrac'd her, saying, "If she be as
virtuous as fair, which I doubt not, since you have made her your
Wife, and be a Catholick, I not only give you my Blessing, but
will do all that is necessary to make you great and happy." Here
*Charlotta* was surpriz'd, being a Protestant, and was ready to sink;
but Don *Medenta*, squeezing her by the Hand to give her a Hint
to conceal her disorder, reply'd briskly, "Honour'd Sir, she is all
you can desire, virtuous, wise, pious, and will I am certain be an
Honour and Comfort to us both." Then Don *Medenta*'s Sister, the
charming *Teresa*, a most accomplish'd young Lady, coming into
the Presence-Chamber,[2] welcom'd her Brother and new Sister, to
whom she made a Present of some very rich Jewels she had on:
And now all the Court (for so the Governor's Palace was justly
call'd, for he was there as great, and liv'd like a King) was soon
crouded with all the principal Gentlemen and Merchants in the
Town; a mighty Treat was got ready, the Bells were set a ringing,
and after the Supper there was a great Ball; *Charlotta* was so complemented and caress'd,[3] and her Friend *Isabinda*, who accompany'd her as a Companion or Attendant, her Circumstance not

---

1  Saluted with the ship's cannons.
2  Room in which a monarch (or, in this case, a governor) receives sup-
   plicants and guests.
3  Treated favorably.

being mention'd, that she was astonish'd; and being so young, and unus'd to such Greatness, no doubt but she at this instant forgot *Belanger*, and was transported at her good Fortune in getting so noble a Husband as Don *Medenta*. The Ball ended, she was by her Husband conducted to a most splendid Apartment,[1] attended by her Father-in-law, Sister, and all the Company. Here being again complemented, the Company took leave, and an old Lady with two waiting Women,[2] waited on her and *Isabinda* into a Dressing-Room, into which none but *Teresa* enter'd with them; the old Lady undress'd her, the Servants put her on a rich lac'd suit of Night-clothes, a delicate fine Shift, Night-Gown and Petticoats; all which *Teresa* furnish'd for her new Sister, whose Beauty she much admir'd, and highly respected her Brother. *Isabinda* had a fine suit of Night-clothes, Night-Gown and Petticoats given her also, and a Chamber prepar'd next *Charlotta*'s to lie in. *Charlotta* was conducted by *Teresa* to a Bed-Chamber, where the Bed was a rich Brocade, the Hangings Arras,[3] and every thing magnificent beyond any thing she had ever seen in her Life. So soon as she was in bed, *Teresa* and the rest took leave; then Don *Medenta* came in at another Door in his Night-Gown, and went to bed to her: mean time the Governor dismiss'd the Company, and retir'd to his Apartment.

Now it is fit that we inform our selves where *Gonzalo* and the rest of the Passengers were dispos'd of; he and *Domingo* and the Officers belonging to the Ship, stay'd on board to see the Ship clear'd and laid up[4] in the Harbour, Don *Medenta* having not thought it proper the Moor should appear with *Isabinda* till he had acquainted his Father with their Story; and therefore it was resolv'd that he should come to the Governor's the next Morning with the Captain, who was oblig'd to wait on him, and give an Account of his Voyage every time he return'd from Sea; *Domingo*'s two Chests, in which was all his Wealth, were to be likewise brought to the Castle: the Moor, who was much inclin'd

---

1   Suite within the castle.
2   Female attendants.
3   Most eighteenth-century beds had curtains around them to provide privacy and to keep their occupants warm in an age before central heating. Those around Charlotta's bed are made of brocade (fabric with a raised pattern woven into it). Around the walls of the apartment are tapestries or "hangings" made of arras (fabric in which scenes are woven in color).
4   Emptied of its cargo and anchored.

to Jealousy, pass'd the Night very ill, and thought the time long till the rising Sun appear'd; he had his little Boy a-bed with him, whom he hugg'd and kiss'd all Night; and rising at Daybreak, took a rich Habit out of one of his Chests, and dress'd himself like a Petty-Prince,[1] as he really was by Birth in his own Country; he likewise put a rich Cloak on little *Domingo*, which *Isabinda* had made him with some scarlet Cloth and Silver-lace,[2] the Moor had brought her for that purpose from the Islands he us'd to trade to. Thus he waited, ready to attend the Captain and Monsieur *du Pont* to the Castle, to which they went about ten a Clock, by which time Don *Medenta* was risen, and had acquainted his Father with *Isabinda*'s Story and *du Pont*'s; the Governor welcom'd them all, *Domingo* he embrac'd, and promis'd him his Protection and Favour. Don *Medenta* conducted him to *Isabinda* and *Charlotta*, who were together in their Apartment entertaining a great many Ladies, who were come to pay their Compliments and breakfast with them. And now nothing but feasting and joy were thought on by all but these two Ladies, who having been both bred Protestants, were in a great Consternation how they should behave themselves. *Charlotta* had reason'd that Morning with her Lord on this subject, and he had convinc'd her that she was under a necessity of dissembling her Religion; for if his Father and Family discover'd she was a Protestant, she must expect to be hated and slighted, nay that he should be ruin'd, and perhaps parted from her. These Thoughts almost distracted her, and she had communicated them secretly to *Isabinda* when she came into her Chamber in the Morning; they both wept, and found too late they must be of their Husbands' Religion, or be wretched. *Charlotta* even repented her breach of Faith with *Belanger*, and began to apprehend the Misfortunes that the change which she had made would bring upon her; but she conceal'd her Thoughts, and they went to Mass every day, which made them highly caress'd by the whole Court, and much oblig'd their Husbands.

*Domingo*, who was impatient to retire with his Wife, being very uneasy at the liberties the Gentlemen took in looking on and talking to her, sollicited Don *Medenta* to procure him some little Seat in the Country, and had it forthwith granted; for the Governor sent him to a little Market-Town about twenty Miles from the City, to a House of Pleasure which he had there; and here he found a little Paradise, a House so neat and richly

---

1 Minor prince.
2 Braid wrapped with silver wire.

furnish'd, such lovely Gardens, Fish-Ponds, Fountains, Fields and Groves, that his Imagination could not have form'd a more beautiful Retreat. Having view'd it, and got all things ready, that is, two Servants, and the Rooms air'd, he came back to the Castle to fetch his Wife, and return Thanks for his fine Being. But when *Isabinda* took leave of *Charlotta*, they both wept, and *Charlotta* promis'd to go every Summer and pass her time there. Here *Domingo* and his little Family liv'd happily the remainder of their days, having many Children, and *Isabinda* by his persuasions became a true *Roman Catholick*. But *Charlotta* continu'd some time a Protestant in her Heart; yet at last she was truly happy in her own Thoughts, and pleas'd she was Don *Medenta*'s Wife; for she had all that Mortal could wish for, a noble Fortune, lovely Children, and a Husband who lov'd her beyond expression, and deny'd her nothing.

And now we must mention the Pirate-Captain, who was safely landed on this Island, and cured of his Wounds; the Pirate-Ship which *Gonzalo* had taken and sent away before, with the Pirates he had taken aboard of it, being arriv'd at *St. Domingo* before *Gonzalo*'s Ship: This Gentleman, who was kept a Prisoner in the Town, hearing of Don *Medenta*'s Marriage with *Charlotta*, sent her a Letter to ask her Pardon for what was past, protesting he was truly penitent, and that he honour'd her Virtue as much as he had lov'd her Person; and beg'd she would procure his Enlargement from that dismal Place. This Letter she shew'd not her Lord; but without relating what had pass'd between her and the Pirate, spoke in his behalf; and told him, that he was a Catholick, and a Man nobly born, and forced against his Will to become a Pirate, and that she beg'd the Favour of him to release him, and some way provide for him in the Fleet or Garison. This Don *Medenta* readily granted; and after speaking to his Father, went to the Prison and releas'd him and two other Gentlemen whom he pleaded for, saying they were his Countrymen and Friends, and not guilty of any Crimes but what they had been forc'd to. The common Sailors of the Pirates were order'd on board the *Spanish* Galleons, and these three Gentlemen follow'd their Benefactor to the Castle, to return their Thanks to the Governor, Don *Medenta* presenting them to his Wife and Father. *Charlotta* look'd on the Pirate-Captain with some disorder; but he address'd himself to her in these terms, making a profound bow, "Madam, I am doubly indebted to you both for my Liberty and Reformation; I am by your Reproofs and Generosity freed from both the Means and Inclinations to sin, and now resolve to live so, that my Actions may witness my Love to God, and Gratitude to you. I will henceforth endeavour to be an

Honour to my Country and Religion." This Speech much pleas'd
her, who perfectly understood his meaning: And in a short time
after, the Governor gave him a Commission of a Captain who
dy'd in the Garison, and he marry'd a Merchant's Widow in the
Town, who brought him a great Fortune. His two Companions,
according to the Custom of the *Irish*, made their Fortunes there
also, and settled in that Island.[1]

And now we must return to the unfortunate *Belanger*, whom
we left at *Virginia* much indispos'd, which prevented him from
coming to the Island of *St. Domingo* for some time. Monsieur *du
Pont* being highly caress'd by Don *Medenta* and all his Friends, as
being *Charlotta*'s near Kinsman, soon obtain'd Money and a Ship
to go to *Canada* in search of *Angelina*, promising to stop at that
Island in his return, before he went home to *France*.

### CHAP. XII.

Monsieur *Belanger*, after ten Months' sickness, being recover'd,
employ'd his Kinsman *Lewis de Montandre* to hire a Bark secretly to
carry them to the Island of *St. Domingo*, fearing Madam *de Santerell*
should get knowledge of his Design, and again follow him; beside,
he knew her Passion would be so violent, that he should scarce
be able to leave her. She was now in a deep Consumption, and
had been so kind to him, that he was oblig'd to withdraw himself
with great reluctance; and had he known *Charlotta* was dispos'd
of, no doubt but he would have marry'd this unfortunate Lady,
who now dearly paid for her parting him from her Rival; for she
had like to have dy'd with Grief after he left her. His Kinsman got
a Bark, and acquainted his Father with their Design; who, to forward it, having nothing to object against it, since *Belanger* and the
Lady were contracted, as he assur'd him they were, took Madam
*de Santerell* with him to a Lady's who was related to him, and had
a fine Plantation not far from his, persuading her it would be good
for her Health to stay there a few days. *Belanger* promis'd to fetch
her home soon, and taking leave of her, found himself in so great
disorder, that he was like to swoon, conscious that he design'd to
see her no more; and stung with a sense of his Ingratitude to her
who so passionately lov'd him, he was in the utmost disorder. She

---

1 The Irish were often regarded by the English as fortune-hunters, so
their "custom" here may involve following their captain's lead and
marrying rich widows or heiresses.

likewise, as if apprehensive of her Misfortune, let fall a shower of Tears: thus parted, never to meet again, as he suppos'd. He went a board with his Kinsman, and set sail for the Island, where he was to meet with greater Misfortunes than he ever yet met with. So soon as the Ship was gone off the Coast, Monsieur *de Montandre*, *Belanger*'s Uncle, who was a Widower, and was fallen in love with Madam *de Santerell*, glad of this Opportunity (as he hop'd) to cure her of her Passion for his Nephew, rid over to his Kinswoman's, where he had two days before left her, to acquaint her with his being gone, aggravating the Baseness of his leaving her thus treacherously, and vile Ingratitude to her: But she, as one thunder-struck, made little reply; but casting up her Eyes to Heaven, with a deep sigh cry'd, "'Tis just, my God, I am the Criminal, and he is Innocent; Affection cannot be forc'd: I vainly strove against thy Decrees, and ask no more but to be forgiven, and to die." She fainted away, and was carry'd to her Chamber, where the Lady of the House endeavour'd all she was able to comfort her: And to her she related all her Story, not concealing the subtile Stratagem she had made use of to get *Belanger* from her Rival, saying, "'Tis but just that I should suffer for my Crime and Folly in persevering to love him, who cannot return it as he ought." She so abandon'd her self to these sad Thoughts, that her Sickness daily increas'd, and they despair'd of her continuing long alive. She was very sensible of her own Condition, and seem'd much pleas'd with the thoughts of Death: for besides the loss of the Man she so excessively lov'd, the sense she had of her own Folly, and the desperateness of her Circumstances, being left in a Stranger's care, (with whom indeed *Belanger* had left Money to provide for, and carry her home to *France*; but thither she was asham'd to return; besides, it might be long e'er her Health would permit her to take such a Voyage). All these sad Reflections overwhelm'd her, and had doubtless kill'd her, had not Providence mercifully prolong'd her Life to be happy. Monsieur *Montandre* shew'd the greatest Concern and Affection for her that a Man could possibly make appear; professing he desir'd no greater Happiness on Earth than the continuance of her Life, and would give all his Fortune to save her. All the Physicians of note in the Place were made use of, and at last, Art and Nature join'd together, rais'd her from her sick Bed; and then Reason took place over Fancy, and she hearken'd to *Montandre*'s Proposal, whose Generosity put in the Balance with *Belanger*'s Ingratitude, and the impossibility of her being his, prevail'd with her to accept of his offer. Thus she was happily provided for, and *Belanger* lost great part of his Uncle's Fortune which he had design'd to give him, never designing to marry again, till he saw this young Lady, by whom he had many fine Children to inherit what he could settle on them (without injuring his eldest Son) which was very considerable.

In few days after his departure, *Belanger* arriv'd safely with his Kinsman at the Island of *St. Domingo*; and being a Stranger there, got the Captain of the Bark, who was us'd to trade there, to take them a Lodging, thinking it most prudent not to appear too openly in a Place where his Rival's Father was Governor, till he had got information how *Charlotta* was dispos'd of; which he soon learn'd to his inexpressible Grief: for his Kinsman making inquiry after her of *Gonzalo*, the Captain of the Ship that brought her thither, whom he met with at a Coffee-House to which he was directed; he told him of her Marriage and good Fortune, as he term'd it. And indeed so it was, had her Lover never come to ruin her Peace. *Belanger* was quite distracted with this news; his Kinsman wisely advis'd him to return to *Virginia*, and never see her. "She cannot be blam'd," said he, "she was left in your Rival's Power, and has wisely chose rather to marry, and be his Wife with honour, than to be his Mistress by compulsion, and be ruin'd; and now it would be cruel and ungenerous to revive her Grief by seeing her: Besides, should her Husband be inform'd of your speaking to her, it might make her miserable all the rest of her days; and this would be an ill Proof of your Love to her." This, and a thousand things more, he said to persuade him to be gone; but all to no purpose: he was deaf as the Winds, and behav'd himself like a Madman. At last he resolv'd to go to the Church she us'd on Festival-days, disguis'd in a *Spanish* Habit, which the Captain of the Bark procur'd him, and have a sight of her, promising not to attempt to speak to her. It was the Cathedral-Church;[1] and the Sunday following, *Belanger*, who had not stirr'd out of his Lodging from the day of his arrival, which was on the Wednesday before, went with his Kinsman to the High-Mass, where he saw the charming *Charlotta*, who was great with Child, standing by her Husband and Father-in-law next the Altar, and the lovely *Teresa* by her, four crimson Velvet Chairs being placed within the Rails on a rich Carpet for them.[2] She was dress'd in a *Spanish* Dress, rich as Art could make it, and

---

1 The principal church of a diocese, from which a bishop oversees the surrounding parishes.

2 The altars in Catholic churches were separated from the rest of the church by a rail. Officially, the laity were not allowed on the altar side

had store of Jewels in her Hair and on her Breast; thus adorn'd, he thought her more beautiful than ever, and felt such Tortures in his Soul, that he could not govern his Passion, but dropt down in a swoon, which occasion'd some disorder among the People; the Crowd was so great, that he could not be carry'd out, but was unfortunately brought near the Rails: *Charlotta* turning her Head, soon knew his Face, gave a great Shriek, and swooned, falling back into one of the Chairs. Don *Medenta*'s Jealousy was presently awaken'd, and he too truly guess'd who was in the Church; but *Belanger*'s Kinsman prudently fearing a discovery, got him carry'd out into the Air, and muffling his Face up in his Cloak, led him home to their Lodging, being come to himself so soon as he came into the open Air. *Charlotta*'s fainting was suppos'd to be occasion'd by her being surpriz'd at the Noise in the Church, or with Heat, being with Child; this past with all but her Lord, who upon her recovering, led her to his Coach, and went home with her, being impatient to question her what she saw that so much disorder'd her: She said she thought the *Spaniard* that fainted, was so like *Belanger*, that being surpriz'd, she could not but be so discompos'd. He desir'd her to go no more into publick Assemblies till she was up again;[1] resolving in himself to set such Spies at work, that if *Belanger* was arriv'd there, he should soon be sent farther off, or dispatch'd.[2] She promis'd to do whatever he would have her, and he seem'd contented. But his Soul was so inflam'd with Jealousy, that he could rest no more till he was satisfy'd of the truth, and had secur'd his Rival. It was not many Hours before those he set at work to discover who this Person was that had occasion'd this disorder in the Church, inform'd him, that two Gentlemen were arriv'd in a Ship from *Virginia*, and lodged privately in the Town; that one of them made inquiry after *Charlotta*, meeting *Gonzalo* at the Coffee-House. In fine, his suspicions were now confirm'd, and he persuaded *Charlotta* to go to *Domingo*'s in the Country, to pass a Month with *Isabinda*, saying it would be better for her to be in a place where she would be freed from receiving ceremonious Visits, and could better indulge her self in that sweet Retirement; and that she should continue there till she was near her time,[3] if she pleas'd. She

---

of the rail, but exceptions were sometimes made for those of very high social rank.

1   Had recovered from giving birth.

2   Murdered.

3   Almost ready to deliver.

willingly consented, being now deeply melancholy, and glad of an opportunity to be alone with her dear Friend *Isabinda*, to whom she could unbosom[1] her Thoughts. He carry'd her thither, and left her, pretending he had business that oblig'd him to return to his Father; concluding in his own Thoughts, that *Belanger*, who no doubt was impatient to speak with her, would soon learn where she was, follow her, and venture to pay her a Visit, he being absent. The old Lady or Governess, who attended her, was his Creature,[2] and he left her a Spy on all her Actions. He took his leave as usual, with all the Tenderness and Concern imaginable; saying, he should think each Day a Year till he return'd to her. All things were transacted as he foresaw; *Belanger* learning he was absent, and *Charlotta* at the Country-House, went with his Friend disguis'd in their *Spanish* Dresses to the Village where she was, and took a Lodging in a Peasant's House, where they kept very private for two Days; then his Friend *Montandre*, who ventur'd abroad for Intelligence, being certain that he was not known by Don *Medenta*, having seen her walking in the Gardens with *Isabinda*, inform'd him of it; so they consulted what to do: And *Belanger* fearing to surprize her a second time, resolv'd to write a Letter to her, and send it by his Friend: The Contents of which were as follow.

Still charming tho perjur'd *Charlotta*,

    *After a tedious Sickness, occasion'd by my Grief for the Loss of you, which long confin'd me to my bed, and brought me almost to the Grave, I am come to this Island, where I have learn'd the cruel News that you are now another's. I shall make you no reproaches, nor ask any thing but the Honour of one Hour's Conversation with you, after which you shall never more be importun'd or disorder'd with the sight of me. I love you as passionately as ever, and only desire to prove it by dying at your Feet. Let it be soon, lest Grief deprive me of that Satisfaction; for my Soul is so transported with Despair, that only the hope of seeing you once more, keeps me alive. My Angel, name the Place and Time to my Friend; and for the last time oblige*

Your constant undone
*Belanger.*

    This Letter was deliver'd into *Charlotta*'s Hand by *Montandre* the next Morning: For he ventur'd to go into the Gardens before

---

1  Reveal.
2  One who is dependent upon and willing to do another's bidding.

day over the Stone-Wall, and there hid himself in a Summer-House[1] till *Charlotta* came into the Garden to walk with her Friend *Isabinda* alone. He took this, as he thought, lucky opportunity, and at their coming into the Summer-House to sit down, presented himself and the Letter to her. She was a little startled, but believing *Belanger* was not gone from the Island, she expected to hear from or see him, concluding he would by some means or other find a way to send or come to her; so she immediately guess'd who he came from. She read the moving Lines, and shedding a flood of Tears, said, "Sir, tell the unfortunate *Belanger* it was his Misfortune, not my Fault, that we are separated; his leaving me, put me under a fatal necessity of giving my self to him in whose Power I was left. I am now dispos'd of to a noble Husband, whom I am bound to love and honour. It is altogether improper for me to admit of a Visit from the Man whom I have lov'd, and still have too much Inclination for: Besides, it is inconsistent with my Honour, and may be both our Ruin. I make it my last Request to him therefore to leave this Island immediately, and conjure him, as he values his own Life, or my Peace, not to attempt seeing me, or to stay here a day longer. My Husband is already alarm'd, and has, I fear, brought me to this Place with design to betray him. For Heaven's sake persuade him to fly hence, and not render me intirely miserable. Tell him, I beg him to remember me no more, but in his Prayers, and to submit with a Christian Resignation to the Will of Heaven. This is all I can say to him, and my final Answer."

At these Words she rose, and went out of the Summer-House, leaving *Isabinda* to let him out at the back Gate with a Key which she always carry'd in her Pocket, to let them into a Grove which was behind the Garden. *Isabinda* hasten'd him away, intreating him never to return. *Charlotta* retir'd to her Closet, and there gave way to her Passion; her Love to *Belanger* was now reviv'd, and she had the most dreadful Apprehensions of his Danger that can be conceiv'd. She perus'd the dear Lines he had sent her a hundred times over, and wash'd them pale with her Tears. Whilst she was thus employ'd, Don *Medenta*, who had lain all the time in the Village, and had receiv'd information of the Strangers lodging at the Peasant's, and of *Montandre*'s being in the Garden (*Charlotta* having been watch'd by the old *Dovegna*[2]) knock'd at the Closet-door: She ask'd who was there; and hearing his Voice,

---

1 Building used for recreation in warm weather.
2 An older spelling of *duenna*: chaperone.

clapt the Letter into her Bosom, and open'd the Door in such a disorder that her Lord would have been much surpriz'd at, if he had not known the Cause of it before. He took her in his Arms with a forc'd Air of Affection, but his Eyes flash'd with Rage; he trembled, and spoke in so distracted a manner, that she too well perceiv'd he was inform'd of what had past, and was so overcome with Grief, that she fainted in his Arms: he laid her gently on the Couch, and took the Letter out of her Bosom, read it, and putting it there again, call'd the old Governess who waited without, and presently fetch'd Cordials to bring her to her self; but they try'd all means in vain so long, that he thought her dead, and indeed began to abandon himself to Passion. *Isabinda*, who had retir'd into her Chamber, seeing Don *Medenta* go into the Apartment as she was going to give *Charlotta* an account that the Gentleman was gone away in safety, hearing his Complaints, came in, and also thought her dead: The Physicians were call'd, and by their Aid she was brought to Life, but immediately fell in Labour, being seven Months gone with Child. This caus'd a great deal of Confusion in the Family, where nothing was prepar'd for her lying-in,[1] it being design'd to be in the Castle with the utmost Magnificence. At three in the Afternoon she was deliver'd of a Son, who liv'd but a few Hours, and was therefore by the Physicians' advice baptis'd so soon as it was born. Don *Medenta* was highly afflicted at his own Imprudence in surprizing her, and shew'd the utmost Tenderness and Concern for her, kneeling by her bed-side on the Floor, kissing her Hands, professing that he lov'd and valu'd her above all earthly things, and could not live without her; till at last the Physicians intreated him to quit the Room, and leave her to repose: So the Chamber being darken'd, and none but Nurses left to attend her, poor *Charlotta* was deliver'd up to her own sad Thoughts, which soon threw her into a Fever which had like to have ended her Life. And now Don *Medenta* was ten times more enrag'd against *Belanger* than before, looking upon him as the Cause of his Child's death, and perhaps of his beloved *Charlotta*'s, for which he now resolv'd to be reveng'd of him. In order to this, he immediately set four Bravoes,[2] whom he had before hir'd, and plac'd ready to seize him, to watch his Lodgings: they were all disguis'd, and hid themselves in a Field behind the Peasant's House; towards the dusk of the Evening they perceiv'd *Belanger* and his Friend go forth, and take the way to *Domingo*'s; they follow'd, and

---

1 Labor, delivery, and recovery from the birth of a child.
2 Assassins.

so soon as they saw them enter the Grove, seiz'd them. *Montandre* had dissuaded him from this Attempt all he was able, but he was determin'd to see *Charlotta* or die; and since his Friend had so easily got to the speech of [1] her, flatter'd himself he should have the same good Fortune; but when he found himself seiz'd by Villains, gagg'd and bound, with his generous Friend, who was like to be made a Sacrifice for his Folly, he bitterly repented his Rashness. They were thrown a-cross a Horse like Calves, their Legs and Hands being fasten'd with a Cord under the Horse's Belly, a Sumpter-horse-Cloth[2] was thrown over them, and thus they were carry'd all Night, guarded by the four Bravoes, who were well arm'd, and had a Pass from the Governor's Son, so that none offer'd to stop them. By break of day they arriv'd at an old Castle, well fortify'd, on the North-side of the Island, where an Officer and twelve Soldiers were in Garison, who had receiv'd orders before what to do with these unfortunate Gentlemen, whom he was to keep secure in the Castle-Dungeon, being Pirates, desperate Villains, and reserv'd to make Discoveries, by the Rack,[3] if they would not do it voluntarily. Don *Medenta* confirm'd all this to the Officer by a Letter he sent him some days before: Into the Dungeon they were accordingly carry'd, put in Irons, and left to live upon the Allowance the Officer was order'd to give them, which was very sufficient: for Don *Medenta* was not willing to load his Conscience with the Guilt of murdering them, but only desir'd to secure his own Repose and his Wife's Honour, and would willingly have sent them to any place, and set them at liberty, could he but have been secur'd from their ever returning to *St. Domingo*. To *Belanger*'s Friend he had no prejudice; nay he rather had an Esteem for him, for the generous Friendship he had shown in risking his Life for his Friend. These Gentlemen thus secur'd, the Bravoes went back to Don *Medenta*, who on this News was more at ease, and apply'd his whole Thoughts about *Charlotta*'s Indisposition. She was many days light-headed, calling often upon *Belanger*, which stab'd him to the Heart. It was more than six Months before she was able to go out of her Chamber. In this time she often ask'd *Isabinda* if she could tell any news of *Belanger*, and was much troubled that she could hear nothing

---

1 Spoke with.
2 Heavy piece of cloth draped over the back of a pack horse to protect it from being chafed by its burden.
3 To be tortured on the rack, a device used to painfully stretch a prisoner's body.

of him. Sometimes she flatter'd her self that he had prudently took her Advice, and left the Island; yet inwardly reproach'd him with want of Affection: then reflecting on his daring Temper and Constancy, which his venturing thither after her did evidence, she concluded he had heard of her Illness, and lay still conceal'd there: Then she trembled with the thoughts of his being discover'd, or ruining himself and her by venturing to speak to her; another while she fear'd he was murder'd. So soon as she was able, Don *Medenta* carry'd her to the Castle, where his Father receiv'd her with much joy, and all the Ladys paid her Visits, congratulating her Recovery. The Ship that brought *Belanger*, set sail, having waited two Months, and return'd to *Virginia*, at which his Uncle and Madam *de Santerell* was much surpriz'd, but concluded that (mad with his Disappointment) he was gone home to *France*; and they were much concern'd at young *Montandre*'s not returning or writing; but were fain to rest satisfy'd, expecting to hear from them.

## CHAP. XIII.

When the wretched *Belanger* saw himself and his Friend in this dismal Place, no words can express the tortures of his Mind; and indeed it was a Providence he was at that time fetter'd, or else his despair might have drove him to destroy himself: He sigh'd deeply, and the big Drops ran scalding down his Cheeks; Grief had so benum'd his Facultys, that his Tongue could not utter one word; so that he remain'd silent, with his Eyes fix'd on his Friend, who bore his Afflictions calmly; for he had not Love and Despair to combat, had lost no Mistress, lov'd his Friend, and had a Soul so generous, that he was even glad, since it was his fate to be thus confin'd, that he was a Partner of his Fortune, and reserv'd to comfort him in that sad place. "Why" (said he to the afflicted *Belanger*) "my dear Friend, do you thus abandon your self to Grief, and are so cast down at an accidental Misfortune? Could you expect less than this from an incens'd Husband? Is it not a Mercy you are still alive? When we went from our Lodgings, we were determin'd to run all risques, and are you shock'd at a thing you had before arm'd against? Your jealous Rival's Rage will in time diminish; and when he comes to reflect on this Action, he will doubtless repent, and permit you to depart this Island: if he persists in his Revenge, Death is the utmost we can fear; and can there be a Place more fit to prepare for it in than this? Here we may live free from the Temptations of the World, and learn the state of our own Souls; nay, converse with our Maker by Contemplation, and enjoy that Peace of Mind, that we were Strangers to whilst we liv'd at large. Consider how many brave Men have perish'd for want abroad, and how many pious Persons have retreated to dismal Caves and Desarts, and left all the Delights of this Life, to enjoy that Quiet and Repose which we may here possess. *Charlotta* has already, doubtless, suffer'd for your Imprudence; and in pursuing her, you offended Heaven, who having thus punish'd you, on your Submission will (I doubt not) free you hence. As for my own part, I am so far from repenting I accompany'd you, that I rejoice that God has been pleas'd to preserve me, and bring me to this Place to comfort you; nor would I leave you, tho I were freed." *Belanger* having been very attentive to all he said, reply'd: "Was ever Generosity like this? What a miserable Wretch am I, that by my Follys have ruin'd the Peace of her I loved, and subjected my faithful generous Friend to Fetters and a Dungeon? I merit all that I can suffer; but your Presence puts me on the Rack, yet I will hope. My God, thy ways are marvellous; in thee I'll trust, and strive to bring my stubborn Will to submit to thine." The first Transports of his Passion being thus conquer'd, he began to be resign'd: And now Food and Wine being brought to them, they eat thankfully what was provided, and for some Days convers'd and pray'd together, like Men prepar'd for all Events; but the damp unwholesom Vapours in the Dungeon threw 'em both into such an Illness, taking away the use of their Limbs, that the commanding Officer, who was a *French* Man, sent to Don *Medenta*, to know what he should do with them; assuring him they would die, if not soon removed: On which he sent Orders to him, to remove them to an Apartment on the top of the Castle, where they might walk on the Battlements and take the Air, have a Bed, and Chambers to walk about, and their Fetters taken off. His Conscience touch'd him, and he would willingly have freed *Montandre*, but that he fear'd he would make a Clamour about his Friend. These Orders were punctually obey'd by the Officer, and the Prisoners soon recover'd: And he sometimes paid them a Visit, and so became inform'd of the true cause of their being brought thither, and pity'd their Condition. At last he contracted so great a Friendship with them, that he said he would willingly free them, could he be assur'd he should not lose his Commission by it: But it would not be long, he suppos'd, before he should be reliev'd by another Officer and Band of Soldiers, it being customary for the Garison to be changed every six Months; and then he would furnish them with Ropes to let themselves down from the Battlements, on that side of the Castle next the Sea, which beat against the Walls; and that they need not fear drowning, the Water being shallow at Ebb.[1] "Thence" (says he) "you may get to the Shore, and disguis'd in two Soldier's Coats, which I will give you; hide your selves in the adjacent Wood. This you must do in the Night, and get off the Island, if possible, as soon as Day breaks, for fear of being taken; for search will doubtless be made for you so soon as you are miss'd. You may effect this by seizing the first Fishing-boat you find on the Shore, of which there are many, plenty of Hutts being in these parts on the Coast, where Fishermen dwell during this Summer-season; and you will find their Boats, which are every Night haul'd up on the Shore. This is all I dare do to serve you, and this perhaps will cost me my Life, if discover'd." They not only thank'd him in the most expressive terms, but promis'd if they ever liv'd to reach *Virginia* again, to shew their Gratitude: And he promis'd to give them intelligence of whatever befel *Charlotta*, by the Captain who brought them thither, whom they resolv'd to send to that Island yearly, he giving them a Direction where they should always inquire for him. This concluded on, *Belanger* and *Montandre* grew chearful.

At last Orders coming for the Officer to depart thence, he faithfully perform'd all he had promis'd, leaving them Ropes and red Coats; nay, when he took his leave, which he did with much Affection, he presented *Belanger* with a good Purse of Gold, which he had much ado to make him accept of. But indeed it was necessary they shou'd not want Money, of which they had no great store about them, having left all their Clothes and Money at the Lodging in which the Captain of the Ship had plac'd them at their landing in the Town; for they brought nothing to the Peasant's House in the Village, but some Linen and about twenty Pistoles in Gold, and some *Spanish* Ducatoons[2] in Silver, in their Pockets.

The very Night after the Captain was gone they made their Escape, *Montandre* venturing down first from the Battlements, having sworn his Friend should not venture till he had try'd the Danger; for it was a vast height from whence they descended, and had the Rope broke, he had run a great risque of losing his Life. They fasten'd two Ropes to the top of one of the Battlements, and putting their Gloves on, slid down one after the other into the Sea,

---

1  Low tide.

2  Large silver coins, typically Italian or Dutch, each roughly equivalent to 5½ shillings.

which then was so high, it being young Flood,[1] that it almost took them up to their Breasts, and the Waves beat so strong, that they had much ado to reach the Shore; from whence they fled to the Wood, and pass'd thro it to the other side: There shelter'd by the Trees from the view of the Garison, they stood a while to see what Boats lay on the Shore; and chusing such a one as they thought they were able to manage, and launch into the Sea without help, they drag'd it into the Water, and getting into it, hoisted Sail, and put off. But alas! their condition was worse than ever, they knew not well how to steer the Boat, and were so weak and tired before, that they could scarce row or guide it. They had no Provisions aboard but a little Bisket and salt Meat,[2] that they found stow'd in the Fisherman's Locker in his Cabin, with a Bottle of Rack,[3] and a small Barrel of fresh Water. And now all their hopes were to reach some Island not belonging to the *Spaniards*; they steer'd for *Jamaica*, from whence they were certain they could get a Passage to *Virginia*, where *Belanger* resolv'd to remain with his Uncle and Friend till *Charlotta* was dead, or a Widow; and never return to *France* again without her, whilst she was living. They were in sight of *Jamaica*, when the Wind began to blow and the Waters foam: then a terrible Storm began, which drove them for four Nights and Days quite out of their knowledge; in which time their Provisions were spent, and their Strength so decay'd, that they were forc'd to lie down, and leave themselves to Providence. But nothing afflicted them so much as Thirst; all their fresh Water was gone, and drinking salt, so increas'd their drought, that they fear'd to repeat it. Thus they continued for three Days more drove by the Winds and Waves: In these three Days Hunger so prest them, that they ransack'd every corner of the Boat to find a Morsel to eat, and devour'd every bit of mouldy Bisket they could find: but alas! that was so little, it only tantaliz'd, not satisfy'd their craving Stomachs. And now they began to reflect, that it had been better for them to have continued Prisoners, than have expos'd themselves to such Miserys. Thus Experience tells us, that when we have obtain'd our own Wishes, not easy in the state Providence has plac'd us in, we are more unhappy than we were before. And now the generous

---

1  First two hours after low tide, when the water is beginning to rise again.

2  Meat preserved by salting.

3  Araq: liquor distilled from grapes and anise, popular in the eastern Mediterranean. Sometimes the term was used more generically for any liquor distilled from ingredients not typically used in Europe.

*Montandre* beg'd his Kinsman to kill him, and preserve his own Life, by feeding on his warm Flesh, and sucking his Blood, saying, "We must now both inevitably perish, unless one supply the other's Wants." *Belanger* was so shock'd at this Proposal, that his very Soul shiver'd. "No" (says he) "before I would destroy you, I would eat my own Flesh: No, we will live and die together: We have this Night pass'd over many Banks of Sand, and are doubtless near some Shore; now pluck up your Spirit, and let us redouble our Importunity to God to send us a Deliverance." Before the Words were out of his Mouth a Wave toss'd a large Dolphin into the Boat, which they kill'd with the Oars, and fell to eating, sucking the warm Blood and raw Flesh more greedily than ever they had done the most delicious Food prepar'd for them. This greatly refresh'd them, and towards Sun-setting the Wind abating, they laid by their Oars, and fell to eating more of the raw Fish, but sparingly, not knowing how long they had to live upon it. Whilst they were at this strange Supper they spy'd Land, on which they apply'd themselves afresh to their Oars, and about Midnight reach'd the Shore; but not knowing where they were, drag'd the Boat up on the Sand, and lay in it till Day-break, having been driven in by the Tide with such violence, that they could not stop her before she struck on the Sands. When Day appear'd they found they had enter'd into the Gulph of *Mexico*, between the Isles of *Cuba* and *Jucatan*, and were landed on that Coast where the *Spaniards* were Masters:[1] They thought it best to pretend they were *Frenchmen*, who, being cast away in a Ship, had escap'd Death by getting into that Fishing-boat, which the Wind had (as they suppos'd) drove out to Sea from the *Havana*, near which they pretended the Ship they were in perish'd; for tho they had Soldier's Coats on, yet their *Spanish* Habits shew'd they were Gentlemen, and their Behaviour shew'd their Breeding. The *Spaniards* receiv'd them kindly, and a Merchant took them into his House, where he entertain'd them very generously, and invited them to continue there till they could find means to go to *Virginia*, telling them it was their best way to do so by some trading Vessel, which he suppos'd they must wait some time for. This Merchant had a Bark ready to sail with Goods for *Carolina*,[2] from whence it would not be very difficult for them to go by Land to *Virginia*: He offer'd them a Passage in this Ship, which they gladly accepted of; and in few Days went aboard, and

---

1 Presumably the Yucatán peninsula (see map, p. 275).
2 North and South Carolina did not become officially separate colonies until 1729.

got safe to *Carolina*. They hired a Guide to conduct them thro the Country to *Virginia*; but passing by the *Apalattean*[1] Mountains, a Party of *Indians* came down upon them, and carrying them away over the Mountains, plunder'd them of their Money and Clothes. Amongst these *Indians* they continu'd four whole Years in the greatest Misery, being oblig'd to live after their barbarous fashion as Slaves; till going out with a Party to cut Fewel in the thick Woods, they took their opportunity to make their Escape, being desperate, and hid themselves in a Cave in the Night, chusing rather to venture being devour'd by wild Beasts, than spend their Lives in Slavery. They lay conceal'd in this place till the *Indians* were gone farther on; and then, destitute of Food, and in their Slaves' Dress, they fled towards one of the *Spanish* Forts,[2] which they could never have reach'd had they not met with an old Hermit, who liv'd in a poor Cottage near a Wood: He was standing at his door, and seeing two poor Slaves, who look'd like Death, come towards him, suppos'd they were in want and Christians, so invited them in, to their great Surprize, and gave them Bread and Drink, asking where they were going. They gave him this account, That they were cast away in a Ship, sav'd in a Fishing-boat near the *Havana*, driven on the Coast of *Jucatan*; from thence went in a Bark to *Carolina*, and going cross the Countrys for *Virginia*, were taken and made Slaves; and weary'd with the Miserys they endured, were now endeavouring to escape to *Fort-Philip*.[3] He told them, he would conduct them thither in Safety the next Morning. They staid with him all night, lying on Straw (as he did) with warm Coverlids: And being very importunate to know the Reasons of his living this solitary Life, he told them his Story in these Words.

---

1 Appalachian.
2 There were no Spanish forts anywhere in Virginia or the Carolinas (and hadn't been for more than a century). The closest ones were in northern Florida (then a Spanish colony).
3 There was no fort of this name anywhere in the region in the early eighteenth century. There was, however, a Fort San Felipe built by the Spanish on what is now Parris Island in South Carolina in 1566. It was destroyed a decade later. Aubin may have seen the name and location on an old map. Or it may simply have been a lucky guess at a probable name (the King of Spain at the time of the publication of *Charlotta Du Pont* was Felipe V).

## CHAP. XIV.

"I am," said he, "by Birth a Frenchman; I was the younger Son of a Counsellor,[1] who had a great Estate, and was put in a good Post under my Father so soon as I was able to understand Business, having a Clerk's Place in the Salt-Office.[2] Here being from under my Father's Eye, I contracted an intimacy with a young Gentlewoman who liv'd with her Aunt, a Person who, tho wellborn, was fall'n to decay, and they maintain'd themselves by their Needles,[3] and some small income the Aunt had left, very genteely, but with much difficulty. It was my fortune to see this young Woman at Church, she was very beautiful and genteel. I follow'd her home, made love to her, and was well receiv'd. I pretended an honourable Affection; but, alas, had no other design in my wicked Heart but to debauch her. Their Circumstances made them willingly receive the Presents and Treats I gave them, not thinking it dishonourable, since I pretended Marriage; glad was the innocent Creature to be so provided for: Their Conversation was charming, and their Conduct so reserv'd and modest, that I was a great while before I could venture to make any attempt upon her Virtue; but then I was repuls'd with such Scorn and Reproofs, that I almost despair'd of effecting my base design; but knowing that it would be my Ruin if I marry'd her, and being now so much in love, that I knew not how to live without her, I still persisted in my Visits and Importunities, and tho refus'd the sight of her frequently, and always receiv'd with Reproaches, yet I could not desist; and finding all my Attempts were in vain, and that I could not seduce her to my Will, at last I consented to marry her privately, on condition that she should keep it a secret. This she gladly consented to, and so we were marry'd by a Cordelier[4] who was her Confessor: and then I was made happy in the possession of my dear *Louisa*, who was the most virtuous and most charming Woman breathing." Here he shed some Tears, and could scarce go on; but recovering, he continu'd his Discourse thus: "And now, Gentlemen, I am going to relate a part of my Life, that fills my Soul with horror, and will, I hope, deter all that hear it from committing such Crimes: We past some Months as happily as we could wish, and

---

1 Judge in one of the Parlements in France, which functioned as the appelate courts for their respective provinces.
2 Administrative office that oversaw the taxation of salt.
3 Earned a living from sewing.
4 Franciscan friar.

she grew great with Child; but my Expences increasing, and a prospect of more charges coming on, made me grow something uneasy; to add to which, my Father began to press me about a Marriage that was proposed to him much to my Advantage. This put anxious Thoughts into my Head, and made me reflect how imprudent I had been: My eager Desires were satisfy'd, my Love diminish'd, as my Ambition and Avarice were encreas'd; and in fine, I wish'd her dead, and meditated on nothing but how to get rid of her. Thus my disobedience in marrying without my Father's knowledge and consent, drew down Heaven's Anger upon me, and the Devil tempted me on to proceed to more flagrant Crimes. I did not visit my Wife so often as usual, but humour'd my Father in visiting the young Lady proposed to me, who was every way agreeable, and had the most prevailing Argument on her side to engage Man's inconstant Heart, that is, a great Fortune: she was the only Daughter of a rich Banker, had taken a fancy to me, and her Parents doating on her, resolv'd not to cross her, for which reason they made the Proposal to my Father: Such Advances were made on their side, that I could find no pretence to delay the Marriage longer. And now I foresaw that I must either incur my Father's hatred, and be ruin'd, (for he was a Man of an implacable Temper, and would, I knew, abandon me, if he discover'd my Marriage) or else that I must rid my self of *Louisa* forthwith, and then I might be great, and, as I vainly flatter'd my self, happy. This wicked thought I indulg'd, and long revolv'd in my Mind, till at last, I resolv'd to put it in execution; and tho I was grievously tormented in my Conscience, yet I persever'd in this wicked Design, and bought Poison, which I made an infusion of in Wine, and putting it into a Vial in my Pocket, I went to my virtuous Wife to lie all Night: She receiv'd me with open Arms; I appear'd more chearful and kind than usual; we sup'd, and after supper I pretended I was not well, and desir'd we might have some burnt Wine,[1] which her Aunt presently got: I slily pour'd the Poison into the Cup, which I presented to my dear Wife, pretending she and her Aunt must drink with me; they readily comply'd, always studying to oblige me: But when I saw *Louisa* swallow it, my Soul shiver'd, my Conscience flew in my Face; and when she came and kiss'd me as I was going to bed, I felt Tortures not to be express'd, or indeed conceiv'd, but by such Wretches as my self. She had not lain long in my Arms, but Convulsions seiz'd her Nerves, and I call'd her Aunt and Servant up, shewing the greatest Concern; but neither

---

1 Brandy.

of them suspected what was the matter, nor need I counterfeit, for at that instant I was fill'd with such Horrors, that I would have given the whole World to save her. From this Moment my Peace was broke, and I became the most miserable Man breathing. She expir'd in my Arms before day, with the dear murder'd Infant in her; saying the kindest things to me and praying for me even in the last Agonies of Death. The innocent *Louisa* thus dispatch'd, I took leave, giving Money to her Aunt (who was almost distracted with Grief) to bury her. They had kept a Maid-servant ever since my Marriage, and I left them in the House, and excus'd my self from being present at her Burial, lest my Father should hear of it; promising the Aunt to be always kind to her. Having left these melancholy Objects, I went to the Tavern, drank a Quart of Wine to revive my Spirits, and then went home to my Father's. And now my whole business was to divert my thoughts as much as possible; I went abroad every day, drank, danc'd, went to the Play, and so lull'd my self with variety of Pleasures, that the Terrors of my Conscience were something silenc'd. The sad Impressions of *Louisa*'s Murder wore off, and I was marry'd; but the Bridal-night I was no sooner in bed, and the Candles extinguish'd, than as I was going to take my Bride in my Arms, the Curtain at my Bed's-head was drawn back, and turning my Head, I saw *Louisa* standing by my side, big with Child, and the fatal Vial in her Hand, which she seem'd to shake, and look'd upon me with a Look that struck quite thro my Soul; the cold Sweat trickled down my Face, and the Bed shook under me, every Nerve shiver'd, as if the Agonies of Death had seiz'd me. Thus I lay, with my Eyes shut, not daring to lift up my Eye-lids, till the Day-break had freed me from this dreadful Vision, which made such an impression on my Soul, that I fancy'd her ever in my sight, and could not relish nor take any Satisfaction in any thing I possess'd. I conceal'd this from the World, and did all that was possible to oblige my new Wife, who was dotingly fond of me, and had brought me so great a Fortune, that we wanted nothing that Wealth could purchase, to make us happy in a moderate way of Life. But Wealth could not cure my wounded Conscience; I had a load of Guilt upon my Soul, and was continually upon the rack; this soon destroy'd my Health, and so afflicted her, that she was almost as unhappy as my self. Being thro great Weakness, attended with an intermitting Fever, confin'd to my bed, I seriously prepar'd for Death, and confess'd my self to a *Franciscan*, a Man of great Wisdom and Piety, who so eloquently laid before me the Enormity of my Crime, the Terrors of eternal Punishment, and the infinite Mercies of God on a sincere Repentance, that I heartily lamented my Sins, and endeavour'd to reconcile my self to God; on which he was pleas'd to raise me up again, and prolong my Life. My Wife was now great with Child, and had never had the Small-Pox, which she unfortunately caught by going to an Opera, where she saw a Person newly recover'd, and at her coming home was taken ill, and dy'd of them. Being now left a Widower, the thoughts I had had in my late Sickness, came a-fresh into my Mind, and I resolv'd to retire from the World; but my Father and Friends much oppos'd it, being desirous I should marry again, because my elder Brother was consumptive, and tho marry'd seven Years, had no Child. The prospect of having all my Father's Fortune prevail'd with me not to enter into the Church into any religious Community; but being still uneasy in my Mind, thinking I ought to do something to atone for my Sins, I resolv'd to retire to some remote part of the World to do Penance for them by Fasting, and Prayers, and Alms-deeds.[1] I therefore put all my Estate into my Confessor's hands, to distribute the income of it every Year to the Poor, and return me forty Pounds a Year to this Place by the hands of a Gentleman who is an Officer in *Fort-Philip*, to which you are design'd to go: with him I came to this part of the World, being my intimate Friend and near Relation. He receives my Income, and when I want Provisions or Money, I repair to him. My Poverty and manner of living, makes the *Indians* never molest me, nay they love me, and supply me with any thing I want: Besides I am a kind of Physician amongst them; for having took delight in studying Physick, I am arriv'd to some knowledge in it, and well acquainted with the Nature and Use of all the medicinal Herbs that grow in these Parts. I am also part of a Surgeon, and dress their Wounds and Sores, and by this means have many Opportunities of saving their Bodies and Souls, by instructing them in the Christian Faith. I speak their Languages, and often procure the Freedom of those Christians, who like you have unfortunately fallen into their hands. Thus I have liv'd for these eight Years, and am now so inur'd to this solitary way of living, and so satisfy'd with this poor retreat, that I do not think ever to return to *France* again, or venture into the World any more; and hoping I have made my Peace with God, I wait my death as a Man who places his hopes on an eternal State."

Thus he concluded his Story. *Belanger*, who during this Discourse was fill'd with admiration, yet never interrupted him,

---

1  Acts of charity.

now broke silence: "Monsieur *du Riviere*," said he, "what transport can equal mine to find you here? I have news to tell you will recall you soon to *France*. I shall tell you wonders." "Is not your Name *Belanger*" (said the amaz'd Hermit) "and have I the Happiness to meet with and entertain the Youth whom I so dearly lov'd?" "Yes," said *Belanger*, "I am that Man whom you were pleas'd to honour with your Friendship in so peculiar[1] a manner; and to convince you that the Almighty has accepted your Repentance and Alms deeds, am doubtless sent to this Place to set your Mind at ease, and restore that Peace of Conscience that you have been so long a stranger to. *Louisa* is, I hope, still living; she was in perfect Health six Years agone[2] when I left *France*." "*Louisa* living!" (said the Hermit) "amazing Wonder! my ravish'd Soul can scarce credit the strange Report, tho from my best lov'd Friend. Speak, tell me the manner how she was preserv'd from Death, whilst my list'ning wounded Soul is heal'd with the soft sound of your sweet Speech." "I will make haste" (said *Belanger*) "to satisfy you. So soon as you had left the House, *Louisa*'s Aunt, who had been before inform'd of all your Actions, knew your Courtship to your new Mistress, and frequent Visits there, had mark'd your Coldness to and Neglect of *Louisa*, and made Observations on your Behaviour that fatal Night, and her sudden Illness and surprizing Death; the Minute you turn'd your Back, ran to the Convent, which you know was not a stone's throw from the House, and call'd up the honest Cordelier, who had marry'd you, a Man who was a good Physician as well as a Divine, and told him with Tears the strange manner of *Louisa*'s Death, which he immediately suspected to be the effect of Poison; and taking some strong Emeticks[3] with him, ran to the House as fast as his Legs could carry him, and finding her Body warm and pliant, pour'd enough down her Throat to effect his good design; for it so wrought, that it soon brought up the baneful[4] Drug, and with more proper Applications, at last restor'd her opprest Facultys to their use, and her to Life and Health, with the innocent Child, so that both were preserv'd, and she perfectly recover'd in a few days; which they kept a secret by his Advice. 'Since your cruel Husband' (said he) 'has this time fail'd of executing his wicked purpose, he will no doubt repeat the Attempt, and may at last succeed; to avoid which, you shall retire

---

1 Remarkable.
2 Ago.
3 Medicines that induce vomiting.
4 Lethal.

to a Convent of our Order, where my Sister is Abbess, there care shall be taken of you and the Child. Let him suffer by the Remorse of his own Conscience, and smart for his Sin, nor be freed from his torments by knowing you are sav'd. When he dies, I will do justice to the Child if it lives, and seize the Estate. Mean time you shall know how he fares with his new Choice, and be freed from those fears which his knowledge of your being alive will subject you to.' She consented, and has continued in this Convent ever since, with her Son, who was born there. All this I was inform'd of by her Aunt, my near Kinswoman, who had made me privy to your Marriage, and ingag'd me not to disclose it; but now it ought to be no longer a Secret to you, since you are truly penitent." The Hermit fell on his Knees, and with a flood of Tears return'd Thanks to God, in such moving Expressions, as drew Tears from *Belanger* and *Montandre*'s Eyes. Then they related the Particulars of their Adventures; and rising as soon as day appear'd, set out together for *Fort-Philip*, resolving to go to *Virginia* by the first opportunity, from whence *du Riviere* might easily get Passage to *France*, being impatient to see and ask Pardon of his injur'd *Louisa*. Being arriv'd at *Fort-Philip*, they were kindly entertain'd by the Hermit's Friend, who furnish'd them with Clothes, and a Guide, with some Soldiers to guard them to *Virginia*, and protect them from the Indians. This Officer being acquainted with his Friend's Story and *Belanger*'s, gave them Money to defray their Charges on the way to *Virginia*, from whence *Belanger* promis'd to furnish *du Riviere* with all necessarys[1] for his return to *France*.

And here we shall leave these Gentlemen to inquire what is become of Monsieur *du Pont*, *Charlotta*'s Kinsman, whom she met with in the Cottage on the desolate Island, and brought with her to the Island of *St. Domingo*, from whence he went in a Bark to *Canada* in search of *Angelina*. He arriv'd safe at *Quebeck*, where he was inform'd the *French* Captain had been to trade, but here he could get no news of her; he visited all the Coast in vain, till he came to find out a *French* Merchant, who assur'd him the Ship was gone to *Newfoundland* to trade; he immediately went aboard his Bark, and set sail for that Place: And here he got intelligence that *Angelina* had been seen there very much indispos'd, and that the Captain had carry'd her thence with design to return to *France*. Monsieur *du Pont* was overjoy'd at this news; and returning to the Island of *St. Domingo* with the Bark, acquainted Don *Medenta* and *Charlotta* with this good news, and resolv'd to go for

---

1 Necessities.

*France,* hoping to find her there before him. An opportunity for this he quickly found, and got safe thither in a *French* Merchant-Ship. At his arrival he found his eldest Brother dead, and took possession of his Estate again, and would have sat down in repose, had *Angelina* been there. But no other news could be got of her, but that the Ship she was in was taken by the *Algerine* Pirates,[1] and none return'd to *France* to give any account of what was become of her and the other Persons on board of it. He well knew it was in vain for him to attempt a farther search for her, and therefore retir'd to a little Seat in the Country, where he gave himself up to Contemplation, and liv'd the Life of a Man that had quitted the World; whilst poor *Angelina* being made a Slave, was sold by the *Algerine* Pirate to the Bey[2] of *Tunis,* whose Steward, a Moor, that us'd to purchase the handsome *European* Virgins for his Master, bought her, and carry'd her home to his Seraglio.[3] The *French* Captain had done all that he was able to debauch her himself, but in vain: he was so inamour'd, that he could not part with her, tho an old Man, and having carry'd her from place to place to no purpose, resolv'd at last to bring her back to *France,* and restore her to her Friends; condemning her Mother's proceedings, and himself for being instrumental in so wicked a Design. But now he was also a Slave, and punish'd for his Crime. The virtuous *Angelina* thus lodg'd in the Seraglio, with others as unhappy as her self, being a Lady of an heroick Spirit and consummate Virtue, bravely resolv'd to die, rather than submit to a Mahometan;[4] and thus determin'd, began to consider what to do to deliver her self; in order to which she thought it best to apply her self to one of those unfortunate Beautys, who seem'd well acquainted with that Place and Life, appearing to have some Command there. This proved to be a *Venetian* Lady, to whom she address'd her self with Tears, saying, "Madam, your Face speaks you a Christian as I am, I beg that you would inform me what I am to be done withal in this strange place." "Alas, sweet Creature," said she, "you are destin'd to be ruin'd, and depriv'd of your Liberty during your Life. I have liv'd here these four Years, and never hope to see the outside of these Walls again." Then she took her by the Hand, and led her into her Chamber, saying, "We shall be observ'd, let us shut the Door and

---

1  Corsairs operating out of Algiers. For more on North African captivity, see Introduction, pp. 39–42.
2  Governor.
3  Harem.
4  Muslim.

talk alone." Being seated in this Room, which was richly furnish'd, the Seraglio being the finest in the whole City, in which there were Apartments for twenty Women and their Attendants, with fine Gardens to walk in, inclos'd with Walls of a great Height; *Angelina* told her the whole Story of her Life and Misfortunes, which drew Tears from the lovely *Catherina*'s Eyes; for so the *Venetian* Lady was named. She related her Life in this manner.

## CHAP. XV.

"I am the Daughter of a noble *Venetian*, my Brother is a Knight of *Malta*,[1] my Name is *Catherina Belamanto de Farnaze*. I was placed in a Monastery as a Pensioner, being but twelve Years old; there a young Gentleman courted me secretly, the younger Son of a noble Family, who was a Captain in the Service of the State, and had no other Fortune but his Commission, which indeed was sufficient to support him nobly, but was not considerable enough to answer that great Fortune my Father design'd me,[2] or to answer his and my Brother's ambitious Expectations, I being an only Daughter. This Gentleman's Person and Sense gain'd my Affection, so that I prefer'd him in my Heart before all others, gave him my Hand and Promise to be his; but it was not long e'er it was discover'd that some Conversation had pass'd between us, and I was sent for home, and question'd, but confess'd nothing. This distracted my Lover, and he was impatient at my being kept from him: so that at last he made use of a Stratagem to get me, which he thus effected: He sent me a Letter by a Servant to my Father's, which he doubted not would be intercepted; in which he acquainted me, after abundance of passionate Assurances, that he would ever love me; that fearing I suffer'd much constraint and uneasiness on his Account, he was resolv'd to sell his Post, and go for *Spain*, having some great Relations there by his Mother's side, who was a *Spanish* Lady, by whose Interest he doubted not to get a better Post; and this was the most generous Proof he could give me of his Affection, being resolv'd to make himself miserable to render me happy. My Father, who broke open this Letter, was very glad, and had me narrowly watch'd, till he saw that he did

---

1 Member of a Catholic military order descended from the medieval Knights Hospitaller. They governed the Mediterranean island of Malta.
2 Expected me to receive when I married.

what he pretended, which he quickly did; for he sold his Post, and took leave of his Friends, and went aboard a Ship for *Spain*, as he pretended. Then I was sent back to the Monastery, where I soon receiv'd a Letter from him by means of another Pensioner who was our Confident;[1] in which he inform'd me, that he lay conceal'd at a Village hard by,[2] and that he conjur'd[3] me to get away with the first Opportunity, and come to him. This I did the next Evening at the close of the Day, and got safe to his Friend's House where he was conceal'd. Here he receiv'd me with open Arms, and his Friend's Chaplain marry'd us that Night. We went away thence before Day the next Morning, in his Coach, which carry'd us to the Port where the Ship's Boat lay ready to receive us, he having hir'd the Vessel on purpose. We went aboard, weigh'd Anchor, and set sail for *Barcelona*; but before we could reach that Port, we were unfortunately taken by an *Algerine* Pirate, and brought to this dismal Place, where I was parted from him, and sold to this vile Infidel, to whose curs'd Bed I have been forc'd, and have had the Misfortune to be lik'd. He has been absent these four Months, being gone to his Country-Seat to pass the Summer Season, where he has other wretched Women to divert him; he is to return hither in three days, and then you must be a Victim to his Lust no question."

Here she let fall a flood of Tears, and *Angelina* bore her Company. "You have," said she, "told me a Story more unhappy than my own, since I have still preserv'd my Virtue, and am now resolved rather to die than yield, since Providence grants me three days for my Escape. I'll use that time, and bravely venture to get hence, or die in the Attempt; if you will venture with me, speak, I'll lead the way, Death is preferable to such a Life as this." "You say you are a Christian, heroick Maid," said *Catherina*, "would you commit Self-murder? Is no other way left to free us, or must we kill each other?" "Far be that dreadful Thought," said *Angelina*, "from my Soul; no, I have thought of other means in the short time I have been here. I have observ'd a Moorish Slave whom I saw enter the Gardens with a Key at a Door that leads to the Sea, as near as I can guess; that Key I am resolv'd to purchase by his Death. Do you contrive some strange Disguise to cover us, and pack your Jewels up, or what you have of Value else, ready to carry

---

1 Confidante.
2 Nearby.
3 Beseeched.

out with us, and I will meet him at the Gate when he enters at the break of Day, as I suppose his Custom is, and stab him with a Pen-knife[1] I have hid about me. Could we get the Habit of an Eunuch[2] for each of us, it would be the safest Disguise we could put on; the Bey being absent, and few of his Servants left here, and those less on their Guard, and more negligent than when he is present, it will not be so difficult to get away as at another time." "I can procure such Habits," said *Catherina*, "and doubt not, tho our Apartment is lock'd up every Night, yet the Windows are not so high, but we may easily venture down, tying the Sheets of our Beds together, by which we may slip down into the Garden, where in a Chamber on one side the Seraglio Door, two white[3] Eunuchs lie to guard it; next this Chamber is the Wardrobe: if one of us can but get in at the Window of this Place, and they not hear us, we may have Clothes of any kind, and Jewels too." "I will attempt it," said *Angelina*, "and would prefer all Dangers, and even Death, to Infamy and Slavery." "And so will I," said *Catherina*. Being thus resolv'd, they waited till Night came on, when hearing all things still, *Angelina* crept to her Friend's Chamber, who had bundled up her Jewels and some Linen: they got down from the Window, and then went to the Wardrobe, the Moon shining very bright, and were some time before they could contrive how to get in at the Window, it being very high; but at last *Angelina*'s Wit, which exceeded her Sex (tho Women ever were esteem'd more quick and subtile than Mankind at cunning Plots and quick Contrivances) soon found the way to enter; she got on *Catherina*'s Shoulders, and went in there trembling; she got two rich Vests, two Turbants,[4] two pair of *Turkish* Boots, and a Box, whose rich outside and weight, tho small, made her believe it worth the carrying away: these she bundled up, and threw out of the Window to her Friend: but then she was at a mighty loss how to get out again, which she in vain attempted, it being impossible for her to get up to the Window from whence she had dropt down into the Room; no way

---

1  Small knife used to carve or repair the tip of a quill pen.
2  Man who has been castrated. Eunuchs were often used as guards in seraglios (because they supposedly posed no threat to the women therein).
3  Of European descent. Most "white" eunuchs were drawn from areas within the Ottoman Empire, such as the Balkans or what is now southern Ukraine (i.e., becoming a eunuch was not a common fate for men captured by North African corsairs).
4  Turbans.

was left but to pass thro the Eunuchs' Chamber, and this necessity prevail'd with her to do. She took down two rich Scymiters[1] that hung up in fine embroider'd Belts, and having drawn one, pass'd thro the Chamber where the Eunuchs lay fast asleep, resolving if they stirr'd, to kill them, or to die by their Hands. Upon the Table there stood a silver Bowl half full of Wine, of which no doubt they had took their fill, altho their Prophet does forbid it them; for few Mussulmen[2] refuse to drink it in private:[3] this Bowl she took, with a bunch of Keys which lay by it; and going to the Door, found the Key in it, so she gently unlock'd it, and putting it to[4] after her, went out safely to her Friend, who stood trembling and almost dead with fear. *Angelina* shew'd her the Keys, one of which she fancy'd would open the Garden-Gate, to which they hasted, and to their great Satisfaction found it so: being got out at the Gate, which they lock'd after them, they stood to consider which way to go, and resolv'd to get away from the Town to the next Wood or ruin'd Building they could meet with; they had not gone above two Miles, when they enter'd a Grove, at the farther end of which they found an old ruin'd Mosque, which they went into with great fear, lest some old *Turkish* Brahmen[5] or Saintoin[6] should live there: but hearing no Creature stir but Bats and Screech-Owls, and such Vermin as live in unfrequented Places, they took courage, and the Day beginning to break, they laid down their Bundles, and changing their Clothes, put on their *Turkish* Habits, which instead of being mean, such as Slaves wear, belong'd to the Bey himself, being both Cloth of Gold,[7] the Buttons of the one was Rubies, and the other Emeralds; the

---

1 Scimitars: single-edged swords with curved blades, primarily used in the Ottoman Empire.

2 Muslims.

3 The Quran's injunction to abstain from alcohol was not nearly as strictly observed or enforced in the eighteenth-century Ottoman Empire and its client states as it now tends to be in most Islamic countries. So the narrator's assertion here, while unkind and perhaps offensive, is not wholly inaccurate.

4 Closing it.

5 Brahmin: a member of the highest caste in Hindu society. Here, though, it seems just to mean something like "priest" and Aubin does not appear to be concerned with the huge differences between Muslim and Hindu religious practices.

6 Santon: French and Spanish term for a Muslim hermit.

7 Fabric with gold wires woven into it.

Turbants were suitably rich, and full of Diamonds, Pearl, and other Jewels: so that they had an immense Treasure, had they known how to dispose of it. But at this time they would willingly have parted with it all for some poor Habit to conceal them, fearing they should be pursu'd and taken, not knowing where to hide themselves: they were weary, faint, and had no Food, and search'd every Corner of this ruinous Place to hide themselves; at last they found a Door which seem'd to lead down some Stairs into a Vault, where they suppos'd the Dead were bury'd, and that they should meet with nothing there but Skulls and Bones and noisom Vapours; yet had they had a Light, they would gladly have gone into it to hide themselves, nay liv'd, and chose to sleep and eat amongst the Dead, rather than to live luxuriously with Infidels. They sat down upon the Stairs however to rest their tir'd Limbs; so that if any should pass by, they might shut the Door upon them. As they sat thus consulting what to do, they heard a Noise, and saw a Man enter the Mosque with a dark Lanthorn[1] in his Hand and a Loaf under his Arm, with some scraps of Meat, and Fish in a little Basket; he had a long coarse frize[2] Garment on, his Face and Hands were tawny, he had only Sandals on his Feet, and a strange fashion'd Straw-Hat upon his Head; he sat down his Basket and Bread, and opening his Lanthorn, turning the light side towards them, came to the Door, and was going down Stairs, when *Catherina* giving a great Shriek, fell into a Swoon upon *Angelina*, and had like to have beat her down the Stairs.[3] It is impossible to express her Thoughts at this instant; for tho she was a Woman of great Courage, and had a dauntless Soul, yet she was shock'd at the instant, as was also the Stranger. He look'd upon them with Amazement; the Beauty of their Faces, the Splendor of their Habits, and the strange Place he found them in, astonish'd him. *Angelina* at last recovering her self, view'd him attentively, and reason'd with her self that he was but a Man unarm'd, and in all probability as much in distress as themselves; mean time he concluded they were Women disguis'd, and doubtless fled thither for shelter; that they must be *Europeans*, and Persons of birth by their Beauty, delicate Hands, Shape and Complexions. He said thus in *French* to *Angelina*, "In the Name of God what are you, and from whence? Speak, if you understand me, tell me if you are

---

1  Lantern with an apparatus for concealing light (usually some sort of metal slide).
2  Rough woolen cloth.
3  Knocked her down the stairs.

in distress, that I may help you." "We are by Birth *Europeans*, and profess the Christian Faith," said she, "as I doubt not you do, since you speak my native Language; we are fled from Ruin, Infamy and Slavery, and got into this dismal Place to screen our selves from the Fury of the Infidels whom we this Morning fled from. Assist us to escape their hands, and find us means to get hence, and all the Riches we have about us shall be yours." At these Words the Man shedding some Tears, took her by the Hand with an air that spoke him a Gentleman. "Fair Creature," said he, "I will assist and defend you, and that lovely Friend that you support, with my Life; fear not to descend with me into the Vault, where I have liv'd above three tedious Years, and where we may without fear of discovery talk our Misfortunes over." He took the Loaf, and *Catherina* being now something recover'd from her Swoon, made way for him to go down before them with the Light; at the bottom of the Stairs they found a Room all of Stone, clean, tho dismal, in which were three Doors which open'd into three other Rooms like that; in one of these lay a great quantity of Bones and Skulls, which this poor Hermit had clear'd the other Rooms of; in that he liv'd in, was a Bed made of Straw and Rushes, into which he used to creep, covering himself with nothing else but an old Mantle,[1] in which he us'd to wrap himself in Winter: near this his miserable Bed, there lay two square Stones, one about a Foot higher than the other; the highest was his Table to eat upon, the other his Seat to sit upon: this with a poor Lamp was all his Furniture, except two Earthen Dishes, and a Stone-Bottle[2] that us'd to keep Water for him to drink. And now desiring his Guests to sit down, lighting his Lamp, he pull'd a small Bottle of Arrack out of his Pocket, desiring them to drink, which they did. Mean time viewing *Catherina* more attentively, he leap'd up and catch'd her in his Arms with such transport, that *Angelina* was amaz'd and terrify'd, fearing he had some ill design upon them; but she was quickly undeceiv'd, for he cry'd out, "My *Catherina*! my Angel! have I liv'd to embrace you again? Is it possible? And do I hold in my Arms my Wife? 'Tis too much: Such Joy is insupportable." At these Words, being extreme weak, he fainted, for he was even starv'd with this poor way of Life, and grown a perfect Skeleton. *Catherina* was so surpriz'd, she could not utter one Word; but *Angelina* pour'd some of the Arrack into his Mouth, and in some time he recover'd, and the most passionate Discourse pass'd

1 Loose cloak.
2 Bottle made of stoneware (a particularly hard kind of ceramic).

between him and *Catherina* that can be imagin'd: For what Joy could exceed hers to meet her dear Husband again? She beg'd to know how he came to live in that Place; and all that had pass'd since they were parted, which he related in these Words, kissing her Hands, and gazing upon her all the while, as if his glad Soul, which seem'd to sparkle in his eager Eyes, would feast it self on that delightful Object.

## CHAP. XVI.

"My Life," said he, "the fatal Day that we were parted, and you were sold to the cursed Bey of *Tunis*, who has no doubt enjoy'd that lovely Person" (then he sigh'd deeply, and she wept) "I was dispos'd of for a Slave to an old Jew, who drove me home into the Country before him, with my Arms pinion'd.[1] Being come to his House, he put me into the Garden to work, there I was made draw Water, dig, and labour hard all Day, at Night chain'd like a Dog in a Hole under his Summer-House on Straw; my Food and Labour were so hard, that in a few days I fell sick of an Ague[2] and Fever; so that fearing I should die, he took me into the House, making me wait at Table, whet the Knives, go on Errands, and such trivial things; but my Weakness increasing, I was at last confin'd to my Bed. This frighten'd him so, that he told me (finding I was a Gentleman, and unfit for Service) if I would write to my Friends, and procure a tolerable Ransom, he would let me go. Then I told him that there was a young Gentlewoman who was taken with me in the same Ship, and that if he could get me Intelligence where she was, and find on what terms she might be freed, then I would send to *Spain* to my Friends for a Ransom for both, tho they were but in mean Circumstances; for I dar'd say no other, because the Villain would have been extravagant in his Demands: and I told him unless he could do this, I did not think it worth my while to write, or care what became of me. This vext him horribly. In short, I lay ill so long, that had not his Daughter, a handsom Jewish Maid, privately supply'd me with some rich Wines and good Food, I had surely dy'd: for tho a kind of a Doctor he employ'd, gave me

---

1  Bound.

2  General term for a disease that causes high fever, chills, and shivering. Most commonly it referred to what we would call malaria, which remained a problem in the Mediterranean well into the early nineteenth century.

some Medicines that conquer'd my Disease, yet I had never recover'd Strength enough to get away without her help; but being able to walk about, and little notice being taken of me by the Servants, I left the House one evening, and resolv'd to get back near *Tunis*, where I hop'd to get some news of you. This Jew's Country-House was fifteen Miles off it, and I was two Days and Nights a crawling to this ruinous Place, into which I enter'd to rest my self, being quite spent. I had a Bottle of Wine, and some Bread and Meat ty'd up in a Cloth in this little Basket, in which I us'd to gather Fruit for the Table. After I had eat and slept here, I began to consider what to do; if I enter'd the City, I should run the risk of being taken up perhaps and examin'd, and so be sent to Prison for a Runaway, or sent back to my Master, which was almost as bad: so a thought came into my Head, that if I could find means to subsist and live conceal'd in this Place, I might have some fortunate opportunity of finding where you were. Then I began to view the Place more narrowly, and found this Door: I descended into the Vault, but it was so dark I could not discern what was in it, but groping about, I thought I heard a Groan, and turning my Head, discern'd the glimmering of a Lamp in one of the inner Rooms: I enter'd it, tho in some disorder, and there I saw one of the most dismal Objects that ever Eyes beheld, it was an aged Man dress'd in this coarse Coat that I have on, his Beard reached to his Waste, his Bones appear'd ready to start thro his parched shrivel'd Skin, his Eyes were sunk, his Voice fail'd, and he seem'd to be in the last Agonies of Death, as indeed he was. I could hardly recollect my Spirits, I was so mov'd at this dreadful Sight. He fix'd his Eyes upon me, and seem'd desirous to speak to me. 'In the Name of Jesus,' said I, 'what are you that are thus come to dwell amongst the Dead?' 'That Name,' said he, 'is sweet indeed; speak it again, dear Christian, and comfort my departing Soul.' At these Words charity made me haste to give him some of my Wine, of which he swallow'd but a little with much difficulty; yet that a little reviv'd him, and I beg'd him to get down some more. In fine, he was so refresh'd, that I hop'd I should have sav'd his Life, but was deceiv'd.

'I know,' said he, 'your Curiosity is great to know who I am, and the strange Adventures that have brought me to this dismal Place and End; and I will endeavour to reward your Kindness, if I am able, with the Story of my Life. I was the eldest Son of a noble Family in *Spain*, it was my fortune to fall in love with a young Lady, the Daughter of a Grandee;[1] I got her Father's permission

---

1  High-ranking Spanish noble.

to court her, but was receiv'd but coldly; in fine, I found I had some Rival who supplanted me in her Affection, and made it my whole study to discover who he was; and it was not long e'er I was satisfy'd that a young Cavalier us'd to be admitted thro the Gardens frequently, in the dead-time of the Night, to her Apartment. I passionately lov'd her, and this discovery so enrag'd me, that I resolv'd to kill him. In short, I lay in ambush with three of my Servants, in a Grove behind the Gardens, and saw him enter, leaving his Horse and one Servant to wait his coming out, which was not till the break of day. I advanc'd at the head of my Servants, and shot him dead, and made off immediately without discovery, being mask'd; my Coach waited about two Miles off the Place; so I quitted my Horse, and went into it, reaching my own Home in the City before it was broad Day: by Noon the news was spread all over the City that Don *Emanuel de Cervantes* my Cousin-german was kill'd, but none could discover by whom. I conceal'd my Thoughts, appearing much concern'd for his Death, and being unable to live at quiet without *Belemante*, I press'd for our Marriage so earnestly, that her Father consented, and we were join'd by the sacred Rites, not to be happy but wretched; for she was so sincere in her Affection to her murder'd Lover, that she could never be happy with another; and having too well convinc'd my self the first Night, that my Bride was no Virgin, I grew furiously jealous and unkind to her. This usage put her upon measures to be reveng'd: and her Charms soon procur'd me such a Rival, that I knew not how to cope withal; a Duke made me that modish thing a Cuckold, and to prevent my having any Opportunity of being reveng'd, not only came always well attended to my House, but procured me a great Post in the Army, which oblig'd me to be absent from home most part of the Year; yet my Wife lost no time, but curs'd me with a Child every Year, so that I began to look on her as a vile Strumpet, and the Children as Vipers and Serpents produced by her Lust and my Dishonour. At last I plotted the Destruction of her and them, and having contriv'd this Villany to destroy them, and ruin my own Peace and Soul, laid all things ready to escape from Justice, I came home, and at one fatal Supper in my Wife's Apartment, poison'd her and her three Children. At Midnight I took Horse, and reach'd the next Sea-Port by Day-break, where a Bark lay which I had hir'd to carry me to *England*, having remitted a vast Sum of Money thither in order to provide for me there, knowing I must never return to *Spain* again. I went on board, met with a great Storm which drove us towards the Straits,[1] where an *Algerine* Pirate met with and took us; being brought to *Tunis*, I was sold for a Slave to a Bassa,[2] who kept me in extreme Misery seven Years: he being kill'd in the Wars, I fell into the hands of his Son, who was an Officer of the Guard to the King of *Fez*[3] and *Morocco*; with him I travel'd many thousand Leagues, carrying Burdens, and running by his Horse's side. All this I look'd upon as a just Punishment inflicted upon me by Divine Justice for my enormous Sins, and must confess the Horrors of that Guilt that loads my Soul, were always more grievous to me than the bodily Pains I suffer'd, tho they were almost insupportable. At last, quite weary'd out and desperate, I fled over the Mountains, and after wandering about in the Disguise of a poor Dervise,[4] which is the Habit I have on, by means of which I pass'd undiscover'd to this Place, in which I chose to reside, and have liv'd five whole Years unmolested, I got my Bread by begging in the adjacent City and Suburbs, being held in great Veneration by the common People, by reason of my Dress, which made me pass for a religious Mahometan. All this time I have been labouring to make my Peace with God by Prayers and Tears, hoping to wash away my Stains, and purify my Conscience; this I hope thro the Merits of my Saviour. I have done: It is about ten Days since, coming to my dismal Cell,[5] I saw two Persons strugling as if one was going to rob or kill the other, and stepping in between them, one of them, which I suppose to be the Thief, stabb'd me into the Thigh with a poison'd Knife, as I since conclude, and then fled; the Person I had rescu'd, seem'd very thankful, and desirous to know who I was, to reward me; but I was shy of that, so he gave me a Purse of Gold and left me. I hasted home to dress my Wound with some Salve I had by me, but the next Morning could not rise; I have lain here ever since in extreme Torment, have had no Food these three Days past, and believe my Thigh is mortify'd.'[6] He related all this, often faltering in his Speech, and groaning, nay fainting several times; but I spare to make particular mention of these things. He concluded thus: 'And now,' said he, 'I shall die by a violent Death, as those I murder'd did; may God accept of these my Sufferings and Repentance here, in compensation of the Ills I

---

1  Of Gibraltar.
2  Pasha: high ranking military officer in the Ottoman Empire.
3  One of the four kingdoms that comprised the Empire of Morocco.
4  Dervish: Muslim ascetic.
5  Dwelling for a hermit.
6  Affected by gangrene.

have done, and then I shall be happy.' I kept him alive with the Wine that Night, but the Mortification ended his unhappy Life the next Morning. I drag'd his Body into the next Room, and shut up the Door as close as I could, to avoid the Stench of it, and concluded to live here, putting on his old Coat as a sure Disguise: I took the Purse of Gold also, which was a great help to me, and having dy'd my Face and Hands with the Juice of an Herb to make me look thus tauny, have liv'd undiscover'd all this time. I learn'd at my Jew-Master's to make Straw-Hats, and Baskets for to gather Fruit in: these I make here in the heat of the Day, and sell for Bread and Meat, which if I get none ready dress'd,[1] I broil upon some Coals, making a Fire of Sticks in the Mosque, in one Corner of which I have made my self a kind of Fire-place with Stones; then I bring down some of the hot Coals upon a Tile into this Place to warm and dry it, else I should die with the Dampness of it. I am so well acquainted with the Country now, that I am confident I could find out some more commodious Place to live in: but fearing to go farther off the City, and so be less likely to hear news of you, made me continue here; but since Providence has been so merciful to bring you hither, you shall take up with this sad Being some few days, till I can procure such a Disguise for each of you as I have on, and colour your Faces like mine, which will wash off again; and then I'll provide some better place near the Sea-side for us to dwell in, till God is pleas'd to send some Ship to carry us off from this sad place. The rich Vests and Turbants you have on would surely betray us; we will take the Jewels off, and hide them in the Vault among the dead Bones, where none will seek them, and to morrow I will buy two Coats, and Boots, with Flannel to make you long Tunicks to your Heels, to keep you warm, and hide your fine Linen underneath; your Heads shall be cover'd with Flannel-Hoods, like Cowls, with Straw-Hats." This resolv'd on, they sat down, and eat thankfully of the Scraps he had brought home. Thus with a good Conscience, Men may live contented, nay be even happy in the most miserable Circumstances. A Charnel-House now entertains these two Ladies, who are better pleas'd to eat Scraps, and lie on Straw and the cold Stones, than dwell in a fine Palace, and sleep on Beds of Down with infamy. After this poor Repast, they pray'd, and laid them down to rest, Don *Sancho de Avilla* having fasten'd the Door of the Vault within-in-side as he used to do, to prevent wild Beasts from entring there. The next Morning he went to the City, and bought what they

---

1 Already cooked.

wanted, yet not at one place, but at several, for fear of suspicion, and return'd soon; then they sat down to work, and made the Flannel Tunicks and Hoods, as he directed them; he had brought Meat, and dress'd it in the Mosque above, whilst they work'd in the Vault below: by Night they had finish'd their Disguises; and he, impatient to remove them from that dismal Place, went out after they had din'd, and searching along the Shore, found an old ruinous Cottage on the side of a Rock, so built in a Cleft of the Rock, that it was well screen'd from the bleak Winds or parching Sun, and so shadow'd with Trees that grew round about and over it, that it was not easily seen. No body liv'd in this place but an old Fisherman and his Wife. Don *Sancho* told them he was a poor Dervise whose Cottage was tumbled down, and if they would quit this for him and two more Hermits to live in, he would pay them to their Content; the poor devout Peasants, reverencing his sacred Person and Profession, gladly consented: so he paid them a small matter, tho to them a great Sum, and they quitted the Place, retiring to another Cottage at a little distance from it; these poor People he employ'd to buy two Quilts, some Coverlids, and what else was wanting, to make this Place a convenient Cell for him and his two Friends; and in three Days' time, all being ready, they remov'd in the dusk of the Evening from their dismal Vault to this clean wholesom Cottage, where they liv'd for some Months very happily, hiding the rich Jewels and Clothes in a Hole in the Rock: the poor Fisher and his Wife were very serviceable to them, fetching what they wanted, and supplying them with Fish; and having a good strong Boat, they hop'd by his means to get to some Ship, he having promis'd to go on board the first *European* Ship he could get sight of at Sea, for which service Don *Sancho* assur'd him, he would give them ten pieces of Gold. During the time of our female Hermits' abode in this Place, they never went into the Town; but Don *Sancho* neglected not to go frequently to sell his Straw Baskets and Hats, which the Ladys learn'd to make with great dexterity; so that they made enow[1] to supply them with Bread and Meat in way of exchange. And now he thought it would not be improper to convert some of the Jewels into ready Money, which might stand them in stead, in case they found cause to remove or means to get off. In order to this, he carry'd some of the Jewels *Catherina* had brought away in the fine Box she took out of the Bey's Wardrobe, which they had broke open, and found to be full of Jewels and Gold; a few of these he went with to a

---

1  Enough.

Jew-Merchant in the City, whom he told that he had found a Box with these Jewels, and some other things of Value in it, on the Sands, as he was walking on the Sea-shore, and suppos'd to be part of some Shipwreck: the Jew did not much trouble him with questions, but finding he should have them a good pennyworth,[1] car'd not how he came by them, and bid him a thousand Pieces of Gold, but Don *Sancho* insisted upon two thousand, to which the Jew at last agreed, and paid him down the Money, the Jewels being no doubt worth twice as much; but this Sum was sufficient for our Hermits. And now Don *Sancho* could boldly go to him, and buy what they wanted, without fearing to give occasion of suspicion, since the Jew would not wonder how he came by Money. All the Diversion the Hermits took, was to walk on the Sea-shore in the Evenings and early in the Mornings, in hopes to discover some Ship to get off. One Morning, a dreadful Storm having blown in the Night, they went out to see what mischief was done; and *Angelina* being foremost, perceiv'd something floating on the Sea: she stood still to observe it, and soon saw it was a Man, with his Hands fast clench'd on a Chest, his Habit was lac'd with Silver; she cry'd out to Don *Sancho* to come to help this poor Wretch: he ran, and stepping up to his middle in the Water, caught hold of the Chest and drag'd it to shore. Then they took the Man up, who appear'd to be dead, but Don *Sancho* holding him up by the Heels, the Water pour'd out of his Mouth in great Quantity, after which some signs of Life appear'd; they carry'd him home to their Cottage, gave him Rack, and put him into a warm Bed, and so brought him to Life; he was a very handsom Gentleman, and his Linen and Clothes spoke him a Man of no mean Quality. Don *Sancho* left him with the Ladys, whilst he call'd the Fisherman to help bring the Chest to the Cottage, supposing it to contain some-thing worth saving. The Stranger view'd the Ladys with wonder, their strange Habit and tauny Complexions ill agreeing with the sweetness of their Features, and delicate Hands and Limbs: he thought he knew one of them, yet was in doubt. Mean time they were very busy in tending him, giving him burnt Wine, and talking in *French* to one another, a Language he was no stranger to, for he was a *French* Gentleman by Birth. At last he address'd himself to *Angelina* in this manner: "Madam, if my Eyes do not deceive me, I have the honour to know you, your Name is *Angelina*, the unfortu-nate Daughter of a Mother who barbarously sent you out of *France*. Speak, are you a Stranger to Monsieur *du Pont*?" At this

---

1 At a good price.

Discourse she chang'd colour, and shedding some Tears, reply'd, "I am indeed the unfortunate *Angelina*, and too well know that name, since I am never like to see, or if I did, can ne'er possess what I so dearly lov'd." "Yes," said he, "you will I doubt not do both, for he is safely arriv'd in *France*, and a Widower, having sought for you all over *Canada* and the *West-Indies*; he came home a little before I left *France*." Here he told her all the Story of her Mother's Death, and the manner of their living together; that he was now possess'd of a vast Estate, and retir'd from the World on her account. By this time Don *Sancho* and the Fisherman brought in the Chest; and *Angelina* proceeded to ask the Stranger who he was, not being still able to recollect. He told her immediately that his Name was *Abriseaux*. "Good Heavens!" said she, "are you that charming gay young Captain who us'd to visit and court my dear Friend Madam *de Belanger*, when we were Pensioners in the Monastery together?" "Yes," said he, "I am that unfortunate Man, who have marry'd and brought that lovely Maid from *France* to lose her Life I fear, and then it had been well for me to have perish'd with her; for if she's dead, Life will be a Hell to me. I beg you therefore to add to the charitable Office you have done in saving me, by searching all the Coast hereabouts carefully, for she was holding fast on the Chest, when my Senses forsook me, and then we were not far from the Shore: I hope therefore that she may still be alive; if I do not find her, Grief will perhaps finish that Life that you have now restor'd me to. I saw a Boat near us when I fainted, and conclude if she had been drowned, she would have kept her hold on the Chest, as People generally do; for this reason I flatter my self the Fisher-Boat took her up, and neglected me, whom they might conclude dead, or that some Wave might drive me out of their reach." Don *Sancho* sent the old Fisherman to make inquiry, who was acquainted with all the others on that Coast, the Stranger being so weak he could not rise. And now they intreated him to tell them his Adventures, and the manner of his coming to that Coast; which he related in these Words.

# CHAP. XVII.

"After you, fair *Angelina*, left *France*, I continu'd my Addresses to
Madam *Belanger*, whose Brother, soon after you were gone, went
away for *Virginia*, being highly disgusted with his Guardians,
resolving to apply himself to an Uncle he has there, who had considerable Effects of his in his hands, and he persuaded himself
would assist him against his other Uncles: Madam *de Santerell* follow'd him, and no News of them has come to *France* since they
left it. Madam *Belanger* was soon remov'd from *St. Malos* to *Calais*,
and I following, she was sent to the Convent of *Augustine* Nuns at
*Paris*. Mean time my elder Brother dying, I became Master of a
Fortune sufficient to answer hers: so I apply'd my self not only to
her obdurate Uncles, but to the Bishop and principal Merchants,
who importun'd them to consent to our Marriage, but to no purpose; for they were resolv'd never to part with her and her Fortune,
tho I proceeded so far, that I offer'd to divide it with them; but this
they rejected with a pretended Scorn. In fine, I saw all I did was
to no purpose, so I resolv'd to steal her away, and fly to *Virginia* to
her Brother, who being now come of Age, might greatly assist me,
as I will him. I set out for *Paris* with this design, but was strangely
disappointed when I came there, for she was remov'd thence to a
House of her Guardian's (an old Stone Building, strong as a little
Fort) in a Village in *Normandy*. Here they placed her under a kind
of Guard, for they put an old Hag in the Chamber with her, who
never let her stir out but on the Leads[1] (for it was the uppermost
Room in the House;) two stout surly Fellows liv'd below, and took
care of the Gate. I took a private Lodging in this Village, disguis'd
like a mean Person,[2] leaving my Servants and Horses at a Market-
Town three Miles off; and pretended to the old Farmer where I
lodg'd, that I had been sick, and was come to that Place for my
Health, being a Tradesman at *Coutance*;[3] this pass'd very well with
the Country People. The House my dear *Janetone* was kept in,
was moated round and had a Draw-bridge, which was seldom let
down but when any of the Servants went out or in. I walk'd round
it several Days, to consider what course to take, and there I had
the Pleasure, or rather Torment, of seeing my dear *Janetone* walking with the old Hag upon the Leads. I did not dare to make any
Sign to discover my self to her; and being convinc'd that it was

---

1   Lead roof.
2   Of low social status.
3   Town in northern France.

impossible to get at her by fair means, I resolv'd to use force; in order to which, I sent the old Farmer's Man to the Market-Town, with a Letter to my Valet-de-Chambre, whom I had left with two Footmen and four Horses, to come to me next Morning, which they accordingly did. I took them to a Place in sight of the Prison where my Mistress was, and we staid conceal'd under the shelter of some Trees, till we saw one of the Men-servants come out, the Bridge being let down: We rid up with Pistols in our Hands, seiz'd on the Bridge, which my two Servants kept, whilst my Valet-de-Chambre and I forc'd the Servant at the Gate to give us entrance; for I caught him by the Throat, and clapping my Pistol to his Breast, bid him bring me to Madam *Belanger*, or I would kill him. He beg'd for Mercy, and I held him by the Arm, and ascended the Stairs with him to the Room where she was. You may believe she was extremely surpriz'd at seeing a Man enter the Room thus rudely, but she quickly recover'd her Fright at the sight of me. The old Hag scream'd and roar'd like one distracted, but that I little regarded; so I bid my Mistress follow me, and we ran down Stairs; I mounted her upon my Horse behind me, on which I had purposely put a Pillion,[1] and my Men breaking down the Draw-bridge, threw it into the Moat, and so prevented our being pursu'd for some Hours; in which time we made off to a Curate's House cross the Country, about twenty Miles farther: Here we were marry'd, and lay conceal'd for above a Month, in which time the Search made after us was over, and they concluded we were gone out of the Kingdom. Then having disguis'd her in Man's Clothes, and a Ship and Money, with Bills of Exchange, being got ready for us at *Diepe*, we set out from the Curate's, attended by two Servants, and got safe off.

Now we thought our selves happy, and had a prosperous Voyage, till we came thro the *Straits*; but then a dreadful Storm arose, driving us on this Coast; and our Ship (which was but small) striking upon a Rock, sprung a Leak, and we had no way to save our selves, but by getting into the Long-boat: my dear Wife was my chief care, I got her one of the first in, and the Captain and several Sailors and Passengers leap'd after in such disorder (all being willing to save their Lives) that they over-set the Boat, and we were all thrown into the merciless Sea. I catch'd hold of my dear Wife, and seeing a Chest floating, and that we were not far from the Shore, I caught hold of it, bidding her throw her self

---

1 Pad attached behind the saddle on the back of a horse to permit a second rider (typically a woman).

upon it: Thus we remain'd, till my Strength was so spent, that I could no longer sustain the Waves beating against me, and fainted at the moment I saw a Fishing-boat making towards us; and now all my hope is, that she was taken into it."

Soon after he had ended his Relation, the old Fisherman enter'd, with the good News, that a Fisherman standing on the Shore, saw the Lady taken up by the Boat, from whence they threw a Rope, which she catch'd hold of; and that the Man on the Chest was carry'd off towards the Shore by the Waves. He said the Woman rung her Hands; and seem'd to call after him; but that the Boat made away out of his sight, from the Shore. Monsieur *Abriseauz* lifting up his Hands, cry'd, "My God, I thank thee with my soul, that her Life is preserv'd: Let thy Angels keep her safe, and direct me to her: strengthen my Confidence in thee, that the improbability of our meeting again may not drive me to despair."

The Hermits did all they could to comfort him, and procured a Habit like theirs for him: They resolv'd to be gone the first opportunity, but he could not be persuaded to leave the Place without his Lady; nay, his impatience was such, that he often ventur'd out in a Morning early, and would go many Miles along the Seashore, making Inquiry of the Fishermen: but alas! he was deceiv'd in looking for her there, for she was otherwise dispos'd of. Some Months pass'd in this manner, so that he began to despair of finding her, or they of getting thence; but Providence, whose ways are unsearchable, and always tend to our good, detain'd them there for the preservation of the virtuous *Janetone*.

Don *Sancho* one Morning going out very early alone, to go to the City to sell his Straw-ware, and buy Provisions, as usual, passing by a Wood, heard the Voice of a Woman making great Lamentations in the *French* Tongue: he turn'd aside to see if he could discover where she was, and following the Voice, enter'd a great way into the Wood, in the thickest part of which he perceiv'd a Woman sitting on the Ground; she had a *Turkish* Habit on, was very young and beautiful; she held her Hands upon one of her Legs, which was much swoln; her Face was pale as Death, her Eyes sunk with weeping and Famine; she look'd upon him as a Person resign'd to Death, and utter'd not one Word. He spoke to her in *French*, saying, "Madam, what ails you? how came you to this place? I am a Christian, and can help you." "Alas!" (said she) "I fear all help comes too late; I have been here three Days with my Leg broke, and have had neither Food nor Help, so am not able to move, or follow you; I fled from Ruin and Infamy, and have met Death: I was sav'd from the merciless Seas, to perish on the more inhospitable Shore." "Is not your Name *Abriseaux?*" (said he.) "Yes," (said she) "but ———." Here she swooned, he was troubled that he had nothing to give her, but was forc'd to run back to the Fisherman's Cottage, which was half a Mile, yet nearer than his own: here he got some Brandy, and made him follow him with a Blanket: They ran all the way, and found her lying as dead, with her Teeth clinch'd; he had much ado to get some of the Brandy down her Throat, but at last she began to breathe and move: Then they put her into the Blanket, and carry'd her betwixt them home to Don *Sancho*'s, where the transported *Abriseaux* was so divided betwixt Grief and Joy, that he scarce knew what he said or did. The Ladys got her into Bed, and gave her hot Spoon-meat;[1] but when they came to look upon her Leg, they shrunk back amaz'd, for she had broke it short at the Instep, the Bone being split, came thro; her Leg and Foot was so swell'd, that had the best Bone-setter in the World been there, he could not have set it at that instant. *Catherina* had some Skill, she presently made a Fomentation[2] with Herbs and Wine, and apply'd Stoups[3] dip'd therein to it, which gave the poor Lady great Relief in some Hours: what to do more they knew not, for they did not dare to send for a Mahometan Surgeon, and there was no Christians of that Profession, and they all fear'd a Mortification, but Monsieur *Abriseaux* was almost distracted. At last Don *Sancho* went to the Jew, and told him he had occasion for a Surgeon, and desired his assistance. He told him, a Friend of his had bought a Christian Slave of that Profession, who had been Surgeon to a *French* Ship; he would direct and recommend him to that Friend. He went with a Letter from this Jew to the other, who freely lent him his Slave. So they went together, and Don *Sancho* talking with him by the way, found he was Surgeon to the Ship which brought *Angelina* from *Canada*. He acquainted him with her being in his House, and his own Story, not fearing to be discover'd by a Christian, whom he offer'd to redeem from Slavery of the Jew; an Offer the other gladly accepted of, no question; for tho we often live as ill as Heathens, who profess our selves Christians, and whilst we live together are often at variance; yet none but such as have experienced it, can tell the Joy and Comfort poor Christians find, in meeting and conversing together when in Slavery, and amongst Turks and Heathens; then true Charity glows in their Breasts, and

---

1 Soft food that can be fed to an invalid with a spoon.
2 Warm medicinal liquid.
3 Pieces of cloth used to apply the fomentation to an injury.

they gladly assist one another to the utmost of their Power.

This Surgeon was caress'd by all, but especially by *Angelina*, who knew him to be a very honest Gentleman. He drest the poor Lady, and miraculously restor'd her Leg to such a state, that in six Weeks she could walk with a Crutch, tho never able to go upright, but was ever lame, it being impossible to cure it otherwise, having lain so long without help. *Angelina* asked him what was become of the Captain? He told her he was dead, he believ'd, of the Wounds he receiv'd in the Fight; a just Reward for his Crimes in using her as he had done. And now Madam *Abriseaux* being able, acquainted them how she came into this condition, and the occasion of her flying to the Wood where Don *Sancho* found her.

## CHAP. XVIII.

"Being pull'd into the Boat" (said she) "by means of the Rope they threw out to me, I expected them (having shewn so much Charity to me) to have made after you" (addressing her self to her Husband;) "but they seem'd deaf to my Intreatys; neither did they understand me, I believe, because they were Strangers to my Language. They made away for *Tunis*, to which they were going, it being a Fishing-boat belonging to a Bashaw[1] who lives there, and sent them out the Day before to get Fish for his Table, as his Custom was. They certainly imagin'd they had got a Prize in me, seeing me young and tolerably handsome. When they had brought me to shore, they led me directly to the Bashaw's (their Master's) House, where I was deliver'd to a Black, who seem'd mighty glad, and view'd me so curiously,[2] that my Face was over-spread with Blushes. By him I was led to a fine Apartment, where an old Maid-servant, who spoke *French*, came to me; the Grief and Surprize I was under made me glad to meet with some body, to inform me what I was to be done with: I ask'd her many Questions, and was answer'd, that I was to be Mistress to one of the handsomest and most powerful Men in the Place, that he was his Prince's chief Favourite: in short, she prais'd him up to the Skys. I told her I was already marry'd, and must rather die, than admit of another's Embraces. She laugh'd at that, and taking off my wet Clothes, brought me up a *Turkish* Dress. Thus I remain'd many Days confin'd in this Place, being furnish'd with all Necessarys of

---

1 Alternate spelling of bassa.
2 Closely.

Food, Habit, and Lodging; in which time walking in the Gardens, I saw and convers'd with some of those unfortunate Women who had been purchas'd for his Pleasures, *Europeans*, now made Slaves to the insolent Mahometan, who was at this time at a Country-house about two Miles distant from the Wood in which Don *Sancho* found me, so that it was some Months before I was expos'd to the Infidel's view. During my Abode in this Place I made some Attempts to escape, but could never effect it, for the Slaves so narrowly watch'd us, that there was no hopes of getting away. And now being almost overwhelm'd with Sorrow, I apply'd my self to God to deliver me. Indeed, I wonder'd that I continued so long without seeing this tyrannical *Algerine*; but at last I learn'd the Reason, he was sick of a tertian Ague[1] and Fever all that time: at last being recover'd, he order'd me to be brought to him; to his Country-house having had such an advantagious Character given him of me, that he was impatient to see me. I had contracted a kind of Friendship with a young Creature, who had been brought there at ten Years old; her Name was *Henrietta Belbash*, a *French* Peasant's Daughter; who being God-daughter to a Lady, whose Husband was a rich Merchant, and went to settle in the *West-Indies* with his Family, she took this beautiful Girl along with her, and the Ship being unfortunately taken, and brought into *Tunis*, she was sold to this Bashaw, whose Mistress she had been five Years when I came to that unhappy Place. She was fair as an Angel, witty, and highly sensible of her Misfortune. She had brought him a Daughter, which was carry'd away from her soon after it was born. She pity'd me extremely, and assur'd me that it was almost impossible to escape thence. She seem'd resign'd to her Misfortunes, and said, since God had been pleas'd to suffer her to be reduc'd to such a way of life, where she could have no opportunity of practising her Religion, or avoiding the Infidel's Embraces, she hop'd he would not lay any thing to her Charge as a Crime, since it was Compulsion, not Choice. But all her Arguments seem'd weak to me, and I resolv'd on Death, rather than to yield. At last, one Morning the old *French* Woman enter'd my Chamber, and bid me prepare my self to go to the great Man, whose Favourite I was to be. She brought me a rich Habit and Linen, and dress'd me to all the Advantage such a Pagan Habit could be put on with, whilst I stood weeping, careless of what she did, and meditating what to do. At last she threw a Vail over me,

---

1 Ague in which fever, chills, and shivering go away every other day and then recur.

and led me thro the Garden to a kind of Horse-litter,[1] into which the black Slave put me. I perceiv'd that there were seven or eight ill-look'd[2] Slaves to guard me, so that it was in vain to resist. I was about three Hours upon the Road, and had refus'd to eat any thing before I set out; so that I was so faint when they came to take me out, that two of them were fain to lead me into the House, which was a kind of earthly Paradise, adorn'd with fine Paintings, and such Furniture, that I was surpriz'd. Being conducted to a delicate Chamber, where there was a Bed made after the *European* Fashion, and Velvet Stools and Chairs, things very uncommon in these parts of the World; they left me, and in a few Moments after a Gentleman, in a rich Night-gown and Turban, enter'd: he was tall, slender, and delicately shap'd, his Eyes were black and shining, his Skin moderately fair, his Air and Mien so soft and engaging, that I stood confounded." At these Words Monsieur *Abriseaux* redden'd; she perceiving it, with a Smile said, "My Dear, don't be jealous, for his Beauty and Persuasions did him no further Service with me, but to raise my Pity; for I soon perceiv'd he was a *European*, and had bought his Greatness here by renouncing his Faith. He bow'd, and stood looking upon me for some time without speaking; then, like a Man waken'd from a pleasant Dream to substantial Joy, he catch'd me in his Arms, and said in *French*, 'Fame has done you wrong, sweet Creature; you are fairer than Fancy could conceive; take to your Arms a Man that adores you, and knows how to value such a Treasure; no Barbarian or fierce Moor, but one who was born in the politest part of the World: I am an *Italian*, whom Injurys drove hither; who being ruin'd by my Fellow-Christians, have fled for Succour to Barbarians, who have advanc'd and made me great enough to make you as happy as the World can make you.' My Soul was fill'd with Horror at these Words. 'Have you renounc'd your Saviour' (said I) 'and think a Christian can look upon you without Abhorrence? My Religion and Honour are so dear to me, that I will die for either; and tho I am in your Power (as you imagine) whilst I remain firm in this Resolution I am safe, and your Attempts are vain.' He us'd all the Persuasions possible to gain me, nay, stoop'd to beg and pray; but finding me inflexible, and growing faint, being still weak with his late Illness, he call'd for Wine, Sherbet,[3] and Sweetmeats,

---

1 Bed slung between two horses, used to transport invalids.
2 Evil-looking.
3 Sweet drink flavored with fruit juice and sometimes cooled with snow (a luxury in an age before refrigeration).

courting me to eat and drink; but I refus'd. Then he ask'd me if I design'd to be my own Murderer, and damn my self? I answer'd, No; but that I did not think it safe to eat and drink with a Person who had base Designs upon my Virtue, and might, perhaps, deprive me of my Reason by some stupifying Drug, and ruin me: therefore I would abstain from eating till Providence supply'd me with some wholesom Bread and Water, or any thing that might satisfy Hunger without danger. He seem'd surpriz'd at my being so resolute, and no doubt but his Conscience prick'd him when he saw me so well perform my Duty, which he had thro Cowardice and Ambition acted contrary to. At last he took leave, bidding me reflect, that no human Power could free me from him; that I must at last yield to his Desires; that he would much rather gain me by Courtship, than Force; but if I continued obstinate, he must be oblig'd to constrain me to be kind:[1] then he left me, a Slave keeping the Door. This Civility, I believe, was owing to his weakness; but being now left alone, I sat down in a Chair, and fell into a serious consideration of my wretched Condition: I had no Weapon to defend my self, or harm him; the Doors were guarded; then I view'd the Windows, and they were so high, that a Leap from thence seem'd to threaten certain Death: I disputed in my Conscience the lawfulness of such an Action. Thus I sat till Evening, being often interrupted by his officious Slaves, who brought me choice Wines and Presents from him, all which I refus'd; yet at last fearing want of Sustenance would render me unable to resist him if he offer'd Force, or Faintness seize my Spirits, and deprive me of my Reason, I made the Slave that brought in the Wine, drink a Glass of it before me, and then I took two Glasses full my self, and eat some Bread. When it grew dark they urg'd me to go to bed, but I refus'd. They brought in two Wax Lights,[2] and retired, shutting the Door; and now I trembled, fearing what follow'd. About Midnight the Apostate[3] Bashaw enter'd the Chamber, and fastening the Door, came to me, using all the softest Persuasions and Intreatys: in short, finding me deaf to all his Sollicitations, he proceeded to use Force; but then some kind Angel sure assisted me, for I grew strong, and he soon tired, renew'd his Intreatys. At last he swooned at my Feet, and then being distracted with my Fears, I resolv'd to use those happy

---

1  Sexually available.
2  Wax candles. The most elegant and expensive form of lighting; most candles were made from animal fat.
3  Someone who has renounced his religion.

Moments; so without standing to deliberate, I catch'd the rich Sash off that ty'd his Night-Gown, and fastening one End to one of the Bars of the Windows, slid down; but that being not above three Yards long, I fell down from a great height, and lay for some time quite stun'd; but recovering, found I had not broke my Bones, and rising on my Feet, fled towards the next Wood, it being a very Moon-light Night: I thought it not so far off as it prov'd, for it was near two Miles, as I guess, and I had hardly Strength left to reach it, but Fear drove me on. When I enter'd the Wood I was fill'd with more dreadful Apprehensions, and fancy'd the wild Beasts would devour me; to avoid which I got up into a Tree, whose Trunk, being old and hollow, I easily climb'd: There I seated my self, and pass'd the remainder of the Night till Daybreak; but then I fear'd to descend, lest I should be pursu'd; nor did I know where to go. Whilst I was thus musing Sleep prevail'd over Thought, and I fell into a Slumber, and drop'd down from the Tree, which Fall broke my Leg. What I endur'd for three Days that I lay there, you may imagine: I expected nothing but Death, as I had reason to do; but Providence preserv'd and reliev'd me by your means, for which I will be thankful whilst I live."

All the Company join'd in Praises to God, and were fill'd with Admiration: They pass'd the time for some Weeks very agreeably, till the good old Fisherman, whom they had converted to the Christian Faith, together with his Wife, acquainted them, that he had that Morning met at Sea with a *Spanish* Ship, had been aboard it, and inform'd the Captain of their being there: that he had promis'd to send his Long-boat that Night to a Creek behind the Rocks, to fetch them. "It is," said he, "a Ship of good force, and fears no Pirate, being well arm'd and mann'd." Don *Sancho*, on this News, went away to *Tunis*, and gave his Friend the Surgeon notice, who went back with him. The Ladys in the mean time pack'd up their Jewels, Money, and some Linen; and all being ready, they went away to the Creek in the dusk, and waited the Boat's coming. They offer'd to take the Fisherman and his Wife along with them, but they chose to end their Lives in their own Country, pleading their Age: so they left them all their Furniture, and twenty Pieces of Gold, a sufficient Provision for them. The Ship's Boat came about eleven of the Clock at Night, and carry'd them off safely to the Ship, Don *Sancho* promising to assist *Angelina* and the Surgeon to return to *France* by Land, and he and *Catharina* doubted not of a good Reception from his Friends at *Madrid*. Besides, the two Ladys had brought such a Treasure in Jewels from the Bey's Seraglio, that (being divided) was sufficient to provide for them all. Monsieur *Abriseaux* and his Lady were presented with a part of them, and his Chest having been sav'd, was a Provision for them; and they were prevail'd upon to desist from their intended Voyage to *Virginia, Angelina* promising, that Monsieur *du Pont* should stand by them against her unjust Guardians; so they determin'd to go home to *France* with her. The *Spanish* Captain receiv'd them with transport, and now they had leisure to entertain him with an account of all their strange Adventures.

They arriv'd at *Barcelona* in good health, sold part of their Jewels there, highly rewarded the Captain, and Don *Sancho*'s Friends provided nobly for him and *Catharina*, who writ to her Parents at *Venice* an account of all her Sufferings, and safe return to *Europe*. The *French* Ladys and Gentlemen staid some days to recover themselves of the Fatigue of their Voyage, and then set out for *France*, promising never to forget the Civilitys they had receiv'd, and the Friendship they had all contracted with one another in their Misery. And now 'tis fit that we leave the barbarous *Algerines*, and return to *Charlotta*, and the unhappy *Belanger*, whom we left travelling to *Virginia* thro *Carolina*.


## CHAP. XIX.

Monsieur *Belanger* and his generous Kinsman *Montandre*, with the Hermit Monsieur *du Riviere*, came safe to *Virginia*, where they were gladly receiv'd by the old Gentleman and his new Wife. *Belanger* was much pleas'd that she was now his Aunt, and *Montandre* lik'd her well enough for a Mother-in-law; yet she could not look upon her Nephew without Blushes and some kind of disorder; this was observ'd by her Husband, and he began to wish his Kinsman thence. He well knew that she marry'd him in a Pique, not out of Affection. In short, having been inform'd of all that had befall'n him and his Son in their Voyage to the Island of *St. Domingo*, he calmly advis'd him to return to *France*, having honourably accounted with him for all the Moneys and Effects left in his Hands, and made him a handsom Present of Sugars, Tobacco, and other Commodities which that Country produces, to a great Value; saying, "Nephew, I always design'd you something, and tho I have now a prospect of more Children, yet I will do what I intended; you are now of Age, and your Guardians can no longer detain you from your own; it is time you should settle in the world, and the young Woman you lik'd being dispos'd of to another, you must use your Reason; conquer that Passion which is now unlawful and injurious to your repose, and look out for a Wife in your own Nation, to bring Posterity to keep up your Name, and be comforts to you in your declining Years." *Belanger* thank'd him for his good Advice and Present, but was determin'd not to follow his Counsel, tho Monsieur *du Riviere* press'd him extremely to go with him to *France*; but *Belanger* would not consent to leave *Charlotta* behind. Young *Montandre* did likewise spur him on to let him go back to the Island to inquire after her: but alas, he had another design than that only in view; he had seen the charming *Teresa*, Don *Medenta*'s Sister, and her bright Image so fill'd his Soul, that he could not rest. We easily consent to what we desire. *Belanger* deals with the Captain that carry'd them thither before, to go back again with *Montandre*. Mean time he finding his Uncle look cold upon him, invited Monsieur *du Riviere*, no Ship being at that time ready to go for *France*, to go with him to see another Plantation of his Uncle's, and view the Country. The Ship goes off with *Montandre*, much against his Father's Will; but he arriv'd safe at the Island, and resolv'd to lie on board the Ship every Night, and not take a Lodging on shore, for fear of discovery; in the Day he ventur'd to walk about the Town, and went to the great Church to Mass on the next Sunday after his arrival, there he saw the charming *Charlotta*, with her little Son and Daughter standing by the Governor her Father-in-law, dress'd in a Widow's Dress, and *Teresa* in deep Mourning.[1] This was a very agreeable sight no doubt to him; he did not dare to venture to speak to her, but was fain to wait for an Opportunity some other time, which he suppos'd would not be extreme difficult, now Don *Medenta* was gone; but he was mistaken, for he had engag'd his Father on his Death-bed to prevent, if possible, her ever seeing *Belanger* again. "My dear Lord and Father," said he, "he is the Cause of my Death, he ruin'd my repose, and if he returns, will rob my dear Children of their Mother; her Affections are still inclin'd to him. I have brought her to the Catholick Faith, he is a Hugonot, and will seduce her from her Religion and Children; do not let my Fortune serve to enrich my hated Rival, nor my Children be wrong'd." He likewise charg'd *Charlotta*, as she valu'd his Soul's repose, not to marry him, or leave that Island and his Children. Thus the revengeful *Spaniard*, even in Death, continu'd to hate his brave Rival, who had a prior Right to her Heart, and endeavour'd to prevent his Happiness, even when he could no

---

1 Black clothing worn by close relatives after a death.

longer enjoy her himself. For these Reasons the Governor, who was inconsolable for the loss of his Son, desir'd *Charlotta* to live in the Castle with him, where she was respected as a Queen, and had all the Reason in the World to be contented. *Teresa*, who was courted by the greatest Persons in the Island, kept her Company, and there was the greatest Friendship imaginable between them. *Teresa* had not as yet felt *Cupid*'s Tyranny; she seem'd invincible to Love. *Montandre* having waited some Days in vain for an Opportunity to speak to *Charlotta*, grew weary, and resolv'd to give her a Letter in publick. He thought in himself, "she is now a Widow, and free to chuse whom she pleases: why should I fear to remind her of her Vows and Engagements with my Friend?" He dress'd himself very fine the next Festival-day, and went to Mass earlier than before, and there waited till they all came; then he went boldly up to *Charlotta*, and with a profound Bow, presented the Letter to her: this he did with such a grace and mein, that *Teresa*, looking upon him, was seiz'd with such an unusual liking to him, and so disorder'd, that she could scarce conceal it; and Love at this fatal Moment enter'd her Breast. He withdrew to the other side of the Altar so soon as he had deliver'd the Letter, and there plac'd himself on his Knees right against them, with design to observe *Charlotta*'s Countenance, by which he hoped to judge of her Sentiments in relation to his Friend, as likewise to have the Pleasure of looking often upon the charming *Teresa*, to whom his eager Glances spoke his Passion, whilst her unguarded Looks and Blushes assur'd him he was taken notice of. Mean while the Governor observ'd him, and watch'd *Charlotta*; who having look'd on the Superscription of the Letter, guess'd that it brought news of *Belanger*, and remember'd *Montandre*'s Face. This threw her into a mighty disorder; she put the Letter into her Pocket, not daring to peruse it in so publick a Place: but the distraction of her Mind caus'd her in a few Minutes to faint. This confirm'd the Governor in his suspicions, and he whisper'd one of his Gentlemen, whom he beckon'd to him, to take care that Gentleman was secur'd as he went out of the Church, and kept under a Guard till he examin'd him. Prayers being ended, he gave *Charlotta* his Hand to lead her to the Coach, so that she had no Opportunity to speak to *Montandre*. A young Cavalier, who courted *Teresa*, did the same by her, inflam'd with Jealousy at her Behaviour towards the Stranger, who imprudently follow'd them, in hopes to speak to one of the Ladys; but he was seiz'd at the Church-door as they were going into the Coach; he struggled, and demanded a reason of the Soldiers and Gentlemen that laid hands upon him, but could get no other answer but that it was the Governor's Order: so he was carried to a Room in the Castle, and kept till the Governor, having conducted the Ladies to their Chamber, came and examin'd him, asking him what the Letter contain'd that he had given his Daughter-in-law, whence he came, and who sent him: To all which he answer'd boldly, and told the Truth, saying, "My Lord, I do not think I have done any thing but my Duty. She is a Widow, was promis'd to my Kinsman before, and forced unjustly from him; he is her Equal, and her first Choice, and I cannot imagine why you should detain her from him." "Your Friend," reply'd the Governor fiercely, "by his imprudent coming hither, ruin'd my Son's Peace, and broke his Heart; he beg'd me with his dying Breath never to let him see her more, to rob his Children of her Presence, whom I will never let her carry hence; and he has bound her by the strictest Injunctions never to marry again; and to be brief with you, I am determin'd, if ever he sets foot on this Island again, to take such measures to secure him, that it shall never be in his Power to disturb her or me any more. As for you, I'll try whether a Prison cannot hold you, and if you escape hence again it shall be my fault." At these Words he left the Room, and *Montandre* was hurry'd away that Night under a Guard to a strong Prison into which they us'd to put Criminals of State,[1] ten Miles from the Town; here he was lodg'd in all Appearance for his Life.

*Charlotta*, so soon as her Father-in-law left her with *Teresa*, open'd the Letter and read it aloud to her; she could not conceal her Joy to hear *Belanger* was alive and constant. "Ah! my dear Sister," said she, throwing her Arms about her Neck, "why did your revengeful Brother lay me under such cruel obligations not to marry this dear Man, to whom my Faith and Heart was given before? He forc'd me from him. Is it just, that having been a faithful Wife to him, I should not be at liberty to dispose of my self to him to whom I do of right belong now he is dead? Your generous Soul, tho yet a stranger to Love, is sensible of Pity, and cannot but compassionate my Distress, my Soul being divided betwixt Duty to my dead Lord, and Affection to my living." *Teresa* embracing her with Tears, reply'd, "Alas, my Sister, I participate of your Griefs, and fear that I am born to be unhappy too, I love the generous *Montandre*; his Person, and noble Friendship to *Belanger* charms me; and if I am not deceiv'd, I am not indifferent to him.

---

1 Those convicted of crimes against the state, such as sedition or treason.

I will do all that I am able to assist you, but I fear my Father will undo us both; I saw his furious Looks, and fear the effect of his Resentments: just as we enter'd the Coach, I saw the People gather in a Croud, and fear some Mischief." As they were talking, *Teresa's* Woman, *Emilia*, enter'd as pale as death: "Madam," said she, "there is a strange Gentleman seiz'd, and brought under a Guard into the Castle, I saw him carry'd along just now up the great Square." This News extremely alarm'd them, and confirm'd their Fears; they employ'd *Emilia*, not daring to be too inquisitive themselves, to get intelligence, for she was Mistress to Don *Fernando* the Governor's Gentleman,[1] who had the Charge of *Montandre*; but he setting out with him that Night for the Prison to see him secur'd there, she could get no account till the next Morning, when she got the Secret out of *Fernando* where he was. This news overwhelm'd the Ladies with Grief, and *Charlotta* grew so incens'd, that she quarrell'd with her Father-in-law, complaining that she was not treated as she ought to be, and that if the Gentleman was not freed, she would complain to the King of *Spain*, that she had been taken away from *Belanger* by fraud, and compel'd to marry Don *Medenta*; that she was a Subject of *England*, and tho his Daughter-in-law, yet that he had no Power to command or restrain her from going off the Island, and marrying whom she pleas'd. This so inrag'd the Governor, that he told her, that since he found she had so little sense of her Honour, and Respect for her Husband's Memory and her Children's good, or his dying Commands, he would take care to keep her to her Duty, and prevent her Disgrace; that *Belanger* was of too mean a Rank to be receiv'd in the place of that noble *Spaniard* his dear Son, who was descended from an illustrious Family, and had demean'd himself in marrying her; that he had hitherto treated her for his sake with too much indulgence, which he perceiv'd she had no grateful sense of; that *Montandre*, tho a good Friend to *Belanger*, yet was a venturous Fool to return thither on so vile an Errand, as to bring Love-Letters to another Man's Wife; that he began to doubt whether his Son had dy'd fairly, or not, and to suspect she had by some cursed slow Poison destroy'd him, else they could not have known the time when it was fit to come to her, and knew she was a Widow: in short, he loaded her with bitter Reproaches and Taunts, and confin'd her to her Apartment under a Guard, suffering none to go near her but *Teresa*

---

1   Valet. Part of what defined an actual gentleman was not being dependent on anyone, so if someone is another person's gentleman, he is, by definition, a servant, albeit a high-ranking one.

and some few of his Relations, who teaz'd[1] her continually with the Respect she ow'd her dead Husband, and how she ought never to marry another inferior to him. The Governor little suspected his Daughter was any ways concern'd in *Montandre*'s Welfare; but, alas, she was as much afflicted as *Charlotta*, and ventur'd to send *Emilia* with a Purse of Gold to him. He would have sent a Letter back, but was deny'd Pen, Ink and Paper. *Emilia* lent him her Table-Book,[2] in which he wrote a most passionate Letter to *Teresa*, declaring his Love, and begging her to let the Captain who brought him thither, be inform'd of what had happen'd to him, and sent back to *Belanger* to warn him not to come thither. On the receipt of this Letter, *Teresa* dispatch'd *Emilia* to the Captain, who presently weigh'd Anchor, and set sail for *Virginia*, to carry these joyful and sad Tidings to *Belanger*; first that *Charlotta* was a Widow, and next that *Montandre* was in Prison, and she under a Guard on his account. *Belanger* in a short time was inform'd of all, the Ship coming safe to *Virginia*; and no persuasion of his Uncle, Aunt and Friends could deter him from going over to the Island, to demand his Lady, and release his Friend: but the Captain of the Ship refus'd to go back, saying he was sure he should be imprison'd and lose his Ship. And now it was some Months before he could get a Vessel to carry him; during which the Governor was inform'd by his Spies of *Emilia*'s Visits to *Montandre* in the Prison, and caus'd him to be secretly remov'd to the old Castle where he had been before a Prisoner; there the commanding Officer had such a strict Charge given him to take care of him, that he was secur'd from any possibility of an Escape, not being ever permitted to go on the Battlements, but confin'd to a Chamber with two Centinels at the Door Night and Day, being relieved every four Hours. The haughty Governor having thus secur'd him, laid wait to catch *Belanger*, not doubting but he would soon follow his Friend, when he heard the News from the *Virginia* Captain, of whose departure out of the Port he had had intelligence, and would have stopt the Ship, which he had a good Pretence for, it being a time of War between the *English*, *French* and *Spaniards*;[3] but only he concluded it best to let it go to fetch *Belanger*.

---

1 Pestered.

2 Two small wooden panels connected by a hinge and covered with wax or another erasable surface, used to take notes or jot down short messages.

3 The War of the Spanish Succession (1701–14) pitted England (and then, after 1707, Great Britain), the Netherlands, and the (*continued*)

*Charlotta* fell sick, and *Teresa* grew very melancholy and much alter'd; no news could be got of *Montandre*. At length she fell dangerously ill, insomuch that her Life was in danger, and being light-headed, call'd perpetually on *Montandre*. This open'd the Governor's Eyes, who finding she lov'd this Stranger, lost all patience. She was now his only Child, and all his ambitious Hopes were comprehended in her being nobly disposed of. The noblest and wealthiest Gentlemen in the Place made their Addresses to her, and would have been proud of having her: but she was attach'd to a Man whose Father was only a Merchant, marry'd to a second Wife, by whom he had younger Children to lessen his Fortune; besides he was a Protestant, and that alone was enough to make him reject the Match; in fine, he was at his Wit's end; the Physicians told him Medicines could do no good, he must resign her to Death, or bring the Person to her whom she lov'd. This expedient was death to him, yet he could not consent to lose his Darling, the lovely *Teresa*; at last he sent for *Montandre*, who was brought pinion'd under a Guard like a Criminal, and expected nothing but Death; he had been sick a considerable time of an Ague and Fever, which was turn'd to a yellow Jaundice,[1] so that he was so alter'd, that his Friends would scarce have known him. Being brought to the Castle, and carry'd up into a Room, the Governor came to him with Looks that express'd the inward distraction of his Mind. "Stranger," said he, "what would you do to gain your Freedom?" "Nothing," he reply'd fiercely, "that should be injurious to my Honour or Conscience: I am now indifferent to Life, and would not thank that Man who, having injur'd me, should ask me Pardon and release me; you may use me as you please, you have treated me so ill already, that I expect neither Justice nor Favour from you." The Governor could not but admire *Montandre*'s Bravery in secret, but yet seem'd angry; and answer'd, "Sir, do you consider whom you speak to, and that your Life's at my disposal?" "Yes I do, Sir," said *Montandre*, "and have spoke my Thoughts." "Well Sir," said the Governor, "I acknowledge I have us'd you somewhat roughly; but had you lost such a Son as I have, kill'd by your Friend's rash attempt, which has broke my Son's Heart and *Charlotta*'s Peace, you would doubtless have acted like me; but I have now but one Daughter" (here he wip'd off the

---

Holy Roman Empire against France and Spain. Aubin's husband fought in this war.

1 Condition in which the skin and eyes turn yellow.

falling Tears) "do you respect her?" *Montandre* alarm'd at these Words, answer'd hastily, "Yes, and honour her above the World, nay dare to tell you that I love her, and that it is my greatest Ambition to die at her Feet, if Fate would permit me; nor is there a thing on Earth for which I would wish to live beside her self." "For her sake," answer'd the Governor, "you shall not only live, but be freed." At these Words he took him by the Hand, and calling in a Servant, who unbound him, he led him to *Teresa*'s Chamber, who was so weak that she had been many days confin'd to her bed. "Here my dear Child," said the Governor, "is the Gentleman you so much respect; I shall leave you together." He was so disorder'd, being forc'd to stifle his Resentments and constrain his Pride, that he immediately withdrew. *Teresa* lifting up her Eyes, view'd *Montandre* with much concern, unable to speak, his alter'd Face too well inform'd her of the Treatment he had met withal; whilst he seeing her, whom he so dearly priz'd, in a Condition so unlikely to recover, fetch'd a deep Sigh, and falling on his Knees by the Bed, catch'd her Hand, and pressing it to his Lips, said with a low Voice, "Must we then meet to part so soon again, and must Death deprive us of that Happiness we might now possess? Speak, divine Creature, what hopes?" "If," said she, "there be a Cordial to restore me to Health again, it is the Sight of you, a Blessing I despair'd of. Say, does my cruel Father relent, will he consent to make us happy? and has he granted you your Liberty? If so, I will endeavour to live." At these Words, he fell into a great Transport; and the Governor entring, said a great many obliging things to him. In fine, *Teresa* in a short time recover'd, and was marry'd to *Montandre*, on his promising to reside there, and not return to *Virginia* to live. But poor *Charlotta*, tho glad of her Sister's good Fortune, and pleased to converse with *Montandre*, of whom she learn'd all that had befallen the unfortunate *Belanger*, yet could get no Satisfaction, or find means to go to him, the Governor having took such Measures that no Person could enter or go out of the Sea-Ports without his knowledge. *Montandre* could not as yet propose going to *Virginia*, but supposed his Friend would shortly arrive, and that *Teresa*'s Interest, and his, with his Father-in-law, was sufficient to procure his Consent to *Belanger*'s Marriage with *Charlotta*. Thus they flatter'd themselves: but a *Spaniard*'s Revenge must be gratify'd; and they never, or very rarely forgive an Injury. *Belanger* having procured a Vessel to carry him, and taking a considerable sum of Money from his Uncle, set sail from *Virginia*, and arrived at the Island of *St. Domingo* about a Month after *Montandre*'s Marriage. He no sooner set his foot upon the Shore, fill'd with Expectations of seeing his dear *Charlotta*, but he was seiz'd by Ruffians, bound hand and foot, and carry'd aboard another Ship, where he was put in Irons, and sail'd the next Morning, but he knew not whither. The same Night that he was seiz'd, the Captain of the Ship that brought him, receiv'd a Message from the Governor to depart the Island that moment, or expect to be treated as an Enemy, and his Ship to be seiz'd. He obey'd immediately, finding that neither Threats nor Intreatys could avail him. This News never reached *Charlotta*'s Ear; and poor *Belanger*, overwhelm'd with Despair, was carry'd up the great River *Oroonoko*,[1] and set on shore amongst the Savages, being carry'd in a Boat up to the River *Paria*, where he expected nothing but to be murder'd, and eaten by the barbarous *Indians*, who dwelt in Huts, and are under no civil Government. They speak no Language, but a Jargon that no *European* understands. The cruel *Spaniards* unbound him, gave him a Sword, a Gun, and a Horn of Powder, with a Pouch full of Bullets and Shot; telling him if he offered to make the least attempt to follow them, they would kill him on the spot. He little regarded what they said, being both weak and over-whelm'd with the dreadful Prospect he had before him of being left in a strange Place, from whence there was no probability of escaping; a Place which we *Europeans* are little acquainted withal amongst Savages, whose Language and Customs he was an entire Stranger to, that he sat down upon the Ground, and casting his Eyes round wept bitterly: then looking up to Heaven, besought God to look upon him, and deliver him from the Miserys of Life. Whilst he was thus employ'd, the Villains retreating to their Boat were set upon by a Party of Savages, about a hundred in number, many of whom fell by the *Spaniards*' Shot, who discharged their Guns and Pistols at them, which obliged the Indians to give back.[2] The *Spaniards* being but eight in number, and some of them wounded, retired towards the Shore to get into their Boat; but, to their great Surprize, found it gone; for their Companions that were left to take care of it, being shot at with Arrows by the Savages, who from the Rocks shot down upon them, concluded their Companions dead, and made off to their Ship with all the Speed they were able. The cruel *Spaniards* now too late repented the wicked Deed they

---

1  Orinoco, river in present-day Venezuela that terminates in a large
    delta. One of the branches of that delta connects to the Gulf of Paria
    that separates the mainland from the island of Trinidad.
2  Retreat.

had done, and seeing Death at hand, trembled at future Punishments; Despair urg'd them on, and they turn'd back and pursu'd their Enemies, who fled before them to the place where poor *Belanger*, rouz'd with the Noise of their Guns and Swords, was standing as a Man who was prepar'd for Death, and unconcern'd at whatever happen'd: but when they call'd to him to help them, crying "forgive, and join with us"; Christianity, and the Generosity of his great Soul, made him forget the Injuries they had done him; and like a Lion rouz'd from his Den, fall on the Savages till they had all left the Place. Then thinking it unsafe to pursue them further, he advised the *Spaniards* to retreat towards the River under the Covert¹ of some Rock; they consented, and hasted thither, there they found a great Cavern in the side of a Rock, into which they enter'd with Joy, and being quite spent; and three of them dangerously wounded, they sat down on the Ground to rest, destitute of Food or any Necessaries. That Night the three wounded Men expir'd; a sad Admonition to the rest, who were conscious they deserved no less. They were now sincerely penitent, and consulted with *Belanger*, whom they resolv'd to obey in all things, what was best to be done; they knew they could not live without Provisions, and tho they hop'd the Boat would return to fetch them, yet that being uncertain, they must find some way to subsist. At last they resolv'd to go out of this dismal Place before it was broad Day, and if possible seize upon one of the Huts of the Savages, and secure them, and so keep them as Hostages, sending one at a time to fetch Food for them, and by Signs threaten to kill the rest if he fail'd to return. They charg'd their Fire-Arms, and crept along the Shore till they came to a Hut, into which they enter'd, and found two Savages, a Woman, three Children, and an *European* Man, as his Complexion shew'd, asleep; they seiz'd the Savages, but for the white Man, who appeared to be of a great Age, he arose and embraced them, crossing himself; and lifting up his Hands as a Man over-joy'd, he spake to them in the *Latin* Tongue, desiring to know who they were and whence they came. The *Spaniards* afraid to speak the true Cause of their coming thither, said they were come on Shore in their Boat in search of fresh Water, and being set upon by the Savages, had been detained there whilst the Boat went off; those they left in it being as they suppose frighted away by the Noise of their Guns. Then the old Man spoke to the *Indians* in their Tongue, and they immediately fell at the *Spaniards'* Feet, kissing them, and bowing

1  Cover.

down their Heads in token of Obedience. The old Man told *Belanger* that he had liv'd twenty Years in that Country; that he was a *Benedictine* Monk, born at *Valladolid*[1] in *Spain*, and thence sent to *Peru*, from whence he had travel'd to this Place by land; that he had learn'd the Language of these Savages, and living amongst them, gain'd their Esteem, and converted many to Christianity; that these poor Savages were some of them, with whom he chose to live, being very honest People; that he would undertake they should supply all their Wants, and be very serviceable to them; that the Savages they had fought with were the Enemies of the Prince that govern'd that part of the Country, and us'd frequently to invade him, and carry off some of his People, whom they eat, as his Subjects did them; but that now he had persuaded a great many from doing it, and pretty well broke them of those barbarous Customs. Then he desir'd the *Spaniards* to sit down with him, and take some Refreshment without fear. After which he said he would conduct them to a place where they might live securely, till he could find means to procure their Return to the Island of *St. Domingo* or *Virginia*, offering to be their Guide to *Cartagena*,[2] from whence they might get Shipping to either Place. *Belanger* return'd him a thousand Acknowledgments, and in his Soul greatly admir'd the Providence of God, but wanted an Opportunity to inform him of the *Spaniards'* Villany in bringing him thither, and to warn him not to be too free in discovering any secret Retreat to them, which he was desirous to conceal, tho his Countrymen; for tho they appear'd sincerely penitent, yet he fear'd to trust himself with them to return to the Island of *St. Domingo*, resolving to go to *Virginia*, and not venture to go there any more; concluding in himself, that if *Charlotta*'s Affection for him continued sincere, she would now being a Widow, find means to get away and come to him thither; and that if at his return to *Virginia*, he could hear nothing of her nor his dear Friend *Montandre*, he would apply to the *Spanish* Vice-Roy[3] at *Mexico* for Justice; and being a Native of *France*, he doubted not of obtaining

1  City in northern Spain.
2  City in what is now Colombia; it was one of the principal ports for the Spanish Empire in the Americas.
3  Ruler of New Spain on behalf of the Spanish Crown. New Spain was composed of the portions of Central and North America claimed by Spain (including present-day Mexico), along with its Caribbean and Pacific colonies, including Cuba, what is now Puerto Rico, Santo Domingo, Guam, and the Philippines.

it, since *France* and *Spain* were at Peace. He and the rest sat down with the good Monk; the poor Savages, who were by Profession Fishermen, set Bread and cold dress'd Fish before them, with some Meat and Broth which they had boil'd the Day before for the humble Priest and themselves; this they had warm'd over a Fire which they made in the Hut with a few Stones set in form of a Hearth, with a Hole made in the Ground, setting the Pot on the Stones, and making a Fire underneath: they gave them also Drink and Rum, which greatly refresh'd them.

*Belanger* whisper'd the Monk that he wanted to speak with him alone; he took the Hint, and after eating, advis'd the *Spaniards* to lie down on the clean Straw which the poor Savages had laid for them in one Corner of the Hut, the only Bed he and they had us'd to lie upon; "there," said he, "you may repose your selves, whilst your Leader and I discourse." They readily comply'd, glad to take some Rest. So he and *Belanger* walk'd out over a Hill, then they descended into a fine Valley, at the bottom of which was a little kind of Copse or Thicket, compos'd of stately tall Trees and close quickset[1] Hedges. By the way[2] *Belanger* told him his Story; and the Monk detesting their Baseness, told him he should return no more to them, but abide with those that he had plac'd in that little Cell to which he was going to carry him: "there you will find," said he, "a Gentleman and Lady whose Conversation will make you think the time no way tedious whilst you stay here; it is a Month since they were cast away upon this Shore, and by my means, thro the Mercy of God, preserved as you have been. I heard a dreadful Storm in the dead of the Night, and walking out on the Shore so soon as Day-break to see what Mischief that sad Night had done, discern'd at some distance two Women, one richly dress'd, the other like her Servant, wringing their Hands, and lamenting over a Person who lay on the Sands, as I suppos'd, dead; the Lady expressed the most extravagant concern that ever I beheld. I made what haste I could to their Assistance, and at my approaching her was extremely surpriz'd; she was young, and fair as an Angel, her Hair was hanging loose, and wet as was her Habit, but she had a Necklace and Pendants[3] of Diamonds, with a Stomacher[4] that

---

1  Dense and thorny.
2  Along the way.
3  Earrings.
4  Triangular, sometimes jewel-encrusted fabric panel used to cover the front of a woman's corset.

dazled my Eyes; she was dress'd in a *Spanish* Dress, her Vest[1] was black Velvet, her Petticoat gold Tissue, Bracelets of Pearl; and in fine, I never saw a Person of greater Beauty, or who appear'd more like a Woman of Quality than the distress'd *Elvira*, for that is her Name: the Man that lay at her Feet as dead, appear'd her Equal in all kinds; he was young, handsom, richly dress'd, and seem'd just drown'd. I staid not to deliberate, but lifted him up, saying in *Spanish*, which I suppos'd she spoke, 'God comfort and help you; sweet Lady, has this Gentleman been here in this Condition any time?' 'Oh no,' said she, 'he is just cast upon the Shore.' 'Then' said I, 'there is hopes'; I immediately turn'd his Head downwards, and a great deal of Water pouring out of his Mouth, he shew'd some signs of Life. Having thus given his Stomach some relief by this Discharge of the Water, I set him upright on the Ground, chafed his Temples, and taking a little Bottle of Rack, which I always carry about me, pour'd some down his Throat; in fine, I brought him to Life, and she and the Maid, her Servant, assisting, we brought him into this little Wood to which we are going, a Place which I had chosen to make me a little Oratory[2] in, and had caused my converted Savages to build with some Boards, making me a kind of little Chappel with an Altar, and a small Chamber or Dormitory behind it to repose in in the heat of the Day. Here I us'd to perform the holy Duties of my Office, to baptize, and give the blessed Eucharist, having under the Altar a way into a little Vault, where I keep poor Vestments and what else belongs to the Altar. I brought them to this Place, fearing the Jewels she had on, and her Beauty, might tempt the Savages to some Wickedness: for should the savage Prince *Manca*, who governs this part of this barbarous Country, hear of or get sight of this fair *European*, he would have her for his brutish Pleasure in spite of all Intreaties or Resistance; therefore I secur'd her here, where she has remain'd a whole Month conceal'd. Her Adventures, and the brave *Gomez* her Husband's, you shall know from themselves: in this Place and Company I will leave you, and at my return to your Companions, tell them a wild Beast came out of a Wood and devour'd you, so send them away by the first opportunity, and then I will disguise and conduct you, *Elvira*, her Husband and Servant, to *Cartagena*, from whence we will go together for *Europe*, or where you please; for I am weary with living amongst Savages, and having but a

---

1  Dress, cut in the front so as to display the rich fabric, or tissue, of the petticoat.
2  Place for private prayer.

little time more to live in the World, am desirous to spend it in my Convent amongst my Countrymen and Friends, who may lay me to rest when dead amongst my Ancestors. The Hardships I have indur'd for twenty Years in this Place, have so broke my Constitution, that I am not able to hold it much longer." By this time they were come to the Wood, and so ending their Discourse, the Monk presented *Belanger* to *Gomez* and *Elvira*, who being acquainted with his Adventures, embrac'd and welcom'd him to their poor Habitation, over-joy'd that they should have such Company, and promis'd to go with him to *Virginia*, and procure him all the Satisfaction he could desire of the Governor of the Island of *St. Domingo*, *Elvira* being the Vice-Roy's Daughter. But Words cannot express *Belanger*'s surprize at the first sight of these Strangers; he thought *Elvira* so beautiful, that she excel'd all her Sex; her Air, her Shape, Dress and Face, and the gloominess of the Place she was in, fill'd him with an unusual Veneration and Respect for her. *Gomez* was tall, finely shap'd, and had a majestick Sweetness in his Look that commanded the Respect and gain'd the Love of all that saw him. Their Servant was a young *Indian* Maid, who tho of an Olive complexion, was very agreeable, well shap'd, and had Eyes so black and shining, that it was dangerous to look upon them. The Monk us'd to send them Provisions by this Girl, whose Name was *Philinda*, having been christen'd by *Elvira*, who took her when a Child, and had brought her up. *Philinda* went every Morning to the Hut to fetch such poor Food as the Monk could procure for them; they drank Water from an adjacent Spring, had some Poultry that they kept in the Wood to supply them with Flesh and Eggs, there being plenty of Fowl in those Parts, as likewise Roots: the Country being not very well peopled, they lay on Straw; and there growing very good Grapes in the Valleys, they had hung some up to dry in the Sun upon the Hedges, and squeezing the Juice out of others, drank of it instead of Wine. Thus these great People, who had been us'd to all the Delicacies in Nature, and had never slept but upon Down, and used to have the finest clean Linen every day, were now content to live in the poorest manner, and found that it was possible to live without all those things that a plentiful Fortune furnishes. The Monk having thus introduc'd *Belanger*, and stay'd some time with them, took leave; and then *Belanger* being intreated, entertain'd them with a more particular Account of his Life and Adventures. After which *Gomez* return'd the Favour with the relation of his and *Elvira*'s, being seated under a fine spreading Tree near the Door of their Cottage, it being now the close of the Day, and a fine Evening, *Philinda* being near them milking two tame She-Goats which the Monk had sent thither, and which were of great use to them.

## CHAP. XX.

*Gomez* began his Relation in these Words: "I should first relate my dear *Elvira*'s Birth, and speak of her Family. She was the only Daughter of the Marquis of *Mirandola*,[1] who is descended of one of the noblest Familys in *Italy*, tho born a *Spaniard*: her Mother was *Elvira Mariana Sabriente*, Daughter of Don *Lopez* Lord of *Langora*,[2] a *Castilian*[3] Lord of great Merit and Fortune. The Marquis being a great Favourite to the King of *Spain*, was appointed Vice-roy of the *Indies*[4] in the Year 1692, at which time *Elvira* was thirteen Years of Age. He arriv'd safely at *Mexico* the same Year with all his Family, and has resided there ever since, which is now ten Years. I am the Son of Don *Alvares de Mendoza*, an *Arragonian*[5] Lord, a Man of equal Birth and Fortune with *Elvira*'s Father; but there was a mortal Hatred between our two Familys, by reason of a fatal Accident that happen'd in my Infancy: my Father had a Sister, who was esteem'd one of the fairest and most accomplish'd young Ladys in *Spain*; she was but fifteen when my Father brought her to Court; there a young *Castilian* Cavalier, who was a Colonel of the Guards, and Nephew to *Elvira*'s Father, saw and fell in love with my Aunt, who was already promis'd to a Lord of the first Quality and Fortune in *Arragon*: he courted her privately by means of a Servant, who was in his Interest; and having gain'd my Aunt's Affection, at length obtain'd the last Favour.[6] It was not long after this unhappy Converse had been between them, before the Lord to whom she was promis'd arriv'd, and she was constrain'd to marry him: He suspecting her Virtue, being

---

1 Independent state in northern Italy until 1711, although it was ruled by a duke, not a marquis.

2 Longoria: town in northwestern Spain.

3 From Castile, one of the medieval kingdoms brought together in the sixteenth century to form the kingdom of Spain.

4 Generic term for Spain's overseas colonies. Elvira's father was the Viceroy of New Spain.

5 From Aragon (another of the former medieval kingdoms that comprised Spain).

6 Convinced her to have sex with him.

sensible she was no Virgin, became furiously jealous; yet conceal'd his thoughts from her and all the World, resolving to stay till he had discover'd the happy Rival that had been before-hand with him,[1] before he let his Resentments break forth: For these Reasons he gave her opportunitys of seeing her Lover, carrying her down to a Country-Seat not far from *Madrid*, which he had bought since his Marriage, under pretence of obliging her, but indeed with design to discover the fatal Secret. Here he often left her for a Night or two, whilst he went and staid at *Madrid* with the King; the unfortunate Don *Duante* (her Lover) fail'd not to supply his Place in her Arms, going disguis'd to a Peasant's House at a Village near, from whence (attended only by one Servant) he enter'd the Gardens, and went into her Apartment by a Ladder of Ropes, which she us'd to fasten for him on a Balcony that open'd into her Chamber. Her Lord (the incens'd *Arragonian*) soon discover'd all by means of a Page whom he had employ'd to watch; and one Night he conceal'd himself in a Summer-house in the Garden, having only this Page with him, both well arm'd, and the Moon shining very bright, saw Don *Duante* go into her Chamber by the Ladder, which he left hanging in order to[2] his Retreat, as usual. He staid till he suppos'd he was undrest and gone to bed; then he mounted the Ladder, follow'd by his Page, and coming into the Chamber, where a Wax-light was burning on the Table, approach'd the Bed softly. Don *Duante* having heard some little noise, was started up, and sat upright in the Bed: This gave *Alonzo* a fair opportunity for his Revenge, and he stab'd him to the Heart with his Dagger; the poor Lady shrieking out, he tore her out of bed by the Hair, cut out her Tongue, and discharging one of his Pistols in her Face, which he had loaded with small Bird-shot on purpose, left her on the Bed blind, her Eyes and Face being in a most dreadful condition, all tore to pieces, and full of the Shot.[3] Never was a more tragick Scene than this Chamber appear'd; she look'd like the wrong'd *Lavinia*,[4] and the unfortunate *Duante* lay weltering in his Blood, expiring on the Floor.

---

1  Who had had sex with her before he could.

2  For.

3  Birdshot: load of small lead pellets that can be fired out of a gun to hit multiple targets at once.

4  The raped and mutilated heroine of William Shakespeare's *Titus Andronicus* (1594) or Edward Ravenscroft's 1686 adaptation of it, whose hands were cut off and tongue severed so that she could not name her attackers. Ravenscroft's adaptation had been performed (*continued*)

Thus one imprudent sinful Action occasion'd the ruin of three noble accomplish'd Persons; nay, involv'd their Familys in the greatest Misfortunes, and have intail'd them upon their Posterity;[1] the first Ground of which was the Lady's Parents, who not consulting her Inclination, match'd her against her Will; want of a firm Virtue in her made her yield to another, when she was pre-ingag'd by them: and an unchristian Spirit of Revenge govern'd her Husband, and made him commit two dreadful Murders, and incur the Anger of Heaven, and the Justice of the Laws; which, tho he escap'd by Flight and his Prince's Favour, yet it ruin'd his Peace and Fortune. I hope it will be a warning to all who hear this dismal Story, to avoid the like Crimes. The distracted *Alonzo* having thus discharg'd his Fury, thought of his own Safety; and taking some Gold and his Wife's Jewels out of a Cabinet in that Room, descended the Ladder, and attended by his Page, went out of another Gate than that by which his Rival had enter'd; and mounting his Horse, which he had left there with his Page, they rid away as swift as possible to a Place twenty Miles farther, where he took shelter in a Convent of *Benedictine* Monks.[2] Don *Duante*'s Gentleman finding his Master staid longer than usual, grew uneasy, and quitting his Horse ventur'd up the Ladder, thinking he might be asleep; but entering the Room, he was fill'd with such Horror and Amazement, that he alarm'd all the Servants with the Out-crys he made. The poor Lady was not dead; she was such an Object as would have excited Compassion in the Heart of a Barbarian. It was easy to guess the cause of all these dreadful Deeds, had the Gentleman not reveal'd them by his Lamentations over his dead Lord; but he conceal'd nothing in his Passion, but too well explain'd the Lady's Crime and his Master's.

Not to detain you longer on so sad a Subject, a Surgeon being fetch'd, the poor Lady was put into bed, and her Face dress'd; but there being little appearance of her Recovery, which indeed would have been a greater Misfortune to her than Death, her Confessor was sent for, who pray'd for her, and gave her all the spiritual Comfort he was able; and tho she could not speak, yet

---

eleven times in London in the decade leading up to the publication of *Charlotta Du Pont*. Shakespeare's version was known only through reading.

1 Imposed those misfortunes on their heirs or descendents.

2 In some Catholic countries, including Spain, fugitives could seek sanctuary in churches and monasteries and be immune to arrest as long as they remained on the premises.

by Signs she testify'd her Repentance. He staid with her many hours, till finding the anguish of her Wounds and loss of Blood took away her Senses by a strong Fever, he left her to the Care of her Servants, and assisted Don *Duante*'s Gentleman to remove his Master's Body into a Herse the Servants had brought to carry him to his own House at *Madrid*. Then he return'd to the Lady, to whom he administer'd the last Rites of the Church, and about four in the Morning she expired.

I need not tell you how enrag'd my Father, and all our Family, was against the cruel *Alonzo*, when this Story was known; nor were Don *Duante*'s Friends less afflicted: but *Alonzo*'s Family did all that was possible to obtain his Pardon of the King, pleading the enormity of her Crime, and the justice of his Procedure; and that he could do no less than sacrifice both her and her Paramour to repair his Honour; that the Injury was unpardonable in both; that the Cruelty he had exercis'd on his Lady was excusable, considering the greatness of the Provocation. In fine, they said all they could in his defence, whilst her Family and Don *Duante*'s us'd all their Interest against him, and were so potent, that tho the King was inclin'd to forgive and only banish him, yet he defer'd to declare himself, and so gave him time to get off[1] with much Wealth, having sold off secretly and made Conveyances[2] of his Estate, before a Process[3] could be got out against him: however, he was sued and condemn'd, when he was got out of the reach of the Laws. My Grandmother broke her Heart for her unfortunate Daughter. *Elvira*'s Father and Family, and mine, tho they join'd in prosecuting Don *Alonzo*, yet conceiv'd a mortal Aversion to one another, and much Blood was spilt on both sides by Duels and Rencounters;[4] so that some few Years after the King honour'd her Father with this great Post in the *Indies*, to prevent a farther effusion of Blood, and Quarrels. I was too young at this fatal juncture, when these Misfortunes happen'd; but *Elvira* and I growing older, my Soul was charm'd with her Beauty; and tho I could foresee no hopes of ever gaining her's or her Father's Consent, yet I could not forbear loving, or desist from pursuing her: my Quality and Fortune made way, and having nothing to urge against me but a Family-difference, the charming *Elvira* consulting Reason and

---

1 Escape.
2 Legal transfers of property.
3 Lawsuit.
4 Spontaneous duels (as opposed to those that have been arranged in advance).

Religion, saw the Folly and Injustice of that Procedure, and gave ear to my Persuasions: At last she generously confess'd a Passion for me, and promis'd to be mine provided I could gain her Father's Consent. Then I apply'd to my Father, who acquainting the King with our mutual Affection, and pleading that this was the only way to reconcile the two Familys, and put an end to that fatal Strife that had been of such ill consequence to both, prevail'd with his Majesty to propose it to *Elvira's* Father; but he delaying to give a positive Answer, having before obtain'd the Viceroyship, went off without it, and so oblig'd me to follow him. I obtain'd a Letter from the King, in which he even commanded him to give me *Elvira*, and let our Marriage be forthwith consummated: my Family and hers all join'd in this, and I departed *Spain* with a whole Packet full of Letters to this effect. I was certain of not being refus'd now, since he did not dare to disoblige or disobey the King. I arriv'd safely at *Mexico*, and was well receiv'd according to my expectation, and soon after marry'd to my dear *Elvira*: and now being completely happy, we study'd how to divert our selves, and take all the innocent Diversions the Land and Sea afforded; and being at a Pleasure-house of the Governor's on the Lake, we went a-board a Yatch[1] one Evening to take the Air on the Sea, it being fine weather, and resolv'd to spend the Night in Mirth and Pleasure. We had several Ladys and Gentlemen with us, with Music. We supp'd, danc'd, and were very merry; but about Midnight a terrible Storm blew, and after having been toss'd about many Days and Nights, not knowing where we were, we were driven upon a Bank of Sand near this Shore. Here we lay bulging[2] till such time as the Yatch was torn to pieces, and then every one shifted for himself: *Elvira* and our Friends were got into the Boat, I plac'd my self next to her, resolving to bear her to shore, if possible, on my Back, in case the Boat should not hold out the Storm to the Shore, as it happen'd, for it was soon swallow'd up in the Waves: I catch'd fast hold of her, bidding her throw her Arms about my Neck; and it being now Day, I made for the Shore which I saw before me; but my Strength being almost spent before I could reach it, just as I felt the Land under my Feet I fainted; she laying hold of me, pull'd me up and sav'd me. *Philena*[3] having got hold of a Plank that was floating, being part of the Ship, to which she clung very fast, was by the Providence of God sav'd;

---

1  Yacht.
2  Leaking below the waterline.
3  Presumably Elvira's Native servant or enslaved person, previously referred to as Philinda.

and the Wind blowing directly to the Shore, she was thrown upon the Sands before us, and seeing my Distress and *Elvira*'s, ran to her assistance, who had otherwise doubtless perish'd with me. They drag'd me on shore out of the reach of the Waves, which would have wash'd us away; and there the good Father came to our Relief. Thus the Divine Providence has preserv'd our Lives and yours in a miraculous manner, and will, I hope, furnish us with means to return to our homes in health and safety."

Thus Don *Gomez de Mendoza* ended his Relation, and they pass'd a few Days as agreeably as the dismalness of their Abode would permit, the Monk visiting them every Day, when the Savages were gone a fishing. One Evening the Monk returning home, saw some white Men, who appear'd to be *Europeans* by their Habit, sitting round a Fire boiling a Pot on the Shore; their Fire-Arms being Muskets, lay by them. He saw that a Pinnace[1] lay on the Shore, and discern'd a Ship lying at Anchor about half a League off: he made Signs to them to permit him to come near; they answer'd, and he hasted to them, and found they were come from the Island of St. *Christopher*'s,[2] and bound to *Spain*: He told them of the *Spaniards* that he had sav'd, and prevail'd with them to take them on board their Ship; so he went and call'd them, and they were overjoy'd to get thence, and meet with such a lucky opportunity; and the Monk thank'd God that he was rid of them, being uneasy whilst they were on that Shore, lest they should discover his conceal'd Friends whom he dearly esteem'd, but these he abhor'd, as being Villains. They went away that Night, returning many thanks to him, and seeming very sorry that *Belanger* was not still alive to go with them; but hoping in themselves, as it afterwards prov'd, that when they got to the Island of St. *Domingo*, the revengeful Governor would reward them highly, designing to tell him that they had dispos'd of him in the Woods, where he had been devour'd by the wild Beasts. The glad Monk carry'd the good News of their departure to his Friends the next Morning. And now they consulted about getting to *Carthagena*; by Land it was very dangerous, and by Sea very difficult; for they had the Savages to fear as they travel'd, and dreadful Mountains and Woods to pass thro; and no Boat of strength sufficient to carry them and Provisions enough for a Voyage of so many Days at Sea; and what was worse, no Pilot to guide the Vessel, if they had had one. In fine, they knew not what course to take: at last they resolv'd to venture to cross

---

1  Boat used to assist a ship (e.g., to ferry people to shore).
2  St. Kitts: island in the eastern Caribbean, then an English colony.

the great River *Oroonoko* in the Savages' Fishing-boat. This being resolv'd, trusting on Providence, they prepar'd to go; but the Night before they were to depart, they saw a Man running down the adjacent Hill, pursu'd by a fierce Tyger: He had a drawn Sword in his Hand, and a strange-fashion'd Coat made of Beasts' Skins: he had no Shoes or Stockings, but pieces of Bears' Skins ty'd about his Legs with Twigs; his Head had a strange Fur Cap on; his Face they could scarce distinguish, till coming into the Wood, he climb'd up a Tree, and the Beast pursuing him to the Foot of it, *Belanger*, who had fetch'd a Gun, shot it dead, having perceiv'd the Man was a White, and his Countenance no *Indian*. No sooner was the Beast kill'd, but the Man leap'd down from the Tree, and ran to embrace his Benefactor, whose Surprize cannot be exprest when he saw his Face, and heard him call him by his Name, and knew it was the honest Captain of the Ship who liv'd at *Virginia*, and had carry'd him and his Friend *Montandre* to the Island of St. *Domingo*. *Elvira* and the brave *Gomez*, who were retired at the Stranger's approach, hearing them talk, came forth, and invited him in, being together in the Hermitage,[1] for that was properly the name of their Cell: they ask'd him to eat, a Favour he gladly accepted of; *Philena* set what Provisions they had before him, as cold Fowl, Goat's Milk, Bread, dry'd Grapes, and Water, and Wine made of their Juice; a noble Feast to a Man who had liv'd for above five Weeks on Roots and Fruits, such as the Woods produced, and had not tasted any dress'd Food, neither Bread, Meat nor Fish. Being much refresh'd, he related to them the manner of his coming thither.

"I was going on a Voyage for some Merchants," said he, "to *Barbadoes* about six Weeks ago, my Ship being heavy laden with Goods for that Place, at which I was to unload, and take in others for other Islands: I had a fair Gale of Wind and good Voyage, till I came near the *Summer-Islands*; then a Storm arose and drove the Ship up this River, where it was dash'd to pieces against some Rocks, amongst some unknown, and I suppose uninhabited Islands. I had but eight Men and a Boy aboard, two of whom were blown off the Shrouds[2] into the Sea: those that were left got out the Boat, and we quitted the shatter'd Vessel, which was full of Water above the first Deck,[3] and committed our selves to the

---

1  The dwelling of a hermit.
2  Lines connecting the hull of a ship to the top of its masts, typically made in the form of rope ladders so that sailors could climb up and adjust the sails.
3  Lowest deck.

Mercy of God. The Night was dark as Pitch, and we knew not which way to steer. At last the Boat, unable to hold out against the dreadful Waves that bore her up to the Skys one moment, and then opening, seem'd to sink her into the bottomless Deep, the Wreck being fill'd with Water by a great Sea that wash'd over her, sunk; and then we gave our selves over for lost, and were all separated, never to meet again in this World, I fear. Nature taught me, tho hopeless, to struggle for Life; and it being just break of Day, I discern'd the Shore, and made for it; the Wind sitting fair,[1] help'd me greatly. At last I reach'd it half dead, and sitting down on the side of a Rock to recover my self, look'd round to see where I was, and soon found that I was cast on this inhospitable Shore, where I must expect to be devour'd either by Men or Beasts; this made me almost repent that I had escap'd drowning. I had no Arms nor Food, and my Soul being full of horrible Apprehensions of the Cannibal-Savages, I sought for a Place to hide my self in, and looking about, crept into a Hole in a great Rock, not far from that on which I sat down; and being quite spent with the Fatigue of the past Night, I fell into a profound Sleep, out of which I was awaken'd some Hours after by two Savages, who were stripping me, and had already got my Shoes and Stockings; but going to pull off my Coat and Wastecoat, which they could not do without lifting me up, I awaked, and looking up, caught one of them by the Throat; and wrenching this Sword out of his Hand, he broke from me, carrying away my Clothes, which he held so fast that he tore my Coat and Wastecoat off as he broke from me, and they both fled with incredible Celerity.[2] I was now left almost naked, and fearing they would return with more Savages, and fall upon me, I fled up into the Woods, not knowing where else to hide my self, but amongst the Trees and Bushes. And now being ready to faint with Hunger, I search'd about for wild Fruits and Roots, and eat whatever I could find, which, alas! instead of satisfying my hungry Stomach, made me sick. I sat in a Tree all that Night, and the next Day, so soon as it was light, crept down to the Shore, to see if I could espy[3] a Boat, or any of my Sailors who might have escap'd like me to the Shore; and there, to my great surprize, I saw my Boat lying on the Sands, and was transported to find her there, thinking I might get off with her the next Tide, and reach some of our Islands.[4] So soon

---

1  Blowing in the right direction.
2  Speed.
3  Catch sight of.
4  Caribbean islands that were British colonies.

as the Water flow'd,[1] and the Sea coming in, set her afloat; I ran down, and leaping into her, steer'd her by the Rudder along the Shore, but found I was not able to govern her at Sea: I wanted Strength and more Hands, had neither Oars nor Sail, yet I fear'd to lose her; and finding I could not venture out with her, I resolv'd, if possible, to secure her in some Place where the Savages should not find her, in hopes that I might meet with some Christians here whom Chance had brought, like me, to this barbarous Land, who would be glad to escape hence, and assist me to get away in her. I brought the Boat accordingly along the Shore, till I came to a kind of a Creek, so cover'd with Trees, that it was almost impossible to perceive any thing that lay there. I brought her into this Creek, at the end of which was a very thick Wood; and having hal'd[2] her on shore, broke down a great many of the green Branches of the Trees, and made a kind of Bower over it, so that it lies quite cover'd, and I have lain aboard it every Night since: I have every Day rang'd about for Food, and liv'd chiefly on the Eggs of the Sea-Fowl and Turtles, which I found in the Rocks and on the Sands; nor did I dare to attempt to make a Fire to dress any thing, for fear of discovery; so I sustain'd Life by sucking them, and eating Turtle raw, laying the Flesh in the Sun till it was thorow hot, and then I eat it as savorily as if it had been the greatest Dainty in the World. I knew not what to do for Clothes; but one Day finding two Bear's Cubs in a Wood, I kill'd and flea'd[3] them, hanging their Skins on the Hedges to dry; these I made into the strange fashion'd Coat I have on: I kill'd some young Goats also, and eating the Flesh, made me a Cap and Spatterdashes,[4] as you see.

But I must now acquaint you with the most surprizing Accident that ever befel any Man living. One Morning roaming about a Wood, I met with a young Woman fair as *Venus*, but pale as Death; she was wrap'd in a piece of Sailcloth, having nothing under but a fine Holland Shift, a white Dimity-Petticoat and Waistcoat, and no Headclothes, but her Hair, which was the finest light brown, hung in Curls down to her Waist; but all this was hid under her Canvas-wrapper; she seem'd half famish'd, and was so surpriz'd at the Sight of me, supposing me a Savage, that she ran away from me as fast as she was able. I follow'd her till she ran into a Cave,

---

1  The tide rose.

2  Hauled.

3  Flayed: skinned.

4  Coverings for ankles and calves, traditionally used to keep one's stockings clean while riding.

into which I enter'd, and getting hold of her, spoke in *English*, asking her who she was, and of what Nation. She seem'd surpriz'd to the last degree, and said, 'pray do not kill or be rude with me; I am a poor unfortunate Maid,' said she, 'who by cruel Guardians was trepan'd and sent away for[1] *Jamaica*; but our Ship being drove on this Coast, was lost, and I with one young Man, who was the Captain's Kinsman, were sav'd on this unhappy Coast; here we liv'd together for three Days, but the fourth, going out of the Cave as usual to seek for Food, he never return'd, and is, I fear, murder'd. I have liv'd in this dismal Place two Months all alone under the most dreadful Apprehensions imaginable, almost famish'd, and pinch'd with Cold and Damps, not daring to go far from my Cave for fear of meeting the Savages.' I was charm'd with her Face, and pierced to the Soul with her Condition. I told her my Story, and beg'd her to go along with me, and live in the Boat, promising to protect her with my Life, and provide her with such Food as I could get; nay more, that I would offer no rudeness to her. She with some difficulty yielded to my Request; so I conducted her to my Bower, and we have liv'd together three Weeks. I left her there about two Hours since, when going out for Food, I met with the ravenous Beast you kill'd, and fear'd to retreat towards my Boat lest he should follow and fright her, or having got the scent of Food, some Bones and remains of Turtle which we could not eat, being scatter'd up and down, surprize her in my Absence; for these Reasons I drove him over the Hill, led by the Providence of God doubtless to this Place. And now with your leave, I will haste and fetch my dear *Lucy*, whom I have promis'd to make my Wife, so soon as I reach a Christian Shore. She is in pain for my return, I am certain." "You shall make your Promise good to her," said *Belanger*, "to-morrow Morning; we have here a worthy Christian Priest who shall marry you; and since you have a Boat able to carry us all, he shall furnish us with Provisions sufficient for a Voyage to one of the Summer-Islands, from whence we may get a Ship to carry us to *Virginia*, and thence to what other place we think fit." The Captain hasted to fetch the Lady, who in less than an Hour reach'd the Hermitage, and was joyfully receiv'd by *Belanger*, *Gomez*, and *Elvira*, who never saw such a Figure as she appear'd wrap'd in her Canvas-shroud, for such it seem'd, a Habit which very ill suited her beautiful Face and charming Mien. After eating together with thankful Hearts, as much transported at this Meeting, as if they had forgot their Misfortunes, they laid

---

1 To.

them down to sleep on Straw, having recommended themselves to God; and rested sweetly, having no load of Guilt upon their Consciences, but Minds resign'd to the supreme Disposer of all things. Next Morning the Monk visited them, and was entertain'd with the History of these new Guests, whom he immediately marry'd, saying, "My Children, it is not fit that you should live in sin; and since the Necessity of your Condition obliged you to live together, and a too near intimacy has I find ensu'd, it is fit that you should be join'd by the holy Bands of Matrimony, that none amongst us may incur God's Anger, but that Blessings may attend us." And now they thought of nothing but preparing for their Departure from this Place. The Monk inform'd the honest Savages, whom he offer'd to take along with them, and they executed his Commands with such Alacrity, that he was surpriz'd. In three Days they got out the Boat and victual'd her, carrying aboard boil'd Fowls, salted Fish, and store of Bread, with fresh Water in Jars. The Savage and his Son made Oars, well understanding the management of a Boat, and fasten'd their own Fisher-boat to her loaded with Provisions; they were perfectly skill'd in all the Turnings and Rocks in this great River, knowing every Island and Bank of Sand; but when out at Sea, the *Virginia* Captain must direct them. All things being ready, our joyful Christians went on board, and the three Women and Children lay down in the Boat, being cover'd over with some Boughs of Trees; the Monk, *Belanger*, the Captain, and Savages row'd and steer'd the Boat, having made Sails of what the poor Savages procured; they pass'd safely out of the River, and being at Sea, steer'd for *Barbadoes*, which they reach'd in few Days, having a fair Wind and fine Weather: they were well receiv'd by a Merchant there, who was the Captain's Friend, and soon got a Passage to *Virginia*; *Gomez* and *Elvira*, with their Maid *Philena*, going with them, because they could get no Ship to carry them to *Mexico* by reason of the War. When they arriv'd at *Virginia*, *Belanger* had the agreeable News that *Montander* had in his absence sent a Bark with Letters for him from himself and *Charlotta*, to acquaint him that the Governor was dead, and that they design'd to sell off all their Effects in the Island of *St. Domingo*, and come for *Virginia*, leaving only *Charlotta*'s two Children behind, whom her Husband's Friends[1] would not part with. He was so transported with this News, that he could hardly be persuaded to wait her coming, but would fain have gone to fetch her. But four Days after his arrival,

1  Extended family.

she and *Teresa*, with his faithful Friend *Montander*, arriv'd with an immense Treasure. Never was a more moving sight than the meeting of these three Persons; *Belanger*, clasping *Charlotta* in his Arms, stood motionless, as if he meant to die in that Posture, and that his ravish'd Soul would make its way out of his panting Bosom into hers; his Eyes seem'd fix'd on her Face, the big Drops escaping them, whilst fiery Love sparkled in his Eye-balls, as if the raging Flame within sent forth those chrystal Drops: she hung upon his Neck, and cry'd, "Do I live, and again see *Belanger!* Blest God, it is enough." Mean time *Montander* wak'd them from this blissful Dream, saying, "My Friend, my Kinsman, have you forgot me? And must I not claim a second Embrace after *Charlotta* has receiv'd your first?" At these Words *Belanger* turn'd, and catch'd him in his Arms, saying, "My dearest Friend, next *Charlotta* you are dear to me: the Obligations I have to you, are so great, that words cannot express the grateful Sense I have of them, nor my whole Life suffice to make returns to you and her, tho wholly employ'd in your Service." Old *Montandre* and his Lady interrupted them, or doubtless they had never known when to leave off this tender Conversation. *Belanger* was so impatient to secure his Happiness, that he never gave over importuning *Charlotta* till she consented to marry him that very Night; and the Monk accordingly wedded them, and they were mutually pleas'd: For what greater Satisfaction can Mortals attain in this Life, than to possess the Person they ardently love, especially when they have so long languish'd for one another, and been so long separated? this is a Pleasure none but Lovers can have a true Notion of. Eternal Bliss is comprehended in this one thing, *viz.*[1] to possess all we desire, or is worthy our Affection; and whilst we are mortal, and on this side the Grave, nothing can equal the Pleasure of possessing the Person we love. *Gomez* and *Elvira* were sharers of their Friends' good Fortune, and were desirous to continue with them some Months, with the Monk, who resolv'd to go with *Belanger* and *Charlotta* to *France*, they offering to provide for him so long as he pleased to stay there.

During their Residence at *Virginia*, they past the time very agreeably together: old *Montandre* and his Lady, who still retain'd an Affection for *Belanger*, entertain'd them very nobly; and *Charlotta*, who was now a sincere Roman Catholick, prevail'd with the Monk to be her Chaplain, and to promise to continue with her the rest of his Days: they took all the Diversions the Place

---

1 Abbreviation of Latin *videlicet*: namely.

afforded, walking, riding, dancing, and feasting. One Evening *Charlotta* intreated the Monk to relate the Adventures of his Life: "certainly," said she, "they must be very extraordinary, since you have pass'd thro so many Countries." He smiling, answer'd, "Yes, Madam, I have met with many strange Accidents, and am ready to oblige you and the Company with the Relation of them; nay, I will own my Weaknesses, and give you the Story of my youthful Follies." They all sat down under the Shade of some Trees on the Banks of a little Rivulet by which they were walking; and being all silent, he began his Narrative thus.

## CHAP. XXI.

"I was born in *Valladolid* in *Spain*, my Father was a Grandee of a noble Family, but having been refus'd a Post at Court, to which he believ'd himself to have a Right, he too freely spoke his Thoughts, and gave his Enemies an opportunity to traduce[1] him to the King, whose Favour he lost, and so retir'd in discontent to his own Seat at *Valladolid*. I was all the Children he had, and design'd to be the Heir of his Honours and Fortune. I was a Student at a College about sixteen, when it was my Misfortune to see a Farmer's Daughter, whose Beauty made me her Captive. I stole out alone into the Fields behind her Father's House every Evening for a Month together before I spoke to her, and there saw her playing with the Lambs, and feeding the young Goats; her plain Dress and innocent Behaviour, made her look more charming in my Eyes than Gold and Diamonds; her Beauty and Modesty were irresistible, and I lov'd her to distraction: In fine, I spoke to her, told her my Passion, and found her Wit and Apprehension exceeded her Face and Years. I succeeded according to my Wishes, gain'd her Love, and resolv'd to marry her; but being not old enough to be master of my self, and having no Fortune in my own Power, I was forc'd to defer doing it till I was of Age, and had got some Settlement in the World: for these Reasons I pursu'd my Studies with great Application, resolving to be a Physician or Lawyer, that I might soon be able to provide for my self; in the mean time I promis'd my dear *Leonora* to maintain her as my Wife, and accordingly paid her Father the half of the Pension my Father allow'd me for her Board; bought her silk Petticoats, Ribbons and Laces; so that I half starv'd my self, and grew very penurious in

---

1 Slander.

my own Expences to provide for her: and she soon grew to be so fine, and so like a Lady in her Air and Behaviour, that the Farmers' Daughters, and other Country Maids envied her, talk'd loudly of this strange Alteration; which, with my continual Visits at her Father's, tho I thought none observ'd me, confirm'd their suspicions of her being a Mistress to me. This Report soon reach'd the Principal of the College's Ear, and he had me watch'd, and sent my Father word, who immediately sent for me home, and school'd me sharply, commanding me to declare the Truth; on which I ingenuously[1] confess'd my Ingagements with *Leonora*, and declar'd boldly, that I would marry her or die. This so inrag'd my Father, to see his ambitious hopes thus cross'd in me also, that he proceeded to Threats; in short, he was very severe with me, put me into the hands of a rigid Tutor, who kept me as a Prisoner ever in his Sight. I was now eighteen, and fancy'd my self a Man sufficient to manage my self. *Leonora*'s Father was threatned, and turn'd out of his Farm and Livelihood by my Father's Instigation, who was a true *Spaniard* in his Resentments. Poor *Leonora*, who was now look'd on as the Ruin of her Family, was drove to Despair; she sent many Letters to me, but none came to my hands; my Father intercepted them all. She, and her poor Father and Mother were retir'd to a Village twenty Miles further, and had there got into a little Farm where they could just get bread. I fell sick with the distraction of my Mind, and was like to die; but Youth and Medicines recover'd me, or rather the Providence of God, which reserv'd me for other Uses. So soon as I was able to creep abroad, I went into the Fields with my cruel Tutor, and resolv'd to try to make my Escape, let the Consequence be what it would; but knowing that without Money I should be no ways helpful to *Leonora*, or be able to travel far without Discovery, I consulted what Course to take, and at last concluded to rob my cruel ambitious Father, whose strong Box[2] was never without a good Sum of Gold in it; it stood in a Closet in his Chamber, and it was impossible for me to get at it but by going in at the Window from the Garden. I revolv'd in my Mind many days what to do, before I could find what Course to take; at last I thought of an expedient, which was this: My Tutor lay with me,[3] I ply'd him with Wine at Supper, so I rose in the Night when he was fast asleep, clap'd a

---

1 Frankly.
2 Safe.
3 It was not unheard of for tutors to share a bed with their pupils, either to economize or to keep an eye on them.

Gag in his Mouth, ty'd his Hands and Feet with my Garters,[1] tho
not without much struggling and some Noise; for tho I had made
all ready before I went to bed, and fastned his Hands to the Bed-
post before he stir'd, yet when I went to tie his Feet, he wak'd, and
opening his Mouth to speak, I clap'd the Gag, which was a piece
of hard Wood, between his Teeth, stretching his Jaws sufficiently,
yet he roar'd strangely, till I threaten'd to kill him with my Pen-
knife, which silenc'd him, for he was a great Coward: then I got
down from my Chamber-Window by a Vine that grew against the
Wall; and finding a Ladder which the Gardiner always left in a
Green-house, the Door of which I broke open, I set it against my
Father's Closet-Window, and went in, taking the strong Box,
which was not above two foot and a half Square, but very heavy. I
hasted down with it, and set the Ladder against the Garden-Wall,
which I got over, and stood some Minutes consulting which way
to go; and consider'd that if I was taken, my Father would not hurt
me farther than to chide and lock me up: I was but weak, and
could not go far, so I made towards a River, where there us'd to be
a Ferry-Boat constantly, thinking to offer the old Ferryman, who
knew me, a piece of Gold if he would carry me over, and convey
my Box for me to some Town where I might get a Disguise, and a
Horse to carry me to *Leonora*'s Father's, whose removal to the
poor Village I knew nothing of. It was about two a Clock in the
Morning when I left my Father's, and a very light Moon-shine
Night, nor was it above three Miles to the Ferry; but I was so
weak, and the Box so heavy, that I was three Hours before I
reach'd it. I found the old Man just launching his Boat; he lift up
his Hands at the sight of me, I knew it was in vain to dissemble
with him, so told him my Story: the good old Man's Heart melted
with my sad Tale, he condemn'd my Father, pity'd me, and offer'd
to serve me faithfully on my Promise not to let my Father ever
know of it: and I have made it my observation, that there is more
Compassion and true Friendship amongst the Vulgar" (said the
good Father) "than amongst the Great; for they are so engag'd in
their own private Interests and Designs, and so much at Ease, and
unacquainted with Misfortunes, that they have very little Sense of
other People's, and forget that they may at one time or other stand
in need of a Friend themselves; whereas the meaner People, who
are sensible of the Miseries of a low Condition, and daily meet
with Disappointments, have a great deal of Compassion, and

---

1 Bands of cloth fastened around the leg, either above or just below the
knee, to keep stockings up in an age before elastic.

readily assist others. This good old Man wept at my Story, carry'd me over, and leaving his Boat in his Son's care, went with me to a Fisherman's Cottage, where he dress'd me in old Boots, the Man's old Coat, thrum Cap[1] and worsted[2] Mittins like a poor Fisher-boy; then he ingag'd the Man[3] to go along with me wherever I pleas'd, fearing his going with me himself would discover me: and now being to pay him, I knew not how to open the Box, and had no Money about me; besides, carrying the Box was the ready way to betray me. I therefore resolv'd to break it open, and empty it, and throw it into the River, which I accordingly did, and was greatly surpriz'd to find two thousand Pistoles, and many gold and silver Pieces of foreign Coin and Medals in it, besides all my dead Mother's Jewels, with her Picture[4] set round with brilliant Diamonds, and the chief Deeds of my Father's Estate; in fine, enough to make *Leonora* and me completely happy in an humble Retreat. I paid my old Ferry-man to his content, dispos'd of the Money and other things about me, sewing the Jewels and Writings[5] into my Clothes, and posted away with my Guide to the Town where I had left *Leonora*; there I was inform'd of what had befall'n her Father, and where they were gone to live. I hasted thither, and discharg'd my Guide before I went to the House, sending him back with the Horses he had hir'd to bring us; and then enter'd the poor Cottage where she was, in so great a Transport of Joy, that running to her as she was sitting in a Chair at work,[6] I fell down in a Swoon at her Feet; she had not time to know me before I fell, but yet did not fly from me, but lifting up my Head to help me, saw my Face, and giving a great Shriek, fainted; her Mother com-ing in at the Door, saw us both lying on the Floor, and crying out, wak'd me from my Trance: I rose and embrac'd her and my reviv-ing Mistress; I told them in few words how I got from my Father's, and what I had brought; that my design was never to leave *Leonora* any more, but to live and die with her. And now the good Man[7] being call'd, we all rejoyc'd at our happy meeting, and consulted what was next to be done; it was altogether improper for me to stay there but a Day, for there my Father would be sure to look for

---

1 Made from scraps left over from weaving.
2 Knit.
3 His servant.
4 Miniature portrait, usually oval.
5 Legal documents (here the deeds).
6 Sewing.
7 Male head of a household (here Leonora's father).

me, and where else to go or how to part with *Leonora* on any account, I could not resolve; at last the good Man proposed to me to go to a Benedictine Monk who was his Confessor; and trust him with the whole Affair; and ask his Advice and Assistance; he was a Man of singular Integrity and vast Experience, a Person of noble Birth and great Years. I consented to this Proposal, we went to him, he receiv'd us kindly in his Cell; and after giving me some gentle Reprehensions for my Undutifulness to my Father, finding me resolute, and determin'd to marry *Leonora*; and fearing, I suppose, that if he refus'd to do that Office for us, we might live together in a sinful State, he at last consented to my desires, and promis'd to serve us in all he was able. He sent me to a Widow-Lady's House five Miles thence near *Soria*,[1] who was his Aunt, and sent *Leonora*'s Father to fetch her thither also; in the Evening he came to us, and that Night I was made Possessor of that lovely virtuous Maid, whom I at his request suffer'd to return home with her Father the next Morning, on condition that she should return to me at Night: this we did with design that if my Father sent, they should find her there, which would induce them to believe that I was not yet arriv'd, and would divert their pursuit of me for some days, and give us time to get over the *Pyrenean* Mountains[2] into *France*, whither we were resolv'd to retire. All things succeeded as we expected; about Noon Officers came to search my Father-in-law's House, examin'd him and *Leonora*, her Mother, and their Man and Maid,[3] who all pretended Ignorance; and finding they could get no satisfaction or intelligence where I was, they went away. This *Leonora* gave me an account of at Night. Father *Dominic*, the good Benedictine, provided us Horses and a Guide for the next Morning, and gave me Letters of Recommendation to several Priests and Persons of Quality in *Gascoigne*,[4] advising me to settle at or near *Bearn*.[5] My dear *Leonora* and I, returning a thousand thanks to him and the Lady, took leave; I presented the Father with twenty Pistoles as a Present for his Convent, gave three amongst the Lady's Servants; and being both dress'd in Men's Clothes like Servants in Livery-Coats, being some of the Lady's Servants' Clothes, we departed. I had given *Leonora*'s Father a hundred Pistoles, and agreed that he and her Mother

---

1 City in northern Spain.
2 The Pyrenees form a natural boundary between France and Spain.
3 Male and female servants.
4 Province in southwestern France.
5 French province on the south edge of Gascony.

should come to us so soon as *Leonora* and I had taken a House, and were settled; we had very fine Weather and a safe Journey, tho much fatigu'd in passing the *Pyrenean* Mountains: and having presented my Letters to the Persons to whom they were directed, I was received by them with such Civility, and so treated, that I was amaz'd, and no ways repented my leaving *Spain*: The Gentry and Clergy seem'd to vie who should be kindest to us; the Ladys courted and treated *Leonora* so highly, that she soon became as free and unaffected as they were, and so improv'd, that I thought her every Day more charming. So soon as we arriv'd in *France*, I sent back our Guide and Horses, with Letters to the good old Father, the Lady, and my Father and Mother-in-law; on the receit of which, Father *Dominic* writ to my own Father, acquainting him that I was marry'd to *Leonora*, and gone out of the Kingdom, that I was extremely sorry he had constrain'd me to leave him in such a manner, and was willing to return to him, if he would forgive me, and receive my Wife into favour; in fine, he urg'd all he could think of to reconcile us, and receiv'd an answer, by which he found my Father was implacable, and so incens'd against me, that it was in vain to hope for any accommodation between us, at least for some time. My Father and Mother-in-law came to us, and having taken a pretty House and some Lands, he manag'd our little Estate, and my Wife and I kept the best Company in the Province, and liv'd at ease; it did not please God to bless our Marriage with any Children, but every thing else prosper'd with us. I writ often to Father *Dominic*, sending him Presents of what I thought might be acceptable, particularly Wine, of which I had enough, having now bought a little Vineyard: He sent to my Father to let him know that I was well, and long'd to visit him, but for seven whole Years could never perceive by his Answers that his Displeasure was abated. All this while he never acquainted him where I was; at last my Father falling sick, relented, and sent to him to send for me, and that I should bring my Wife along with me. I no sooner receiv'd this joyful News, but I made ready to go to him; and leaving all to the Care of my honest Father-in-law, my Wife and I, attended by two Servants, set out for *Valladolid*, where we soon arriv'd, and were receiv'd by my Father with much Tenderness. But alas, my oversight had drawn him into another; during my absence, he had taken a young handsome Kinswoman into the House and debauch'd her; this was a Secret could not be long hid from me: she was saucy and insolent to my Wife, which I resented, and desir'd my Father's leave to return to *France*; he desir'd me not to leave him any more, and would know the Cause of my

Disgust, and who had offended me: at last I modestly told him, our pert Kinswoman took too much upon her; he colour'd, and said it should be remedy'd; but, as I afterward discover'd, he had two Sons by her, and knew not how to get rid of her: this made her insolent, and finding I had made my Complaint to my Father of her, she was fir'd with Revenge, and resolv'd to destroy my Wife, who was now to my inexpressible Joy with Child; she disguis'd her Thoughts, seem'd sorry for what she had done, and so behav'd her self, that *Leonora*, who was all Goodness, forgot what was past, and grew kind to her; but the Viper ill return'd it: for drinking Chocolate one Morning together, she put Poison into my dear *Leonora*'s Cup, of which she languish'd about a Month, and then dy'd; the Physicians were of opinion that she was poison'd, and when she was dead, I had her open'd,[1] and was too well convinc'd of it: My Affliction was so great, that I was inconsolable. I suspected my Father, and could not believe his Strumpet dar'd to have committed such a Deed without his knowledge and consent. I seiz'd her, and had her examin'd before a Magistrate, but she deny'd all, and I had no proof of the Fact; so I took leave of my Father, having had some sharp words with him, and return'd to *France* the most disconsolate Man living. And now I had time to reflect on all the Actions of my past Life, and too late became sensible that my Disobedience to my Father first drew God's Anger upon me, who had accordingly punish'd me in bereaving me of her who had been the occasion of my Sin, and was in some kind culpable her self, tho more excusable than I, yet had paid her Life for her Fault; that my Father, who had been too severe, and ought to have had more indulgence for my Youth, and less Ambition, was punish'd by the divine Justice in being permitted to become a Slave in his Age to a vile Passion, no ways just or honourable like mine, and blasted his Fame. These Considerations inclin'd me to quit the World, and dedicate the remainder of my Life to God, being then but twenty nine Years old. I accordingly settled my Affairs in *France*, leaving my Father and Mother-in-law in possession of my Estate there, taking only for my own support a thousand Pistoles and my Mother's Jewels, which I had still reserv'd, and order'd my Estate to go to a Convent in the Town where it lay near, after their decease; and taking my Mother's Picture, and the Writings I took from my Father, set out for the Benedictine Convent where Father *Dominic* lived. I acquainted him with my design, he approv'd of it, and then I waited on my Father to obtain

---

1 Autopsied.

his leave and blessing. There I found the wicked *Isabella*, my Father's Mistress, had been her own Executioner, having gone distracted with the remorse of her Conscience, and so had cut her own Throat, having in her Madness discover'd all the Circumstances of the Murder she had committed on *Leonora*. My Father was so struck with the manner of her Death, and Shame, his Crime with her being now made publick, that he seldom went out of his Chamber. Our meeting was at this time very different from our parting; I fell at his Feet with the greatest submission, and with Tears beg'd Pardon for the Follies I had committed in my Youth; he wept over me, and lifting me up, embraced me, unable to utter one Word: then his Countenance express'd the Confusion of his Thoughts; he blush'd at his own Weakness, and could not look me in the Face: at last he said, 'My Son, we have both offended God, but I more grievously; God pardon me, as I do you.' A tender Conversation ensu'd, and we pass'd some Days together in pious Discourses, I hope much to our Advantage. I beg'd him to make some Provision for the two unfortunate Children he had had by this ill Woman, and settle his Affairs, as I had mine; he told me he would be wholly directed by me. In few days he fell sick, and continu'd ill for six Months: having in that time settled his Affairs, by my desire the Estate was given to his Nephew, a worthy young Gentleman, with several Legacies to his poor Relations and the Church; he expir'd in my Arms with great Piety and Resignation; I bury'd him nobly,[1] and then retir'd to the Convent, where I liv'd many Years, being receiv'd into that Fraternity: At forty Years old I was chosen by our Superior to be sent to *Peru*, and from thence went amongst the People where you found me, among whom I indured great Hardships, it being long before I could acquaint my self with their Language and barbarous Customs; yet the austere Life, and good I did them in curing their Sicknesses and Wounds, with my Discourses of God and Christ, so wrought upon these Savages, that they listned to me and rever'd me. I was several times taken Prisoner by different Parties of these Barbarians, who are ever at variance with one another; but they still spared me, having a Notion that I was a holy Person: Those I converted to Christianity were very hard of Apprehension,[2] and yet very devout when once instructed. I had lived seven Years with the poor Fisherman and his Family, whom we have brought with us, and was doubtless preserved by Providence to be the means of your Deliverance: and

---

1 In accordance with his high social rank.
2 Had great difficulty understanding.

now I hope to spend the remainder of my Days in that pleasant Country where I was once happy with my dear *Leonora*, whom I might still perhaps have enjoy'd, had we never left it; but it was Heaven's Will that I should be what I am, and therefore won't repine." Here he ended his Relation with a deep Sigh, all the Company being much pleased with the manner of his relating it, and the strangeness of his Adventures; admiring the Wisdom of God which had preserved him amongst Savages, and placed him where he was the means of their Preservation.

## CHAP. XXII.

*Gomez* and *Elvira*, with *Philena* their faithful Slave, having hired the Bark to stay that brought *Charlotta* and her dear Friend, and Sister, to *Virginia*, to carry them to the Island of St. *Domingo*, and from thence to *Mexico*, having made *Charlotta* and *Teresa* Presents of two rich Jewels, part of those *Elvira* had on when she was cast on the barbarous Shore, making great Acknowledgments for all the Favours received, took leave, promising to continue their Friendship by a constant Intercourse of Letters; and that if they ever return'd to *Spain*, they would make a Tour to *France* on purpose to see them: for *Charlotta* and *Teresa* had contracted so great a Friendship, that the latter had made her Husband promise to go settle in *France*, his Religion being no hindrance, because he was a Subject of *England*, being born in *Virginia*, and therefore had nothing to fear.[1] As for *Belanger*, he was persuaded by his Wife and the Monk to be a Roman-Catholick, which he had been bred at first. *Gomez* and *Elvira* returned Thanks to old *Montandre*, his Lady, the Captain, and *Lucy*, and all that had visited, and treated them, offering to serve them all in Trade, or otherwise, whatever was in her Father's Power; and departed with a fair Wind, and arriv'd safe at *Mexico*, as they were afterwards inform'd by Letters from them, and considerable Presents which they received some Months after, by the same Bark that carry'd them. And now young *Montandre*, who had received a great Fortune with *Teresa*, agreed with his Father, who had Children by his young Wife, to take a

---

1 French Protestants were harassed and persecuted with the aim of getting them either to convert to Catholicism or to leave the kingdom. But Protestant subjects of other monarchs who resided in France were largely left alone, although they risked forfeiting their estates to the Crown after their deaths.

certain Sum of Money to be remitted in Goods to *France*, as his Fortune; and began to prepare for going thither, where *Belanger* and *Charlotta* long'd to be. The poor Savages were settled in old *Montandre*'s Plantation, he having given them a little House and Ground to live on, at his Son's and the good Monk's Request. A Ship being got ready, and loaded with their Effects, *Charlotta* and *Teresa*, with their Husbands, went on board, where they took leave of the good old Gentleman *Montandre* and his Lady, with the honest Captain, and *Lucy* the fair Maid, whom he had made his Wife, and who hearing part of *Charlotta*'s Story, had conceal'd her Thoughts to this moment; when going to take leave of *Charlotta*, after a noble Entertainment which *Belanger* and *Montandre* had given them on board the Ship, threw her Arms about *Charlotta*'s Neck, saying, "I cannot part with you, Madam, before I reveal a Secret to you that nearly concerns you: Are not you the Daughter of Monsieur *Du Pont*, who lived near *Bristol*, and marry'd a second Wife from *London*, by whom he had a Daughter named *Diana*? and were you not trepan'd to *Virginia* by that Mother-in-law?" "Yes," answered *Charlotta* much surpriz'd, "I am the Daughter of that unfortunate Gentleman, and was by that wicked Woman betray'd and expos'd to a thousand Misfortunes. But who are you? for I am impatient to know." "I am," said she, "that Daughter *Diana*, and your Sister by the Father's side, by the Justice of God for my Mother's Sins, doubtless, exposed on the Seas, and more barbarous Lands; but by his Mercy saved, and honestly disposed of to this generous Man," turning towards the Captain her Husband. All the Company, but especially *Charlotta*, were impatient to learn her Story; which, being all seated, she in few Words related.

"My unjust Mother," said she, "having got rid of you, whom she made my Father and the World believe were drown'd coming back from the Ship with her and Captain *Furley*, apply'd herself wholly to amass a Sum of Money to provide for me and her self, resolving to return to *London*, and pursue the same unhappy Course of Life she had before follow'd, which I am too much confus'd at the mentioning of to explain farther: for her shame is in some measure mine; tho I bless God I have never been guilty, but ever had an aversion to all wicked Actions. In order to accomplish this Design, she took up Clothes and Money of every body that would trust her; and in a short time my Father was persecuted on every hand, and unable to raise Money fast enough to answer his Creditors' Demands. You may imagine that this caused a great many Quarrels between my Father and Mother: but she minded nothing he said, but continued her Extravagancys so long, that at last he was arrested by Captain *Furley*, who pretended that she owed him a hundred Pounds by a Note under her hand; and having before mortgaged his Estate, it was not easy for him to get Bail immediately.[1] The Night he was taken to the Officer's House in hold,[2] my Mother packed up the Plate and Linen, and all that was worth carrying away; and taking me, went aboard a Hoy[3] bound to *London*, which *Furley* had provided, and left him. What is become of my poor Father since, I know not; but I fear he is (if alive) in very bad Circumstances." At these Words Madam *Belanger* wept; and her Husband wiping away her Tears, kiss'd her, and said, "Come, my Dear, be chearful; you and I will fetch him from *England*, and take care of him. If he is dead, being a good Man, doubtless he is happy, and does not need our help." *Diana* continued her Discourse thus: "Being arrived at *London*, my Mother went directly to *Westminster*, to her Friend *Miranda*'s, but found her gone from the House, and well marry'd to a Sea-Captain, with whom she lived very happily and honestly at *Portsmouth*,[4] as the old Baud inform'd her, to whom she went for Information: so she took a Lodging in the Baud's House, and soon got a rich Gallant, an old Merchant in the City: for tho she was still very handsome, and had very rich Clothes, yet she was now in Years, and not of an Age to attract the young Fops and Rakes. I was about eight Years old when she went for *London*; and, doubtless, she design'd to advance me to be some great Person's Mistress, or some rich Fool's Wife. She had robb'd my Father of near two thousand Pounds; but *Furley* pealed[5] her of a good deal of it. She kept me very fine, carry'd me to the Parks, the Plays, and had me taught to dance, sing, and play on the Spinnet:[6] in fine, she took pains to make me agreeable, but none to instruct me in Virtue and Goodness; yet God had given me the Grace to abhor her way of living; and I often wept for her Sins in secret, and wished my self in Prison with my good Father, or if he was poor and at liberty, that I might beg for him, rather than be a Mistress: in short, in about two Years' time, in which we had chang'd our Lodging at least ten times, and my Mother had broke[7]

---

1  In most circumstances, a husband was responsible for his wife's debts and so could be arrested for them.
2  In custody.
3  Small ship used to carry passengers and cargo along the coast.
4  Port on the southern coast of England.
5  Stripped.
6  Keyboard instrument, similar to a harpsichord.
7  Bankrupted.

two or three Merchants and a Linen-Draper,[1] she was struck with Sickness, and the Rheumatism took away the use of her Limbs, so that she lay a long time unable to help her self; then she broke out into Boils all over: in short, she became full of Ulcers, and died in a most miserable Condition, to my great Grief, I fear little sensible of her Sins, and destitute of all spiritual helps, having only the vile old Baud about her, and the People in the House where we lodged. Being dead, every one plunder'd something; and my Mother having made a Will, tho no Widow, which was left in a Tally-man's[2] hand, who was her old Acquaintance, and together with Captain *Furley*, were her Executors and my Guardians; the Tally-man came and bury'd her privately, and indeed poorly, and carry'd me home to his House, *Furley* being gone on a Voyage to *Ireland* with his Ship. I know not what my Mother left me, but believe it was considerable, because she had often told me she could give me a handsom Portion. I was but meanly treated at this vile Tally-man's; and being ready to break my Heart, begg'd Day and Night to be sent down to *Bristol* to my Father: but that was not his, nor *Furley*'s Interest; for they well knew my Father would call them to an account for my Mother's Effects. Old *Gripe*[3] told me, so soon as *Furley* arrived, they would consult what to do with me; accordingly they pretended to send me to my Father, but putting me into a Waggon, sent me to *North Wales*, to a Place where I could hear nothing but *Welch*, and lived four Years miserably; all which time I could not tell how to escape to *Bristol*, having not a Penny of Money, nor any but poor ignorant People to talk to, who could not help me. At last being now fourteen, I apply'd my self to the Minister of the Parish, and told him my Story. He was a very good Man, and writ up to *London* to a Friend, whom he order'd to find out the Tally-man, and threaten him, and try to find what they design'd to do with me, and what my Mother had left me. This Gentleman did so, and *Gripe* laid all the Fault on *Furley*, and promised to send for me up to *London*; which he immediately did. At my arrival, he treated me kindly. Then *Furley* and he contrived to get rid of me for good and all; so they seem'd mighty ready to send me to my Father, in order to which they went with me on board a Ship that lay in the River, bound, as they pretended, for *Bristol*, and ready to sail. They had bought me new

---

1 Merchant who sells linen.
2 One who sells goods on an installment plan.
3 One who lends money at exorbitant interest (as installment plans often involve).

Clothes, and given me my Mother's Watch: and being young and ignorant, I did not suspect their Villany. *Furley* pretended he would go along with me, and the Tally-man gave me a Broad-piece[1] at parting, and went from us at *Greenwich*:[2] but *Furley* went with me as far as *Sheerness*;[3] but there pretending to go on shore about some Business, left me, and I never saw him more. I knew it was a great way to *Bristol* by Sea, yet was every Hour asking when we should get thither, and how far we were got. But a young Man, who was the Captain's Nephew, and a very honest Youth, taking pity of me, told me, That I was not going thither, but to *Jamaica*: that he heard his cruel Uncle bargain with my cursed Guardians to carry me thither: 'they have,' said he, 'pay'd your Passage, and he has promised not to sell you, but to get you a good Service; but be assured he will strip you of all your Clothes so soon as he does reach *Port-Royal*,[4] and sell you for a Slave.' I thought I should have died at this News, but the young Man beg'd me to take no notice of his discovering this Secret to me; 'for if you do,' said he, 'I am undone, my whole Dependance being upon my Uncle, and he will discard me.' I told him that in return to the Obligation he had laid upon me in trusting me, I would conceal it, and trust him. Then I told him all my Story, and of the Fortune I had, of which these Villains wrong'd me, and that if he could find means to get me ashore any where in *England*, and would go with me to my Father, I would give him what part of my Fortune he should desire in reason, when it was recover'd, as it would soon be. He answer'd, That he had other Terms to propose, which was, that I would promise to marry him in case he deliver'd me, and that then he would free me out of his hands, tho I went to *Jamaica*, which he fear'd I must do now, because we were past the Land, and out at Sea: 'for so soon as we land,' said he, 'I will go to the Governor, swear that you were trepan'd thither, and tell him all the Circumstance. I have an Uncle there, who, I am sure, will take my part in such a Case: besides, if you will marry me so soon as I can get you ashore, he cannot sell you.' I readily consented to his Proposals, thinking any honourable way to escape the Miserys I was like to fall into ought to be accepted of: besides, I was very sensible, that if I refused this honest Offer, I should certainly be ruined on the Island by some

---

1 Older English gold coin worth £1. They had not been minted since 1663.

2 Town on the eastern edge of London along the River Thames.

3 Port on the east coast of England.

4 Port on the southern coast of Jamaica.

Villain, who would doubtless buy me for that vile Use, and force me to comply with his wicked Desires. After this Mr. *Stephen*, for that was his Name, study'd how to oblige me, and took such care of me, that tho there were two wild young Men, a Merchant's Son and a Mercer's[1] aboard the Ship, sent by their Fathers for no good doubtless, yet he engaged a very honest Gentlewoman, a Passenger, to keep me always in her Company; so that I went very safe: and being near *Jamaica*, our Ship was drove up the River *Oroonoko*, and shipwreck'd, as you have before heard related; and there this unfortunate young Man has, I fear, met with his Death from the *Barbarians'* Hands, whose Virtue and Piety deserv'd a better Fate; tho as for my part, I have made a Choice much more to my liking in my dear Husband," turning her self to the Captain.

*Charlotta* ran and embraced her, saying, "Dear Sister, our Fates have so much resemblance, that I am astonished at the Almighty's Justice. Be assured if I live to see *England* again, I will see Justice done both to you and our dear Father." At these Words the old Captain bow'd, and saluted *Charlotta* and *Belanger*, saying, "I think my self very happy to have such worthy Relations, and doubt not but you will assist my Wife in all things: her Virtue I am convinced of; and as I took her without the Prospect of a Fortune, shall value her no less, tho she never has any." They all persuaded him to take his Wife, and go along with *Charlotta* for *France* and *England*; but the good Man being in Years, and having a plentiful Fortune in *Virginia*, did not care to run any more hazards; so they took leave, and went ashore with old *Belanger*, his Lady, and the other Friends who came with them on board, and the Ship set sail the next Morning, and in ten Weeks safely arrived at St. *Maloes*, where *Belanger* was agreeably surpriz'd with the News of his Guardian's Death, and also that *Angelina* and his Sister, with her Husband Monsieur *Abriseaux*, were all safely arriv'd in *France* by the way of *Spain*; that *Angelina* was in Health with Monsieur *Du Pont*; that *Du Riviere*, who had long before left *Virginia*, was now living with his dear reconcil'd *Louisa*. *Charlotta*'s Arrival and his was soon spread abroad; and it was not many Days before they and all their Friends sent or came to congratulate them, and to invite them to their Seats. In few Days these now most happy Relations and Friends met all together at *Belanger*'s House, who was now possess'd of his Estate: his Sister having received her's before his Arrival, entertain'd them nobly; and they entertain'd one another with an account of the strange Adventures they

---

1 One who sells cloth, especially luxurious fabrics like silk or velvet.

had every one met withal. Monsieur *Du Pont*, who had retired to his Country Seat in despair of ever seeing his dear *Angelina*, recounted the manner of their meeting thus: "I was," said he, "sitting by a Fountain in my Garden, when a Servant came and told me, that there were two Ladys and two Gentlemen in a Coach said they must speak with me. 'They are utter Strangers,' said he, 'Sir, and I deny'd them entrance as you have order'd me, saying you were busy and would not see Company; but they will not be refus'd, and one of the Ladys said she would see you tho you were dying.' At these words I rose and flew to the Gate, where my *Angelina* was standing without; but no words can express the transport I was in at the sight of her. I catch'd her up in my Arms, and ran into a Parlor with her; there setting her down, I sometimes gaz'd upon her, and then kiss'd her, saying and doing I knew not what, nor did I remember my Kinswoman and Monsieur de *Abriseaux* were present, tho they stood by me, or Monsieur *Morine* the Surgeon, who all laugh'd: but at last *Angelina* reminded me of our Friends, and I welcom'd them in few words; nay I was so distracted to know *Angelina*'s Adventures, that I hindred her from sleeping by my impertinent Questions half the Night."

Just as he spoke these Words, Monsieur *Riviere* and *Louisa* enter'd the Room; *Belanger* and *Charlotta* saluted her: "Dear Kinswoman," said he, "I sent your Wanderer home to bless you with his Presence, and repair the Injuries he did you." "Indeed," said she, "when he came to the Grates of the Convent to ask for me, I could scarce credit my Eyes, he was so chang'd; but I soon threw aside my Veil, and fled to his Arms with as much Affection as at the first Months of our Marriage." "You are," said he, in some confusion, "all Goodness, and I beg you would make no more mention of my Crime, since I hope God and you have forgiven it." "Where is your Son?" said *Belanger*; "at home," said Monsieur *du Riviere*, "well, and such a one as merits a better Father than I: he will be here by and by to wait on you." Many days past in Visits and Entertainments, too tedious to recite the particulars of; but after some Months were past, *Charlotta* being big with Child, and Madam *Montandre* near her time,[1] *Charlotta* continually importun'd her Husband to go with her to *England*, it being the Year of the Peace which King *William* made with *France*;[2] but he was afraid of venturing her upon the Sea in that Condition, and offer'd to go himself: Madam *Montandre* also

---

1 Almost ready to deliver a baby.
2 1697. An inconsistency on Aubin's part. If we follow the previous

would not part with her before she was brought to bed.[1] "My dear Sister," said she, "will you leave me in this Condition? Have I come so far with you out of Affection, and left my Relations and Country for you, and can you consent to go from me at this time?" In short, *Teresa* was deliver'd of a Daughter, and *Charlotta* of a Son two Months afterward, and not able to go to Sea for two Months more; at last being recover'd of her Lying-in,[2] she and *Belanger* went over to *England* from *Calais*, and landed safely at *Dover*,[3] from whence they hir'd Horses to *Bristol*. There were few in the Place who knew *Charlotta*; but from them she learn'd the sad News that her antient Father was in Prison, and had lain there five Years, his Wife's Debts which she had wickedly contracted having intirely ruin'd him; she would not stay a Moment after this Information, but flew to the Prison wing'd with filial Piety and tender Affection: she ask'd for him so earnestly, that the Goaler was startled; but clapping half a Crown in his Hand, he let her in; she quickly saw her dejected Father, who was creeping along the place clothed in nothing but Rags, his white Beard[4] was grown down to the leathern Thong which girded[5] his poor Coat about him; he lifted up his Eyes which were before fix'd on the Ground, at the sound of her Voice, when she said, "Sir, let me speak with you"; and seeing a fine Lady and Gentleman, put out his white wither'd Hand, expecting an Alms, but had not the least remembrance of her Face, or notion of her being alive, as indeed it was impossible he should. She was in so great disorder, that Monsieur *Belanger* fearing she would swoon, went to draw her aside. The Tears stream'd down her Face, and her Voice falter'd, so that she could utter no more, but clasping her Arms about the old Man's Neck, said, "My dear Father," and fainted. These words caus'd such a Tumult in his Soul, that he seem'd like a Man wak'd from a frightful Dream; he trembled, held her fast, and gaz'd upon her, without speaking one Word. *Belanger* was so mov'd with this

---

evidence for when this narrative is set, Charlotta, Belanger, and their friends returned to France c. 1703 or 1704.

1 Had given birth.

2 Recovered from her delivery.

3 Port on the southern coast of England directly across the narrowest part of the English Channel from Calais.

4 European men in the eighteenth century were generally clean-shaven; only those in desperate circumstances (for example, shipwrecked or in prison) would be bearded.

5 Belted.

sight, he could scarce constrain his Tears; but he taking hold of him gently, said, "Sir, be not surpriz'd, God can do wonders, there is a Mystery in my Wife's words, which if you will recollect your Spirits a little, we will inform you of." The old Gentleman staring on him, cry'd out, "It cannot be! 'tis all Wonder, 'tis my Child's Face, 'tis her Voice, and yet ——" At these Words he drop'd down. *Belanger* call'd for some help, two or three Prisoners came, whose meagre Faces and poor Habit spoke their Miseries; they assisted him to lift Monsieur *du Pont* into a poor Room, where his Bed lay on the Floor, and *Belanger* carry'd *Charlotta* in his Arms, who by this time recover'd; he call'd for Wine, of which he gave some to the old Gentleman; after which they talk'd and wept together: *Charlotta* defer'd to tell him the particulars of her Adventures, till they were out of that sad Place, sending the Goaler to fetch his Creditors; but that being a Work of time, she deposited into a Merchant's Hands the whole Sum her Father was charg'd withal, which was but three hundred Pounds, he having paid as long as he had any thing left, and took him out with her, the Merchant giving the Goaler his Bond to indemnify him: they went home with this Merchant, where they refresh'd, and new clothed and shav'd the old Gentleman, who still wept for Joy, and praised God with his whole Heart and Tongue in such a manner, that every stand-er-by seem'd to participate of his Joy, and being warm'd with his Zeal, wept with him: nor could he be less mov'd, who had in one Moment receiv'd such a miraculous Deliverance from the Miserys of a Prison, the greatest Trial this Life can subject us to, and such a Child, who was restor'd to him even from the Grave. This to a Man who had outliv'd hope, and had not the least Prospect of any Deliverance but by Death, was enough to revive all his Faculties, and fill his Soul with the most exquisite Transports of Joy, and highest Sense of Gratitude to God. He enter'd a clean bed at Night with more Joy than he had ever done in his Prosperity; the next Morning he appear'd so reviv'd and alter'd for the better, that *Charlotta* could do nothing but look upon him with the greatest Pleasure. His Creditors came, and pretended to be sorry for what they had done; but he and she treated them with such scorn and reproaches as their unchristian treatment of him deserv'd. And now all his old Friends and Acquaintance, who many of them had left him in his Distress, came to visit and congratulate him, and see *Charlotta*; she treated them all very civilly, but those who had reliev'd him in the Prison, she caress'd and entertain'd splendidly: lastly she sent to the Goal, and freed those poor Wretches who had been his Companions and Fellow-Sufferers in that dreadful

Place, which were but five Persons, People of mean Condition, whose Debts amounted to 120 *l* a noble Gift from her, by which she obtain'd their Prayers and Blessings, which were better worth than the Money; and having furnish'd her self and Father with whatever she wanted from *England*, she, he, and Monsieur *Belanger* return'd in the same Vessel that brought them, to *St. Malos*; the old Gentleman being under no Apprehensions of any Troubles about his Religion, being now so very antient, and so long absent thence, that none but his Friends and Relations could remember him; but he resolv'd, if he was any ways molested, to remove to the Island of *Jersey* or *Guernsey*,[1] from whence he could pay or receive a Visit from his Daughter once or twice a Year. *Angelina* gave them an Account of all the strange Adventures she had met with in *Barbary*,[2] which fill'd them with Admiration.

One Morning (a *French* Ship having come into the Port in the Night) an old Man in a very poor Habit came to young Monsieur *du Pont*'s House, and desired to be admitted to speak with *Angelina*. She was at Breakfast with her Husband, and bid the Servants admit him; but was extremely surpriz'd when she saw his Face, and knew that he was the old *French* Captain who had carry'd her to *Canada*. "Madam," said he, "I am come to beg your Pardon before I die: God has been pleas'd by a severe Slavery to punish my Sin, of which I had before a true Sense; and at last in his Mercy has brought me back to my native Country. But I could not live or die in Peace till I knew what was become of you, which having learn'd last Night when I landed, and went home to my House, I hasted to your Presence to obtain your Pardon, and beg your Favour in the behalf of two Christian Strangers, who escap'd with me from *Tunis*; they are a Gentleman and Lady who have been Slaves, and have nothing to support them when landed, or to carry them to their home." Monsieur *du Pont* and *Angelina* told him, they were glad he had escap'd, and should be ready to assist the Strangers in any thing. *Du Pont* said, "I can hardly forgive you what you have done by my Wife, but as a Christian I won't resent it: Bring the innocent Strangers, and we will do something for them." The Captain took leave, and about an Hour after return'd with the Gentleman and Lady: She was very handsome, her Shape, Stature and Mien were delicate and engaging. The Gentleman was tall, slender, and had a Face so lovely and majestick, that he seem'd the Offspring of *Mars*

---

1  Islands in the English Channel off the coast of France. Aubin's husband was from Jersey.
2  North Africa.

and *Venus*.[1] Their Dress was as mean as their Persons were noble, being such as Charity had furnish'd them withal. *Angelina* saluted and welcom'd her to *France*, not knowing whether she understood her or not. Monsieur *du Pont* answer'd the Gentleman's Civility in the same manner, who thus address'd himself to *Angelina*. "Madam, you doubtless wonder why my Wife and I have presum'd to visit and apply our selves to you, before any other Person, at my Arrival in *France*: but when I tell you that her Name is *Silvia de Mount-Espaigne*, who was your Companion in the Convent, and was in a particular manner honour'd with your Friendship; you will not be surpriz'd that she comes to ask the Protection of her Friend." At these Words *Angelina* ran and embrac'd her, and Monsieur *du Pont* said, "Then you are my dear School-fellow *Charles du Bois*: My God! where have you been this Age, and what Providence has preserv'd you, whose death I have mourn'd for so passionately? Come, sit down, and tell us all your Story, for we must not part again; my House is at your Service, and my Fortune. We shall be proud to procure your Happiness in all things, to the utmost of our Power." *Angelina* was the mean while weeping with *Silvia*, being both so transported with Joy, that they knew not how to contain or utter their Thoughts. At last Monsieur *du Bois* took upon him to relate their strange Adventures.

"You know," said he, "that my Father dying whilst we were School-fellows, I was left in the Hands of the two rich *East-India* Merchants, Monsieur *Dandin* and Monsieur *du Fresne*: *Dandin* had but one Daughter, who was as deform'd as *Esop*,[2] and as ill-natur'd as she was proud and ugly. My Fortune was very considerable, and his whole aim was to match me to *Magdelain*, and so secure it to his Posterity. I was but thirteen, and he wheedled me into signing a Contract with her; and she being twenty, was not a little pleas'd to have such a fine young Husband. She took much upon her,[3] and so tutor'd and school'd me upon every occasion, that my Aversion daily encreas'd towards her. I was fain[4] to hand her about[5] to every place she was pleas'd to gad[6] to; and at

---

1 The Roman god of war and goddess of love.
2 Aesop was the legendary ancient Greek author of a series of fables. He was traditionally described as extremely ugly and misshapen, though the accounts differ as to the nature of his condition.
3 Was conceited.
4 Obligated.
5 Escort.
6 Go idly from place to place.

last it was my fortune to go with her to a Chappel near the Monastery where you and my dear *Silvia* were Pensioners; there I saw you and her together: you I knew, because my Friend Monsieur *du Pont* had shew'd you to me; for Students always tell their Amours to one another, and I am younger than he, so that he had a Mistress[1] before me. I was so charm'd with her, that had not my Fury[2] been along with me, I had follow'd you to the Convent: but I soon found an opportunity to go thither, and found you gone. I got to the Speech of her, and in some time gain'd my Charmer's Consent to marry me secretly. She, you know, was an Orphan, who being related to the Abbess your Aunt, was bred there with design (having but a small Fortune) to be made a Nun. Being but a Pensioner, it was no difficult thing for her to come to me; but my keeping our Marriage a Secret till I was of Age, was a hard thing to be done. My Guardians did not keep me short of Money, so that I fancy'd I could easily maintain her if I could but get some faithful Friend for her to live withal privately in the House with his Wife and Family, or else a private Lodging. This last I thought most secure, and accordingly took a Chamber in a Widow-woman's House in a Village. Having thus provided a Retreat, and engag'd my Confessor to marry us, I gave her notice, and she got out the next Morning with another Pensioner, on pretence of going to Church to the little Chappel I had seen her at: I waited for her in a Coach near the Chappel, and coming out in the Croud, she slip'd from her Companion, and turning back into the Church, went out at another Door, where I took her into the Coach, and drove away with her to the Fryar's Cell, where we were marry'd. Thence we went away to the Village, to our Lodging, where I had provided a Dinner and all things for our Reception. The Widow's Daughter, a very modest young Maid, I had hired to wait on her. Here I staid all night, having pretended to old *Dandin*, my Guardian, that I was to go out of Town with a young Gentleman whom I kept Company withal, and whom I had trusted with my Secret, and engag'd to ask me to go with him before my Guardian and *Magdelain*, my crooked Rib[3] that was to

---

1 Girlfriend.

2 The Furies were ancient Roman goddesses of vengeance and so, by extension, a term for angry women.

3 Unwished-for wife (a reference to Eve being created from Adam's rib in Genesis 2.21–23, although the biblical narrative does not specify that the rib was crooked; that was a later addition to account for the supposedly "crooked" nature of women).

be. In fine, I kept my dear *Silvia* here some Months, tho a great Search was made after her, being very cautious in my Visits. She was in that time with Child, but miscarry'd. She never stir'd out of Doors without a Mask, or when I fetch'd her out in a Coach; but finding it was inconvenient to have her so far off, I remov'd her to St. *Malo*'s, and took a Lodging for her at a Widow's House in a back Street, in a very private Place, with a Garden, and Back-door into the Fields. In this Garden *Silvia* us'd to walk, and venture sometimes to look out of her Windows into it. A young Lord who often pass'd by that way, saw and fell in love with her: he soon inquired who kept the House, and learn'd that it was a Widow who had a young Gentlewoman and her Servant lodg'd with her. He, embolden'd by his Quality and Fortune, went to the House in a Chair,[1] richly dress'd, and ask'd to see the Lady, the young Gentlewoman that lodg'd there: The Woman seeing his Attendance[2] and Habit, was daunted. He ask'd no leave, but going by her, went up Stairs, and found *Silvia* sitting in her Chamber reading: She was doubtless surpriz'd, but he told her his Business was Love, and in fine would take no denial, or be gone. He sup-pos'd her a Mistress[3] by the Place she resided in, being so mean and obscure, and resolv'd to possess her whatever it cost. She told him she was married; but he turn'd that into ridicule: before he went he presented her with a fine Diamond Ring, which she refus-ing, he left it upon the table. He went not away till Midnight; the next Morning I found her in Tears, she told me what a Misfortune had befallen her. I was now but seventeen, and the Expence of maintaining her and a Servant, so sunk my allowance, that I had no Money by me; and being something indebted to the Widow, I knew not how at present to remove her. In fine, this young Nobleman, who was mad in love with her, continued frequently to visit her, and set Spys to discover who kept her, who quickly got knowledge of the Secret. This young Lord, who was one of the most powerful Persons, and had the greatest Fortune of any Nobleman in the Place, knew my Guardian, and sent privately for him, telling him, as out of Friendship, the Matter. 'Monsieur *Dandin*,' says he, 'you have a young Heir who is contracted to your Daughter, who will be ruin'd; he keeps a Mistress in such a Place, 'tis your Duty and Interest to put an end to such an Intrigue, and

---

1  Sedan chair.

2  Servants.

3  Here, a woman in a sexual relationship who is financially maintained
   by her lover but not married to him.

save the Youth from being undone.' My Guardian promis'd never to reveal who told him, and return'd him a thousand Thanks; so he came home and took no notice to me, but watched me the next time I went out, and dog'd me to *Silvia*, and at my return home, told me I must go travel, or marry his Daughter next Week. I was ready to go distracted before, but now I was quite overwhelm'd. I found I was watch'd, and dar'd not go to *Silvia*. The next Morning when I was in bed, he enter'd my Chamber, search'd my Pockets, took away all the Money I had left, with my Watch, and told me, 'Young Gentleman, I am inform'd you keep a Mistress, your Allowance shall be shortned; you are like to prove a good Man and an excellent Husband, that begin so well.' I was so enrag'd, I lost all Patience; I told him I would never marry his Daughter, and that so soon as I was of Age, I would call him to a strict Account. I know not what I said, but we quarrel'd to that degree, that I rose and went out of the House, protesting that I would never set foot in it again. I went directly to *Silvia*, but cannot express the Transport of Sorrow I was in when I came there, and found the poor Widow and the Maid in Tears, who told me; that at twelve a Clock the preceding Night, somebody knocking softly at the Door, they suppos'd it to be me; and the Maid rising, and going to it, ask'd, who was there? Somebody answer'd, 'It is I, *du Bois*'; at these words she open'd the Door, and a Man in a Vizard[1] caught hold of her, clapping a Pistol to her Breast, three more rush'd in all mask'd, and ran up Stairs, dragging *Silvia* out of Bed; she saw them bring her Mistress down bound hand and foot, and put her into a Chair; one Man staid till the Chair was gone, as she suppos'd, a good way: then he bid her shut the Door and make no noise, for if she did, he would come back and kill her. The poor Creature was so frighted, she had not Power to stir for some time; at last she went up to the Widow, and acquainted her with what had happen'd. This was all I could learn, and enough to make me desperate. I return'd to my Guardian like an enraged Lion, demanded my Wife, declaring my Marriage: this made him as furious as I; he threatned to sue me for the Contract with his Daughter; I apply'd my self to several of my Relations and Friends to assist me against him, but no body car'd to meddle; for he was known to be a very rich and a very cunning Man; then I challeng'd the young Lord, charging him with stealing her, but he only laugh'd at and ridiculed me. At last, being unable to get any news of her, I resolved to travel, believing they had murdered her. I was

---

1  Mask.

deeply melancholy; and my Guardian, who indeed knew not what was become of *Silvia*, was willing to be rid of me, and readily agreed to my going to travel. I design'd to go first to *Rome*, and from thence to make the Tour of *Europe*, and return to *France* so soon as I was of Age, to be reveng'd of my Guardian. He agreed to make me a handsome Allowance, and gave me five hundred Pistoles to defray my extraordinary Expences, being willing to be reconcil'd to me before the Day of Reckoning came. Attended by a Servant, I set out on my Journey, and reach'd *Rome*, having view'd all that was curious in my way thither thro *Spain*. I resolv'd to stay there some time, and took a Lodging for that purpose. One Morning my Servant wak'd me, saying there was a Youth, who said he was come post[1] from *France* to me. I bad him call him up; when he enter'd my Chamber, he made a Sign with his Hand that I should send away the Servant; I did so, and then he ran to me and catch'd me in his Arms: But good Heavens! how was I at that Moment transported when I saw it was *Silvia*. I shut the Chamber-Door, and then she told me, that being (as I knew she was) pretty far gone with Child, the fright had thrown her into such a Condition, that when the Villains, who had carry'd her away, came to take her out of the Chair, she seem'd half dead; they carry'd her up Stairs into a Chamber richly furnish'd, and laid her upon a Bed, and so left her; that the young Lord came into it immediately, and told her that she must now consent to his Desires, that he would never part from her again; that it was in vain to resist, or call out for help: in fine, nothing but the Condition she was in preserv'd her; for telling him she was in Labour, and should die if he did not call somebody to her Assistance, begging him with Tears to pity her Condition, she pre-vail'd with him to defer the execution of his brutish Design, and he call'd an old Woman and her Daughter to her. She had no other help but these Women; and falling into a Fever, lay sick in her Bed three Months, unable to rise; all which time the young Lord con-tinually visited her, bringing a Physician several times: at last recovering so as to be able to walk about her Chamber, she began to consider how to make her escape. By this time, as she after-wards learn'd, I having declared our Marriage, the young Lord refrain'd from visiting her some days.

One Afternoon he came, and being alone with her, he said thus to her, '*Silvia*, I am come to ask your Pardon for the Injuries I have done you; I thought you a Mistress, not a Wife, and my

---

1  Had come as quickly as possible (as the mail traveled).

Passion for you was so excessive, that it blinded my Reason. I believ'd you ruin'd by a Man who was pre-ingag'd to another, and was not half so well able to take care of you as my self: had you been a Virgin, I would have marry'd you, but finding you are virtuous, and Monsieur *du Bois*'s Wife, I am heartily sorry for what is past, and ready to restore you to him. He is gone to *Rome* in discontent. So soon as you are able to travel, I will furnish you with Money, and a Servant to wait on you thither. Believe me, *Silvia*, I love you no longer with an unlawful Passion, but with a tender Affection as a Sister. I will so soon as your Husband is of Age, assist him to the utmost of my Power against Monsieur *Dandin*, who has been the Cause of all this Mischief.' Here he discover'd to her what had past between him and *Dandin*, and how they had contriv'd together that he should steal her away, and carry her to this his Country-House, where the Servants were at his Devotion,[1] who suppos'd she was some young Lady whom their Master had got with Child, nor dar'd inquire farther than by supposition: in fine, so soon as my Wife found her self able to sit a Horse,[2] she by his Advice put on a Man's Habit, and having receiv'd a thousand Pistoles from him, set out for *Rome*, attended by one of his Servants. Nothing could be more welcome than she was to me, and I concluded that the Disguise she had on was the best in the World to conceal her till I was of Age, and prevent farther Misfortunes, which her Beauty in a female Dress might again occasion. I now wanted but a Year and half of being of Age, and had no mind to return to *France* till that time was elaps'd; so we remov'd to a Lodging some Miles from *Rome*, where *Silvia*, who pass'd for my Kinsman, liv'd with me; we pass'd the time very agreeably: At last we embark'd aboard a Vessel bound for *Marseilles*,[3] and set sail with a fair Wind; but in a few Hours a terrible Storm drove us out to Sea, and we were driven for eight and forty Hours before the Wind, in which time our Ship was so disabled, that she sprung a-Leak, and had not a Ship come up, we had all perish'd in the merciless Seas: but alas, it had been better for many of us that we had done so; for it prov'd to be a Corsair of *Tunis* belonging to a great Bassa there, and we were all put into Irons and carry'd thither. How inexpressible my Concern was for my dear *Silvia*, you may easily imagine. At our coming on Shore we were carry'd to this Bassa's House, who viewing the Prisoners,

---

1 Command.

2 Sit astride a horse (and so ride as a man would do).

3 Port on the southern coast of France.

made choice of her and me for Slaves, supposing we were Prisoners of Birth, and that he should have a large Ransom for us. He examin'd what Nation we were of: I answer'd that we were Natives of *France*, and Brothers, that we had been at *Rome*, to which our Father, a private Gentleman,[1] had sent us, and were returning home. He seem'd satisfy'd, and us'd us gently, making us write, or attend him into the Country, riding by the side of his Litter; but I soon perceiv'd he had a wicked Design on *Silvia*, whom he dress'd in a fine *Turkish* Dress, and treated with great Indulgence. I was seiz'd with such dreadful Apprehensions at this Proceedure, that I resolv'd to run all Hazards to escape his hands. This put us on a Project which we happily effected; the *French* Captain who brought us home, was at that time his Slave, he had been so to his Father, who was a General, and had treated him very cruelly: by his Death he fell into this *Muly*[2] *Melee*'s hands, who was a good natur'd Man; and finding him skill'd in Sea-Affairs, had made him Master of a very neat Pleasure-Boat he us'd to go out to Sea in for his Diversion; he likewise trusted him to go out in her with other Slaves, Natives of *Tunis*, to fish for him. The *French* Captain was generally thus employ'd in the Summer-Season, and was much in his favour. I was often sent aboard with him, but *Silvia* never. I contracted a Friendship with him, and we contrived our Escape thence in this manner; he had got knowledge of the Christian Fisherman and his Wife, where you had liv'd; he directed me thither, and we agreed that *Silvia* and I should retire to that Place, which was not very difficult for us to do, since we had the Liberty of walking the Town, and that he should send some of the Slaves on shore, and bring the Pleasure-Boat about in the Dusk of the Evening, and take us in. All our hope was to get to *Malta* in this slight Vessel, a very dangerous Undertaking; but our Condition made us resolve to trust to Providence, and venture all Risques to get out of the Infidel's hands. There was a lovely Maid who had been sold to this Bassa some Months before, whose Name was *Margaretta des Sanson*; she was a Farmer's Daughter at *Poictou*,[3] who was in quality of[4] a Servant with a Lady that was going with her Family to her Husband, a Merchant, who was settled in the *West-Indies*; and the Ship being taken by a Pirate of *Tunis*, she was made a Slave, and

---

1 Gentleman who does not hold public office.
2 Mulai: North African ruler.
3 Poitou: province in western France.
4 Acting as.

so fell into *Muly Melee*'s Hands. With this Maid the Captain was fall'n in Love, so he sent her along with us to the Fisherman's. All things being ready, and the Bassa absent, being sent for to the Court, we got away, as agreed, and the Captain came according to Appointment; and it pleased God that we arriv'd safely at *Malta* in four Days' time, the *Algerine* Slaves not in the least suspecting our Design till they saw the Vessel enter the Port: they were but five in number, and unarm'd, so that we had not any thing to fear from them, being on our Guard. Here we were receiv'd as became Christians, and furnish'd with Clothes and Refreshments, having brought nothing but the Clothes on our Backs with us: from hence we got a Passage in a *French* Ship that put in there. And now Providence having brought us back to our own native Country, we must beg your Assistance to get *Dandin* to deliver up my Fortune." "That," said Monsieur *du Pont*, "is easy, for he is long since dead, and his Daughter is marry'd to a very honest Gentleman, Monsieur *de Fontain*, the Banker, who I dare promise will gladly restore to you all that is your due." *Angelina* entertain'd them nobly, and the *French* Captain having marry'd *Margaretta*, brought her to wait on her. In few Days Monsieur *du Pont* having manag'd the Affair, procur'd an Agreement between Monsieur *du Bois* and *de Fontain*, who honourably paid him what Moneys *Dandin* had in his hands of his; and Monsieur *du Bois* enter'd into Possession of all his Fortune. Thus divine Providence having by various Trials and strange Vicissitudes of Fortune, proved[1] the Faith and Patience of these heroick Christians, whom neither Slavery nor the fear of Death could prevail with to forsake their Faith, or distrust their God, they were all happily preserv'd and deliver'd out of their Troubles, and at last brought home to their own native Lands. *Charlotta*, whose filial Piety and extraordinary Virtues make her justly claim the first Place in our Esteem, as well as in this History, had the Satisfaction of seeing her dear Father die in Peace in a good old Age; was blest with an excellent Husband, and many Children fair and virtuous as her self: nor was her Prosperity interrupted by any Misfortune. The virtuous *Teresa* and *Angelina*, and all the rest were blest with all earthly Happiness. These Examples should convince us, how possible it is for us to behave our selves as we ought in our Conditions, since Ladys, whose Sex and tender manner of Breeding, render them much less able than Men to support such Hardships, bravely endured Shipwrecks, Want, Cold, and Slavery, and every Ill that

---

1 Tested.

human Nature could be try'd withal; yet we who never feel the Inclemency of foreign Climates, that never saw the Face of barbarous Pirates, or Savages, are impatient at a fit of Sickness, or a Disappointment, shake at a Storm, and are brave in nothing but in daring Heaven's Judgments. Let us blush when we read such Historys as these, and imitating these great Examples, render our selves worthy to have our Names like theirs, recorded to Posterity.

## FINIS.[1]

---

1 Latin: the end.

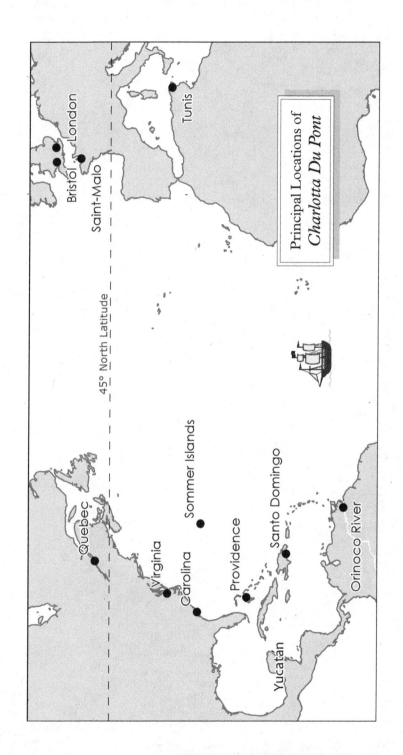

Principal Locations of *Charlotta Du Pont*

Tunis

London

Bristol

Saint-Malo

45° North Latitude

Quebec

Virginia

Carolina

Sommer Islands

Providence

Santo Domingo

Yucatán

Orinoco River

# Appendix A: Aubin Theorizing Her Own Work

[The principal place in which late seventeenth- and early eighteenth-century writers of prose fiction theorized what they were doing and why it mattered was in the prefaces that appeared at the front of their books. It was in prefaces that writers described the genre in which they were working (or that they were trying to create) and related it to or distinguished it from other genres—and sometimes specific texts—likely to be known by their readers. It was in prefaces that writers put forth claims as to what their work could do for their readers or the world more generally. And it was in prefaces that many of the issues now central to the study of prose fiction (e.g., the nature of fictionality, what constitutes realism, what is involved in sympathizing with or imitating a character) were first explored in an at least semi-systematic way that readers could then test against their own experience of the texts in question. Not all works of prose fiction had a preface, and some of this thinking was also done in dedications to aristocratic patrons or narratorial commentary.[1] But until the advent of periodicals devoted exclusively to reviews of non-learned books in English around 1750, most published discussion of prose fiction was conducted in prefaces and by the writers of such fiction, rather than by scholars, journalists, or general readers.

This appendix includes the most significant passages (except for those in *The Life of Madam de Beaumount* and *The Life of Charlotta Du Pont*) in which Aubin explicitly reflects on her own work and the effects that she hopes it will have. As the Introduction details, there has been some scholarly disagreement over the past few decades concerning how seriously we should take the claims that Aubin makes about her intentions, but regardless of what we decide about the tone and function of these texts, they are all that we have and it would be foolish to

---

1 Leah Orr estimates that approximately one-fifth of the works of prose fiction published between 1690 and 1730 have prefaces that reflect on genre in some way (20).

ignore them as we are investigating the pleasures and insights to be had from her work.[1]]

## 1. From Penelope Aubin, *The Strange Adventures of the Count de Vinevil and His Family* (1721)[2]

### PREFACE TO THE READER.

*Since serious things are, in a manner, altogether neglected, by what we call the Gay and Fashionable Part of Mankind, and Religious Treatises grow mouldy on the Booksellers' Shelves in the Back-Shops; when Ingenuity is, for want of Encouragement, starv'd into Silence, and* Toland's[3] *abominable Writings sell ten times better than the inimitable* Mr. Pope's Homer;[4] *when* Dacier's[5] *Works are attempted to be translated by a Hackney-Writer,[6] and* Horace's *Odes turn'd into Prose and Nonsense;[7] the few that honour Virtue, and wish well to our Nation, ought to study to reclaim our Giddy Youth; and since Reprehensions fail, try to win them to Virtue, by Methods where Delight and Instruction may go together. With this Design I present this Book to the Publick, in which you will find a Story, where Divine Providence manifests itself in*

---

1  For dozens of additional examples of such theorizing (by writers other than Aubin), see Millet; Williams.

2  For the full title and publication details of this and the other works in this appendix, see the Works Cited and Select Bibliography.

3  John Toland (1670–1722) was a religious "freethinker" who argued that the only true Christian beliefs were those that made sense rationally (which left no space for faith in miracles or other instances of divine intervention). He regarded the supernatural elements of Christianity as either phenomena that could be wholly explained (his enemies would say explained away) or as inventions of the priesthood to control naive believers.

4  Between 1715 and 1720, Alexander Pope (1688–1744) published a translation of *The Iliad* into heroic couplets.

5  André (1651–1722) and Anne (c. 1645–1720) Dacier were prominent French scholars and translators of literature from classical antiquity.

6  A writer who works for anyone willing to pay, a description that arguably fits John Ozell, William Broome, and William Oldisworth, whose translation of *The Iliad* into blank verse (1712) was based upon Anne Dacier's prior translation of it into French prose (1699).

7  Horace (65–8 BCE) was the most celebrated lyric poet of ancient Rome. His *Odes* were translated into prose by David Watson and "a Gentleman well-skilled in this sort of Literature" in 1712.

every *Transaction, where Vertue is try'd with Misfortunes, and rewarded with Blessings: In fine, where Men behave themselves like Christians, and Women are really vertuous, and such as we ought to imitate.*

*As for the Truth of what this Narrative contains, since* Robinson Cruso *has been so well receiv'd, which is more improbable, I know no reason why this should be thought a Fiction.*[1] *I hope the World is not grown so abandon'd to Vice, as to believe that there is no such Ladies to be found, as would prefer Death to Infamy; or a Man that, for Remorse of Conscience, would quit a plentiful Fortune, retire, and chuse to die in a dismal Cell. This Age has convinc'd us, that Guilt is so dreadful a thing, that some Men have hasten'd their own Ends, and done Justice on themselves.*[2] *Would Men trust in Providence, and act according to Reason and common Justice, they need not to fear any thing; but whilst they defy God, and wrong others, they must be Cowards, and their Ends such as they deserve, surprizing and infamous. I heartily wish Prosperity to my Country, and that the* English *would be again (as they were heretofore) remarkable for Vertue and Bravery, and our Nobility make themselves distinguish'd from the Crowd, by shining Qualities, for which their Ancestors became so honour'd, and for Reward of which obtain'd those Titles they inherit. I hardly dare hope for Encouragement, after having discover'd,*[3] *that my Design is to persuade you to be vertuous; but if I fail in this, I shall not in reaping that inward Satisfaction of Mind, that ever accompanies good Actions. If this Trifle sells, I conclude it takes, and you may be sure to hear from me again; so you may be innocently diverted, and I employ'd to my Satisfaction.*

Adieu.

---

[the final paragraph of the text]:

Thus Divine Providence, whom they confided in, try'd their Faith and Vertue with many Afflictions, and various Misfortunes; and, in the end, rewarded them according to their Merit, making them most happy and fortunate.

---

1  Daniel Defoe's *The Life and Strange Surprizing Adventures of Robinson Crusoe of York, Mariner* came out in 1719 and was an immediate success. Like many early eighteenth-century works of prose fiction, *Robinson Crusoe* claimed to be a true story.

2  Suicides in London increased 40 percent in the wake of the South Sea Bubble (the meteoric rise and then crash in 1720 of the stock of the private company used to manage the national debt).

3  Revealed.

## 2. From Penelope Aubin, *The Noble Slaves* (1722)

THE PREFACE TO THE READER.

*In our Nation, where the Subjects are born free, where Liberty and Property is so preserv'd to us by Laws, that no Prince can enslave us, the Notion of Slavery is a perfect Stranger.[1] We cannot think without Horror, of the Miseries that attend those, who, in Countries where the Monarchs are absolute, and standing Armies awe the People, are made Slaves to others. The* Turks *and* Moors *have been ever famous for these Cruelties; and therefore when we Christians fall into the Hands of Infidels, or Mahometans,[2] we must expect to be treated as those heroick Persons, who are the Subject of the Book I here present to you.[3] There the Monarch gives a loose to his Passions, and thinks it no Crime to keep as many Women for his Use, as his lustful Appetite excites him to like; and his Favourites, Ministers of State, and Governors, who always follow their Master's Example, imitate his way of living. This caused our beautiful Heroines to suffer such Trials: The Grand Signior[4] knowing that Money is able to procure all earthly things, uses his Grandees like the Cat's Paw,[5] to beggar his People, and then sacrifices them to appease the Populace's Fury, and fills his own Coffers with their Wealth. This is* Turkish *Policy,[6] which makes the Prince great, and the People wretched, a Condition we are secur'd from ever falling into; our excellent Constitution will always keep us rich and free, and it must be our own Faults if we are enslav'd, or impoverish'd.*

---

1 Slavery here means both a lack of political liberty (the possession of which was supposedly part of what distinguished the subjects of Great Britain from those of the absolutist monarchies on the Continent) and the ownership of persons by other people. As the Introduction details, the enslavement of European Christians by North African Muslims was better known to most Britons in the period than the (far more familiar today) enslavement of persons of African descent on plantations in the Americas (pp. 39–42).

2 Muslims.

3 Ottoman and North African Muslims ("Turks and Moors") were often proclaimed by Europeans to be tyrannical, cruel, lustful, polygamist, manipulative, and untrustworthy.

4 Italian: Great Lord. "Le Grand Seigneur" was the standard way in which the French referred to the Sultan of the Ottoman Empire, the heart of which was what is now Turkey.

5 A person used as a tool by another.

6 Cunning (especially political cunning).

*But to leave this unpleasant Subject, let us proceed to reflect on the great Deliverances of these noble Slaves: You will find that Chains could not hold them; Want, Sickness, Grief, nor the merciless Seas destroy them; because they trusted in God, and swerv'd not from their Duty.*

*Methinks now I see the Atheist grin, the modish[1] Wit laugh out, and the old Letcher and the young Debauchee sneer, and throw by the Book; and all join to decry it: 'tis all a Fiction, a Cant[2] they cry; Virtue's a Bugbear,[3] Religion's a Cheat, tho at the same time they are jealous of their Wives, Mistresses, and Daughters, and ready to fight about Principles and Opinions.*

*Their Censures I despise, as much as I abhor their Crimes; the Good and Virtuous I desire to please. My only Aim is to encourage Virtue, and expose Vice, imprint noble Principles in the ductile[4] Souls of our Youth, and setting great Examples before their Eyes, excite them to imitate them. If I succeed in this, I have all I wish.*

*The charming Masquerades being at an end, our Ears almost tir'd with* Italian *Harmony,[5] and our Pockets empty'd of Money, which must prevent extravagant Gaming, unless our private Credit outlives the Publick;[6] it is possible that we may be glad of new Books to amuse us, and pass away that time that must hang heavy on our Hands: And Books of Devotion being tedious, and out of Fashion, Novels and Stories will be welcome. Amongst these, I hope, this will be read, and gain a Place in your Esteem, especially with my own Sex, whose Favour I shall always be proud of: Nor have they a truer Friend, than their humble Servant,*

Penelope Aubin.

———————————

[opening paragraph of the narrative]:

A *French West-India* Captain just return'd from the Coast of *Barbary*, having brought thence some Ladies and Gentlemen, who had been Captives in those Parts, the History of whose Adventures there are most surprizing, I thought it well worth

———————————

1  Fashionable.
2  Empty moralizing.
3  Bogeyman.
4  Easy to instruct.
5  This text was published at the end of the season for masquerades and operas.
6  Public credit had taken a serious hit in the preceding two years with the South Sea Bubble.

presenting to the Publick. It contains such variety of Accidents and strange Deliverances, that I am positive it cannot fail to divert the most splenetick[1] Reader, silence the Profane, and delight the Ingenious; and must be welcome at a time when we have so much occasion for something new, to make us forget our own Misfortunes. The Providence of God, which Men so seldom confide in, is in this History highly vindicated; his Power manifests it self in every Passage: and if we are not better'd by the Examples of the virtuous *Teresa* and the brave Don *Lopez*, 'tis our own Faults.

---

[the last four paragraphs of the narrative]:

And now it is fit that we make some Reflections for our own Improvement, on the wonderful Providence of God, in the Preservation and signal Deliverances of these excellent Persons in this Narrative.

A great number of Christian Slaves are at this time expected to return to *Europe*, redeem'd from the Hands of those cruel Infidels, amongst whom our noble Slaves suffer'd so much, and lived so long;[2] and no doubt but amongst these, if we enquire, we shall find some whose Misfortunes, if not their Virtues, equal these Lords and Ladies. It is in Adversity that Men are known: He is only worthy the Name of a Christian who can despise Death, and support even Slavery and Chains with Patience; whom neither Tortures or Interest can shake, or make renounce his God and Faith. How frequent is it for us, who boast so much of Religion, to sacrifice our Consciences to Interest? How impatient are Men for small Injuries or Disappointments?

The Gentlemen in this Story well deserve our Imitation; the Ladies, I fear, will scarce find any here who will pull out their Eyes, break their Legs, starve, and chuse to die, to preserve their Virtues. The Heathens, indeed, shew'd many Examples of such

---

1 Easily irritable.
2 A little more than three months before *The Noble Slaves* was published, there was a procession through London, culminating in a special service at St. Paul's Cathedral, of 280 men who had recently been ransomed from North African slavery. To visually mark what they had undergone, they were all wearing what remained of their "Moorish" clothing. Perhaps this passage was written in anticipation of that procession and then publication did not proceed as quickly as expected.

heroick Females; but since the first Ages of Christianity, we have had very few: The Nuns of *Glastenbury*, who parted with their Noses and Lips to preserve their Chastity, are, I think, the last the *English* Nation can boast of.[1] 'Tis well in this Age if the fair Sex stand[2] the Trial of soft Persuasions; a little Force will generally do to gain the proudest Maid. But I forget that to give good Advice, and not to censure, is at present my Business; I shall therefore sum up all in few words.

Since Religion is no Jest, Death and a future State certain; let us strive to improve the noble Sentiments such Histories as these will inspire in us; avoid the loose Writings which debauch the Mind; and since our Heroes and Heroines have done nothing here but what is possible, let us resolve to act like them, make Virtue the Rule of all our Actions, and eternal Happiness our only Aim.

### 3. From Penelope Aubin, *The Life and Adventures of the Lady Lucy* (1726)

TO The Right Honourable THE Lord *COLERAIN*.[3]

*My Lord,*
It has hitherto been my study to endeavour to discourage Vice, and inculcate Virtue, in the Minds of those, who, either out of Curiosity, or good Nature, read my Novels, the amusements of some melancholy Hours; and I always dedicate them to such Persons, as both by their Quality and Virtues, are an awe to the Vicious, and bright Examples for the Virtuous to imitate.... For my own part, I could think of no better way of manifesting my Satisfaction and Respect, than by offering this little Present to

---

1 According to sources written several centuries after the incident in question, the nuns of the monastery of Coldingham (in what is now southern Scotland) cut off their noses and upper lips to deter Vikings from raping them. It is unclear why Aubin should have associated this story with Glastonbury, except that it also had a monastery that was raided by Vikings.

2 Withstand.

3 Henry Hare, Baron Coleraine (1694–1749), was the husband of Anne Hare (*née* Hanger) to whom Aubin had dedicated *The Noble Slaves*. However, the couple had separated in 1720, after only three years of marriage. Aubin's husband seems to have been at least an acquaintance and perhaps a friend of Lord Coleraine.

your Lordship: the Adventures of the unfortunate Lady which it contains, will move your Compassion; and her deliverance from Death, and reconciliation with her Husband, your Admiration, and I doubt not but you will be agreeably diverted for some Hours; and your Name being plac'd at the entrance of the Book, will be a sufficient Recommendation of it to the good and virtuous part of this Nation....

---

## THE PREFACE TO THE READER.

*This is the fifth Attempt that I have made of this nature, to entertain the Publick, and not with ill Success; which has encouraged me to proceed. The Story I here present to the World is very extraordinary, and I fear my own Sex will now be displeas'd with me, for* Henrietta's *Story; but I was oblig'd to follow Truth, and I hope that one ill Woman, amongst a great many others of singular Virtue, will be no injury to the good Opinion which I would fain persuade all my own Sex to deserve, and Mankind to have of us, who are the sole Authors of our being wicked, whenever we are so. But let me give this Word of Advice to the vicious Woman; let her Station be ever so great and high in the World, nay, let her Crimes be ever so well conceal'd from human Eyes; yet, like* Henrietta, *she will be unfortunate in the End, and her Death, like her's, will be accompanied with Terrors, and a bitter Repentance shall attend her to the Grave: Whilst the virtuous shall look Dangers in the face unmov'd, and putting their whole trust in the Divine Providence, shall be deliver'd, even by miraculous Means; or dying with comfort, be freed from the Miserys of this Life, and go to taste eternal Repose.*

*I hope that my own Nation, can furnish a great many Women of all degrees, whose Characters and Virtues are unquestionable: And I intreat all marry'd Men to consider, from* Albertus's *Story, the dangerous Effects of Jealousy, and not to give credit to Appearances, but to examine well into the Truth of Things, before they treat a Wife unkindly, or abandon her; for we are very often deceiv'd, and condemn the innocent, whilst we love and caress the guilty. Let us be always tender of other People's Characters, and not only slow to condemn, but apt to forgive oversights in both Sexes, that we may both live and die like Christians; and let him who has done anything revengeful like* Albertus, *like him repent and make atonement for his Crimes, and not sleep supinely in a Mistress's Arms, and pass the time in Luxury and Folly, till Death overtakes and snatches him away, to render an Account of his Deeds at the great Tribunal above, from whence no appeal can be made. We* English

*are neither revengeful nor cruel, and therefore need not fear such treat-*
*ment from our Husbands, as the poor Lady* Lucy *met withal: from her's*
*yet we ought not to be less cautious than the Ladys of other Nations,*
*of giving just occasion, of Jealousy, for fear of ruining our selves and*
*Familys; and 'tis a poor Excuse to say we have unkind Husbands, when*
*we prove false our selves, tho I own a Husband's cruelty often occasions*
*a Wife's inconstancy. I wish both Sexes would amend their Lives, which*
*would be the greatest Satisfaction of their devoted Servant,*

Pen. Aubin.

---

[the final paragraph of the text]:

And thus ends a History full of very extraordinary Events; and
I hope it will be of use to all who read it, and prevent Men from
entertaining that dangerous Enemy to Man's repose, Jealousy, and
teach them to be very cautious in suspecting their Wives' Virtue, or
giving credit to Appearances, which very often deceive the Wisest:
and may the unhappy *Henrietta*'s Crimes and Death, make my
own Sex take care to avoid the like Fate, and strive to imitate the
virtuous Lady *Lucy*, that like her they may die in peace, and their
Memorys be ever dear to all that know them, and reverenc'd by
all Posterity. But I forget the Age I live in, where such things as
Religion and Virtue are almost grown out of fashion, and many
of both Sexes live as if they had neither; when there is scarce any
Truth, Honour, or Conscience amongst Men, or Modesty and
Sobriety amongst Women. The few Good and Virtuous will, I am
sure, read this with pleasure; the Vicious I do not strive to please,
but to reform; may they rather be touch'd to the inmost Recesses
of their Soul, at the reading of this History, and amend, that they
may have pardon, and God be glorify'd.

## 4. From Penelope Aubin, *The Illustrious French Lovers* (1727), translation of Robert Challes, *Les Illustres Françoises* (1713)

### THE PREFACE TO THE READER.

*The* French *Historian*[1] *avers all the following Histories to be true; and*
*that he had them from such Hands as he could entirely confide in: Nay*

---

1 Robert Challes (1659–1721), the author of the text that Aubin is
translating.

more, that he was personally acquainted with several of the Heroes and the Ladies, whose Lives he here presents to the Publick, being the Labours of his leisure Hours; which he thus employ'd, because he thought such Histories were useful to excite those Virtues in others, which these illustrious Lovers practised. And thus he gives the Moral of each History.

Monsieur des Ronais's Story, says he, makes appear that if all Parents would act with regard to their Children, as Monsieur du Puis did with his Daughter, they would be always honoured and respected by them, and not end their days in Misery, by putting their Children into the Possession of all their Fortunes before they are dead; who are often so unnatural and ungrateful as to despise and neglect them, when they have no more to give.

In Madam de Contamine's History, he shews, That a wise and virtuous Maid may both hope and pretend to the greatest Advantages, and gain a Husband of superior Quality and Fortune, by her Virtue and prudent Conduct.

Monsieur and Madam de Terny's Story makes appear how greatly Parents are to blame, who go to force their Children to do things contrary to their Inclinations: And that tho they may hinder them (and sometimes with Reason) from marrying according to their Fancies, yet they ought never to force them to marry against their Wills; or to become Religious,[1] especially when they find them much averse to it.

Madam de Jussy's Story shews, That when a young Lady has once had the Weakness to yield to a Lover, she ought to repair her Fault by keeping the Promise she has made to him, of being only his, even to Death; and by her Constancy to her first Engagement, shew that it was no vitious Inclination that induced her to oblige him, but only Love, and the entire Confidence she had in him: which, if he proves a Villain to her, will make her pitied, and him scorn'd and despised.

Monsieur des Prez's History, shews the Fruits of a too violent indiscreet Passion on both Sides; and that a Woman should always give ear to a good Husband's Advice; and that when she is bereft of him, the whole World slights her: And that even our nearest Relations, if they are of mean, mercenary Dispositions, are not to be trusted with any Secret, because they will sacrifice all things to Self-interest.

Monsieur des Frans's melancholy Story, is an Advertisement to all Womankind, to be ever upon their Guard; and the more Beauty and Merit a Woman has, the more doubtful and cautious she must be of giving any Opportunities to the faithless Sex, who always plot the Fair One's ruine, not trusting to her own Virtue alone: And here appears what Rage and Jealousy can spur a Man's Passions on to act even

---

1 To join a monastic order (e.g., compel a daughter to become a nun).

*upon the Woman he loves most, and what cruel Tragedies Love and Revenge occasion in the World.*

*Monsieur* du Puis's *mad Adventures, are a Lesson to warn us of being Libertines in our Youth; and his Conversion to Virtue, after having acted the Part of a Rake and a Hero before, shew the Power a virtuous Woman, who has sense, may gain over the most vitious Man. His Justification of* Silvia, *in discovering the Secret of* Gallouin's *manner of gaining her;* Gallouin's *turning Friar, and strange Death; all shew, That the Man who is most addicted to his Pleasures, even to the sacrificing of his Fortune and Conscience for them, if he does but once give himself time to reflect, as a Christian, on his life past, he will not fail to repent and change his manner of life, and generally make a good End.*

*In fine: Monsieur* Vallebois *and* Charlotte's *History does shew, That Strangers are oft-times more touch'd with our Misfortunes than our nearest Relations; and that we must not judge of Persons by their outward appearance only, since, like* Charlotte, *noble Minds may be lodged under mean Habits. 'Tis also a Warning against that ruinous Vice, Gaming; which reduced Monsieur* Vallebois *to such mean wretched Straits.*

*The Reader, says our Author, will not here find any of those strange and surprizing Accidents and Turns of Fortune which we are frequently entertain'd withal, in fictitious Stories and Romances,*[1] *because here is nothing but what is really true and natural; which I thought, says he, it would be a Crime to embellish, and set off with Falsities of my own Invention. Nothing appears romantick*[2] *but Monsieur* du Puis's *falling upon his Sword for Madam* de Londe; *but it is really matter of Fact, and therefore could not be omitted. The Stories are, says he, in my Opinion, very particular and extraordinary, and very different from any I ever saw in print: And if they had fallen into the Hands of such as are used to steal, from other People's Works, the Stories they turn into Novels and Romances, they might have been very easily improved into several Volumes. But I have related them just as they were related to me; in the same Style, and as few words as if I were relating them to some of my Friends in private. And if the Publick gives these a good Reception, I hope to oblige them with something else of the same kind no less diverting and instructive....*

*This is what the* French *Author says in behalf of his Work. And all I*

---

1  Possibly a jab on Aubin's part at Daniel Defoe's *The Life and Strange Surprizing Adventures of Robinson Crusoe of York, Mariner* (1719), which claimed to be a true story. Challes is concerned with probability and what is "natural" in the counterpart to this passage, but doesn't mention the "strange," "Turns of Fortune," or fictionality.

2  Improbable, as romances were sometimes charged with being.

*can say of mine, is, That I have endeavour'd to translate it both faithfully and in good Language, and a familiar Style, like his; and I hope it will meet with a kind Reception, since I am still pursuing my Design of recommending Virtue and Piety to the World, and presenting new Examples worthy our Imitation to the Publick, who have hitherto shew'd me a great deal of Favour, which if continued may encourage me to publish something more valuable out of the* French *Tongue, to oblige my own Nation; which none has a greater love and respect for than their*

Devoted Servant,

PEN. AUBIN.

## 5. From Penelope Aubin, *The Life and Adventures of the Young Count Albertus* (1728)

To her G— the D. of —[1]

MADAM,

*It was with the utmost Satisfaction that I receiv'd the Honour of your G—'s Letter, in which you seem pleas'd with the unfortunate Lady* Lucy's *Story, and to intimate, that you would be glad to know what befel her Illustrious Son, who had been so miraculously preserv'd from Death, and of whose Adventures you have had some slight Account, but only such as could raise, not satisfy your Curiosity. This was enough to excite me to use the utmost diligence to get Knowledge of this brave Man's Life, Actions, and Death; and tho his Life was not very long, yet it was pass'd with such Honour, and his End was so pious and heroick, that it well deserves to be transmitted to Posterity. And having now gotten a perfect Account of all Particulars, I have composed this short Narrative, and presum'd to send it to your G—, hoping it will contribute something to your Diversion, in your leisure Hours....*

[from the final paragraph of the text]:

Thus this great and good Man, whose Birth and Infancy was attended with such wonderful Circumstances, who was indeed miraculously preserved alive, and whose whole Life had been in a manner a Series of Misfortunes and Deliverances. After having travell'd over the greater part of the Universe, and been surprized

---

1 The dashed-out phrase presumably stands in for "To Her Grace the Duchess of" somewhere, but it is unclear whether Aubin is being discreet with respect to the identity of her dedicatee or if the duchess in question does not actually exist.

and exposed to the most imminent Dangers amongst Barbarians, and again restored in safety to a Christian Country where he might have lived and died in Peace: yet could he not restrain that ardent Zeal for God's Glory which filled his Soul, but must again launch out and run the Hazards of a long and dangerous Voyage to convert Infidels and Pagans to Christianity, and gain that Crown of Martyrdom which so few in this unthinking Age do court or endeavour to obtain, sealing the Truth of the Doctrine he had taught with his Blood. An Account of his Death, and the Manner of it was brought into *China* by some of the Christians who had been taken Slaves along with him into *Tartary*,[1] and redeemed some time after by being exchanged, and thence an Account was transmitted by the Missionaries at *China*[2] to *Spain* to the Bishop of *Toledo*,[3] who published it with Design to do a just Honour to the Memory of so excellent a Man, and with intent to excite others to follow so holy and brave an Example. But I forget that I am speaking in a Nation and to a People who are the greatest part of them more fond of Pleasure than Martyrdom, and care not to be reminded of Death; yet I hope there is a great number of good Christians amongst us who are truly zealous for God and Religion, and would not scruple to lose their Lives and Fortunes in a good Cause: These I honour, and to these I dedicate this History, hoping they will excuse any Oversights which I have committed in the writing of it, and admit me into the Number of their Friends.

## 6. From Penelope Aubin, *The Life of the Countess de Gondez* (1729), translation of Marguerite de Lussan, *Histoire de la comtesse de Gondez* (1725)

TO THE READER.

*I am here going to present to my own Nation the History of a* French *Lady's Life; which, tho it is not filled with a great number of strange Events and uncommon Transactions, yet has something in it very instructive and very uncommon: For first, she was a great Beauty and a great Fortune, and chose an old Count for an Husband when she was not eighteen; and tho she fell in Love with a young Lord, who was handsome and charming, and pursued her with all the Arts of Love, yet she kept her Virtue, preserved her Reputation, and never was guilty of*

---

1  See p. 92, n. 1.
2  Jesuits.
3  City in central Spain.

*one Slip for above three Years that her old Lord lived with her. But what*
*is yet more extraordinary, she mourn'd him dead without Hypocrisy,*
*kept still up to the Dignity of her Character, and refus'd to marry the*
*Man she lov'd, till she had pay'd all the Tribute of a long Mourning,*
*more than Duty required, for her deceased Husband; and that being*
*past, and her Lover making some false Steps, she conquer'd her Passion,*
*and prefer'd a nobler and more constant Lover before him. And thus she*
*has set her Sex a noble Example; but I fear it will not be much follow'd*
*here, for we daily see Widows from twenty to eighty, trip to Church in*
*their Weeds[1] to marry worthless Rakes and Libertines; and Virtue is too*
*seldom the Companion of Greatness and Beauty: The Age is grown so*
*corrupt, that Vice seems to reign; and both Sexes are so lost to all sense*
*of Honour and Fame, that Merit and Virtue are unregarded; 'tis Riches,*
*Pleasure and Preferment which all pursue: these are the Idol Gods they*
*worship. The daring Lover bribes high[2] to debauch the unwary Fair,*
*and gains his Ends; Wives and Husbands hate, and mutually pursue*
*unlawful Pleasures; some Wives leave good Husbands and live at large,*
*whilst some for Profit wink at their fair Spouses' Crimes,[3] and blush not*
*at Dishonour. Yet it must be confess'd, that the* English *Throne has this*
*last Age been singularly happy, in being filled with Princesses who have*
*been the greatest and most shining Examples of Virtue; and we have*
*now one who is such, and ought to be a Pattern for Conjugal Affection.[4]*

I always have endeavour'd to inspire Virtue and noble
Principles into my Readers' Breasts: Still I pursue the same
Design, and still I hope to find such Patrons as will defend bright
Virtue's Cause, and help to shame the Vicious into Virtue: and 'tis
these I love and honour, and to these I dedicate all my Labours.

---

1  Black clothing worn by widows.
2  Pays a significant bribe (presumably to someone, like a lady's maid,
   who controls access to the woman he hopes to "debauch").
3  May be a reference to the practice of husbands suing their wives' lovers for "criminal conversation" (sometimes for large amounts: a year
   after this text was published, a jury awarded £10,000 in damages to a
   husband). There were periodic rumors that some husbands colluded
   in these affairs and so their lawsuits were merely a means of cashing in
   on the situation, rather than an attempt to restore their lost honor.
4  There may be a jab at the Hanoverians here: George I's wife, Sophia
   (1666–1726), was imprisoned by her husband on suspicions of adultery for more than thirty years and the "pattern for conjugal affection"
   set by George II's wife, Caroline (1683–1737), included putting up
   uncomplainingly with her husband's infidelities—though there is
   some evidence that they genuinely did love one another.

# Appendix B: Reshaping Aubin's Reputation

[As the Introduction details, Aubin has spent most of the past three centuries being regarded as "strenuously pious" in ways that (supposedly self-evidently) limited her importance and narrative appeal. In part, this has been the result of our often impoverished and unimaginative ways of thinking about what constitutes good prose fiction and good women writers (and the doggedly literal habits of reading her prefaces that tend to accompany such thinking). But it is also the result of two powerful distortions of her reputation on which subsequent scholars have relied far too uncritically: the malicious and factually incorrect biographical account of Aubin by the Abbé Prévost (1697–1763) in *Le Pour et contre*, which, among other things, claimed that she was dead almost four years before she actually died, and the preface to a 1739 three-volume collection of her prose fiction. This preface, which may have been written by Samuel Richardson (1689–1761), offers up a vision of Aubin far more compatible with the prose fiction that Richardson and his followers would be writing in the 1740s and 1750s than with what Aubin actually wrote back in the 1720s. In both cases, scholars could have investigated further and read more skeptically and so uncovered the truth about Aubin's biography and the ways in which her work is doing something different than what we get in a text like Richardson's *Pamela* (1741). But for whatever reasons, such efforts were not seriously undertaken until the present century and we are still very much in the midst of figuring out how best to read Aubin and assess her place in literary history. Part of that work will involve coming to terms with what Prévost and the preface-writer have kept us from seeing or led us to discount (and why it might have been attractive to them to reshape Aubin's reputation in the first place).]

## 1. From Antoine François Prévost d'Exiles, *Le Pour et contre*, no. 58, 27 September 1734, translated by David A. Brewer

[Prévost, often referred to as the Abbé Prévost, was a French priest and writer. Originally trained as a Jesuit, he spent most of the 1720s as a Benedictine monk. In 1728, he left his abbey without permission and then fled France after an order was issued for his arrest. He spent the next five years in England and the Netherlands writing and getting involved in financial scandals. In 1734, he resolved his legal troubles (with a pardon from the Pope) and returned to France, where he remained for most of the rest of his life. He published a number of works of prose fiction that were both praised and denounced for their focus on overwhelming emotion, perhaps most famously the *Histoire du chevalier des Grieux et de Manon Lescaut* (1731), which was banned in France for its sympathetic portrayal of a passionate, but deeply flawed—and decidedly unmarried—couple. Prévost also edited a fifteen-volume collection of travel writing and translated/abridged/adapted several literary texts from English, including John Dryden's *All for Love*, Samuel Richardson's *Clarissa*, and Frances Sheridan's *Memoirs of Miss Sidney Biddulph*. Between 1733 and 1740, he wrote and published a weekly periodical, *Le Pour et contre*, which sought to make English literature and culture better known in France. While he and Aubin were both in London in the early 1730s, there is no evidence that they ever met.]

... For me, who had no other view in the telling of this story, than to publish an extraordinary example of caprice and oddity, I ask the liberty to add to it another tale, that will be no less agreeable.

Death and character of Madame Aubin.
A lady, born in London, although the daughter of a French officer, found herself poorly defended against poverty and its miserable consequences. Her wit was her only resource; for while it seems from her works that she had a heart capable of the most tender passions, she lacked what it takes to inspire them. She was ugly and poor, two qualities that attract little solicitude in the iron century we are in. After having tried her strengths for some time with various small Pamphlets, which she published anonymously,[1] she finally ventured into the light of day with a

---

1   *The Extasy* and *The Wellcome* (both 1708) are the only early works of Aubin's that were published anonymously. Both poems are short

novel that she acknowledged as her work, and which met with some success, because it came from the pen of a woman. But the public's ardor waned with the novelty. The volumes that followed were received so coldly, that she broke pen and paintbrush out of bitterness,[1] with a vow to never take them up again. Parnassus,[2] which did not lose much by this, easily comforted itself. Religion gained more than expected. Madame Aubin, cured of love for the world by her misfortune and by that of her books, turned entirely toward Heaven, and resolved to use her talents to turn her neighbor there as well. She started composing sermons, and for want of preachers wishing to buy them,[3] she took to preaching them herself. In a country where caprice pleases by its very name, it is rare that one refrains from tasting its fruits. The *Oratory*[4] of Madam Aubin was soon filled with a prodigious crowd of audience members of both sexes, who regularly paid their thirty sous[5] to listen to a bad speech that lasted

She preaches.

enough to count as pamphlets, but typically that term was used for argumentative prose. We do not know whether Prévost is referring to these poems or to works that have been lost or attributed to someone else or if he is just making things up.

1 [Prévost's note:] *Frange miser calamos vigilataque carmina dele.* Juven. [Latin. This is a slightly modified version of the ancient Roman poet Juvenal's *Satire* 7:27 and translates as "Break your pens and wipe out those songs" that you have "spent all night" writing (301). This line comes as advice to would-be poets, letting them know that in the current age there is no possibility of making money as a writer.]

2 Mountain that was home to the Nine Muses in Greek mythology and so became a shorthand for the arts.

3 Clergy were generally expected to compose their own sermons, but there were persistent rumors that some, out of laziness or a sense of their own limitations, were actually delivering sermons written by others.

4 [Prévost's note:] We give this name to pious assemblies that do not constitute regular churches. Thus the non-conforming churches, such as the Presbyterians, the Anabaptists, the Quakers, etc. are called simply *Meetings*, that is, places where one meets. The Oratory of Madame Aubin was in *York-buildings*. [Aubin's venue—Topham's Great Room, in York Buildings, Villiers Street—was actually London's first concert hall, not a religious space.]

5 French coins, roughly equivalent to a shilling in terms of their place in the hierarchy of money. However, Prévost here seems to be treating the sou as the equivalent of a penny, since the ticket (*continued*)

about three-quarters of an hour. The success matched that of her books; it lasted no longer than the novelty: but she earned enough in the space of a few weeks to put herself above misery.

She dies rich. Unfortunately Death has just robbed her of the fruits of her labors, having left her so little time to enjoy them that she had only the pleasure of misers; that is, to die in abundance.

Satire against Madame Aubin. Mr. *Bavius*, Secretary of *The Grub-Street Journal*[1] did not act in accordance with the interests of honest people when he pitted himself against Madame Aubin, and set about destroying her reputation. He could, without offense, pleasantly banter about the poor success of her books and her skills in the Pulpit; but what satisfaction did he find in tearing apart her conduct, and tracing her character with such dark colors? Men are odd in the judgments that they make of Women. If they should please them by their beauty, then they are blind to their vices,[2] to the point of

Cause of this satire. recognizing only their perfections and virtues. Ugliness, on the contrary, drives them to the other extreme; thus Mr. Bavius confesses that what provokes him the most about Madame Aubin is the audacity she had in taking the Pulpit; that is to say, in making a public spectacle of herself, with a deformed face. The mere thought of it causes him to get heated. *An ugly woman,* he cries, *dares to take the Pulpit! Dares to seek men's glances from on high! To look them in the eye! And with the usual presumption of her sex, perhaps to imagine that the attention they were giving to her extravagant*

---

prices for Aubin's Oratory ranged from 1s to 2s 6d. At the exchange rates of 1734, thirty sous would be roughly equivalent to 1s 4d.

1 [Prévost's note:] I spoke of this Journal and of Secretary Bavius, No. III. [It was actually no. 2, 29 June 1733, where he called it "the Inquisition of England" and described its editorial persona, Bavius, as "a rare man for impudence," who "would slander the Nine Muses." Scholars have been unable to find a reference to Aubin or her Oratory in *The Grub-Street Journal,* which is not particularly surprising, since, with the exception of one benefit performance in February 1730, the Oratory had ended before the journal ever got going.]

2 [Prévost's note:] *Facta merent odium, facies exorat amorem.* Ovid. [Latin. This is from the ancient Roman poet Ovid's *Amores* 3:11 and translates as "Your actions merit hate, your face pleads winningly for love" (499). It comes as part of an outcry by the speaker regarding how he can neither live with nor without his unfaithful beloved.]

*speech was granted to her charms?* It is such a monstrous disorder, Mr. Bavius continues, that it cannot be too severely punished by satire. I admit that this outburst does not appear serious; but an enemy of Madame Aubin nonetheless might use it as an opportunity to fall upon her character and her morals, and attack them without mercy.

Beautiful or ugly, I agree with Addison that a Woman always deserves the respect of Men for several reasons;[1] and I do not even count the last reason[2] that he reports, because it is not as sound as all the others. It is true that it is in the nature of beauty to excite tenderness and love, and in the nature of wit to give rise to esteem and admiration: but it does not follow that ugliness must produce contempt and hatred. It is only the *lack* of something one cannot give oneself; and if one supposes that even the involuntary deprivation of a good is always a real evil, it should inspire compassion, not hatred or contempt. This sentiment is all the more just for ugly women, as they themselves feel their disgrace only too keenly and surely they suffer from it more than anyone; especially when they are tender enough to wish to put the feelings of their hearts into practice, but it happens that, for want of attractiveness, they do not find any heart that wishes to answer. Without looking for any other example than Madame Aubin, what an idea we form of her pains from reading her gallant works! What mortification! What torment! To be born with such a tender sensibility and so ugly! Mr. Bavius is a cruel man, to have treated a woman of this character so badly. Nothing is so cowardly as to insult misfortune and pain.

*Respect that Men must have for Women.*

*They must have compassion for the ugly. Why?*

An English Author[3] less gallant, by the way, than philosophical, claimed that one should not generally expect from an ugly

---

1  Joseph Addison (1672–1719) championed a new "politeness" toward women in much of his writing, especially his contributions to two periodicals, *The Tatler* (1709–11) and *The Spectator* (1711–12, 1714).

2  [Prévost's note:] Ugly women, he says, differ only in their faces from those we idolize the most.

3  [Prévost's note:] Milord Shaftesbury's *Miscellaneous Reflections.* [Anthony Ashley Cooper, Third Earl of Shaftesbury (1671–1713), repeatedly links the beautiful with the good in his *Characteristics of Men, Manners, Opinions, Times* (1711), which includes his "Miscellaneous Reflections."]

If ugly people are capable of beautiful feelings? woman, nor an ugly man, the same beauty of feelings, as from those who share the favors of nature. He gives this reason: "it is a common notion," he says, "that by the term *feelings* one should understand the manner in which the soul is affected by the movements of the body. Now, it is almost indubitable that the same irregularity that makes ugliness in facial features rules more or less noticeably in all other parts of the machine: from which we must conclude, that the movements being as irregular as the subject who receives them, they cannot create in the soul a feeling more regular than them, or what is the same thing, a beautiful feeling; because it is in regularity that beauty consists."

Reflections on a thought of Milord Shaftesbury's. Without examining whether all the parts of this reasoning are accurate, one could stop Milord Shaftsbury with two reflections: one, that among ugly people, one finds a large number who are only so by accident; and without a doubt this sort of ugliness does not entail irregularity in other parts of the body. In the second place, there is so little to conclude from facial deformity for the rest of the body, that on the contrary, nothing is so common in both sexes, than to see the best built body in the world under the *Sign* of a greatly deformed face. In the case of a total irregularity, such as the English Philosopher supposes, I would be strongly inclined to think like him. It appears that Martial was of the same mind, when he challenged Zoilus to be a honest man[1] with his red hair, his crossed eyes, one foot shorter than the other, etc....

## 2. From Penelope Aubin, *A Collection of Entertaining Histories and Novels* (1739)

[This preface has been attributed to Samuel Richardson on the basis of similarities between its phrasings and ideas and ones known to be Richardson's, some of which are fairly unusual for the period. Richardson also had strong ties, both personal and professional, to several of the booksellers who published Aubin (for details, see Zach; Richardson lvii–lxi). Richardson was an English printer and writer. In 1706 he was apprenticed to a

---

1 [Prévost's note:] *Crine ruber, claudus pede, lumine luseus, Rem magnam praestas, Zoïle, si bonus es.* [Latin. This is a slightly modified version of the ancient Roman poet Martial's *Epigram* 12:54 and translates "Red-haired, ... lame-footed, boss-eyed, it's a great achievement, Zoilus, if you're a good fellow" (cf. *Epigrams*, vol. 3, p. 135).]

printer, which led to a successful career of printing books, periodicals, and legal documents, sometimes for Parliament. However, he also sometimes printed pamphlets and newspapers that were highly critical of the government and sympathetic to Jacobites. At some point in the 1730s, he began to write pamphlets and newspaper articles offering advice to young men on how to avoid the temptations of the city, especially those associated with the theater. From an early age, he had been a prolific writer of letters, sometimes in the voices of other people (for example, as a teenager he would write love letters on behalf of the neighborhood girls). In the late 1730s, he expanded his work in this area, first producing a collection of sample letters to be sent on various occasions, including one that demonstrates how to tell your parents that your employer had been making sexual advances. The latter situation then became the seed for the first of Richardson's three epistolary novels: *Pamela* (1741), which was a sensation and prompted an unprecedented number of responses and parodies, including Henry Fielding's *Shamela* (1741) and *Joseph Andrews* (1742). There were also visual and theatrical adaptations, and a broad range of *Pamela*-related consumer goods. The even longer *Clarissa* (1747–48), which features a virtuous heroine harassed by her greedy family and ultimately raped by a dangerously alluring libertine, and *Sir Charles Grandison* (1753–54) followed. In these novels, Richardson posed as merely the editor of a series of collections of actual correspondence, but his authorship came to be widely known and fan letters poured in. He answered most of these letters, but rarely heeded the advice they offered, even when he had solicited it. Richardson's specificity of detail and his technique of "writing to the moment" (recounting events almost as they were happening) help create an extraordinary sense of access to his heroines' thoughts and feelings, albeit at the cost of considerable prolixity and a rather narrow conception of feminine virtue. Toward the end of his life, he consulted extensively with Edward Young on the latter's *Conjectures on Original Composition* (1759), which influentially theorized the importance of originality, as opposed to the imitation of classical models that had been at the heart of earlier eighteenth-century literary theory. His work has long been regarded as central to the development of prose fiction in English, French, and German, both for good and for ill. Jane Austen supposedly knew *Sir Charles Grandison* by heart.]

# A
# COLLECTION
## Of Entertaining
# HISTORIES
## AND
# NOVELS,

### DESIGNED

To promote the Cause of VIRTUE
and HONOUR.

Principally founded on FACTS, and interspersed
with a Variety of beautiful and instructive
Incidents.

BY

## Mrs. *PENELOPE AUBIN.*

And now first collected
## IN THREE VOLUMES.

## VOL. I.

Containing, The *Noble Slaves* ; or, The Lives and Adventures of two Lords and two Ladies.
The Life and amorous Adventures of LUCINDA, an *English* Lady.
The strange Adventures of the Count DE VINEVIL, and his Family.

## LONDON:

Printed for D. Midwinter, A. Bettesworth and C Hitch, J. and
J. Pemberton, R. Ware, C. Rivington, A. Ward, J. and
P. Knapton, T. Longman, R. Hett, S. Austen, and J. Wood.
MDCCXXXIX.

# PREFACE.

*We present the Publick with a Collection of* NOVELS, *written by the late ingenious Mrs.* PENELOPE AUBIN, *and published by her, at different times, singly, and with no small Success.*

AMUSEMENTS *of this Kind have always been highly approved of in the most polite Nations, both of* Europe *and* Asia: *For such is the Nature of the human Mind, that it cannot be satisfied without Variety; and religious Subjects themselves, though the noblest Entertainments of all others, will sometimes lose their Force and Efficacy, even on serious Minds, when too strictly imposed or pursued, and if nothing be admitted to diversify and amuse. Much more may Subjects of Diversion be needful to regale the gay and sprightly Fancies of the Youth of both Sexes, the Vivacity of whose Tempers, so natural to their Time of Life, require somewhat[1] to allure, to amuse, and to entertain; and who cannot be long kept to any one Subject, though ever so noble or important in itself.*

*As these Kinds of Writings, then, are principally of Use to divert and entertain the Minds of young Persons, the following Rules ought to be inviolably observed in them.* First, *A* Purity of Style and Manners, *that nothing may be contained in them that has the least Tendency to pollute or corrupt the unexperienced Minds, for whose Diversion they are intended.* Secondly, *That the Subjects should be such as naturally recommend all the Duties of social Life, and inforce an* universal Benevolence *to Mankind.* Thirdly, *That when a* guilty Character *is introduced, it should in the Conclusion appear to be signally punished or distressed, that others may be deterred from the Pursuits of those Follies, or Mistakes, which have been the Occasion of its Misfortunes.* Fourthly, *That* Virtue *or* Innocence, *on the contrary, be not finally permitted to suffer; but that a* Prospect *at least should be opened, either* here *or* hereafter, *for its Reward, in order to encourage every one who reads it to Imitation. And, lastly, that the whole have, at least, an Air of* Probability, *that the Example may have the greater Force upon the Minds it is intended to inform.*

*If these, among others that might be enumerated, may be said to be the indispensible Requisites of a good* Novel, *we must confess, with Concern, that they have been too seldom observed by those who have undertaken this Species of Writing, insomuch that it has brought a Disreputation on the very Name. And we are still more sorry to have Reason to say, That those of the* Sex, *who have generally wrote on these Subjects, have been far from preserving that Purity of Style and Manners, which is the greatest Glory of a fine Writer on any Subject;*

---

1 A certain amount of something (in this case, diversion).

*but, like the* fallen Angels, *having lost their own Innocence, seem, as one would think by their Writings, to make it their Study to corrupt the Minds of others, and render them as depraved, as miserable, and as lost as themselves.*

*Our Design is not to attempt to establish this Collection at the Expence of others, or, indeed, on any other Footing, than that of its own Merit: We will not therefore point out the particular Pieces of others, which we think dangerous to be perused by unguarded Youth, and, of Consequence, unfit to be recommended by such as would instil into their Minds the Principles of Virtue and Honour, and that at a Time when they are most susceptible of such Impressions as may be attended with either happy or pernicious Effects on their future Lives and Morals.*

*We shall only therefore observe, that Mrs.* AUBIN *had a far happier Manner of Thinking and Acting. She disdained to paint the guilty Scenes of Folly and Vanity in such Colours as might conceal their natural Deformity, and make the most unlovely and pernicious Vices amiable. She had no contemptible Share of Learning, surpassing what is usual in her Sex: She had excellent natural Talents, which were improved by Reading and Observation, as well as by Conversation with Persons as much distinguished by their Rank as for their good Understanding. She was Mistress of a polite and unaffected Style, and aimed not at the unnatural Flights, and hyperbolical Flourishes, that catch the weaker and more glittering Fancies of some of her Sex, and give their Performances too romantick an Air for Probability; and yet, at the same Time, it is lifted up above that tiresome and heavy Kind of narrative Prolixity, which affords no Entertainment to a brilliant Imagination. In short, she has the Felicity to hit and preserve that happy Medium between both Extremes, in this Particular, in which so few of her Sex, or our own, have succeeded; and which, at the same Time that it gives an Air of Probability to her Stories, equally delights and informs the youthful Mind. Her Relations are interspersed with a very entertaining Variety of Incidents, which flow naturally from her Subjects, and keep the Mind attentive and delighted; so that the longest of them cannot tire: And she mingles every where, as Occasions offer, very instructive Observations and Reflections, all tending to that one uniform End which was the principal Scope of her Writings; the mending of the Hearts of her Readers; the Encouragement of Religion and Virtue; and the discountenancing of Impiety and Vice. And so well has she observed the Rules above set down for constituting a good Novel, that her Heroes and Heroines are generally made successful or unsuccessful, happy or unhappy, according to their Merit: Or, if an innocent Person suffers, it is but for a Time, and then she draws from their Afflictions such Arguments as become a good Christian and wise Moralist. And,* on the contrary, as she generally inflicts an exemplary Punishment on the premeditatedly guilty; so she raises from it such a Doctrine as may caution others to avoid the Crimes and Mistakes which have subjected them to the Calamities under which they labour.

And here it may not be amiss to transcribe a few Lines from different Places of these Volumes, in Confirmation of the Justice we do our Author, and which will best shew the End she constantly had in View in all her Writings; and how safely they may be recommended to the Perusal of Youth, without the least Apprehension of inculcating upon their Minds, those impure and polluted Images which too generally abound in Pieces of this Nature.

To instance then a few Things, in the Preface to her Novel called The Noble Slaves, she tells us, That her only Aim is to encourage Virtue, to expose Vice, imprint noble Principles in the ductile Souls of our Youth, and by setting great Examples before their Eyes, excite them to Imitation. That her only Desire is to please the Good and Virtuous, and is particularly studious of promoting the Instruction and Delight of her own Sex. She censures freely the Infidels of the Times; recommends Trust in God, as the best Security in all Dangers. And concludes that Piece with this Observation, Since Religion is no Jest, Death and a future State certain; let us strive to improve the noble Sentiments such Histories as these will inspire in us; avoid the loose Writings which debauch the Mind: And since our Heroes and Heroines have done nothing here but what is possible, let us resolve to act like them, make Virtue the Rule of all our Actions, and eternal Happiness our only Aim.

In the entertaining History of the Count de Vinevil, she professes to try to allure young Minds to Virtue, by Methods where Delight and Instruction may go together, in an Age where more grave Pieces are too generally dispised or neglected. She tells us, That it is a Story in which Divine Providence is shewn to manifest itself in every Transaction; where Virtue is tried with Misfortunes, and rewarded with Blessings; where Men behave like Christians, and Women are really virtuous and imitable. Would Men, she says, trust in Providence, and act according to Reason and common Justice, they need not to fear any Thing; but whilst they defy God, and wrong others, they must be Cowards and Self-destroyers, and their Ends infamous. She heartily wishes Prosperity to her Country; and that our Nobility would distinguish themselves by the same shining Qualities which gave Being to their distinction.[1]

---

1 The same qualities that prompted the monarch to ennoble their ancestors in the first place.

*The Story of the Lady* Lucy *she thus prefaces, with Regard to a vicious Character in one of her own Sex, and which is well worthy the Consideration of every Lady.*—Let me, *says she,* give this Word of Advice to the vicious Woman: Let her Station be ever so great and high in the World; nay, let her Crimes be ever so well-concealed from human Eyes; yet, like *Henrietta,* she will be unfortunate in the End, and her Death, like her's, will be accompanied with Terrors, and a bitter Repentance shall attend her to the Grave: While the Virtuous shall look Dangers in the Face unmoved, and putting their whole Trust in the Divine Providence, shall be delivered, even by miraculous Means; or, dying with Comfort, be freed from the Miseries of this Life, and go to taste eternal Repose.

*The Life of* Charlotta du Pont *she dedicates to the celebrated Mrs. Rowe,*[1] *with whom she had an Intimacy, as we there see, and may farther reasonably infer from the Tenor of both their Writings, for the Promotion of the Cause of Religion and Virtue, and from that Affinity and Kindred of Souls, which will always make the Worthy find out one another, and create stronger Ties of Union and Friendship than those of Blood.*

*In the same exemplary Manner does she end that beautiful Story, as also every other contained in these Volumes; besides interspersing occasionally, as we have hinted, such Reflections, in the Progress of the Relations, as are worthy of the Design she had principally in View: And therefore, we hope we may safely conclude with recommending this Collection to the Perusal of all such as desire to be agreeably entertained, and instructed at the same Time.*

---

1 Elizabeth Singer Rowe. However, the biographical details given regarding the "Mrs. *ROWE*" to whom *Charlotta Du Pont* is dedicated do not line up with those of "*the celebrated Mrs. Rowe*" (see p. 119 n. 1). It is unclear whether this is an honest mistake on the preface-writer's part or an attempt to retroactively associate Aubin with a writer famous for her piety.

# Works Cited and Select Bibliography

Aristotle. *Poetics*. *Aristotle: Poetics; Longinus: On the Sublime; Demetrius: On Style*, edited and translated by Stephen Halliwell, Harvard UP, 1995, pp. 1–141.

Aubin, Penelope. *A Collection of Entertaining Histories and Novels, Designed to promote the Cause of Virtue and Honour. Principally founded on Facts, and interspersed with a Variety of beautiful and instructive Incidents. By Mrs. Penelope Aubin. And now first collected in Three Volumes*. London, D. Midwinter, A. Bettesworth and C. Hitch, J. and J. Pemberton, R. Ware, C. Rivington, A. Ward, J. and P. Knapton, T. Longman, R. Hett, S. Austen, and J. Wood, 1739.

———. *The Extasy: A Pindarick Ode to Her Majesty the Queen*. London, Printed for the Author, 1708.

———. *The Life and Adventures of the Lady Lucy, the Daughter of an Irish Lord, who marry'd a German Officer, and was by him carry'd into Flanders, where he became jealous of her and a young Nobleman his Kinsman, whom he kill'd, and afterwards left her wounded and big with Child in a Forest. Of the strange Adventures that befel both him and her afterwards, and the wonderful Manner in which they met again, after living eighteen Years asunder. By Mrs. Aubin*. London, J. Darby, A. Bettesworth, F. Fayram, J. Pemberton, C. Rivington, J. Hooke, F. Clay, J. Batley, and E. Symon, 1726.

———. *The Life and Adventures of the Young Count Albertus, the Son of Count Lewis Augustus, by the Lady Lucy: Who being become a Widower, turn'd Monk, and went a Missionary for China, but was Shipwreck'd on the Coast of Barbary. Where he met with many strange Adventures, and return'd to Spain with some Persons of Quality, who by his Means made their Escape from Africa. After which he went a Missionary again to China, where he arriv'd, and ended his Life a Martyr for the Christian Faith. By Mrs. Aubin*. London, J. Darby, A. Bettesworth, F. Fayram, J. Osborn and T. Longman, J. Pemberton, C. Rivington, J. Hooke, F. Clay, J. Batley, and E. Symon, 1728.

———. *The Life and Amorous Adventures of Lucinda, an English Lady, Her Courageous and undaunted Behaviour at Sea, in an Engagement wherein she was taken by a Rover of Barbary, and sold a Slave at Constantinople. An Account of her Treatment there, with several particular Customs of the Turks. Her unexpected Deliverance, with the lucky meeting of her first Love, their Return and Settlement in their own Country, where she at present resides. Written by her self. Intermixed with two diverting Novels, the one call'd Conjugal Duty rewarded, or, The Rake reform'd. The Other Fortune favours the Bold, or, The happy Milanese.* London, E. Bell, J. Darby, A. Bettesworth, F. Fayram, J. Pemberton, J. Hooke, C. Rivington, F. Clay, J. Batley, and E. Symon, 1722.

——. *The Life of Charlotta Du Pont, an English Lady; Taken from her own Memoirs. Giving an Account of how she was trepan'd by her Stepmother to Virginia, how the Ship was taken by some Madagascar Pirates, and retaken by a Spanish Man of War. Of her Marriage in the Spanish West-Indies, and Adventures whilst she resided there, with her return to England. And the History of several Gentlemen and Ladys whom she met withal in her Travels; some of whom had been Slaves in Barbary, and others cast on Shore by Shipwreck on the barbarous Coasts up the great River Oroonoko: with their Escape thence, and safe Return to France and Spain. A History that contains the greatest Variety of Events that ever was publish'd. By Mrs. Aubin.* London, A. Bettesworth, 1723.

——. *The Life of Madam de Beaumount, a French Lady; Who lived in a Cave in Wales above fourteen Years undiscovered, being forced to fly France for her Religion; and of the cruel Usage she had there. Also her Lord's Adventures in Muscovy, where he was a Prisoner some Years. With an Account of his returning to France, and her being discover'd by a Welsh Gentleman, who fetch'd her Lord to Wales: And of many strange Accidents which befel them, and their Daughter Belinda, who was stolen away from them; and of their Return to France in the Year 1718. By Mrs. Aubin.* London, E. Bell, J. Darby, A. Bettesworth, F. Fayram, J. Pemberton, J. Hooke, C. Rivington, F. Clay, J. Batley, and E. Symon, 1722.

——. *The Merry Masqueraders: or, The Humorous Cuckold. A Comedy.* London, T. Astley, J. Isted, E. Nutt, A. Dodd, and J. Jolliffe, 1732.

——. *The Noble Slaves: or, The Lives and Adventures of Two Lords and two Ladies, who were shipwreck'd and cast upon a desolate Island near the East-Indies, in the Year 1710. The Manner of their living there: The surprizing Discoveries they made, and strange Deliverance thence. How in their return to Europe they were taken by two Algerine Pirates near the Straits of Gibraltar. Of the Slavery they endured in Barbary; and of their meeting there with several Persons of Quality, who were likewise Slaves. Of their escaping thence, and safe Arrival in their respective Countries, Venice, Spain, and France, in the Year 1718. With many extraordinary Accidents that befel some of them afterwards. Being a History full of most remarkable Events. By Mrs. Aubin.* London, E. Bell, J. Darby, A. Bettesworth, F. Fayram, J. Pemberton, J. Hooke, C. Rivington, F. Clay, J. Batley, and E. Symon, 1722.

——. *The Strange Adventures of the Count de Vinevil and His Family. Being an Account of what happen'd to them whilst they resided at Constantinople. And of Madamoiselle Ardelisa, his Daughter's being shipwreck'd on the Uninhabited Island Delos, in her Return to France, with Violetta, a Venetian Lady, the Captain of the Ship, a Priest, and five Sailors. The Manner of their living there, and strange Deliverance by the Arrival of a Ship commanded by Violetta's Father. Ardelisa's Entertainment at Venice, and safe Return to France. By Mrs. Aubin.* London, E. Bell, J. Darby, A. Bettesworth, F. Fayram, J. Pemberton, J. Hooke, C. Rivington, F. Clay, J. Batley, and E. Symon, 1721.

——. *The Stuarts: A Pindarique Ode. Humbly Dedicated to Her Majesty of Great Britain. By Mrs. Aubin.* London, John Morphew, 1707.

——. *The Wellcome: A Poem, to His Grace the Duke of Marlborough. By Mrs. Aubin.* London, John Morphew, 1708.

Baer, Joel H. "Penelope Aubin and the Pirates of Madagascar: Biographical Notes and Documents." *Eighteenth-Century Women,* vol. 1, 2001, pp. 49–62.

Baer, Joel H., and Debbie Welham. "Aubin, Penelope (1679?–1738), Novelist and Translator." *Oxford Dictionary of National Biography,* Oxford UP, 2004, rev. 2010.

Bakhtin, M.M. "Forms of Time and of the Chronotope in the Novel: Notes toward a Historical Poetics." *The Dialogic Imagination: Four Essays,* edited by Michael Holquist, translated by Caryl Emerson and Michael Holquist, U of Texas P, 1981, pp. 84–258.

Ballaster, Ros. *Fabulous Orients: Fictions of the East in England, 1662–1785.* Oxford UP, 2005.

Bannet, Eve Tavor. *Transatlantic Stories and the History of Reading, 1720–1810: Migrant Fictions.* Cambridge UP, 2011.

Bekkaoui, Khalid. *White Women Captives in North Africa: Narratives of Enslavement, 1735–1830.* Palgrave Macmillan, 2011.

Bialuschewski, Arne. "Jacobite Pirates?" *Histoire sociale/Social History,* vol. 44, no. 87, 2011, pp. 147–64.

Black, Scott. *Without the Novel: Romance and the History of Prose Fiction.* U of Virginia P, 2019.

Branham, R. Bracht. "A Truer Story of the Novel?" *Bakhtin and the Classics,* edited by R. Bracht Branham, Northwestern UP, 2002, pp. 161–86.

Brewer, David A., and Angus Whitehead. "The Books of Lydia Languish's Circulating Library Revisited." *Notes and Queries*, vol. 57, no. 4, Dec. 2010, pp. 551–53.

Burke, Kenneth. "Literature as an Equipment for Living." *Direction*, vol. 1, no. 4, Apr. 1938, pp. 10–13.

Burwick, Frederick, and Manushag N. Powell. *British Pirates in Print and Performance*. Palgrave Macmillan, 2015.

Challes, Robert. *The Illustrious French Lovers; Being the True Histories of the Amours of several French Persons of Quality. In which are contained a great Number of excellent Examples, and rare and uncommon Accidents; Shewing the Polite Breeding and Gallantry of the Gentlemen and Ladies of the French Nation. Written Originally in French, and translated into English by Mrs. P. Aubin.* 2 vols. London, John Darby, Arthur Bettesworth, Francis Fayram, John Pemberton, Charles Rivington, John Hooke, Francis Clay, Jeremiah Batley, and Edward Symon, 1727.

Choi, Yoojung. "'Between Japan and California': Imaginative Pacific Geography and East Asian Culture in Penelope Aubin's *The Noble Slaves*." *Eighteenth-Century Fiction*, vol. 34, no. 1, Fall 2021, pp. 33–60.

Colley, Linda. *Britons: Forging the Nation, 1707–1837*. Yale UP, 1992.

———. *Captives*. Pantheon, 2002.

Daston, Lorraine, and Katherine Park. *Wonders and the Order of Nature, 1150–1750*. Zone, 1998.

Davis, Robert C. *Christian Slaves, Muslim Masters: White Slavery in the Mediterranean, the Barbary Coast, and Italy, 1500–1800*. Palgrave Macmillan, 2003.

De Jean, Joan. *Tender Geographies: Women and the Origins of the Novel in France*. Columbia UP, 1991.

Denham, John. "On Mr. John Fletcher's Workes." *Comedies and Tragedies Written by Francis Beaumont and John Fletcher, Gentlemen. Never Printed Before, and Now Published by the Authours Original Copies*, sig. b1v., London, Humphrey Robinson and Humphrey Moseley, 1647.

Dooley, Roger B. "Penelope Aubin: Forgotten Catholic Novelist." *Renascence*, vol. 11, no. 2, 1959, pp. 65–71.

Forster, E.M. *Aspects of the Novel*. Harcourt Brace, 1927.

Fricke, Stefanie. "Female Captivity in Penelope Aubin's *The Noble Slaves* (1722) and Elizabeth Marsh's *The Female Captive* (1769)." *Mediterranean Slavery and World Literature: Captivity*

*Genres from Cervantes to Rousseau*, edited by Mario Klarer, Routledge, 2020, pp. 111–31.

Gallagher, Catherine. *Nobody's Story: The Vanishing Acts of Women Writers in the Marketplace, 1670–1820*. U of California P, 1994.

Gillot de Beaucour, Louise-Geneviève Gomès de Vasconcellos. *The Adventures of the Prince of Clermont, and Madam de Ravezan: A Novel. In Four Parts. By a Person of Quality. Done from the French, by the Author of Ildegerte.* 2 vols. London, E. Bell, J. Darby, A. Bettesworth, F. Fayram, J. Pemberton, J. Hooke, C. Rivington, F. Clay, J. Batley, and E. Symon, 1722.

Gollapudi, Aparna. "Virtuous Voyages in Penelope Aubin's Fiction." *Studies in English Literature, 1500–1900*, vol. 45, no. 3, Summer 2005, pp. 669–90.

Gomberville, Marin le Roy, sieur de. *The Doctrine of Morality; or, A View of Human Life, According to the Stoick Philosophy. Exemplify'd in One Hundred and Three Copper-Plates, done by the Celebrated Monsieur Daret, Engraver to the Late French King. With an Explanation of each Plate: Written Originally in French by Monsieur de Gomberville, for the Use of the said Prince. Translated into English by T.M. Gibbs, late of Hart-Hall, Oxon.* London, E. Bell, J. Darby, A. Bettesworth, F. Fayram, J. Pemberton, J. Hooke, C. Rivington, F. Clay, J. Batley, and E. Symon, 1721.

Gowing, Laura. *Common Bodies: Women, Touch, and Power in Seventeenth-Century England.* Yale UP, 2003.

Griffith, Elizabeth. "Character of *The Noble Slaves* and Anecdotes of Its Author, by the Editor." *A Collection of Novels, Selected and Revised by Mrs. Griffith.* London, G. Kearsley, 1777, vol. 3, pp. 47–48.

Hershinow, Stephanie Insley. *Born Yesterday: Inexperience and the Early Realist Novel.* Johns Hopkins UP, 2019.

Horace. *Satires, Epistles, and Ars Poetica.* Translated by H. Rushton Fairclough, rev. ed., Harvard UP, 1929.

Hume, Robert D. "The Value of Money in Eighteenth-Century England: Incomes, Prices, Buying Power—and Some Problems in Cultural Economics." *Huntington Library Quarterly*, vol. 77, no. 4, Winter 2014, pp. 373–416.

Hunter, J. Paul, *Before Novels: The Cultural Contexts of Eighteenth-Century English Fiction.* Norton, 1990.

Johnson, Samuel. *The Rambler* 4 (31 March 1750). *The Rambler*, edited by W.J. Bate and Albrecht B. Strauss, Yale UP, 1969, vol. 1, pp. 19–25.

Juvenal. *Satires. Juvenal and Persius*, edited and translated by Susanna Morton Braund, Harvard UP, 2004.

Kareem, Sarah Tindal. *Eighteenth-Century Fiction and the Reinvention of Wonder.* Oxford UP, 2014.

Keymer, Thomas, editor. *Prose Fiction in English from the Origins of Print to 1750.* Oxford UP, 2017.

Kim, Elizabeth S. "Penelope Aubin's Novels Reconsidered: The Barbary Captivity Narrative and Christian Ecumenism in Early Eighteenth-Century Britain." *The Eighteenth-Century Novel*, vol. 8, 2011, pp. 1–29.

King, Kathryn R. "Elizabeth Singer Rowe's Tactical Use of Print and Manuscript." *Women's Writing and the Circulation of Ideas: Manuscript Publication in England, 1550–1880*, edited by George L. Justice and Nathan Tinker, Cambridge UP, 2002, pp. 158–81.

Kozaczka, Edward J. "Penelope Aubin and Narratives of Empire." *Eighteenth-Century Fiction*, vol. 25, no. 1, Fall 2012, pp. 199–225.

Kulik, Maggie. "What the Bookseller Did: A Case of Eighteenth-Century Plagiarism." Internet Archive, https://web.archive.org/web/20210423124840/http://www.chawton.org/library/files/what_the_bookseller_did.pdf.

London, April. "Placing the Female: The Metonymic Garden in Amatory and Pious Narrative, 1700–1740." *Fetter'd or Free? British Women Novelists, 1670–1815*, edited by Mary Anne Schofield and Cecilia Macheski, Ohio UP, 1986, pp. 101–23.

Loveman, Kate. "'A Life of Continu'd Variety': Crime, Readers, and the Structure of Defoe's *Moll Flanders*." *Eighteenth-Century Fiction*, vol. 26, no. 1, Fall 2013, pp. 1–32.

Lussan, Marguerite de. *The Life of the Countess de Gondez. Written by her own Hand in French, and Dedicated to the Princess de la Roche-Sur-Yon. And now faithfully Translated into English. By Mrs. P. Aubin.* London, J. and J. Knapton, J. Darby, A. Bettesworth, F. Fayram, J. Osborn and T. Longman, J. Pemberton, C. Rivington, F. Clay, J. Batley, and A. Ward, 1729.

Martial. *Epigrams.* Edited and translated by D.R. Shackleton Bailey, 3 vols, Harvard UP, 1993.

Matar, Nabil. *Britain and Barbary, 1589–1689.* UP of Florida, 2005.

McBurney, William H. "Mrs. Penelope Aubin and the Early Eighteenth-Century English Novel." *Huntington Library Quarterly*, vol. 20, no. 3, May 1957, pp. 245–67.

McCusker, John J. *Money and Exchange in Europe and America, 1600–1775.* U of North Carolina P, 1978.

Michals, Teresa. *Books for Children, Books for Adults: Age and the Novel from Defoe to James.* Cambridge UP, 2014.

Millet, Baudouin, editor. *In Praise of Fiction: Prefaces to Romances and Novels, 1650–1760.* Peeters, 2017.

Monod, Paul Kléber. *Jacobitism and the English People, 1688–1788.* Cambridge UP, 1989.

Moore, Steven. *The Novel: An Alternative History, 1600–1800.* Bloomsbury, 2013.

Moretti, Franco. "The Novel: History and Theory." *Distant Reading,* Verso, 2013, pp. 159–78.

Mounsey, Chris. "'… bring her naked from her Bed, that I may ravish her before the Dotard's face, and then send his Soul to Hell': Penelope Aubin, Impious Pietist, Humourist, or Purveyor of Juvenile Fantasy?" *British Journal for Eighteenth-Century Studies,* vol. 26, no. 1, Mar. 2003, pp. 55–75.

———. "Conversion Panic, Circumcision, and Sexual Anxiety: Penelope Aubin's Queer Writing." *Queer People: Negotiations and Expressions of Homosexuality, 1700–1800,* edited by Chris Mounsey and Caroline Gonda, Bucknell UP, 2007, pp. 246–60.

Oakleaf, David. "Testing the Market: and After." *The Oxford Handbook of the Eighteenth-Century Novel,* edited by J.A. Downie, Oxford UP, 2016, pp. 172–86.

O'Quinn, Daniel. *Engaging the Ottoman Empire: Vexed Mediations, 1690–1815.* U of Pennsylvania P, 2019.

Orr, Leah. *Novel Ventures: Fiction and Print Culture in England, 1690–1730.* U of Virginia P, 2017.

Ovid. *Heroides and Amores.* Translated by Grant Showerman, 2nd ed., revised by G.P. Gould, Harvard UP, 1977.

Paige, Nicolas D. *Before Fiction: The Ancien Régime of the Novel.* U of Pennsylvania P, 2011.

Pavel, Thomas G. *The Lives of the Novel: A History.* Princeton UP, 2013.

Pétis de la Croix, François. *The History of Genghizcan the Great, First Emperor of the Antient Moguls and Tartars; in Four Books: Containing his Life, Advancement and Conquests; with a short History of his Successors to the present Time; the Manners, Customs and Laws of the Antient Moguls and Tartars; and the Geography of the vast Countries of Mogolistan, Turquestan, Capschac, Yugurestan, and the Eastern and Western Tartary. Collected from several Oriental Authors, and European Travellers; whose Names, with an Abridgment of their Lives, are added to this Book. By the late M. Petis de la Croix Senior, Secretary and Interpreter to the King in the*

*Turkish and Arabick Languages. And now faithfully translated into English*. London, J. Darby, E. Bell, W. Taylor, W. and J. Innys, and J. Osborn, 1722.

Porter, Cole. *The Complete Lyrics of Cole Porter*. Edited by Robert Kimball, Alfred A. Knopf, 1983.

Prescott, Sarah. *Women, Authorship, and Literary Culture, 1690–1740*. Palgrave Macmillan, 2003.

Probyn, Clive. "Paradise and Cotton-Mill: Rereading Eighteenth-Century Romance." *A Companion to Romance: From Classical to Contemporary*, edited by Corinne Saunders, Blackwell, 2004, pp. 251–68.

Richardson, Samuel. *Early Works*. Edited by Alexander Pettit, Cambridge UP, 2012.

Richetti, John J. *Popular Fiction before Richardson: Narrative Patterns, 1700–1739*. Clarendon, 1969.

Savile, Gertrude. *Secret Comment: The Diaries of Gertrude Savile, 1721–1757*. Edited by Alan Savile, Kingsbridge History Society, 1997.

Snader, Joe. *Caught between Worlds: British Captivity Narratives in Fact and Fiction*. UP of Kentucky, 2000.

Sterling, James. "To Mrs. Eliza Haywood, on Her Writings." *Secret Histories, Novels, and Poems. In Four Volumes. Written by Mrs. Eliza Haywood*. 2nd ed., 1:sigs. a1r–a2v, London, Dan. Browne, Jun. and S. Chapman, 1725.

Thompson, Helen. *Fictional Matter: Empiricism, Corpuscles, and the Novel*. U of Pennsylvania P, 2017.

Todd, Dennis. *Defoe's America*. Cambridge UP, 2010.

Turner, James Grantham. "'Romance' and the Novel in Restoration England." *Review of English Studies*, new series 63, no. 258, Feb. 2012, pp. 58–85.

Virgil. *The Aeneid*. Translated by Robert Fagles, Viking, 2006.

Welham, Deborah. "Delight and Instruction? Women's Political Engagement in the Works of Penelope Aubin." 2009. University of Winchester, PhD dissertation.

———. "The Lady and the Old Woman: Mrs. Midnight the Orator and Her Political Provenance." *Reading Christopher Smart in the Twenty-First Century: "By Succession of Delight,"* edited by Min Wild and Noel Chevalier, Bucknell UP, 2013, pp. 205–26.

———. "The Particular Case of Penelope Aubin." *Journal for Eighteenth-Century Studies*, vol. 31, no. 1, Mar. 2008, pp. 63–76.

Williams, Ioan, editor. *Novel and Romance, 1700–1800: A Documentary Record*. Routledge & Kegan Paul, 1970.

Zach, Wolfgang. "Mrs. Aubin and Richardson's Earliest Literary Manifesto (1739)." *English Studies*, vol. 62, no. 3, June 1981, pp. 271–85.

Zitlin, Abigail. Review of Stephanie Hershinow, *Born Yesterday: Inexperience and the Early Realist Novel*. *Eighteenth-Century Studies*, vol. 53, no. 3, Spring 2020, pp. 510–12.

This book is made of paper from well-managed FSC® - certified forests, recycled materials, and other controlled sources.